The Judge's Apothecary

Emma-Nicole Lewis

ALSO BY EMMA-NICOLE LEWIS

Novels:
The Wishing House
A Shadow Beyond

Novellas:
Three
The Hidden Door

COPYRIGHT

First published in Great Britain by Twilight Moon Publishing 2021.

ISBN-978-1-9161960-1-8

DEDICATION

For my Dad. For being an everyday hero and rock to us all. I count my blessings.
Love you forever, Pops.

Special mentions:
There are a number of people who I really should mention for their support in getting this next novel out there:

For my patient readers who have waited for this next novel and who are endlessly supportive. Your kind comments and enthusiasm truly drive me to keep writing! Thank you – all of you. I hope you will enjoy this next one.

Thank you to my wonderful editor, Anne Louise Booth. You have been amazing and it has been fabulous working with you.

Thank you to those who have kindly furnished me with information on the various settings within this novel and the historical events that take place. Sadly, the business who allowed me access to the upper floors of the Judge Jeffreys building in Dorchester is no longer there, but it was extremely beneficial getting that private access.

FOREWORD

As always, I begin my novels with an idea of the angle I want to take. However, as I fall deeper into my research, I find new strands that make me consider things from a different side.

For anyone with an interest in the infamous Judge Jeffreys, also known as 'The Hanging Judge', you will know that he is usually painted as a very sinister and cruel man. When I was writing this novel, I wanted to look a little deeper and also consider the reasons behind why the sentences he delivered were so harsh, even for those times. Hated and feared though he is by so many in this story, there are key moments that capture what I believe were his own vulnerabilities and fears – as witnessed through the eyes of the main protagonist, Kat.

Whilst many of the characters are fictitious, some are based on people documented in history. One particular example is the legend of a man from Monmouth's rebel army who could outrun a horse. Anyone who has visited Westonzoyland and the nearby Battle of Sedgemoor memorial will be familiar with this tale, albeit there is no concrete evidence I know of that proves it to be true. 'The Judge's Apothecary' elaborates on that story and I have applied my own twists to it.

This novel probably has a bit of everything for those who love history, the supernatural, a dash of romance – and twists. More than anything I hope it gives my readers an interesting and emotive read that will stay with them and inspire a visit to some of the places featured.

PROLOGUE

With a trembling hand she finished the letter before pressing neat folds through it so that the content was concealed. Turning it over, she found the place where she would write the intended recipient's name, so similar to her own. Strange, she thought, how much time needed to pass before this letter was meant to be read. That was assuming it ever would be read. Dread clutched at her heart as she imagined the consequences of the letter getting lost in time. What if she did not correctly set the chain of events that must follow? So much could go wrong between then and now. What wars, disasters and savagery of men would the letter have to survive over the years? She wondered how her soul could ever rest whilst the seal remained intact.

Dipping the nib of her quill in the inkpot, she paused before carefully writing the name and then the number that she had been given. Each stroke of the quill felt unfamiliar as she dated it: a future time so far away and unimaginable. Leaning back in her chair, she shut her eyes and reminded herself that she could indeed picture it. The memories were still there, dulled over time but not forgotten. Snippets of another time and place were buried in the deepest chasms of her mind. There had been lights and warmth and strange, merry music. On occasion, she had even smelled woodsmoke not so dissimilar from her own time.

Shaking her head, she tried to ignore the pain in her chest. If she thought too much of those distant memories, her heart would break all over again.

Reaching for the chain around her neck, she gently tugged to release the pendant from its resting place beneath her clothes. There it was, the black stone clasped in silver resting in the palm of her hand once again. Innocuously inanimate, it looked rather dull and boring in comparison to some of her other jewellery. This was no ordinary jewel though. This was one that could bring future, past and present together. It would make its journey through generations, finding its way into the hands of the most sensitive child, until fulfilling its destiny.

A shout from outside reminded her that her youngest son was due home from his studies. The thought brought a smile to her face as she reached for the wax stick. With the seal in place, she tucked the letter away. Her son would know what needed to be done. She could trust him.

A polite knock at the door of her chamber indicated that her presence was required. As she acknowledged the request, the coughing fit took her by surprise. It was nothing new, but every time, the relentless painful spasming would still leave her breathless, weak and shocked. Pressing a white square of linen to her mouth, she doubled over as her body convulsed and her chest burned from the effort.

From her chair in the corner, the attending maid hurried to her side, fretting alongside futile attempts to soothe her.

The door to her chamber was opened and the sound of more panicked footsteps were outdone by the sound of her husband's voice. His hands replaced the maid's and he gently guided her to the bed with its layers of blankets. As the coughing subsided, he whispered something in her ear and placed a kiss on her forehead, his eyes shining with grief. He knew. She knew. They all knew. It was the unspoken knowledge that seemed to cling to the room, stagnating the air and curdling it. However, they would not speak of it; her husband would not let them. For him, the inevitable outcome was too painful.

The familiar coppery residue on her tongue made her gasp for a drink. Somebody was holding a cup to her lips and it took several sips to regain her composure.

"Master Nathaniel has arrived." The statement was directed at her husband and she did not miss the way that he flinched at the words, as though they were spiked. This was a strained relationship between father and son, one that should never have happened but fate had made it that way. The pendant necklace had ensured it.

"Someone fetch the lad a drink and let him know that I will be with him presently," he replied, the authority in his voice somewhat betrayed by the faint quiver of emotion. He was not like this with their other children, only Nathaniel. Instructing the maid to see that she rested a while, he left the room.

When the window was thrown open, the chatter of birds and smell of fresh grass breathed life back into the room and she looked down at her lap. A bloom the colour of port wine had sullied the crispness of the white linen. It looked like an ugly rose. Her stomach twisted at it. She had seen so much blood in her lifetime. She had always thought that her marriage had been forged from blood. Theirs was a love built from death, deceit and darkness. The nausea continued to grip her as her fingers clutched the sheets and she glanced over at the place where she had tucked the letter.

"Mother?" The sound of his voice released her from the nightmarish thoughts and her heart lifted as she looked at him in the doorway. He looked older, broader, his features more defined. Sunlight bounced from his thick red hair as he regarded her with searching green eyes. She reminded herself that he was only a few years shy of the age his father had been during the summer that had changed their lives forever. "Tell me it is not true, that it is a mistake?"

The attending maid looked away. This was the first time anyone had mentioned it so openly and frankly.

His jaw clenched in the handsomely stubborn way that brought old memories back to her.

Patting the side of the bed, she gestured for him to sit with her and his gaze fell to her knee. The stained piece of linen answered his question. Bowing his head, he tried to hide the tears.

"Tears can come later, my son. There is something that you must promise me you will do first."

Composing himself, he nodded and looked at her as she dismissed the maid and insisted that they must be left alone. Then she unhooked the chain from around her neck and gently placed it in the palm of his hand. "Remember before you left for your studies, I told you that one day I would have much to tell you?"

"I do, Mother."

"That day has come." She nodded in the direction of the table. "Over there you will find a letter that must not be opened for a long time, certainly not in our lifetime or even during the time of your own children, or theirs."

His brow knitted in confusion and she told him that he must pour them both a drink if she was to embark on the story that she needed to impart. "That letter and this necklace will be the making of both history and the future, so it is very important that you do exactly as I ask." She paused as she took the cup offered to her. "The lives of so many in our lineage will depend on that letter surviving the test of time, including yours and your father's."

"I still don't understand."

Enclosing his hand in her fist, she gently squeezed so that his fingers tightened around the black stone pendant. "Listen carefully because what I am about to tell you begins and ends with that necklace. The stone is obsidian. It is extremely valuable and must never be sold or placed into the wrong hands. And it is the reason why I must now share with you the secrets of our past."

CHAPTER ONE

Lady Alice Lisle. The name was on everyone's lips in Winchester. From behind the counter of her grandmother's apothecary, Kateryn Fox carefully scooped some hartshorn into a small box. She glanced at her grandmother whose face remained stern as she listened to the news the last customer of the day had brought into the shop.

The old woman pursed her lips and gripped the edge of the counter as she stared at Mistress Hemingway. "A terrible business," she agreed as she handed over the remedy that Mistress Hemingway had come in for. Kat was unable to fathom whether her grandmother supported or opposed the news of the noble woman's arrest for her evident part in the rebellion against King James. Word of the Duke of Monmouth's execution had swept across the country only weeks before and now the King's men were scouring the land for those who had supported his treasonous quest. This latest turn of events seemed preposterous though. By all accounts Lady Alice Lisle was a woman of grand age and title whose New Forest estate had been used to harbour some of the rebels. But this was not what had Mistress Hemingway so excited. She had fresh news. Snapping the lid of the box shut, Kat pushed it across the counter towards her.

A curt glance and smile in Kat's direction demonstrated that she was vexed by the unwelcome interruption to her story. Returning her focus to Kat's grandmother, she cleared her throat to continue. "It is said that they're holding her at Fisherton." Her eyes twinkled as she imparted her newly gleaned knowledge. "She will be brought here, to Winchester, when the assizes open."

"Fisherton, you say?" Shocked by the revelation of where the noble woman was being held, Kat's grandmother put her hand to her chest. "The gaol in Salisbury? But that is full of felons!"

Nodding, Mistress Hemingway spared no pity of her own. "Indeed. The King will show the traitors no mercy."

"She is an old woman and a gentlewoman." Kat's grandmother was still struggling to digest the news. "A woman of a frail disposition, so I have heard."

Kat said nothing. She knew where the conversation would go after Mistress Hemingway had left the shop. It had been the same topic of conversation most days since her husband Gideon had left. It was a bad time to be travelling on business; it was a bad time to be travelling at all. There had been barely any notice given before Gideon was required to accompany him on his business. Even when he had left, word was out that the country was littered with men intent on bringing a pretender to the throne. Kat had begged him to reconsider, to swallow his pride and return to the Stour estate but full of ambition and giddy on whatever false promises his new employer had made, Gideon had left anyway. There had been no word from him and no money sent to help her pay the rent or keep food on the table, so she had taken to working for her grandmother in the apothecary shop.

Leaning towards them, Mistress Hemingway pressed down her coins for payment. "I do not think that sex, age or status should come into it, do you?" There was a calculating look upon her face as she silently dared either of them to challenge her. Kat knew her type and how difficult she could make things for her grandmother and the apothecary business. "Do not forget that she is the widow of a regicide," she reminded them with a haughty sniff. "She is of a Presbyterian household. It was her late husband who had the head of our first King Charles put to the bloc. God rest his soul."

"Quite right, Mistress Hemingway," Kat agreed through gritted teeth, although she wondered how the actions of men nearly two score years before could confirm an old woman's guilt of treason against the current King. She took the money and turned away so as to disguise the irritation on her face.

"Treason is a despicable crime," her grandmother added. "Wishing you a good day now," she said with a tight smile.

When the bell of the shop tinkled for the last time that day, Kat went to lock up before turning to her grandmother. "That woman is as sour as turned milk and a dreadful gossip," she remarked, dusting off her hands. "Don't you agree, Darling?" Darling was the affectionate name that Kat had coined for her grandmother ever since she had been a child and, at her grandmother's insistence, the term of endearment had remained. She said anything else made her sound old and withered. At nine and sixty years, Darling was almost the same age as Alice Lisle. The thought of anything so awful happening to her made Kat's legs feel weak.

Her attention on the shop ledger, Darling wrote out the details of the last purchase. "People talk," she said before adding, "as I have warned you."

The familiar fist of irritation clenched Kat's chest. "I do not care for loose tongues." She shifted her gaze to the bumpy nub on Darling's hand, where the little finger had once been. Kat did not know the full story behind the missing finger, only that Darling had found herself to be the unfortunate source of gossip on more than one occasion during her lifetime and had paid the price. It was the sad consequence of the mind she had been gifted with. Most people were not like Kat's grandmother and that bred fear. It had been instilled in Kat that they were to do all they could to avoid unwanted attention or gossip.

Pressing her lips together, Darling glared back at her. "That may be so, but loose tongues care for scandal, Kateryn. I do not want more trouble brought to my door." Lifting her hand to her chest, she rubbed the ugly nodule that had once been a finger.

Kat knew what it was that she was insinuating. "Gideon will be home soon and then you will have no need to worry about any troubles being brought to your door." A prickle of heat crawled over her skin. It was followed by the nauseating sensation that always came with thoughts of her husband. As a footman, he often accompanied his employer on long journeys, sometimes even overseas if necessary. There had been rare occasion when this had happened but he had always returned when promised, or ensured that news was sent to her if his absence was to be prolonged. Not this time though. He had left in early June and had promised that he would return by the height of summer. They had argued. She had not wanted him to go. She had thought him mad for leaving his respectable position in Hampshire so that he could return to his previous employer, Lord Granville. Gideon had worked for Lord Granville after they had first married. She had left a comfortable family home and sacrificed her dowry to be with Gideon and had moved to his home town, Dorchester, where they had lived in a modest cottage. Lord Granville was crooked as a stick and the employment had not lasted for long before Gideon had found himself a more secure and coveted role working for the Stour family in Hampshire. It had meant that Kat could be near to her beloved grandmother again. For a while they had been happy, but Gideon had always been so full of ambition. He carried a great burden on his shoulders for the very fact that he had been the reason for Kat losing her family and her dowry. It had never occurred to him that she was happy as things were and had never wanted for the finer things her mother had always craved so much. Whatever promises Lord Granville had made to Gideon had been of great influence though. It should have been no surprise to Kat. Crooked though the man was, he was one full of charm and persuasion.

Darling's expression darkened with disapproval. "It has been weeks, Kateryn and you have not had any word. He was not treating you well before he left either. I saw the sadness he caused you."

"Husbands and wives have disagreements. That has no bearing on where he has gone. Besides, the country is torn in two. I cannot expect word to come so easily as it has done before."

"That man has brought you nothing but misery."

Shaking her head, Kat pushed past her into the kitchen. "Now you sound just like mother. Gideon is my husband and I love him." No matter what reserves she had about Gideon's travels, she would always defend him. "Gideon may be ambitious but he is a good man. He assured me that this trip brings with it opportunity and if that makes him happy, then a few more weeks will do no harm."

Darling was not to be convinced. "What sort of opportunity is available to a footman, Kateryn?"

Anger misted her vision as she noted the judgement in Darling's tone and expression. "There you go again, just like mother and father. Why should it only be men of noble bloodlines who can rise up in the world? How is that fair?"

"Have a care for your words, Kateryn," Darling warned. "You are in danger of sounding like those who support the Whigs."

Kat dismissed the insult. "Of all people, I expected that you would support and respect any person seeking better favour in life. You did it. You were an unmarried woman with bastard children, and now you own all of this." She pointed at the shelves full of jars and bottles, the wooden drawers labelled with all kinds of foul and exotic substances and the bunches of herbs hanging from the walls. "If a woman can rise to this on her own, why can a footman, who works harder than any other man I know, not rise to the ambition of a better life?"

Rounding on her, Darling's cheeks flared with angry colour. "A better life? You had the chance of a better life, Kateryn. After you refused to marry the suitor your parents found and your father threatened to withdraw your dowry, I offered you a role here, as an apothecary in training. If you had not followed Gideon and his fanciful dreams, the Company of Apothecaries may well have recognised you as qualified to trade. You had a future with us, but he took you away. A youthful dalliance with a mere footman blinded you. You lost your dowry for him, your family, and now that he has gone, you have lost your reputation."

Feeling the familiar sting of the words her family reserved for describing Gideon, Kat's eyes welled up with tears. "Gideon has done nothing to harm my reputation. He will be back!"

"He has run off to chase fool's gold when the country is at war again. You said before that the Granville fortune is rumoured to be crumbling, that Lord Granville is a drunk and a gambler. I cannot understand why Gideon has to be so stubborn-minded in trying to become a man that he is not, and all to impress your father who is a hard and unforgiving man. Even if he was to be invited to the Royal court as an honoured guest, it would not be enough.

Nothing will melt your father's cold-heartedness towards him. In his eyes, Gideon stole his only daughter. This dalliance will only make matters worse. Gideon should have been out there fighting for the King, as your brothers are doing."

Kat was defiant. "He may not be fighting with the rest of them, but at least he is safe. I would far rather that than the idea of him on a battlefield."

"Foolish girl!" Darling brought her fist to the table in frustration. "Your husband's family home is where all this trouble started, Kateryn. It is a town filled with puritans who hate the monarchy. They still grieve for Cromwell and the false freedoms he promised. You said it yourself when you lived there for the short time that it lasted." There was such bitterness to her tone, such derision, that it made Kat take a step back.

"I do not understand how people can hate each other so. This was why mother and father never approved of Gideon, isn't it? It was not the fact that he was a footman. Mother could have persuaded father over that. You could have done it! Especially you! The reason for all of this scorn is because his parents supported Cromwell. And why not? Why should they not have had a little more ambition? What is it that was so terrible about those who just wanted a little more fairness?"

"Stop it!" The sting of Darling's hand against her cheek took her by surprise. "If anyone was to hear you, you would be accused of treason." Darling's voice was low, like the first distant rumbles of thunder that precede an approaching storm. "You have not lived through troubled waters yet. You have not endured two wars. You did not see the fields soaked with blood, neighbours turning on one another, brothers killing each other when Cromwell ripped the crown from the King's head. Do not speak so lightly of those who suffered. It is thanks to a pretender that more suffering has happened on English soil. Mark my words Kateryn, there will be far more suffering to come. The Duke of Monmouth has lost his head and King James is looking for revenge. Woe betide any man caught up in all of this."

"Or woman," Kat reminded her, her tone bitter as she referred to Alice Lisle.

Darling's bottom lip quivered as she glared at her granddaughter. "Men and women, people will be made to pay and made to pay with blood. It is always the way with these things. It was the man who gave me my bastard children who taught me that." Unable to look at her any longer, Darling stormed out into the garden where they grew their many herbs and plants.

Kat hung her head in shame, only too aware of the damage her words had inflicted. It had been unkind and disrespectful to say those things to Darling. She had forged a life for herself during times that were not easy and Kat's grandfather had broken her heart on many occasions. All Kat knew of him was that he was of great nobility and that Darling had been the secret mistress. He had always looked after her, but not in the way that she had needed. Ashamed by the hasty remarks she had made, Kat climbed the wooden stairs to the privacy of her little chamber. When she was behind the door, she allowed the tears to fall. Darling had been right. It was indeed a bad sign that she had received no word from Gideon. The gnawing doubt bit away at her as she stared unhappily out of the window into the pretty herb garden below. Darling was out there angrily uprooting vegetables and herbs, dropping them into a basket. In spite of what she had said about Kat's marriage, she did not know the half of what had gone on before he had left.

They had rowed dreadfully in the months leading up to his departure. The talk of returning to employment with Lord Granville had changed him. It made no sense. They had a better life in Winchester, near to Kat's grandmother with the security of a position for Kat in the apothecary and Gideon working for a family with a fortune far more stable than the Granville money. Lord Granville had met with Gideon in secret on more than one occasion. Kat had learned the meetings had taken place in a coaching inn on the route between Winchester and Dorchester. The attention had given her husband a false sense of security and importance. She had warned him that he was no equal, no companion. "He is making a fool of you, Gideon," she had told him one evening as she had applied a salve to the blisters on his feet. He had been intoxicated and dismissed her warning, boasting about what a life they would soon have.

"Why ruin yourself over dishonest, drunk men?" she had asked him angrily.

Gideon had appeared crestfallen. It had always been a sore point, the fact that he was not of a high enough social standing to be accepted by Kat's family as a worthy husband. It had become the wedge between them, pushing them apart and pushing him away. The way that she spoke and conducted herself, the fact that she could read and write, it was all a daily reminder to him that she was too good for a man like him. There had been an underlying resentment simmering away beneath her husband's usually charming and happy demeanour and her opinion on Lord Granville's motives had driven him further away. He had refused to share any more details of his meetings or whereabouts with her. He no longer thought to bring home the wild flowers or plants he found on his journeys so that she could place them in the kitchen in the home that she feared they were close to losing. They had stopped talking altogether.

Then one day, as the sky was lightening to dawn, he had returned home after another evening with Lord Granville and his acquaintances. Gideon's eyes had been red-rimmed and the stink of alcohol had been on his breath. "What is wrong?" he had asked her when she had looked upon him with reproach.

Kat had been unable to sleep and was stirring the pot of oats that she had begun to warm over the fire.

"What is it, wife? Do you still see the farm boy from Dorsetshire when you look upon me? Will I never be good enough for your family?" After stumbling against the door, he had fallen onto a stool. Kat had bitten her tongue, hoping that if he was to sleep it off his temper would cool, but he had stood up again and thrown his knuckles into the wall. "I will prove myself better than any man your father wanted you married off to. You will see. But perhaps I shall take another wife, one who will be grateful for all I have done, one who will look pretty in the fine dresses that I will buy her." His words had ripped at her heart and she had turned to see him reeling forwards and backwards as his fingers bled.

Kat had rarely seen him so intoxicated and he had never been so cruel either. There had been such malice on his face as he had glared at her, daring her to challenge him. She had retorted by telling him that perhaps she had made the wrong decision, that she should have wed one of the men her parents had selected so that her heart may not feel so broken. He had shot up from his seat at that, marched towards her and she had flinched. In that moment he had seen her fear and she saw something switch in him. The following night he had stayed at home and he had been so consumed with guilt that he had fallen to his knees and begged for her forgiveness. Relieved to have her old husband back, her legs had buckled so that she joined him on the floor. Her knees pressing against the rough rush matting, she had held his hands and told him that she was his wife, that her heart would always find forgiveness. Between kisses he had promised her a better life, said that when he returned from his next journey as footman that they would start a family. There had been a look on his face though that Kat could not brush aside. It had been the sort of look she imagined belonged to a man guilty of betraying his wife. In that moment, she had wondered if he had bedded another woman, but she knew better than to ask and start another argument. He had made love to her and it had been the first time in so long. Afterwards, they had wept together and she had noticed how much he was shaking in her embrace. The following morning, he had left, promising that he would return before the apple tree in Darling's garden was bending with fruit.

Kat's gaze moved to the corner of the garden where the tree he had spoken of was already beginning to bear its fruitful burden. It would not be long before she and Darling were filling baskets. When would he come good on his promise, she wondered?

There was a knock at the door and Darling appeared with her large black and white dog. He hovered loyally by her side as Darling offered Kat a small posy of red, pink and white flowers picked from the garden. "A peace offering," she said.

Reaching for the flowers, Kat sniffed them. "Thank you." She noted the sadness on Darling's face.

"I am taking Merlin out. I hoped you would come." The dog's ears pricked up. Impatient to leave, he began to bark.

"I'd like that very much."

They took the path that flanked the River Itchen. Behind them, they could hear the wheel of the mill churning through the flowing water. Some of the washerwomen were finishing the last of their work, rinsing and scrubbing late bundles of linen, ready to wring and dry. As they passed them, it was impossible for Kat not to feel a wave of envy upon hearing their exchange of complaints of snoring husbands keeping them awake at night. What Kat wouldn't give to swap her lonely bed for one that was too crowded or too noisy for sleep. She twisted at the band on her wedding finger, recalling the look in Gideon's eyes when he had put it there four years before, promising her everlasting love and loyalty. Sensing her sadness, Merlin nudged her legs with his nose.

Darling suggested that they follow the path through the meadows. It was a glorious summer evening and the river walk was a beautiful one. They chatted about the herbs and plants and the shop and about Nell Deakin three doors down. Nell had just given birth to her sixth. Darling asked if there had ever been any hint of a baby for Kat and Gideon.

"Only the once, but it wasn't to be," Kat admitted with a heavy sigh. She contemplated confiding in Darling about how it had really been before Gideon had left, but it would only make her grandmother's dislike for him grow. Shaking off the temptation to confess any of it, Kat gave the obvious answer: "I should love to start a family, but it is so hard…" They passed by some of the boys from Winchester College. The meadows were their place to play. Both women went quiet, avoiding the sparky looks. They could be cruel for entertainment and two women walking alone would be easy pickings. Eager to return before their curfew, the boys ran along without saying anything and Kat resumed their conversation. "It is so hard, this endless waiting for his return and what with all this trouble, not even knowing if-"

"Do not even say it, Kateryn," Darling warned. She pressed her lips together and her demeanour softened. "You were right earlier when you said that it would not be as easy for word to come from Gideon this time. The country is greatly disrupted. He and Lord Granville will return."

"I wish they would make haste," Kat complained, "Lord Granville made no payment before their trip."

"Kat, you need only ask if you are struggling. Do not let pride get in the way."

"I have enough," Kat lied. The truth was that there was barely enough to pay the next sum of rent and if it was not for Darling's charity, she would be struggling to feed herself let alone keep the cottage on the edge of town.

"Do not fret Kateryn, he will be back soon."

"We could look for him." Kat's words were barely more than a whisper, the suggestion hanging in the air between them.

Ignoring the hint, Darling shook her head. "You know that the country is awash with the King's soldiers and the rebels. Imagine what they would do to two women found wandering the countryside alone?"

"You know very well what I mean," Kat said as she caught her grandmother's eye. "There are other ways." She was referring to Darling's gift of sight. Although it did not always come very easily, she was rarely wrong when it did. Folk suspected it of course, but she had always denied it. Sometimes women would come into the shop asking for remedies to help bring babies and there had even been requests for drinks that could stop a baby from coming. Then there were those who would promise to cross her palm with silver in return for gazing into the future. Darling bent to nobody's will on these matters.

Gripping her by the elbow, Darling pulled her closer, afraid that somebody might be within earshot. "You speak as though I am a cunning woman. Talk like that could land us both in trouble." She turned to check whether anyone was behind them, but the schoolboys were ever shrinking silhouettes as the distance between them grew.

For a while, they carried on in silence before Darling suggested that they return home. Merlin, who had until that moment been obediently sticking to Darling's heel, bounded off. His nose had caught the scent of something and he was heading in the direction of the river's flow. With no choice other than to follow the wayward dog, they called him back, but he was determined. The hems of their dresses trailed against the dried mud of the riverbank and their shoes kicked up the dust of summer-parched earth as they hurried after him. When at last they reached him, they were both short of breath and standing near to the strip of river that eventually meandered beyond the water meadows to pass the magnificent hump of St Catherine's Hill.

Walking towards the water's edge, they stood watching the silver flash and dart of minnows and listening for the splash of trout. "We could keep following the river," Kat suggested, her heart beating wildly at where it would take them.

Darling remained firm. "I would prefer to take the walk back into town. We can make it back before the sun starts to set."

"But sunset is the best time," Kat protested, determined not to give up. The ancient Hill Fort was a sacred place for her grandmother. It was a place where the spirit guides gathered and could be reached. Both women looked to where the splendid green shoulder of the hill rolled upwards, high over the trees that lined the water meadows. "Please, Darling. You once said what a terrible thing it is for a woman to be left neither widow nor wife and with no children. At least if we look, we might find him. We might find Gideon."

"Why can you not write to Lady Granville and ask her when her husband is set to return from this business?"

"I have and she has not replied," Kat clutched Darling's forearm. "Please, Darling. You know that I am worried and I know you share my concerns. Say that you will look?"

Darling sighed heavily. "And what if I do see something? What if I see that his skin is blue, his body beaten, or worse? What then?"

"It would be better than this endless waiting, the not knowing at all!" Kat cried, her arms falling to her sides. "Every night I struggle to sleep and when I do I wake to the slightest noise, hoping it is him and fearing that it is someone coming to tell us that-" She stopped, struggling to admit the fear that had been plaguing her since Gideon had taken off.

"Tell us what, Kateryn?" There was pity in Darling's icy blue gaze as she heard Kat's anguish.

Tears that had threatened earlier welled up in her eyes and she looked longingly at the hill ahead.

Her reserve crumbling, Darling took her by the hand and they began to follow the river.

St Catherine's Hill was a beautiful and special place: an old settlement from times long before Kat could even imagine. It was a place where deep magic resided. A chapel had once stood proudly on the hill. Following its demise during King Henry's reformation almost one hundred and fifty years before, its ruins were hidden amongst an enclave of beech trees.

Darling had always claimed that she had felt the magic of the place. It had pulled her towards it, and as a young girl, Kat had followed her. Even Kat had felt its power running through the roots of trees beneath her feet, like hot blood in a network of veins. It made her fingertips tingle and lit a fire in her belly so that she thought she might explode. It had always been as though an invisible, enchanted thread had drawn them there. It was a place that they had agreed should only be ventured to if there was something to be seen, some future truth to learn. St Catherine's Hill was the place where answers could be found to the questions asked.

Merlin aborted sniffing the ground and looked at Kat with melancholy in his brown eyes. He felt her grief, for he had memories of Gideon too. Kat thought back to happier days, when she had first met him. He had been employed by her father and she had often seen him when she had taken her beautiful mare, Flame, riding through the nearby fields. She had not realised that he had been watching her from afar and one day, just as she had kicked the horse on to a canter across the meadows, he had appeared, running alongside her. Merlin had been a puppy at the time and had joined her on many rides, but even as a much younger dog he had lagged far behind. The young footman had laughed as he ran alongside them, calling out to Merlin. Kat had spurred Flame on faster and faster, but Gideon had effortlessly kept the pace. Even when she had taken Flame to a gallop, Gideon had not tired. Amazed, she had brought the horse to a halt and waited for Merlin to catch up. She would never forget the cheeky twinkle in Gideon's eyes as he had stopped just ahead of her, turned and punched his arm in the air as he had claimed his victory at outrunning the horse. Then he had smoothed Merlin's fur, tickled him behind the ears and laughed as the dog had barked and licked him. She and Gideon had met lots after that, in secret. They had raced through the fields, his smartly kept hair tumbling free so that his auburn locks flowed behind him as he raced past her. They had enjoyed racing each other and Kat had marvelled at his speed and agility. Onlookers had spotted the pair racing and one morning a crowd had gathered. Bets had been placed and people had been cheering. Gideon had won. He had basked in the glory of his short-lived fame and carelessly, so had Kat. Word had got back to her father. Furious, Gideon had been promptly dismissed and forced to return to Dorchester.

Kat had been in disgrace and forbidden to leave the house. It was not long before she was thrust in front of would-be suitors, but she had despised all of them. When Gideon had returned to Winchester to take his chance with her, it had been the best moment of her life. In the still of night, he had thrown small stones at her window and told her to take Flame on a ride to St Catherine's Hill the following morning. There he had informed her of his new position as footman to the Granville family in Dorsetshire. He had said that it was a secure post that paid enough so that he could do what he had been planning with all his heart. Getting down on one knee, he had asked her to be his wife.

They had both known that her father would refuse. The situation escalated and Kat had defied the wishes of her parents. She had left for a new life in Dorchester, where Gideon was already popular and famed for his speed and agility. Lord Granville had enjoyed putting him in races with other notoriously quick footmen. Gentlemen would place bets to see whose footman would win and when Gideon beat every one of them, the competition had turned to outrunning horses and hounds. Her husband had become known as the man who could outrun any beast. She had loved watching him run, the determination on his face and the way his shirt collar parted to show the glisten of his hot skin.

Wrapping her arms about her chest, she looked up at the sky. Those days seemed so long ago.

When they neared the curve of the river, they slowed a little, catching their breath before taking the track that led to the foot of the steep climb that they would need to endure. The chalk stream wended lazily to the right and left before there was a bridge. They crossed it and Kat heard her grandmother slip. She turned to see her stop to catch her breath, her eyes looking into the glassy surface below. Darling brought a hand to her chest and winced. A disloyal thought fleeted through Kat's mind as she recalled the old adage that a witch could not easily travel over water. She looked around nervously, wondering if anybody was near enough to notice. Then she looked down at her feet with shame. Just because her grandmother had the sight, it did not make her a witch.

A dragonfly flew ahead, hovering before resting on some of the taller grass that fringed the river's edges. "Can I help?" she asked Darling, offering her a hand but she shook her head, rubbing at her chest.

"These pains, they come and go. I forgot to take my daily tincture. That is all this is." She waved her on and Kat looked back at the dragonfly. It was right in the spot where Gideon had proposed. The brilliant green and blue glint of its body dazzled her for a moment, then it was gone.

They reached the other side of the bridge and Kat's eyes followed the short length of mud track stretching between them and St Catherine's Hill. After the river, any wildlife they would see would most likely be signs: messengers from the spirit world.

As they neared their destination, the sun had started embarking on its descent, ready to give way to the moon and the creatures that liked to emerge beneath its waning, milky light.

At the foot of the incline, they stopped and looked up. The twisted knots of tree roots snaked their way over the chalky ground, creating nature's uneven staircase up the hill. "Come on," Darling said, her vigour having returned. "No time to dither."

Careful not to lose her footing, Kat climbed. Ahead of them, Merlin scrambled up the chalk face. Foliage rustled as trees took in their winged lodgers ready for nightfall. Higher they climbed, until the chalk fascia mingled with grass. An urgent flapping took Kat by surprise and the ground in front of her was shadowed by the large wingspan of a buzzard. It circled once before swooping, climbing and then circling again. "Do you think it is a sign?" she whispered, noting the look of trepidation on Darling's face.

"I hope not," she answered. "A bird like that is never a good sign."

"Why?"

Darling shot her a sideways glance. "It portends death," she said before pushing on.

As they neared the hill crest, Kat paused, her brow sticky with sweat. The welcome cooler air of evening glanced over her and she pushed up her sleeves, desperate to let it cool her skin.

Allowing her breathing to regulate again, Kat paused and took in the view. Winchester sprawled out beyond the fields and pasturelands of roaming sheep. Save for the evening trill of birdsong and the frantic click of crickets, everything was still. In the distance she could see the cathedral, its magnificent structure gleaming in the low sun, amidst the clusters of townhouses. Kat turned to look towards the clump of beech trees that were hiding the last remnants of a once beautiful and peaceful building. It saddened her to see what would have once been such a tranquil and beautiful place of worship in ruins.

Watching Darling bend to pet Merlin and whisper to him with the instruction to stay, Kat braced herself for what was to come. Obediently, the dog lay on the floor, giving the darkness beyond the trees a wary glare. He knew what to expect too but, loyal to the end, no matter what happened, he would always stay.

Darling took a moment to remove her coif and Kat copied. It was what they always did in this place. Darling said that it made it easier for the spirits to feel them and to come. They walked to the clump, Darling in front of Kat, her hair once liquid sunshine, now faded to the colour of moonlight, tumbled down her back in silky waves. She looked every bit the enchantress.

Beneath a sky that was ablaze with orange and gold, the rock-rose wildflowers appeared as a glowing carpet stretching towards a natural opening in the coppice of trees. Bumps began to rise on the skin of her arms and the hair on her scalp bristled. She felt the presence of the spirit guides. Most were good, but amongst them were others: dark souls, on the periphery between earth and hell.

"Stay near me, Kateryn," Darling whispered as they reached the opening in the trees.

Their fingers laced together as they slowly entered the darkness beneath the dense foliage. Each step felt heavy. Kat could feel the clamminess of Darling's palms. They had to be careful.

Darling reached in to the pocket of her apron and brought out a bag of salt for protection. It was something she always carried.

Kat shivered. She could not shake the feeling that something bad was waiting for her. She could sense it - the smell of the air, the taste on her tongue. In her mind's eye, she could see shapes ebbing in and out of view: silhouettes of the dead, keen to connect once again with the living.

Deeper into the wooded area, she began to feel them reaching out, their ethereal hands emanating an unearthly cold. Her body reacted; she was trembling, nausea rising, the taste of bile in the back of her throat.

"Think not of the darker shapes Kateryn, lest you bring them closer," Darling whispered, guessing her fears. "Focus on those who have left us. Think of those who have crossed over but who, in their mortal flesh, loved us. Feel them near you."

As they walked further into the coppice, stepping over tree roots and into the darkness, Kat began to regret asking this of her grandmother. She wanted to close her eyes, to be in her bed back at the house with the strange and pungent smells that would drift upstairs from the shop, not out on this chalky, untamed grassland where souls that were centuries old gathered.

Exercising her grandmother's advice, she felt the terrible coldness retract and dared to breathe, but fear was quickening her feet as she cumbersomely navigated the uneven ground. Just as she lost her footing, Darling caught her by the forearm. "Do not give them the chance to see any vulnerability," she reminded her. "We are stronger when we are calm, when we embrace the gift bestowed upon me. It runs in your blood too."

Shutting her eyes, Kat focused on the earth, the trees and the ground, solid beneath her feet. Her grandmother was wrong. The gift had skipped her mother's generation and it had skipped her own too. Neither she or her brothers had inherited it.

Kateryn.

The voice was like breath on a gentle breeze. Soft and wraithlike, it seemed to drift above the huge fallen log that they had reached. The log would be their altar. Darling stopped, placed her hands against the wood and began saying something.

Kat watched her silky long hair begin to blow about her shoulders. A wind was whipping up, thrashing through the leaves of the trees. She thought she saw shapes dancing beyond the tall trunks, keeping their distance but allowing her to glimpse them now and again. It was disconcerting and her fear returned. She turned her head to see the burnished glow of the dipping sun through the arch of trees that fringed the edge of the coppice. She wanted to run towards the light, return to what was left of the day. It was too late now though. Darling had already begun the ritual, eager to get it over with. Besides, Kat reminded herself, she was doing this for her husband. They were both doing this for Gideon.

"Join me, Kateryn." Darling motioned for Kat to place her hands on the log, to say the words that would help channel the spirits and bring the message. Kat wondered whether Darling would tell her everything that they would show her, and she wondered whether they would show her anything at all.

Opening her mouth, she took a breath and felt the rough bark graze her fingertips. Then, as Darling used the salt to create a protective circle, Kat removed her shoes. Beneath her feet, the earth was cold from the shade offered by the trees. She would need to remain strong for her grandmother as invoking the spirits and the sight would leave her weak and vulnerable. Kat knew that she had to keep her wits about her so that she could pull Darling from her reverie if she appeared to be fading or weakening. Wriggling her toes, she focused on the sensation of the cool soil as she joined in the chant. It was a ritual that had been practised for centuries by those whose roots were from deep magic.

Their voices danced as one, high notes rising above the wind. The trees continued to rustle and there was an urgent flapping of wings as a flock of birds took flight. Kat imagined their tiny bodies disappearing into the darkening sky as they sought refuge in a safer place. Fear clawed at her insides, her instincts screaming at her to run. Holding her ground, they repeated the words in unison as the wind lashed at them, the force of it stealing her breath.

Aware of other voices, still distant but drawing nearer, Kat kept her ears keen. Then she heard the howls of something else. Her heart hammered against her ribs. No weakness. No vulnerability. No room to let whatever it was in. Looking ahead, she could see the sea of shapes and she searched for those that resembled relatives who had passed to the other side, but found it impossible to single any one of them out.

Blood was rushing through her veins, burning her limbs, colouring the skin of her cheeks. This was not something that she had felt before. She looked at

Darling, who had stepped inside the circle to welcome the spirits and the message that they had. She was asking them for guidance, to show them what Kat needed to know. Kat wobbled on her feet. They hadn't invoked the spirit world often but she knew that she wasn't supposed to feel this strange, unearthly tingle, or the horrific rush of hot and cold throughout her body. Had they gone too far and incited some terrible force from the brimstone of hell?

Focus, she reminded herself. *Do not think of the darkness or the fear. Feel the earth and be aware of the mortal plane.* She continued to chant, changing the words so that she incited a charm of protection. She felt her knees weaken. Something was in front of her. It was not her grandmother, but a shape that was tall, foreboding and bright. A hand, cold as ice, pressed against her forehead. Then there was only blackness.

******

"Kateryn! Kateryn!" The voice was filled with urgency and she could feel a hand tugging her arm. There was a pain in her head and a crawling sensation beneath her skin. "You must get up, Kateryn. It is too dangerous to stay." Darling's breath was laboured as she attempted to haul Kat to her feet and she cried out, pressing a hand to her chest. The sound of her in pain brought Kat to her senses and she got to her feet, swiftly propping her up.

"I am here, Darling. I am with you. What happened?"

"Help me out of here. We must leave this place," she said and she winced as another pain took hold.

"Hold on to me and I will get you home." In spite of her own pain, Kat all but carried her grandmother to the opening in the trees where Merlin was barking. They fell to the ground, catching their breath. There was enough light to see them along the river but it would not last for long. With a groan, Darling turned her head as Merlin licked her cheek. "We must go home. We cannot stay here." She went to push herself up.

"No, Darling! I will fetch help. You cannot manage it."

Batting her hand away, Darling was adamant that she would be fine. "I am quite recovered. It is you who I worry for now. You did not ground yourself. I thought you had become lost."

Still aware of the unpleasant sensation beneath her skin, Kat apologised for losing her concentration and they moved on, walking most of the way back in silence. It was only when they reached the mill that Kat dared ask about what she had seen.

Her jaw set in a straight and stubborn line, Darling shook her head. "I saw nothing of Gideon."

Disappointed and shocked, Kat felt overwhelmed with the hopeless feeling that had been creeping up on her for weeks. "The spirits brought you nothing at all? Can you be sure?"

"I told you that it is unwise to call upon the spirit world for self-serving reasons," she snapped. "I should have done more to convince you otherwise." She refused to say another word as they finished their journey home.

The house was silent upon their return, its emptiness emphasised by nightfall. Merlin lapped at some water that had been placed into a dish by the fire and Darling found some scraps for him whilst Kat collapsed into a chair with sudden exhaustion. Her body felt fatigued and beaten and she tried to ignore the dizzying sickness that was threatening.

"I should think we will both need some of this." Darling placed two cups on the table and the rich and spicy aroma of hippocras filled Kat's nostrils. It was the good stuff, usually saved for special occasions. For a long time, there had been no occasion of any happy note to toast.

"You should not waste this, Darling."

"How can it be a waste when there is not much time to drink it?" Darling tipped the contents of her cup down her throat and poured herself another.

"What did you see out there?" Kat asked, refusing to touch her own.

There was a burden upon Darling's shoulders that was greater than any Kat had witnessed her hold and she looked suddenly frail. Her eyes had pooled and she tried to hide it by taking another drink.

"Grandmother, what did you see?"

Putting down her cup, Darling looked away. "I cannot help you with what you seek, my love. You must find your own way now."

Recalling the buzzard and Darling's warning that portended death, Kat recoiled. "Is he gone?"

She shook her head. "Not Gideon."

"Then what is it?"

She looked at the red patch on Kat's forearm where she had been scratching. "That feeling you have running through your arms and legs, as though something is crawling beneath your skin, I know it."

Retracting her nails from her arm, Kat stiffened.

"And I recognised what happened to you, up there on the hill." She picked up Kat's cup and offered it to her. "Drink. It will get rid of the pain in your head."

"You know?" Kat did not know why she was even asking; her grandmother knew everything.

"It is time, Kateryn, and they have chosen you."

She did not understand what her grandmother was trying to tell her. "You are making no sense, Darling."

"I am not long for this world. The spirits did not show me Gideon's future, they showed me my own and then they took you. That is why you feel the way you do." She hung her head. "I am sorry."

Kat did not know how to reply. Was her grandmother telling her that she had seen her own demise?

Pulling something from her pocket, Darling leaned across the table. A long chain was looped around her fingertips. Clasped into it by a neat silver claw was a shiny black stone. "Obsidian." Darling introduced the stone as though it was another person. It swung back and forth, gleaming.

Kat reached out to touch it, but Darling pulled away. "You have now been blessed and cursed, Kateryn, and so now you must take this. It is a powerful gem. Your grandfather gave it to me after he had spent a long time at sea. It is from the great mountains of a faraway land. Those mountains erupt with hot fire when God is angry. He said that is how the gemstone came to exist. It is for protection." She leaned closer, bringing the necklace nearer again. "And sometimes it can help with finding what you seek, for obsidian is said to show you the future, present and past. You must use it carefully, my love, and never in front of anyone. People do not understand that women like us can still be God-fearing whilst doing what we do or seeing the things that we see." The chain dangled so that its pendant was suspended in front of her, catching the candlelight. "This is precious and valuable. A charm like this must only be passed on down generations and never sold. Do you understand?"

The stone grazed against Kat's fingers and she felt its heat, the power surging from it. Shades of deep purple and green seemed to glint from the surface. "Why did you not give this to mother?"

Giving a scathing chuckle, Darling lowered her hands. "Your mother is too full of ambition. She follows your father's mind, not her own. This would have been sold to the highest bidder had I passed it down to her. Now, if you will." She gestured for Kat to bow her head so that the chain could be fastened around her neck.

Tucking it beneath her clothes and shift, Kat expected to feel some tremendous surge of energy but all she was aware of was the sensation of the stone's smoothness against her skin. "Are you going to die?" She blurted the words out before she had even realised but Darling did not flinch.

"We all have our time, Kateryn. Death comes to us all, beckoning with its icy pull. My time is not up yet but I am an old woman now." It was all she was prepared to say and Kat knew she would not share anything more.

"How will I know how to use it?" she asked as she turned the stone between her finger and thumb.

Leaning forward, Darling gave her a stern look. "Never try to use the stone, Kateryn. You and I, we are not powerful enough for such ventures. It will use you."

"It will guide you." Finishing her drink, Darling scraped back her stool and yawned. "Now, you must let an old woman retire."

When Kat had snuffed out the last of the candles and made her way into her chamber, she could already hear the gentle snores from Darling's room. The conversation they had shared sat uneasy with her as she fell heavily on to her bed. Kat had pleaded with her to look into the future and now her grandmother had paid the price by seeing the end of her days. Stripping to her shift, she gazed into the stone, thinking that there must be some way of stopping it all from transpiring. "Show me what I must do," she whispered. "If you really are so powerful you will show me all of it now." The stone remained dull and with a heavy sigh, she threw it to the floor. She hoped that Darling was wrong about what had she had seen. Kat blew out the candle on the little bedside table and dashed at the tears that had begun to fall. She tried to think of Gideon and of her grandmother, imagining them all together once again but it was not their faces that came to her when she eventually fell asleep…

******

In her dreams she felt different – weaker, frail and slower to move. She lifted her hand and recoiled as she stared at the pale, wrinkled skin. She was an old woman. She felt it beneath her skin, heard it in the creak of her bones and saw it through watery, old eyes.

The pounding against the huge oak doors reverberated through the house and Kat's thoughts became insignificant as she was swamped by the vision that the guides had been waiting to show her. She was no longer Kateryn Fox. She was Lady Alice Lisle.

Holding her breath, she paused, knowing that the visitors would be far from welcome.

Outside, the sun was rising as a brilliant orb of white promising another sunny July day in the New Forest.

From somewhere in the house a window was thrown open and a servant called out to the impatient knocks and bangs.

A man's voice replied. It was loud and commanding. "Lady Alicia Lisle." His tone curdled as he said her name.

Another ripple of voices followed from inside the house and then more pounding. The intruders had no intention of waiting for the doors to Moyles Court to be opened. Alice knew that they would beat them down if necessary.

Clutching the back of a chair, she turned to see that one of her guests had vanished, the other was rushing to her side, taking her hand and insisting that he had not meant to bring her harm. There was fear in his eyes and shadows of a terrible truth upon his expression. Alice felt a sinking despair. With haste, her guest let go of her hand and took to finding a hiding place.

She could hear the heavy bolts being lifted on the entrance doors. The urgent, impatient voices grew louder, their boom travelling up the staircase into the house. Alice felt a cold dread run through her. She had been here before, when the death of their Lord Protector, Oliver Cromwell, and the incompetence of his son and heir had forced her late husband into exile. Alice had been much younger then, able to take on the challenges thrown at the wife of a man in politics. Now she was much older, her bones creaking and her limbs shaky with age. Alice did not think that she had the constitution or the energy for a repeat of anything that had gone before. Her knees threatened to buckle.

The servants' protests were ignored. Heavy heeled boots took to the floorboards and she could hear pikes and musket-butts batter her walls and knock into her treasured possessions.

Steadying herself with her cane, she kept her face calm and her posture as rigid as a lady of seventy-one years could before leaving the temporary sanctuary of the room.

Moyles Court, and all its peaceful grandeur, had surrendered to a cacophony of chaotic voices, stamping feet and upturned furniture. She winced at the sound of something shattering against the floor. The pitch of it echoed through the hallway.

Calmly she walked onto the landing, holding her head high. With every step her reserve remained solid. Holding the balustrade, she looked into the madness below.

The long stems of the last of her beautiful roses had been crushed beneath heavy, careless feet, their crimson heads resembling screaming mouths. Another door crashed open and she could hear the clanging of pots in the kitchen. They were searching for her guests.

Men were shouting at each other, shouting at servants, shouting at her, shouting for people they couldn't see. The old lady wanted to press her hands flat against her ears to shut the noise out. Instead, she remained standing at the top of the landing, a picture of tranquil serenity.

Rough hands took her by the shoulders. She didn't know what was being said to her. Fear had rendered her unable to make any coherency of the words that were being flung in her direction. Struck dumb with the shock of it, she could not and did not respond.

Without knowing how she had even got there, she found herself downstairs, in the entrance hall, staring at the crushed roses from the broken vase, their once beautiful heads pressed to an ugly pulp. Soldiers trampled over them, carrying no regard for the beauty and grandness they had displayed only moments before. She wanted to scream at them, to tell them to stop but she knew that her voice would be of no importance.

Somebody was speaking to her again, pressing demands onto her. It was impossible to understand. She needed to sit down, to think and to come up with an answer. What was happening? What were they accusing her of?

Words spilled into the air, swirling around and threatening to choke her as the hands gripping her by the shoulders pinched even more cruelly. Her head pounded as she tried to focus on what they were saying.

The Duke of Monmouth. Traitors. Treason. Conspiracy.

She wanted to laugh. How could they be associating her, a seventy-one-year-old woman, with these words? It had to be a dream, a terrible dream that she would awaken from, warm in her bed and to the bright sound of birdsong from outside her window.

Moments passed. She was not waking. It was no dream.

Finding her voice, she turned to her interrogator, looked into his hollow, small eyes and swallowed back a gasp as she heard somebody utter his name.

Bells of alarm began ringing in her head, drowning out the aggressive voices that were booming through the usually calm and peaceful household.

Resplendent in his scarlet coat was the man named Colonel Thomas Penruddock. The black plume of his hat ostentatiously tickled the air above him as he stood in front of her full of self-importance. His thin, ruddy pink face wore a smug, cruel expression, as he looked her up and down.

'Penruddock'. She remembered that name well. It took her back to those days of her late husband. The grip on her shoulder tightened even more. Penruddock knew exactly who she was. Just as she knew of him. He had been all of an innocent young boy when, at the order of Alice's husband, he had lost his father to the henchman's axe, just as had happened to the King, but now he was a strong and cold-hearted man. She could see it in his eyes. It was his intention that she would suffer for a vendetta spanning back decades.

Her fear turned to panic as her mind began to run through all of the possibilities of what these men might have planned. They could do what they wished to her, but to harm her daughters would be a torture she could not stand. "Sir, for what reason is it that my house is subject to this mindless plundering?" she asked, her voice deceptively cool as she regarded a soldier appraising some silver from a drawer.

With effort, she tried to listen to his reply, but with her hearing waning and the terrible din that Penruddock's men were making, it was an impossible task. His thin lips curved into a self-satisfied smile as the shouts reached fever pitch.

Hickes. They had found Hickes. He had been hiding with another by the name of Dunne, the man who had brought her guests to Moyles Court the evening before. More shouts indicated that they had been hiding together. The third man, as far as she knew, was still hidden.

To the very end of his life, her husband had worried of this day. Before his death, he had fretted that his actions as a politician in the bloody wake of war would one day be avenged using Alice and his family. None of it had been her doing though. She had even begged her husband to reconsider his actions. She recalled the day bitterly, the cruel shove from her husband who had not recognised her when she had approached him in London, imploring him to influence a different choice for sentencing the King. How her heart had ached and her pride had tumbled. Hickes had been there, giving her support and comfort after the way that her husband had cruelly silenced her in all of his eagerness to exercise the power that Cromwell's victory had bestowed upon him. She had been indebted to the kindness and goodwill of John Hickes for a long time. That was all that her hospitality extended to. How was she to have known what matters he had been involved in? Surely they would understand that?

But she found herself protesting, proclaiming her innocence. Her argument was weak. Not heard, or more likely, not listened to. She was just a woman. She had no voice, just as back then, when her husband had sentenced the King to death, she had no voice. It seemed that the political tides were shifting again, pulling against one another.

Revenge twinkled cold and hard in his eyes as Penruddock began the proceedings to place her under arrest. As his words echoed through the house, the fear that had plagued her late husband began to unfold.

Of course, Alice had been privy to the news that, in previous weeks, the nephew of King James had landed on the shores of Dorset and tried to take the crown as his own, but nobody in her household had supported it. Her son had fought against the uprising. He had helped to bring the rogue army down at Sedgemoor. She had not been a supporter of the rebellion. What reasons could an old lady have to hope for another bloody war on English ground? The truth of the situation she found herself in did not matter. In her heart she already knew that she would be found guilty of harbouring these men as part of a conspiracy. Her innocence would be contested and it would be with a bitter irony that she, a regicide's wife, would have her destiny decided by men doing the bidding of King James – the son of the monarch whose execution her late husband had helped orchestrate.

Rough hands led her from the peaceful sanctuary of Moyles Court to the impatient snorts of horses, eager to carry their riders to the next destination.

The summer air was already feeling close and her body was sweating beneath the heavy material of her dress. Behind her, servants were hurrying to return order to the house. Some were whimpering with fright over the morning's turn of events, whilst others chastised them for being weak of spirit. Nobody knew what was happening or what was going to happen.

Penruddock escorted her away from the hysteria, away from the home that she had grown to love with its beautiful gardens and everything once neatly in its own place. His lips grazed her ear as they walked so that he could utter words that only she would hear: they had not needed to wait for the men to find refuge in her home, they could have intercepted their journey before they had reached the gates of Moyles Court.

Alice understood what this was. They had identified a political opportunity, the chance to arrest somebody with a measure of notability and make an example. It did not matter that she was a woman with no voice or influence over any of the terrible things that had happened. As she listened to the mocking way that he relayed the information, she realised that whatever happened to her would mark the end of an unfulfilled vendetta and the beginning of another.

There was a bang as the doors of Moyles Court were closed on their owner. Alice was shut out from the wail of voices and commotion inside, but she felt no respite. The silence only made it worse. Bitter tears pricked at her eyes as she stepped onto the mounting block and was helped onto the horse. She did not yet know where they were taking her, only that she was expected to ride the full distance and they needed to make good time. The scrape and clatter of hooves echoed about the estate as the horses made haste in their departure. Stones and dust were thrown into the air and Moyles Court began to shrink away. Above the sound of the horses, the sickening truth reverberated through her head. Once again, a woman would pay for the follies of men.

With difficulty, Kat tried to raise her head from her pillow, but to no avail.

In the body of Alice, she listened to the man riding alongside her as he spoke loudly, taking great delight in telling her where she was being taken and what fate was likely to be waiting for her. Salisbury, he told her, and it would be a long ride – a good few hours. There was no need for the rest of his cruel words. Inside, she knew that she would not likely hug her children again, smell the sweet scent of another summer, or know the bitter chill of winter biting at her skin. Nevertheless, she held her head high and looked straight ahead onto the rolling landscape.

It was not long before they broke into a canter and she struggled to keep a hold. Her eyes watered and streamed as they rode against the rising sun, the heat of the day creating a watery haze ahead of them. She could not see for the fine film of tears in her eyes and she had to rely on her horse following the soldier's. So eager he was to get her to the intended destination that he never once had the courtesy to check on her. On more than one occasion, thinking she would fall, she called out to him, but he did not hear, or he refused to listen.

It came as a surprise when her horse suddenly jolted, almost unseating her. He righted his footing but it was soon evident that he was struggling to keep up. Ahead of her, the soldier slowed, aware that she was unable to keep pace. Angry, he shouted, threatening her. The horse was lame though. He had lost a shoe and the pained grunts demonstrated his discomfort. She requested that they stop at a smithy. He regarded her with a mistrustful glare, summing up whether she was plotting something before shaking his head. They were to continue. The beast would be attended to when they arrived in Salisbury. She was furious. This was barbaric. The poor horse continued to struggle, trying to keep up with the one in front. Calling out again, she made clear her demand: they stop at the forge ahead, or she would resist arrest.

There was fear in his voice when he sternly addressed her threat. She knew that she was a high prize, valuable cargo not to be misplaced or to arrive late due to any form of resistance. Her late husband's name was well known to the King. That made her important. The stakes would be high for this soldier if he did not fulfil his duty.

Giving her a mistrustful glare and then looking at her struggling horse, he begrudgingly conceded to her request. The sound of iron striking against steel signalled that the blacksmith's forge was nearby. She knew where the forge was. In her dream, Kat stirred. Then, in a voice very different to her own, she heard herself give instructions.

At the forge, the soldier called out several times before a man greeted them. He regarded her with bright eyes and she could tell that he recognised her. As the soldier made the request for a new shoe for the horse, the man shook his head, stating that he was unwilling to play any part in the arrest of Lady Alice Lisle.

Kat felt frustration that was not her own and she pleaded with him, insisting that it pained her to be riding a lamed horse. Reluctantly he agreed and set to work.

She watched the red glow of sparks fly and enjoyed listening to the sound of the striking and bending of iron. These were sounds that she had taken for granted all of her life, but now they were sounds that she knew she might never hear again. They waited patiently, their horses dipping their heads as they attempted to loosen their bits. At last, the shoe was cooled and ready to be fitted. As the blacksmith did so, she saw the look of regret on his face. It warmed her to think that already, people disagreed with this terrible decision to take an old gentlewoman from her warm bed and make an example of her. It gave her hope.

The man refused to take payment. It wasn't right, he said. None of it was. He stood at the edge of the forge, watching them leave and not moving from his spot until the horses and riders disappeared over the horizon.

Everything became a blur and Kat felt herself growing dizzy. The breath was taken from her chest and she cried out as the ride rattled her bones. She was exhausted.

They arrived in Salisbury to a crowd of people from the streets. People would have no idea who she was upon sight, but it was clear that she was a prisoner and as an old woman, they would assume she was likely to be accused of witchcraft. Some began to make the sign to ward off the evil eye, whilst others looked away and one woman fished a ball of blue glass from her pocket, holding it in front of her, hoping that the charm would enable her to outstare the witch.

The horses came to a halt and rough hands were suddenly pulling at her. A man was urging her to make more haste in dismounting the horse. Nervous excitement from the crowd sounded out.

Peasants! The thought struck her with frightening clarity as she regarded the chaotic scene around her. Peasants on the streets were jeering, hooting, name-calling. How dare they? What did they know of her to say such things? They knew nothing about her but they did not like that she was wearing fine garments, demonstrating that she was well above their post in life, when it seemed that she was here to await trial as a witch.

A building loomed in front of her. Fisherton gaol. The stench of death, pain and decay billowed from it. Somebody jumped near, too near. She felt the unwelcome wet of spittle upon her cheek but her wrists were bound and she could not wipe it away. A man was shoved back into the growing crowd of jeering people. None of them knew the true reason that she been taken as prisoner. Those who hadn't averted their eyes in fear looked at her with both curiosity and malice. Her age, her gender and demeanour - it all went against her.

Another voice called something out. She could tell by the ugly drawl that there was nothing educated about its owner, but at least this one was better informed than the others who had branded her a witch. "Nah, a traitor!" The voice belonged to a man with crumbling teeth and a nose that appeared to have been broken on countless occasions. "She must be one of his lot." As she passed, she saw him lean forward. "Shame on you. God save the King."

There was the crunch of metal and the creaking of hinges. A gate was opened and a draught of putridly odorous air accosted her. She stumbled, but was held upright as she was walked forwards. The smell worsened the deeper into the darkness they descended. Then another gate was opened and she found herself in front of a heavy door. A large set of keys was required to throw back the latch and somebody barked at her to go through.

There was no point in protesting. Obediently, she did so and she waited for the bindings around her wrists to be removed before the door was shut. She remained standing, her hip beginning to throb from being made to walk too fast after an uncomfortable journey on horseback that had stiffened her joints.

She turned her nose up as she noticed the pail in the corner, still full of slop from the previous occupant. Then she looked out of the small square hole in the wall. Strips of sunlight glared at her through the bars, like rays of judgement from heaven. Her stomach churned. If she had broken her fast, she would have been sick. Instead, she doubled over and spat, realising how dreadfully thirsty she was. She wanted to sit down but the floor was filthy. It would be better to remain standing. The stonework of the building did a good job of keeping the place mercifully cool. She did not fancy the idea of collapsing in the heat. It had been a hot summer and even inside the walls of Moyles Court, she had spent some very uncomfortable, hot and sticky days.

Moyles Court.

In her dream, Kat repeated the name given to the estate again and again as though it was the one thing that would keep her sanity.

Time passed and she found herself slumped against the wall of the prison. The sun had long been eclipsed by nightfall. As Alice Lisle, her dignity and pride had been overcome with exhaustion, and she had been given no choice but to rest amidst the muck. They had thrown in fresh straw, intended to make the pitiful cell more comfortable. She had hoped that by now somebody would have come for her, had her removed from the foul place, explained that it was all a dreadful mistake and that a lady of her standing should never have been arrested and thrown into a gaol for commoners who evaded their taxes or committed dreadful crimes. Nobody had come. If they had, the guards had not allowed them past.

The seriousness of her plight began to dawn on her as the night eventually gave way to a crimson sunrise, bleeding through the meagre gaps between the window bars.

During the course of the evening, someone had come and left her food and drink. They had not spoken to her, but she had seen the look on his face, the pity. She had also seen his fear for her. She wondered how long they would keep her there. There was clearly going to be a trial of sorts.

Turning her head to look out at the hints of a new day, she wondered when she would look out at her last. The thought lingered, making her head pound and she felt something tugging at the sleeve of her dress. She turned…

******

"Kateryn, wake up." Darling's voice rang out above the rush and buzz in Kat's head.

Raising her head, she caught her grandmother's melancholy stare. "What did they show you?"

Taking the glass of milk that was offered to her, Kat drank deeply, quenching her thirst before giving her answer. "I had terrible dreams of Lady Alice Lisle."

Sitting on the edge of the bed, Darling cast her gaze to her hands. "It is true then. They have chosen you. The gift must pass on down the line when the time is right." She looked sad and distant and then she sighed. "What of her? Was there a message?"

"I don't know. I don't think so. Should there have been? How would I know?" Kat felt the weight of it all upon her and her eyes blurred.

Darling did not notice. Biting her nails, she began to pace the room. "It is a sign. It has to be. But why her? Why her crime?"

"She did not commit the crime she is accused of!" Kat was aghast, her anger hot and unexpected.

"Then that is the message," Darling said flatly and left the room.

Exasperated, Kat pushed back the blanket and followed her downstairs. "What are we supposed to do with it though?"

Moving the cast iron cooking pot aside, Darling began to bank the fire. "I do not know that yet."

"And what about Gideon? Why has nothing come to us about him?"

Darling blew gently on the glowing embers before answering the question. "I do not know, Kateryn. Perhaps there is no message to give."

A horrifying thought struck her. "Do you suppose that Alice Lisle is somehow connected to Gideon?"

Darling's expression was grave. "Let us pray not. That would not bode well."

Sweeping the wayward ashes, Kat focused her thoughts on Gideon. "I can feel him inside, Darling. He is alive but I sense something else."

"Go on."

Swallowing, Kat realised that her mouth was dry. "I sense fear," she said and felt her stomach knot.

CHAPTER TWO

Every time I shut my eyes all I can see is a sky that appears to bleed, full of fire and smoke, and all I can smell is the gunpowder mixed with marshland. My body shakes. It will not stop. I hear the cries of those whom I left behind and I pray that God will forgive me for my sins. It is a miracle that we have reached the safehouse Lord Granville had told me of. This had never been the plan for our journey, but this is where I find myself.

We are unwanted guests, but favours are owed. As a footman, I hear and see everything. They expect my confidence. I am the silent companion, the one who runs alongside the carriages; the one who runs messages and the one who helps polish the status of my employer with my height, speed and looks that are considered handsome. My good looks, broad shoulders and strong body have always held me in good favour, but none of that will be enough now.

My heart beats wildly in my chest as, not considered worthy enough by my hosts for a bed with feather pillows, I climb into the hayloft. This is not the home of a nobleman, but the home of a wealthy wool merchant. It is big but by no means grand. It is what my employer disdainfully refers to as 'new money'.

The dreadful noises, sights and smells I left behind come back to me again and a cry catches in my throat as I think of my brother. There was so much chaos and he would not come. We argued and we fought. It cost us time. It may have cost him his life.

I wonder where he is now, whether he is still in the ditch that I left him in, caked in mud, determined to find his own way out. Pride stopped him from coming. He thinks that I betrayed him when I married and left him. I suppose I did. I suppose I have betrayed everyone dear to my heart…

I think back to when I left Winchester. Things had been so different back then. I had been so full of hope and certainty that the journey would bring fortunes beyond our wildest dreams. There had been no talk of ordinary men in their thousands, huddled together with permission to swiftly dispose of anyone whose noise threatened the element of surprise.

That night will forever haunt my dreams and plague my waking moments with a sickening dread as I recall the muffled clomp of horse hooves wrapped in cloth and the endless rows of silhouettes of men marching across the wetlands and into their doom. How, I ask myself again, did it come to this? I think of the young man who had marched with me and I squeeze my eyes shut even tighter as I try to think of his name, but my memory fails me. Then my stomach heaves but nothing comes up. I have not eaten in days and all that I have had to quench my thirst has been the water in ditches and streams. My throat is burning.

Only a few short months earlier, things had been so very different. Lord Granville had been so pleased to have me back, said that I would rise far higher in position than a footman back in his employment. He had treated me as a companion, a man of his standing. We had set off for the journey he had said would be the most important in all my life. It was, he had assured me, a journey of honour. I was given a horse, told that I was to save my feet and that when the journey was complete I could keep him.

Our travels took us over moorland and less travelled roads and then we encountered the rebels, swelling in their numbers. Some claimed they were ready to fight just as their fathers and grandfathers had done forty years earlier, others had the look of the devil in their eyes. These were the ones who grew disinterested after skirmishes. They'd had a taste of it, enjoyed the sport and began drifting back home. Lord Granville became unnerved at that. I think he regretted the journey the moment we stepped foot on the soil of Somersetshire. He was right to feel that way. The things we have witnessed: fields awash with blood, men hanging from trees, their bodies mutilated. After leaving my brother, we raced across the moors and through woodland, desperate to reach the destination that Lord Granville insisted we needed to find. He no longer looked like a man of status. I realised that in spite of all the times he had cajoled me into believing that I could be like him, this would be the only time that we were equals – two men running for their lives.

When we arrived there was a conversation - one I was not party to the detail of. I did not care though. All I could think about was home:, the smoking chimney, the warm kitchen smelling of freshly baked bread and the sound of something simmering in the iron pot suspended over the fire and of her beautiful smile – the one that could lift my world.

I move hay and pat it into a suitable bed. The sweat of the horses mingles with my own. My sleeves are still wet from the splash of the pails of water we threw over them to cool their bodies. Grimacing, I take off my boots. They are worn through and my feet are blistered.

I throw my mind back to before Winchester, when we were first married and living in my hometown, Dorchester. We had been happier then, too much in love to care about money or titles, or the differences between us that would always set us apart. Back then, in our small but cosy home, there would be salves and small ale and conversation; we would sit outside looking across at the watermills, beneath the orange blaze of a setting sun.

Before long though, I had tired of that simple life. She missed her own home and how could I blame her? Although she never complained, I could see how the colour had drained from her cheeks and how much thinner she had become. She was used to far finer things than I could give her. It had all seemed so meagre, nothing close to the grandeur that she deserved

- that we deserved. There was once a time when I would have given anything to live in a house like this one that I find myself at now, drinking from fine crystal glasses, eating bountiful feasts of meats, cheeses, custards and tarts. Now I would give anything for a night beneath the stars, the smell of rubbed herbs still on her hands and the vibrant song of crickets. I would give anything to travel back to the summer when I first saw her and my heart slammed against my chest as I watched her from afar, hair untamed and flowing as she rode that chestnut mare across meadows of gold. I would give anything to take back all the decisions that eventually led me here.

CHAPTER THREE

Ruth placed the cards on the table and slipped off her rings. She had learned over the years that removing her own personal items made for a better reading.

In spite of a gloriously sunny but frosty afternoon, the curtains had been drawn and candles lit. The atmosphere of the room was complemented by warm tones of sandalwood.

Flicking back her wrist, she checked her watch. Five minutes to spare before her next client arrived. She hoped that he would turn up soon. Her husband, Grayson, was due back home in just over an hour and he did not like it when Ruth did Tarot readings.

Taking a deep breath, she leaned back in her chair, inhaling the incense and shutting her eyes. In recent months, her psychic ability had been waning and it worried her. Reading the cards were only a secondary source of income to working in the administration department of Winchester University but it was another way to fund her own financial independence and she liked the idea that she was able to help people.

Tarot had come naturally to Ruth. She hadn't even realised her talent until she had bought a pack, enticed by the psychedelic pictures on the other side of a very Gothic looking design. At the time, buying the cards had simply been another addition to the eclectic mix of objects in her student accommodation. She had been young and studying at university in Brighton. Shops selling those sorts of things had littered the lanes and the items in them had adorned her shelving which had been filled with Chinese healing balls, a macabre looking incense holder and several sets of wind chimes. One night, after drinks and tapas with friends, she had been persuaded to try doing a reading. It had all been part of a phase of experimenting with new ideologies and beliefs. Being 'different' had been the status quo. It was that night that Ruth had found her 'different'. With the help of a bottle of vodka and various sickly mixers, she had set about attempting a reading. It had been exciting, a tantalising exploration of another realm – kids' stuff by all accounts. Then she had felt the fizz in her veins, the pulsing in her head, the blurry tunnel that she seemed to travel down every time she turned those cards over. The thoughts had come as a tumultuous waterfall of imagery, the meaning crystal clear, in spite of the unrelenting chaos in her mind. That was as far as her psychic ability took her. She couldn't see spirits, hear them or even sense them. In fact, Ruth often found herself questioning their very existence. The brain, she had decided over the years, was a wonderfully powerful thing indeed. It could make people see what they wanted to see. Perhaps that was the case with her readings. Nobody had ever complained of inaccuracy but Ruth had to admit that the digital era had brought with it the useful tips to be found on social media accounts. It wasn't cheating as such, just a way of getting a better understanding of the person. Statistically, her clients with active social media accounts appeared to result in far more successful readings than those without. It made it easier for her mind to conjure the pictures, the settings and dynamics of situations. Ruth considered it purely a visual aid.

Her next client hadn't given his name and she had been too busy and distracted to ask, so she had scribbled him onto the calendar as Mr X. Ruth's next door neighbour and best friend, Zoe, had laughed when she had seen the entry. "Mr X?! Sounds like a racy new novel," she had said when she had noticed the appointment scrawled in red biro across the calendar Ruth kept in the room where she performed the readings. Then with her eyes twinkling, she had nudged her and said: "Maybe he'll be tall, dark and handsome and undress you with his eyes as he sits there, smouldering in his seat. What on earth did Grayson say when he saw that?"

"Grayson doesn't notice these things. He would barely notice if I was to run around the house in nothing but a feather boa, let alone a bit of scribble on the calendar," Ruth had joked, but the thought had remained with her all week. Grayson had stopped noticing a lot of things over the years and she had stopped caring. It had all started just before Casimir, their only child, had left home. Ruth had felt useless and empty, a hollow bag rather than what she had once been. It had reminded her of the first year after she had given birth, only this time, the eternal stretch of her late twenties was not on her side. In recent years she had felt the changes in her body, the harder bite of her periods and a different shape to her figure that felt alien and wrong. Ruth had seen how Grayson's eyes had glanced disapprovingly at her when he thought she wasn't looking and she had noticed how his gaze, once reserved only for her, had begun to rove. It had made her feel unattractive and as though part of her identity had disappeared.

Ruth thought of the name on her calendar and chuckled to herself about her friend Zoe's remark. Mr X. The name did have an air of mystery to it. She didn't often get male clients for her Tarot or healing, not unless they were recently widowed or just plain weird. Disconcerted, she glanced at her watch. He was late or, more likely, he had changed his mind. Ruth let out a long breath, realising that she was nervous. Lately, she hated running the little business that she had once been so good at. It was as though all her psychic energy had been sapped. More often than not, she was turning people away, full of apologies and insisting they keep their money. A failed reading was such a terrible disappointment. It was mostly those who were at their most vulnerable who would come: depressed, anxious, life slipping away from them, grieving, or loss of all direction.

Drumming her fingers against the table, Ruth told herself that this would be the last one, that she would knock it all on the head for a while. She didn't really need the second income. It was just a way to pass the time and to forget about what Grayson might be doing on all his many trips away. He owned a law firm. That was how they had met. Ruth had started work there shortly after completing her LPC. She had been an associate when she had fallen pregnant with Cas. Returning to her career to work her way up to partner had stolen all the baby and toddler years she could have enjoyed. In the end she had given it all up to be a more hands on mum and, when Cas was old enough, she had got herself a job in the administration department at the local university. It suited the family set-up well and Ruth didn't miss the long hours or high demands that she had previously been used to.

Just as she was giving up on Mr X actually arriving and was preparing to pack everything away, the chimes outside the front door tinkled. Ruth stood up and then paused, taking a deep, calming breath, waiting for the familiar tingle of thoughts and feelings that could rush at her. Still nothing. Maybe there was an energy blockage, maybe she was losing it, or perhaps she was just a terrible fraud? Pushing aside the negative thoughts, she went to answer the door.

The man on her doorstep was by no means tall and dark. He was handsome though. "Ruth Meadows?" he queried offering her a handshake, and she noted that he had an accent.

Ruth took his hand and smiled. "That's right. You found the place no trouble then? The village has that many roads running off it that people often call to say they can't find the house. Can I get you a drink? Herbal tea or water?"

He shook his head, looking slightly nervous.

"Have you done this before?" Ruth asked as she led him through to the small room that she had set up for the readings. "Had a reading I mean?"

Maintaining his silence, the man shook his head again.

"Don't worry." Ruth attempted to keep her voice bright and optimistic, but she was beginning to feel an element of trepidation. She hoped he wouldn't turn out to be one of the weirdos. "I don't see the bad things, only the good." That was a small fabrication of the truth. Sometimes she saw images that suggested bad news of sorts was on the horizon, but she actively chose to filter those out, to look for the more positive element of the message.

Then of course, the unhelpful voice inside her head reminded her, *sometimes you don't see anything at all.* Ruth ignored it and gestured for him to take a seat. She watched him quietly take in the setup of the room. What was it that this man was hoping for? Had he lost someone special? Was he feeling a hollow despair that he just needed filling in some way with good news, a message that might bring him some hope, some reason to exist? Ruth felt a sweat break underneath her arms. Was she about to dash all hopes he might have and add to his despair by being an utter fake?

"So erm, what's your name?" she stammered, unable to keep her own nerves from showing.

From across the table, the man gave her a suspicious look. "I thought you were supposed to be a psychic?" She couldn't tell whether he was joking or not.

Feeling her face flush, Ruth shrugged her shoulders and attempted to keep her tone light. "Sometimes I need a little help with the smaller things. Not that a name is important, it just helps to-" She was waffling, suffering with the onset of verbal diarrhoea.

"I was joking." He interrupted her with a smile that reached his eyes and made them twinkle. "I'm Jeremy Franklyn. I should have introduced myself at your front door but I'm a little nervous, you know."

"Oh right, yes of course." Ruth found herself suddenly speaking in a very English accent. It was a sharp contrast to the soft notes of his New Zealand twang.

"New Zealand?" Ruth asked, praying that something would suddenly leap out at her so that she could give this man the answers that he had come for rather than disappoint him.

He chuckled. "I'll give you psychic brownie points for that. Most people confuse the accent for Aussie."

Slipping the cards from the swatch of green silk she kept wrapped around them for protection, Ruth pushed the deck across the table towards him. "Here, I find I get a stronger reading if you cut the cards." She paused, watching his hand hover near hers. In the dim light of the room, he looked strangely paler, almost translucent.

"Actually, it's not a Tarot reading I've come for." Clearing his throat, he shuffled awkwardly in his seat. "Can you read objects? You know, items of jewellery, that sort of thing?"

Ruth felt uncomfortable. Reading jewellery was the last thing she felt capable of doing. There was nothing at all coming to her. No atmosphere. At least with the cards, she had a visual aid and pictures to guide her. "I'm sorry, Jeremy, I- "

"No, no, it's fine. It probably wasn't very fair of me to come over in the guise of a Tarot reading and then ask something else of you. Let's stick with the cards, shall we?" He took the pile from her and began to shuffle. He gave her a quizzical look. "Have you ever seen a ghost?"

The question took her by surprise. "I've experienced things that are tricky to explain. I don't know that I could categorically state that I have seen a ghost though." She locked onto his gaze, trying to decipher the hidden meaning behind his question. "I don't really deal with ghosts," she added. "I'm not a medium as such. I'm a healer. The Tarot cards are a by-product really."

"A healer?" Jeremy smiled. "You've got a pleasant, calming nature. I can see that."

Ruth looked awkwardly down at the table. "Is there something that you would like to ask the cards? Somebody you would like to ask about?" It was the standard line of enquiry Ruth always invited. Keeping her gaze averted from his, she picked up her glass and took a sip of her water.

Jeremy didn't answer and she lifted her gaze, but he wasn't looking at her. His mind appeared to be elsewhere. There was something profound pooling in his dark eyes. Was it sadness? Grief? What misfortune had brought him to her door?

"Well, not to worry. You don't have to ask a question. Let's just see what they have to say."

Please help me find him. The thought was obtrusive, sudden and unexpected. It was a voice in her head and not her own. Ruth felt her lips twitch, desperate to repeat those words. In the background, she was vaguely aware of the sound of the cards being divided, slotted back together and divided again. Her eyes felt unfocused. The familiar rush through her veins was coming, taking her to another place. Ruth felt giddy, as though she was in a wind tunnel. The sensation was intense. There was going to be a reading.

"I'm ready." That was his voice: Jeremy's. It was quiet and distant, as though spoken from another place.

Ruth's heart began to hammer as she started placing the cards into a Celtic Cross. Nerves didn't usually get the better of her during a reading but she couldn't shake the feeling that she was falling into some sort of abyss. Amidst the silence she could feel an energy. It was as though the walls were watching, waiting, longing for a glimpse into what the cards were going to show her.

Ruth turned the first card. "The High Priestess," she said.

Jeremy watched her with interest. "Is that you?"

Smiling, Ruth shook her head. "The card does not necessarily signify a person, rather it represents a situation." She frowned as the intuition flowed from the image into her mind. "Although in this case, I think it is a person." She looked up at him. "It's not me, but another woman who you have encountered."

Giving nothing away, he shrugged, eager for her continue.

Studying the next picture, Ruth felt the rushing sensation in her ears. The cards were buzzing to tell her something. "There has been a significant change very recently." She closed her eyes, trying to get a grasp of something more concrete to impart. "It's a shift, a huge, life changing shift."

Jeremy's expression remained poker-like.

Her hands quivering with the need to read on, Ruth began turning. "Oh." The word hung in the air between them, waiting for a direction on what kind of 'oh' it was to be. She took a breath. "I see conflict. Two Swords. There has been imbalance, destruction." She turned another over. "The woman who the High Priestess represents has brought her troubles to your doorstep." Ruth felt her mouth opening and closing, the sensation of sound vibrating her lips. There was someone else on the periphery, a darker force. Could it be an affair? The atmosphere shifted and she felt danger. The air was thick with it.

"Have you lost somebody?" she asked, but Jeremy was still struck dumb, staring and waiting for each of the cards to be revealed.

Ruth couldn't stop turning them. A story told through pictures: The Three of Swords to show heartbreak, grief, suffering; the reversed Hierophant to suggest rebellion; the reversed world, depicting that some form of closure was still needed.

The feeling of something beating at her skull persisted. Inside the caverns of her brain, she searched hard. This was the way it happened when she tapped into her higher state of consciousness. It was like finding a secret door and peering through the keyhole. A woman's face had appeared in front of her. She was a beautiful woman, with delicate features framed by wavy dark hair. A wind began to blow, whipping the woman's hair about her face. Then she began to drift backwards, away from Ruth.

"No, wait!" Ruth clutched her head and shut her eyes, unable to stop the whooshing sensation. The secret door was flung open, as though an invisible key had turned in its lock. Ruth was outside, the sweet scent of summer upon her and the warmth of low sun on her face. Ahead of her was the rich, green shoulder of a steeply sloping hill. She recognised that hill. St Catherine's Hill.

At the hill's crest, the sun was dipping rapidly and dusk was beginning to envelop the countryside beneath it. Ruth found herself surrounded by a circle of trees. This was a sacred place, reserved for magic far deeper and more complex than she could hope to imagine or understand. For this was where the eternal priestesses walked, above the ruins of an old chapel.

Somebody was crying out. It was the woman. She was calling for help. Ruth reached out but there was no substance to her body. It was as though she had become a spirit. Was this astral projection? She had heard of it but never experienced it before.

"What is it?" A male voice was drawing her back into the room. "Ruth?"

Ruth wanted to move towards the voice, but she was unable to. The pull from the woman was too strong. Then she felt herself moving again. The motion of travel was so fast that it was making her nauseous. Images streaked past her but she was unable to see anything with clarity. The woman's face was the only thing that remained in focus. Ruth was frightened and wanted her out of her head. "Get out!" she screamed, forgetting about her client sitting opposite. "Leave!" The sensation was growing stronger and she could no longer hear Jeremy. "I said leave me alone!" she shouted again, willing the woman to break her hold.

Faster and faster, she travelled until the giddying sensation of tumbling haphazardly through the air left her feeling as though she was spinning through vast amounts of space. It was as though she had travelled somewhere entirely different. Then a noise: the gentle chink of stones hitting against one another. Something was weighing her down and she was wading through water but she was determined to press on. Behind her, there was splashing and shouting. A man was chasing her. She knew this without looking back. Her arms and legs felt weak and, with a dark and dismal certainty, she knew that she had no choice but to keep going. The shouts from behind stopped but if she was to turn to see how much he had gained on her, it would be her undoing. Above her head, she heard the cry of gulls. The air was salty and surprisingly cold. Something grey was coming towards her - fast. A swelling wave. Cold, unforgiving sheets of water enveloped her. It flooded her mouth and her eyes, blurring her vision. Was she upright, upside down or lying horizontal? Ruth did not know, but her lungs were screaming at her and now all that she could see was a furious shade of red. "Forgive me!" A man's heartbroken, sobbed apology was the last thing that she heard before she was gasping for breath and clutching the edge of the dining table.

Snapping open her eyes, she coughed and spluttered, waiting for her surroundings to settle. Her vision started to clear and she could see the cards spread in front of her. Incense was burning, its soothing scent calming her, flushing away the salty, briny taste from her mouth. Ruth looked up. Opposite her, the chair Jeremy had been sitting in was empty. The pleasant tinkle of her wind chimes echoed through the hallway and she could hear the front door juddering against the doorstop, its spring reverberating from a hard exit.

She stood up but her head was swimming. Steadying herself using the walls, she hurried into the hallway and stared ahead of her, trying to focus her vision. Pea shingle had sprayed onto the lawn either side of her front path. He had obviously left in a rush.

Ruth raked her fingers through her unruly strawberry blonde curls, shaken by what had unfurled in her mind. There had been two women. With a sickening certainty, she knew that both were no longer living. Had Jeremy been responsible in some way? Wrapping her arms around her body, Ruth stared out into the village. In spite of the chaos she had just witnessed, it was a perfectly lovely afternoon. Trees gently swayed in the crisp, wintry air and the purr of a car engine passed by.

Pushing the front door closed until the latch slipped keenly into place, she turned. The house looked darker. Her footsteps echoed against the Victorian tiling. She stepped out of her slippers, feeling the cool enamel beneath the soles of her feet. The duck egg blue walls seemed more of a murky grey and the yellow flowers on the hall table looked decidedly sorry for themselves. It felt unseasonably hot and clammy. Ruth turned down the heating and went to open a window to let some air in. She hesitated at the doorway leading to the Tarot room before going in. It was just as she had left it. Incense burning, candles flickering, a glass of water and a jug on the cabinet at the side, the Turkish ceramic saucer with her jewellery in it next to them and the cards upturned – all but one.

Ruth stared at the rumpled red linen cloth spread across the table. There had been no money left for her. The man had simply run. Pulling open the curtains to let the last of the afternoon light in and open a window, she noticed something glint against the cloth on the table. It was a jet-black stone set in a silver clasp and chain. The silver had dulled considerably with age but the stone was as shiny as the surface of a well-polished mirror. She picked it up. It looked valuable. She couldn't remember the man holding it when he had arrived but he had asked her about reading jewellery. Carrying it over to the ceramic saucer, she put it down and picked up her rings, sliding them all back on her fingers. Then she looked back at the unfinished reading, the way the cards had become scattered across one another, telling a tangled story.

She poured herself another glass of water, drained it and hovered over the last card. The images that had accosted her had already faded, but she could still remember the terrible feeling of water invading her lungs, flooding her mouth, her nostrils, her chest. In all of her time reading Tarot, she had never experienced anything even close to that. What connection did Jeremy have to the two women she had seen and felt?

Ruth felt heat from beneath her fingertips. The card was willing her to turn it over, to reveal the final link of the cross and reveal the outcome. When she did, she gulped back air, falling against the side of the cabinet so that the jug of water fell to the floor, smashing into pieces. As soon as she saw the word, she was able to see another face. This one belonged to a man. In spite of his soft features, there was malice in his expression and he was staring right at her.

In gold lettering, the word was embossed into the glossy card beneath an image of a figure swathed in a dark, flowing cloak and holding a horn marked with a cross: 'Judgement'.

"The judge," Ruth said and her words tripped out as a strangled croak. "The Hanging Judge."

CHAPTER FOUR

His tyres left a spray of gravel in their wake as Jeremy drove out of the courtyard that adjoined the houses belonging to Ruth Meadows and her neighbours. He drove straight to the pub that was perched on top of a hill in the village. After what he had just witnessed, he needed a spark of normality.

It was busy inside. A large group of women, evidently at the tail end of their Christmas lunch, were sitting at a particularly long table. He warily eyed the assorted empty bottles of prosecco and wine whilst attempting to keep a low profile. Women complained about men harassing them, but in his experience, a group of drunken women could be just as bad, sometimes worse. Thankfully, they seemed relatively tame. Approaching the barman, he ordered a pint of lager on tap and took it to a table in the far corner.

The whole episode with the Tarot woman had unnerved him. Everything had started out relatively calmly but then it was as though she had been possessed. She had started screaming things at him, telling him to get out and to leave. Terrified that somebody would think that he was attacking her, he had run. Taking a large swig of his pint, he sat back as the pleasant sensation of creamy froth and cool, nectar liquid flooded his mouth. It had been stupid of him to approach the woman in the first place. Jeremy had never believed in any of that sort of thing. The decision to contact her had been a spontaneous one, driven by the strange things that had been happening that were so difficult to explain and of course, the events leading up to them that he carried such a burden of guilt over.

He hadn't left any form of payment for the reading. It hadn't been intentional. He had just got scared. So, he had run. Jeremy realised that he couldn't leave it at that. The idea of going back was not particularly appealing. He imagined the scene: her screaming at him, accusing him of all sorts, neighbours poking their noses in and incorrect conclusions drawn. That was the problem with small villages; everybody seemed to know one another's business. It was the very reason why Jeremy had decided to rent a small cottage on a farm estate when he had moved to Winchester. His closest neighbours were a retired couple in the farmhouse opposite and the foxes and badgers who liked to roam the surrounding fields at night.

Lifting the pint to his lips, he thought of the Tarot woman again. What had her name been? Ruth, that was it. A striking woman with long strawberry blonde curls, delicate features and bright eyes, she had reminded him of something from a painting of an enchanted forest. It had thrown him, made him nervous. Behind her, the hallway had been a nod to hippy chic: Victorian tiled flooring, an ornate mirror reflecting the bright yellow of a vase of flowers, doors that were part wood, part glass. There had been the heady scent of incense coming from the room that she had led him into. The curtains had been drawn and a staggered formation of candles burning. The card deck had been wrapped in silk the colour of moss. It had seemed very gothic and very surreal. It was the sort of setting that he found unnerving and he had almost changed his mind but he was determined to know why the otherwise inexplicable events kept happening to him. Was it the necklace or something else? Part of him had hoped the visit to the Tarot lady would hit a dead end and prove it was only his mind playing tricks on him.

Engaging with a psychic had been a risk. What if she could read minds? There were things that he had locked away that he had no desire to unearth. He was a man who kept himself to himself. All he had wanted since arriving in the UK was to live a quiet life. Aside from work, he had planned to live as reclusively as possible. The necklace had put an end to all that though and he needed help. The damn thing had been torturing him ever since.

Reaching into his pocket, Jeremy sighed. Maybe it was for the best that he hadn't given it to her. As his fingers slid against the denim of his jeans, fruitlessly digging for something that wasn't there, he felt a surging sense of alarm. The necklace! Where was it?

Frantically, he tried the other pocket and then stuffed his hand into the pockets of his coat. Swearing quietly to himself, he drained his drink and realised that he would have to go back for it. Of course, one night without it might offer him some respite. The woman had seemed honest enough and judging by her house she wasn't exactly short of money. He couldn't imagine her going off and trying to sell it. As soon as he was settled back home, he would give her a call, apologise for his hasty exit and check that she was okay. Standing up, he found his car keys.

******

His cottage was small, dark and a dull contrast to the home belonging to Ruth. Stepping in through the door that led straight into the kitchen, Jeremy threw his car keys onto the table and removed his coat. Thankfully the Aga had done its job in keeping the place heated. He looked around the kitchen with its exposed criss-cross of timber beams. If the landlord had the time and the inclination, he could make a beautiful, modern conversion of the old cottage. Hemmed in by a quaint looking fence and with its wild garden of shrubbery and foliage stripped naked by the breath of winter, the cottage was a lot smaller than the rustic farmhouse opposite. It was cosy though and just what Jeremy needed. He had never been one to care much for the finer luxuries in life. Back home in New Zealand he had been happy with the camper van, long stretches of road and deserted beaches off the beaten track. The ramshackle cottage was definitely a step up, if he was inclined to look at it that way.

There was a gentle sigh from the living room and Jeremy looked through to see Rex, the Scottish Deerhound he was taking care of whilst his neighbours were away. Rex lifted his head slightly to acknowledge Jeremy's return before letting it flop back lazily onto his paws. "Pleased to see you too, Rex. You'd be a terrible guard dog, you know." Jeremy chuckled and went to tickle him behind the ears. "You hungry?" The dog looked up with his dark brown eyes and padded after him into the kitchen.

With Rex contentedly eating his dinner, Jeremy kicked off his shoes and went upstairs to take a quick shower before settling in for the night.

When he stepped out of the bathroom he noticed the light on the screen of his phone. He had a voicemail. Throwing on a sweater and some joggers, he pressed for the messaging service as he headed back downstairs. The voice of Ruth Meadows was on the recording. Her tone was clipped as she explained that he had left the necklace behind. Feeling guilty, he bit down on his bottom lip.

Mulling over whether to call her back straight away, or wait, the impatient grumble from his stomach made up his mind. Pulling a tin of tomato soup from the cupboard, his heart sank as he realised there was no other choice on the menu. He had to start taking better care of himself. Tinned soup and a slice of bread for dinner wasn't the most nutritious of options. Rex regarded him from his spot under the table, appearing to raise an eyebrow as though he was also questioning Jeremy's apparent state of self-neglect. "Don't give me that look, tomato soup is the unsung hero of the soup world. Especially from a tin."

With a look of something like disgust, Rex stood up and lolloped back into the sitting room. Unless there was something in it for him, he had no interest in keeping Jeremy company at mealtimes. Dumping the contents of the tin into a pan, Jeremy planned to return Ruth's call after dinner.

As the soup gently heated, he recalled the words Ruth had said as she had lost herself in what the cards were showing her. She had mentioned St Catherine's Hill. Jeremy knew all about the place. It was a famous and historic beauty spot belonging to Winchester. He had walked Rex up there on several occasions after reading all about it whilst researching the history of the area. The research had seemed like a good idea given that he had just accepted a post as Professor of Modern History at the university. It was after Christmas that he was due to start and he was keen to make an impact. Of course, the history of St Catherine's Hill stemmed much further back than his background of study. In fact, Winchester was steeped in history, especially with its Roman past when it had been known as Venta Belgarum.

The coppice of beeches at the top of the chalk hill had intrigued him, as had the turf-cut labyrinth with its strange history. There were two stories: one that suggested the Bishop of Winchester had carved it so that pilgrims could pay to walk it, and another linking it to the early eighteenth century and a delinquent schoolboy from Winchester College who, after being banished to St Catherine's Hill for bad behaviour, had carved out the Mizmaze. Regardless of the reason for the labyrinth being there, it added to the enigma of the place.

It was the evening after he had first ventured there that he had started experiencing the strange events that had been unfolding. It had been a crisp morning but by the time he and Rex had ascended the steep series of steps built into the hillside, he had been grateful for the cool bite of air on his skin. Then he had noticed the view spanning across Winchester and beyond. Aside from one other dog walker who had passed them on their ascent, they had been alone. As he had been taking in the impressive scenery, something in the enclave of trees had caught his eye. A streak of white had been amidst the foliage. Rex was on the long lead and too busy pawing and nosing a rabbit hole to notice. Squinting, Jeremy had thought he could make out the outline of a woman in a long dress. It was as though she had been watching him and had then run. Curious, he had called Rex over, shortened the lead and entered the coppice. In spite of the wintry sparkle of the morning sun, it had been dark beneath the trees. A makeshift swing had been attached to some of the sturdy branches and he had found it swaying far faster than if it had been caught in a wintry gust. Back and forth it had swung, as though somebody had only just leapt from it. He had shouted out for whoever was there to come out, but had only been greeted by an eerie silence. Then he had heard what had sounded like women chanting.

Mesmerised, he had run further into the density of trees and then he had seen her, just a glimpse but enough to confirm that there was definitely somebody else up there with him. "Hey!" he had shouted and run after her, tripping over the raised roots and stumbling over the uneven ground until he broke through the foliage and into a clearing that gave him a clear view of the landscape beyond. There was nowhere that she could have disappeared so quickly. He had shouted again, his voice lonely and small amidst the ancient magnificence of the place. Then he had felt in his pocket for the necklace he had kept on his person for almost a year. The sensation had been intense heat against his fingertips. With a surprised shout, he had withdrawn his hand and stared incredulously at his fingers. When he had touched it again, the heat had gone but he could have sworn that there had been a face in the stone – her face. For a long time, he had stayed looking for her, but aside from a harrier bird circling above the trees, he and Rex had been alone.

When he had returned home, his first instinct had been to hook the chain around a candlestick on the mantelpiece in the lounge. It no longer felt safe or comforting to keep it on his person. The obsidian gemstone had originally fascinated him but after that day it scared him. Clasped into a claw of silver, it resembled a beautifully striking black mirror. It had been gifted to him in circumstances that should never have happened. Jeremy clenched his fist. There was something wrong with that stone. He had been sure of that as he had stared at it, wondering where its origins were from. There had been no time, no opportunity for him to find out. All he had was the history books and articles that detailed stones like it. He knew it was old and so the stone had most likely been used as a scrying tool. If there had not been such a tragic story attached to how he had come to be in possession of it, he would have considered delving into its original use, making a project out of it that he might have even involved his new students in.

That night his sleep had been disturbed by a noise. Jeremy had slipped quietly downstairs, ears and eyes keen. The house was situated in such isolation that there were no street lamps, so his only source of illumination was the torch on his phone. Then the noise had happened again: a rustling noise, followed by scratching. It had sounded like fingernails against wood.

Creeping towards the living room door, he had sucked in his breath, expecting to see a rat. He didn't want to startle it, he wanted to identify where it would bolt to so he could fill in any entry holes and lay any humane traps. Quietly he had pushed open the door a crack. He had forgotten to shut the curtains before bed and so the moonlight spilled into the room, a pale pool of silver leaching the Persian rug of the rich tapestry of colour that was woven into its design. His eyes had searched the floor and the hearth, slowly working up towards the mantel where the precious treasure was still resting and then eventually to the mirror above it. Jeremy had opened his mouth in shock as he had seen the reflection in the mirror's surface. A woman's face had been staring back at him and it was an uncanny likeness to the one he had seen in the obsidian stone earlier that day. Her hand had uselessly clawed from behind the mirror to the wooden mantelpiece as her fingers had attempted to find purchase with the necklace. With hollow eyes full of despair, gaunt cheeks sunken into her face and long hair falling about her shoulders, she had looked so real and yet, it was only in the mirror that he had been able to see her.

Blinking once, twice, three times, Jeremy had tried to shake off the cobwebs of sleep, discard the remnants of any strange dreams that may have been causing him to see things but the image in the mirror had remained. It had only been as he had started to back away that the impossible reflection had started to fade and the persistent scratching had stopped. The only sound left in that room on that cold and strange night was the swear word that Jeremy had cried out, his breath billowing in front of him from the icy cold blast that had crept in. After the third occurrence of the same nocturnal event, he had contacted Ruth Meadows.

The soup began popping and spitting on the hob as he turned over those particularly disconcerting and chilling memories. Tiny bubbles splattered on his hand, burning his skin. "Damn!" Jeremy licked the hot orange dots from the back of his wrist and turned off the flame. Every time he recalled what he had experienced he lost all sense of what he was doing. It wasn't that he didn't believe in the paranormal, it was just he hadn't considered it much. To believe in the afterlife was to give one a sense of false hope that loved ones were still close; the alternative being that the afterlife gave souls who had been cheated by death the chance to seek their revenge. Jeremy would not allow himself to entertain either scenario.

Pouring the soup into a bowl, he took it to the little table and pulled up a chair. As he dunked a chunk of crusty bread into the soup, he wondered whether he would see his moonlight visitor again that night.

The last number dialled on his phone was the one for Ruth Meadows. He stared at it as he chewed. It didn't seem fair to leave the necklace at her house overnight. Not if there was a vengeful spirit attached to it. Finishing his meal, he made a cup of tea, found a chocolate digestive in the biscuit tin and decided to call her. She answered on the second ring.

"Hi, it's erm, er, Jeremy," he stammered, suddenly mortified by the fact that he had run out on her without leaving any form of payment for the reading. When she didn't respond, he became even more flustered. "I'm the guy who came for the reading earlier. I err, ummm, listen, I'm really sorry that-"

"Sorry you ran off?" Ruth interrupted and her reply could have come across as sarcastic but her tone was filled with understanding.

Jeremy could visualise her shrugging her shoulders, curls tumbling haphazardly over them. "Yes," he gave an embarrassed laugh, "I suppose for that and for failing to pay."

On the other end of the phone there was a pause and an intake of breath. "You never did get around to telling me the question you wanted answered." Her voice was breezy but there was an edge of trepidation to it.

"You didn't really give me much chance, if I'm honest," he replied. "You started shouting at me to leave, to get out."

"Oh. Did I?" It was Ruth's turn to feel embarrassed. He sensed the awkwardness from the other end of the phone. "Sometimes that happens."

"What? You yell at your customers to get out?" It was meant to come across as light-hearted banter but Jeremy realised he sounded as though he was questioning her sanity.

"Well, no. It can be…" She struggled to find the words to explain before giving up on the idea. "Look, this is extremely awkward but I have to admit, I haven't had a reading of that nature before. The strength and vividness knocked me. It was as though I became…. somebody else."

Jeremy felt a chill race up his spine. "I thought you said you don't deal with ghosts."

"What makes you think it was a ghost?" She sounded full of suspicion now and Jeremy realised that she didn't trust him.

"What exactly did you see?" he asked cautiously and his heart began to pound.

Silence. He could almost hear her brain carefully spinning through a range of answers. It was getting them nowhere. Preposterous though it sounded, he had to tell her the truth about the necklace, or at least some of it. "Look, Ruth. If you want to know the reason I contacted you, it was about the necklace that I left behind." He hesitated, contemplating how he might articulate it all without sounding completely insane. "It's a very old artefact and I just want to understand its history a little more." He simply could not bring himself to admit that he thought it was haunted. "My only question was whether you could somehow use your psychic ability to tap into who the original owner might have once been."

There was a sardonic chuckle. "I think I tapped into her alright." Her tone had switched to cold and monotone. Jeremy pushed down on the tide of panic that he could feel swelling inside him. Did she suspect him of something?

Ruth interrupted his worries, impatient to get the call over with. "I suppose you will be wanting your necklace back?"

"I suppose you'll be wanting payment?" he retorted, feeling a little stung by her icy attitude. "Don't worry, I hadn't intended on doing a bunk without leaving the cash. You had just been so intent on yelling at me, that it left me unnerved. The last thing on my mind had been to stop and dig around in my wallet."

"I'll bet." The cold edge was still there.

Sighing, he walked back to where he had left his soup bowl and carried it over to the sink. "It's getting late, so how about I nip over tomorrow, bring the cash and collect the necklace?"

"No!" Her retort was rushed and he realised that she was scared of him. Just what was it that she had seen? "I can meet you somewhere. There's a coffee shop in town. It's a nice place in the Square, just opposite the Eclipse Inn and the museum. It's called The Orangery. I'll meet you there tomorrow afternoon, after work. How does four-thirty sound?"

"Okay, see you then." Disconnecting the call, Jeremy put his mobile onto the countertop. Frowning, he plugged it into the charger. A sense of irritation was growing inside him and he felt distinctly uncomfortable, as though somebody had poked around his brain. Had she unearthed some history that had been deeply buried in his head? As he began to wash the dishes, he wondered if it was normal to feel so violated after a visit to a psychic. It made him feel cross. He had not invited her to dig around in his mind. It had been the necklace that he had approached her about, albeit she had made it clear she did not read jewellery or personal items. Now she had the audacity to behave standoffish and afraid. Her behaviour had been strange to say the least, with all that shouting. There had been no apology on her part and a lot of subservience on his. It was just as well that they were meeting in public. He didn't fancy the idea of being left alone with her and the risk of any more strangely, hysterical behaviour. For all he knew, she could be setting him up to throw some wildly abhorrent accusation at him. Jeremy bit his lip. What could she accuse him of? His mind began to wander down rabbit holes of possibilities. Slamming his hands on the countertop, he stopped himself. Worrying about it would do him no good at all.

Stacking the clean dishes on the side, he picked up his mug of tea but it had long gone cold. After tipping it down the sink, he took Rex out to stretch his legs and do his business in the woodland adjacent to the cottage. It had been a long day and he needed an early night with a good book. He would meet Ruth Meadows the following afternoon, exchange the Tarot reading money for the necklace and leave her to enjoy her coffee. The last thing he needed to disrupt his plans was any kind of trouble or attention.

After returning with Rex, he locked up and flicked out the lights. As he headed upstairs, Rex hot on his heel, he could not help wondering whether he would see his ghost lady again. He really hoped that the reason for her visit was not to bring him some disturbing message from the realms of the afterlife.

******

Taking a sip of her turmeric latte, Ruth curled up on her sofa and pulled her dressing gown across her chest. It was a chilly night and the weatherman had warned of a hard frost in the morning.

After her call with Jeremy, she had taken a long, soothingly warm bubble bath to soak away the distress she was feeling. If the necklace and what she had seen in those cards were associated with some foul play, then he could be dangerous. He had seemed so cagey about what she had seen during the reading and it was obvious that there was something he was hiding. It was a shame she couldn't tap a little further into her psychic abilities to look, but she was exhausted.

Before receiving the call, Ruth had spent the remainder of the evening cleansing the Tarot room. There had been a lot of residue after the reading. Negative energy had been lingering and it needed white sage as well as the crystals. Usually, Ruth felt much better after a cleansing ritual. This one had barely helped at all. She still felt disjointed, as though something, or someone was tugging at her. It was an unnatural sensation, full of disharmony and imbalance.

The sound of the front door opening and closing caused her to jump. After a couple of minutes, Grayson entered the lounge and slumped into the armchair nearest the Christmas tree. "Bloody trains," he complained. "Delays all the way to Basingstoke and then I had to get a taxi from there. Have you eaten?"

"Yours is in the warming drawer," she said, not bothering to point out that he was hours later than he had promised and hadn't even bothered to return her text enquiring about his dinner plans and that it had become very late. The slur to his speech was obvious. Regardless of whether or not the trains had been running on time, he would have been too late for dinner. She knew that he had been out somewhere and she just wished that he would tell her the truth rather than keep secrets from her. It didn't even bother her that he had been out. It was the lies and deception that she didn't like.

Ruth went into the kitchen and he followed, sniffing the air in the hallway. "Don't tell me you've been performing all your hocus pocus again?"

"I had a client visit earlier, yes." Ruth pulled open the warming drawer beneath the oven and flicked the dial to the off position.

"I thought you said that you were giving all that up?" He looked distinctly peeved as he washed his hands at the sink.

"I said that I felt I'd been failing at it lately and that I should probably give it up." She replied, astounded yet not surprised at his complete lack of empathy for anything that she had told him.

Grayson reached for an open bottle of Pinot Noir on the side and poured himself a glass. He didn't think to offer Ruth one. "Probably a good thing the train was delayed after all. All that incense you use really gets into my chest." He coughed to prove the point. "Honestly Ruth, the place smells like a hippy teenager's bedroom."

Ignoring the barbed remark, she put the plate on the table. "Help yourself to vegetables or salad from the fridge."

Grayson grunted a response but she had no idea whether he had really been listening as his head was down and his mind clearly absorbed in something on his phone. She stood in the doorway waiting for him to respond, to give her something that would help her to open up and confide in him about her earlier experience. She thought about the necklace and how when she had picked it up, it had been as though it was scorching her skin, a burning white heat trying to penetrate her soul. In the end she had left it on the saucer on top of the cabinet and shut the door. Grayson wouldn't go in there. It was Ruth's space, just as he liked to keep the study as his private space.

The sound of the cat flap made her look through into the conservatory just in time to see Meg's familiar tabby feline form slink in from her adventures. "Here, Meg," Ruth called, rubbing her forefinger and thumb together and making a sucking noise with her lips.

Meg padded through, head high and proud. It was as though she was walking over to a royal subject rather than her owner. Yawning, Ruth checked her watch. 'I think I'll turn in," she said, tickling the patch of soft fur between Meg's ears. "You coming?"

Meg looked at her with sharp green eyes, contemplating the choice that she had to make, between sitting with Grayson into the small hours or an early night with Ruth.

Grayson did not look up or acknowledge her presence. Giving him a look of disdain so well practised by cats, Meg followed Ruth.

It didn't take her long to get ready for bed and she drifted off to sleep with thoughts of the necklace playing on her mind. She wondered whether it really was old, or whether that was a cover story that Jeremy had concocted because it had once belonged to somebody he knew – or had known. Who were the women she had seen in the vision? What about the face of the man that had suddenly presented itself to her? She recalled those strange words that had come to her when she had turned over that last card: The Hanging Judge.

It was still dark when she awoke. Something had disturbed her. A sound. Ruth looked over at the rise and fall of covers next to her. Grayson was breathing heavily but it had been something else that had woken her. She sat up in bed and flicked on the lamp, looking for Meg. She was no longer curled up in her usual cosy spot at the end of the bed. The indentation in the silver runner at the bottom told her that she hadn't been gone long. Ruth reached out to touch the silky material, still warm from the cat's body. Next to her, Grayson turned over and gave a snort before settling back into his breathing rhythm. Turning out the light so as not to disturb him, Ruth slipped out from under the duvet and tiptoed across the room to the door. She pressed her head against the wood. Everything was silent. She wanted to believe that the sound had just been part of a dream, but instinct made her wait, listening hard. There it was again, a shuffling and scrabbling noise. Immediately, she thought of what Jeremy had asked her about ever having seen a ghost. The thought bristled the hairs on the nape of her neck and drew goosebumps to her arm.

"Grayson?" she called in a raised whisper. He did not respond. "Grayson?" she hissed but there was no waking him. What was the point though? He would only be mad at her for interrupting his sleep and she didn't fancy the idea of a disagreement at such an hour.

Treading as carefully as she could along the corridor, Ruth avoided the squeaky floorboard patches that she knew about. She hoped that Grayson had locked all the doors before coming to bed. Her mind wandered back to Jeremy. There had been something unsettling about the way he had reacted to what she had seen. What if he had returned with the intent to keep her silenced?

By the time she was halfway down the stairs, the shuffling and scrabbling noise had stopped. It occurred to her that it could simply be Meg acting out some of her nocturnal habits, hunting for mice or playing with the little pink ball that Ruth had bought her the previous weekend. At the bottom of the staircase, she held her breath, waiting, listening and hoping that she would hear Meg meow. There was nothing.

It didn't feel safe to put the light on, just in case it alerted the intruder. *Or the ghost*, a voice in her mind chimed out. With a sinking heart, Ruth realised that she had left her phone upstairs and the landline was switched off at the wall, the phone batteries well and truly flat after years of no use. There was no point in regrets. Ruth decided that she was simply going to have to face whatever or whoever was in the house. If necessary, she could scream at the top of her lungs. That would wake Grayson from his slumber and spur him into some sort of action.

Edging along the corridor towards the kitchen, she paused and looked back. There was something or someone in the room she used for readings. She didn't have to be psychic to sense it. The door had been shut when she had gone to bed but it had fallen open from the catch. From the small gap, there was no torchlight or anything else to give anybody away. *A ghost it is then*, Ruth thought as she pushed the door with her fingertips and peered through the crack.

It was too dark to see anything properly. Trying to be brave, she opened it a little wider, allowing the nightlight in the hall to spill through.

Everything was as it should be: the table with its neatly pressed linen cloth, the silhouette of the cleansed cards that she had rewrapped. Nothing on the table had been disturbed, the curtains were still drawn shut and over on the cabinet was the saucer with the necklace draped across it…

Ruth drew a breath, her body preparing for fight or flight mode. A shape was bent over the cabinet. Long, bony white fingers were reaching towards the necklace. A woman with long hair that was hanging in bedraggled strands were obscuring her face and she was wearing a long dress. Ruth knew that she was staring into the face of the stone.

With a gasp, Ruth stepped forward and the woman looked up, startled. There was a small thud as the necklace dropped to the floor.

Ruth pounced for the light switch. It took a split second for the room to flood with light. The woman had gone.

******

She had been staring at the necklace for over an hour. Her cup of coffee had gone cold. After the disturbance during the night, Ruth hadn't slept a wink. Tossing and turning, she had been churning it all over in her head. Had she really seen a woman? Was it a ghost or had the figure been a figment of her imagination, a trick of the light or some other equally rational explanation? There was no logical answer that seemed plausible.

Grayson had slept blissfully through it all and headed off to work with an overnight case packed ready for several Christmas party functions with work and clients, none of which Ruth had been invited to attend. She was too caught up in the events from the night before to feel at all dejected. There had been no more disturbances, but it was as though the energy in the house had shifted.

Meg hadn't returned from her nocturnal antics. Ruth wondered how much of her absence was to do with the shape she had seen. Something was attached to the necklace, an entity. She had no idea whether it was connected to Jeremy or not but the more she thought about it, the more she felt convinced that she had seen a ghost.

Ruth knew the stone to be obsidian and that it could be used for protection and scrying. The night before, when the chain had slithered to the floor, she had been too scared to pick it up, so she had left it and shut the door before returning to bed. It was only in the light of day that she had dared go back and use a tea towel to retrieve it from the floor. Now it was on the kitchen table, resting on the tea towel. The stone resembled a large hollow eye staring back at her.

Even in the light of day, things felt strangely off and the atmosphere was close. The kitchen, a sunshine yellow room of a bright disposition with lush green plants trailing from pots on shelves, pastel ceramics on show and the pretty orangery beyond it, didn't feel as welcoming as usual. Of course, the steady miserable drizzle of sleet outside was doing nothing at all to brighten things. Still, Ruth felt as though the heavy ambience was down to the necklace.

Stretching out her fingers, she held them above it, feeling the energy that was emanating from the stone. She shut her eyes. The image of the woman she had seen the night before came back to her.

Opening her eyes again, Ruth noted what an innocuous and beautifully timeless piece of jewellery the necklace appeared to be; only it wasn't innocuous at all. The necklace had history and a secret. She could feel it all buzzing beneath her fingertips and crackling in the air all around her. Without warning, her hands fell on to the chain. It felt hot, burning. She couldn't let go. The sensation was searing through her body, the blood in her veins heating up like molten lava.

A brilliant shaft of light temporarily blinded her. Before her eyes rolled back in her head, Ruth questioned whether she had just seen the figure again, standing at the opposite side of the table and reaching out to her, clawing at the air between them. It felt as though something was lodged in her throat; she opened her mouth to cough. Instead, words came out and she had no idea what they meant. She tried to stop them but they were bursting from her as though being ripped from depths of her. "The judge is coming. God have mercy on you all."

From somewhere within the house, she thought she could hear the sound of a dog barking and the clatter of something falling to the ground…

CHAPTER FIVE

Sunlight reached through the wool curtains into the chamber Kat slept in at her grandmother's house. Pulling them back, she looked out of the window at the red sky above. "Shepherd's warning," she muttered to herself before plunging her hands into the bowl of lavender and rose scented water.

The power her grandmother had told her was within her now had been growing as the weeks passed. She felt different, as though an energy was coursing through her veins. It made her feel restless and impatient. With it came the certainty that Gideon was looking at the same red dawn. The colour seeped from the orb of sun, spilling across the sky so that it looked like a bleeding heart. Kat was painfully aware of how much her own heart was aching. Did he think of her when he looked up at the sky or was another woman's face emblazoned in his mind?

After washing her face, she removed her shift to bathe her body. As she was rubbing the scented water over her skin, she stopped. Something felt wrong. Placing the cloth down, she reached for her shift and pulled it back over her head. There was something not quite right but she couldn't place what it was. Bringing her fingers to her throat, she realised that the necklace her grandmother had given her was missing, but she had not taken it off the night before. Her gaze roamed the room but there was no sign of it.

Hurrying downstairs, Kat searched the kitchen, hunting in between the woven baskets of fruit and vegetables that were on the floor. Darling had taken great pains to impress on her how precious that necklace was and she would be furious if it had disappeared.

Evidence that Darling was already up was scattered throughout the kitchen. A knife and some apple cores had been discarded on the worktop and the iron pot filled with oats, water, currants and fine slices of nutmeg was already hanging over the fire. Kat called her name but only Merlin trotted through, his face expectant, hoping that Darling had returned from wherever it was that she had gone.

"Sorry boy, she's still not back," Kat said and ruffled his fur before she walked through the archway that led into the shop. Opening the door to the street, she looked out. A carter trundled past, the driver bidding her a good morning, but there was no sign of her grandmother. She must have gone on an early errand somewhere. It was going to be a hot day and the streets were already stinking, the air clammy. Kat was glad for the smell of herbs, liquorice root, fennel, peppermint and even the pungent odour coming from some of the more unpleasant ingredients that they stocked. She pressed her fingers to her temples. Her head felt sore and she was slightly nauseous. A concoction of chamomile with some ginger root to stem the sickness would see her right.

Making her way over to the vast shelving of jars, she ran her finger along the labels. When she had found what she was looking for, she pulled back the thick curtain that separated the dispensary from the shop and began preparing the ingredients for the decoction. She would need to bring a pot of water to the boil in the kitchen so that she could steep the dried flower heads.

Merlin began to growl as the pleasant tinkle of the shop bell interrupted her work and she dropped the paring knife on the workbench. Darling must have returned already. Poking her head around the curtain, she looked into the shop and called out, but there was no reply.

The shop was empty. Merlin was in the doorway, a low warning growl coming from between his bared teeth as he looked through into the main section of the house. This had happened before, when the weaver's boys had thought it funny to sneak in after hours. Darling had told her all about it. Marching around the counter, Kat felt her temper flare. If this were those boys making mischief again, she would see to it that their behinds were tanned. "You may as well show yourselves now," she warned, rounding the counter's edge. "I will not have this nonsense and I will see to it that you are punished harshly if you do not come out now."

Aside from Merlin's threatening growl, everything remained silent. There was a rustling noise, like material sweeping against the floorboards. Following the sound through to the kitchen, Kat was alert. It sounded as though someone was venturing up the stairs that wound up from the kitchen. Merlin began to keen, backing away. "Thank you for your help in chasing away the intruders," Kat muttered sarcastically as she marched towards the staircase. The cheek of it, that these young tyrants should enter the house like this!

Cursing, she took the steps to the top of the house as nimbly as she could. The dog had disappeared. Upstairs it was stifling. The windows needed opening. Her headache intensified and she clutched at the railing, feeling herself grow dizzy. "You'll come out now," she called again, but her voice was beginning to shake. What if it was not just young boys? What if it was someone who had seen her with Darling at St Catherine's Hill and now they meant her harm? Superstition ran deep in some parts and nobody would condone the idea of witchcraft, particularly when it concerned the owner of an apothecary shop.

The rustling sounded again and she strained to see in the dark. Most of the shutters upstairs were still to be opened. Thin shafts of the sun's beam spilled through cracks in the wood, providing just enough light for her to see the figure at the bottom of the corridor. A man with his back to her moved slowly down the length of the building, giving the impression that he was hovering. At first, she thought it could be Gideon and that he had returned at last. She opened her mouth to call his name. Then, with a gasp she pressed herself flat against the wall. It wasn't Gideon. He was too tall and too bulky. Who was this stranger in her house? If he had heard her, he had made no attempt to acknowledge it.

Kat peered through the murk of the corridor, a feeling of unease unfurling inside her. The cloak that he was wearing swept against the floor, creating the rustling noise. Shades of scarlet the colour of the crushed roses she had seen in her vision flashed amidst swirling dust. She could see swathes of thick dark hair falling in waves down his back. He turned to open the door at the far end of the corridor. It was the door to her grandmother's room.

Had this man done something to Darling? Was he the man who was responsible for Gideon's disappearance? Rage propelled her towards him. "Who are you? What are you doing in our house?" she demanded but he did not turn around to acknowledge her. Instead, he disappeared over the threshold, the long, red train of his cloak drifting behind him. The door slammed shut.

Downstairs, Merlin started barking and howling.

In ordinary circumstances, Kat's instincts would have screamed at her to turn back, to get help from neighbours or passers-by in the street, but outrage gave her courage and she marched down the corridor before throwing open the door to Darling's chamber.

Light spilled in from the window. The man had disappeared. There was nowhere he could be hiding. Kat felt her knees threaten to buckle and she began to back out of the room. The air in front of her was moving, shifting and vapour-like. An outline of a woman had started to appear.

"Grandmother?" she asked, her voice small and weak.

This was not her grandmother. This was another woman, with long flowing hair the colour of a gloriously golden sunset. Her eyes shone like polished marble. In her long flowing robe of patterned silk, and with her pale skin, she appeared ethereal looking. The woman reached towards Kat and a long silver chain was looped around her fingers. A black stone, clasped into the chain as a pendant, was swinging gently back and forth. It was the necklace that Darling had given to Kat.

The woman's eyes were wide and unblinking as she opened her mouth to speak. When she did, the words came out with such force that Kat thought she would be blown back against the wall. "The judge is coming. God have mercy on you all."

There was a bark and Merlin bounded through the door before skidding to an abrupt stop.

Terrified, Kat instinctively snatched at the air in front of her, but the woman was disappearing until all that was left was a fine green mist. There was a loud clatter and, with a whimper of terror, Kat looked down at the floor. There, by her feet, was the necklace.

Trying to comprehend what she had just seen, Kat took a step back. Is this what invoking the spirit world had done? Had she crossed a line with the Druids of the ancient Hill Fort by insisting that Darling ask them about Gideon? Darling had warned her but she had refused to listen.

Merlin was still growling and barking when Darling appeared, her face drawn with concern. She silenced him and touched Kat gently on the shoulder. "Kateryn? What is wrong?"

Dumbfounded, Kat stared back at her, unable to describe what she had just seen. She swallowed but her throat was dry and her tongue felt thick.

Darling looked around nervously. "I heard Merlin barking as though there was somebody else here. I came upstairs and then I saw you. Whatever has happened? You have paled so, my love."

Kat looked into her worried face. She did not want to scare her or give her cause to believe that an ancient spirit had been brought into the house. Darling was a superstitious woman and would not take that news well. Stooping to pick up the necklace, Kat managed a weak smile. "Nothing. I thought I heard something but it was nothing. My head is turning like a spinning wheel. I have been feeling a little ailed since yesterday, that is all."

Darling nodded but continued to eyeball her with suspicion. "The sight can do that to you."

"Here," Kat handed her the necklace. "I dropped this. Can you help me fasten it back into place? I only removed it to wash."

With trembling fingers, Darling helped her. Neither of them said anything to one another but it was as though the words that had come from the woman's mouth were bouncing off the walls:

The judge is coming. God have mercy on you all.

******

On her walk back from the butchers' shambles the heavens had opened. With her clothing drenched, Kat shivered in the kitchen as Darling chastised her for the fifth time since her return, telling her she should have waited for the break in the cloud. Outside, the rain had stopped and the sun was making another appearance. With a grateful smile, Kat took the hot posset that was handed to her and perched on the wooden chair in front of the fire. She would dry off and then run the errands needed for the apothecary shop.

"How are you feeling now?" she asked Darling as she took a seat to join her. Darling had not said anything more about the pains in her chest or what the spirits had shown her on the hill.

Dismissing the question, Darling went to finish cutting the rim of a pie she had been making. "I should be asking that of you. How has it been since they chose you?"

Kat shrugged. "I still don't understand why they chose me. I am not like you, Darling. I am ordinary."

Darling chuckled as she cleared the excess pastry and fed a little to Merlin who was waiting with expectant patience. "You are far from ordinary, Kateryn. Mark my words." There was something in her tone that suggested she knew something more than she was prepared to let on. Darling had always been that way – she just knew things.

"I saw somebody in your chamber. The spirit of a woman." The truth tumbled out. Kat could not contain the information any longer, although she took care not to say too much about the woman's appearance being akin to a High Priestess.

Darling dropped the pastry crust that she had picked up to feed to the dog. "A female spirit?" she snapped, rubbing her hands on her apron. "Did you recognise her?"

Kat shook her head. "I did not. But before I saw her, there was something else. I think it was another vision. I saw the back of a man. He was wearing a judge's robes and he was walking away from me. I knew that he was of this time, and not of the spirit world." Kat looked away, conscious of the woman's warning that was still echoing between her ears. "The woman said something to me, a warning."

"What sort of warning?"

"She said, '*The judge is coming. God have mercy on you all*'. I think she was speaking of the assizes that are to be held here at the end of the month."

Darling's shoulder relaxed a little. "It is hardly a useful message. Everyone knows of the assizes."

"What if she was warning me of something linked to them, though? What if she was warning me that Gideon is caught up in them?" Kat felt her legs weaken at the thought. Royal soldiers were herding the rebels, weeding them from their hiding places across the West Country. Word had reached them that the King was sending his most senior and formidable judge to lead the assizes courts, the Lord Chief Justice Jeffreys. His reputation went before him as a hard and cold man, capable of reducing the most educated and highly standing men to a trembling mess. Everyone knew that justice was to be served.

"You think Gideon got himself involved with the rebels?" Darling's glare was sharp and accusing.

Kat was quick to defend her husband. "No. He has not."

"Do not forget that he is from a Puritan family, Kat. Gideon's family will have supported this rebellion." She lowered her voice. "Do you think it is possible?"

Shaking her head, Kat protested. "No! Gideon had no ties with his family after we moved here. His family were just as angry with him for marrying me as you all are. Everything Gideon does is intended to prove to father that he is honourable and worthy as a husband. He knows father's loyalties lie with the King. Gideon is for the King too. He would not do anything to compromise any chance he has of winning his approval."

"Men can be fickle beasts," Darling commented.

"Not Gideon," Kat replied confidently but there was a knot in her stomach as she recalled how changed he had become in the months leading up to his departure; how cruel he had been, pushing her away, snapping at her, irritated by everything.

Seeing the look upon her face, Darling reached out to Kat, drawing her head to her chest. She smoothed the hair that had fallen from beneath Kat's cap. "I am sorry, Kateryn. I know that Gideon is a good man and that he loved you very much."

Kat took a sharp breath and pulled herself from her grandmother's embrace. "Loved? You think he is dead?"

Darling was taken aback by the outburst. "No. I did not mean it that way, Kateryn. You have said yourself that you can feel him, that you know he is still out there." Her lips quivered as she stared back at Kat. Was there something she was not letting on? Darling did not always impart all the news that she was privy to and Kat recalled a time when she had foreseen the death of a mother to be. Kat had queried why she would not tell her or make a concoction that would rid of the child before it was too late, but Darling had insisted that it was God's way and neither the woman or her husband should have that knowledge. She had said that it could be a ripple in time that would change everything God had intended as the natural order of things.

Kat sniffed loudly. "I suppose that if he continued up North, it is a long way to travel. It is very possible that there would be delay. They will be reluctant to travel whilst the country is littered with so many desperate men," she said, feeling a little better as she turned the possibilities over in her head. "Perhaps the message has another meaning?"

"Keep looking, Kateryn. The spirit world brings us signs that are not always clear at first. There is a reason why they want to the bring the message to you and there will be reason enough as to why they are dismissing me. They do not think I can help this time. You simply need to harness your gift. All will be well, my love. All will be well." She turned her attention back to her cooking, her face hidden again. She did not turn quickly enough though, for Kat not to notice the trouble that had darkened her expression.

******

A blistering heat ravaged the southern part of the country in the week leading up to assizes. During that time, neither Kat nor her grandmother had seen any more hints of Kat's vision and she wondered if there had been nothing more to it than warning that they were coming to Winchester.

Kat had gone to market with Audrey early in the morning. Audrey was a young girl apprenticed to Darling at the shop. Darling had always been adamant that she wanted a girl to learn her trade. She wanted to give a woman a chance to make her own way in life. Kat wondered how disappointed Darling must be that both she and her mother had not defied convention like she had and had both married young, dependent on their husbands. Whilst Kat's marriage had been for love, her mother's had been for the ambition of wealth.

Audrey was a timid little thing and Kat had warmed to her quickly, keen to put her at ease and help give her the confidence she needed. The street was busy with traders shouting over the top of one another, each hoping to outdo the other on quality of goods and price. "Stay close to me, Audrey," Kat instructed, clutching the girl's hand and guiding her through the crowds. As one particular stall caught her eye, she pulled the young apprentice along. "Has my grandmother had you negotiate yet?" she asked and Audrey gave her a nervous look.

"Do not look so troubled, Audrey. A pretty face like that and a keen mind, you shall do well." Kat winked at her as they nudged their way through the crowds until they were face to face with a man who had leathery brown skin and smelled strongly of rose water. Looking at all the rare and wonderful items on his stall, Kat's heart skipped a beat. This was an apothecary's dream. Vials of oils, powders and various concoctions lined his stall. Behind him were beautiful silver perfume casks and some of the rarer items that a discerning apothecary might stock.

"Welcome ladies," the man greeted them with an accent laced with an exotic tone. Kat was surprised that the trader had come to Winchester with such expensive and rare items. Even with the interest of the late King Charles II, Winchester was not renowned for being the prosperous place it had once been in its history. With the castle destroyed after the war and the grand beginnings of the new palace dying with the late King, any hope for the town's return to its former glory had been abandoned. King James certainly appeared to hold no ambition for the place.

The man eyed them both up and down. "What are you seeking today?" he asked. "Summat for the pretty young lady?" He smiled at Audrey before glancing back at Kat. "Or will it be summat for yerself? Mind not bewitch me with that beauty of yours either. I can't afford to be giving things away."

Kat felt her hackles go up. Even though he was only trying to charm them, she did not like the insinuation that she could bewitch somebody. "We have come for items far simpler than these," she said sternly. "It is only some of the more usual items we need to replenish in the apothecary shop. The summer cold is rife this year and we need some additional supplies."

The man looked momentarily disappointed, but as Kat selected some of his simpler goods, he brightened. "As a woman skilled with such things, you will understand the need for a good dung. We have elephant's dung." He pointed out a dark green vial. Next to it was another which had been labelled, 'Powdered Mummy'.

Kat picked up the elephant's dung and went to sniff it. She knew the tricks. People all too often would use the excrement of dogs, bottle it and pass it off as something far more unusual. She winced at the stink of it, noting the hard white crust inside. "Good stuff that," the man interrupted. "Shipped in to Portsmouth only yesterday."

"What are those?" Audrey asked, pointing to the array of perfume flasks. His eyes flashed even brighter at that. Kat didn't like it. He looked like a mischievous wood nymph. There was something disconcerting about him. "These, Miss?" He gave a dramatic sweep of his hands as though unveiling something of great magnificence. "These are some of the most beautiful scents your nose will ever smell." He leaned forward, teasing her. "If this one will allow you to take a sniff, I could offer a good price." He went to touch Audrey's hand. It was a step too far.

"Not today, thank you." Kat eased his hand away with a firm pressure and gave him a withering look. "We are not here for perfumes and other such luxuries." When Audrey stepped back, Kat placed herself between her and the leering man. Then she counted out some coins for the things she needed and handed them over.

With surprising force, he closed his hand around her fingers and leaned towards her. "You want to watch yourself, Miss. All high and mighty now but these hands will have blood on them soon enough." He leaned closer, his voice threatening and coarse. "And they will never be washed of the stain."

Pulling her hand away, Kat backed off. "Hear my warning Miss. Be careful of where your heart leads you, for there is darkness in it."

"What did he mean?" Audrey asked breathlessly as Kat dragged her through the crowds.

"He meant nothing," Kat snapped, desperate to get away from the chaos of the market. "That man was a villain if ever I saw one and he wanted to scare us when we wouldn't buy his wares. There is nothing more to it than that."

They hurried away from the street, down the one that led them away from the Buttercross and past the cathedral. Kat could still feel the prickly heat from his sweaty palms around her fingers. She wanted nothing more than to get back to the shop and plunge her hands into rose scented water. It felt as though he had tried to curse her, but she knew that was nonsense. He was just a nasty pedlar man employed by some merchant to sell his goods. That was all.

As they neared the cathedral grounds, Kat stopped by an old timber-framed building and an icy chill coiled its way about her body.

"What is it?" Audrey was perplexed by the swift change that had come over her.

Kat took a step forwards and looked at the whitewashed walls of the building, the dark timber frames and then to the mullioned window at the top. "That's where they'll hold her." The words slipped from her mouth before she could stop them.

"Hold who?" Audrey asked as she stared with misgiving at Kat's strange turn in behaviour.

Shaking her head, Kat looked away but the sudden smell of burning faggots attacked her nostrils. "Do you smell that, Audrey?" she asked, gripping the girl's arm.

Audrey sniffed and screwed up her nose. "It always smells out here. My ma carries a nosegay. If you please, I am surprised that you do not." She smiled with the aim to please. "I could make one for you if we are to work in the garden later today."

"I do not need a nosegay," Kat snapped. "A nosegay will not rid us of that dreadful smell of the faggots burning. Nobody said there was to be a burning today?" She turned around, panicked, aware of the most awful feeling that something was tightening around her neck, strangling the breath from her.

Beside her, Audrey looked confused and frightened. "There is no smell of burning and there has been no news of a burning. What would give you cause to think such a thing?" she asked but her voice had become distant.

"Dear Lord!" Kat exclaimed as the constricting feeling worsened. Gasping for air, she dropped to her knees. People were turning to stare as Kat brought her hands to her throat, retching and coughing.

"Mistress Fox?" Audrey cried before turning her attention to the onlookers. "Somebody help! Help us!"

Nobody dared go near her for fear that it was the plague or the sweating sickness that had taken hold. Audrey cried out for help again and her scream pierced Kat's skull, breaking the nightmare feeling. She could feel the hot cobbles through the material of her skirt and apron and she thought of the faggots for the fire, feeding the greedy flames in readiness to engulf their victim. It took all her willpower not to scream out. The sensation of something around her throat and neck began to subside and the sharp, searing pain in her chest eased.

"Keep away from her," somebody shouted from the gathering crowd. "Could be the sweat. Look at her forehead."

Kat could feel the beads of perspiration gathering against her skin. She knew she had to do something to disperse the show that she was creating. Waving her hand, she called out, "I am quite well. It is just this heat leaving me quite faint. I do not suffer it well."

"Who does?" a woman replied with empathy and poked at her husband to help Kat to her feet. "You're the apothecary's granddaughter, aren't you? Maybe you are with child," she added kindly.

Reluctantly, her husband took Kat's hand and pulled her up, asking her if he could be of assistance in walking them back home. Politely declining the offer, Kat turned to Audrey who was visibly shaken. She was the only one who had heard the words Kat had uttered before dropping to her knees. "Come now, Audrey," she said formally and they hurried back to the shop.

That night, Kat tossed and turned in her bed, lost in the realm between sleeping and waking. Shadows flickered across the walls, mingling with images of Lady Alice Lisle and the strange woman who had warned her of the judge. The obsidian stone felt hot against her chest, as though it was heating up and she thought of the great fiery mountain that Darling had said it had come from. A candle that she had carelessly left by the bedside guttered and spat as it wore down into a stump, bringing the smell of burning faggots into her fitful dreams. In only a matter of days the Winchester assizes would begin and with them, the first trial for treason against the King. As she twisted and groaned in her sleep, her heart hammered in her chest, beating out a rhythm of fear. She knew why she could smell the faggots and hear the hot, hiss of greedy flames. Lady Alice Lisle's trial would find her guilty and she would burn for it.

She was up with the first of the dawn chorus. Grateful that it was wash day, Kat removed her shift, feeling the welcome coolness of morning air against her clammy skin. The shift was stained and discoloured from patches of sweat, Kat would need to scrub hard. One of the washerwomen who worked at the river claimed that her soap brought the white of old linen as good as new. Darling said that the woman's services were expensive but worth it in the heat of the summer months. Kat felt the familiar weight of despair as she reminded herself that since marrying Gideon, she no longer had the privilege of affording luxuries such as the most expensive washerwoman looking after her linen.

Reaching for the pitcher on the little wooden table, she poured the remaining water into the bowl that it rested in. Then she picked up the soap that she had recently made using venison fat she had garnered from Joan Rankin, the butcher's wife. In return for the venison fat, she had promised Joan Rankin two wash balls. It was the arrangement that Darling had put in place for a long time. Kat thought that the fat of venison was the best kind for soap. It gave a creamy texture to the wash balls that she prepared and it mixed well with petals and herbs. To this one, she had added the last of the rose petals from the garden and some lavender. After dipping her hands into the bowl, she picked up the soap and rubbed it between her hands. Using the creamy lather, she cleaned under her arms, between her legs and her cleavage. Then she dipped her washrag into the water and swiftly rinsed herself before finding her clean shift and dressing.

Darling was not up when she went downstairs and so Kat waited for a while, scrubbing down the table top and the counters in the shop before going and tapping on the door of her grandmother's chamber.

A weak voice called her through. Darling was still in bed, her face ashen. "Oh Kateryn, I have taken a little turn. It is this heat, I tell you." With a small moan she tried to shift her position.

Rushing to her bedside, Kat felt her forehead. "You are running a fever," she stated and stood up. "I shall go and fetch you something for it. Audrey can run the shop with me today. You rest."

There was no argument from Darling, who rested back against her pillow, her eyelids fluttering rapidly at her discomfort.

Making up a cooling tincture laced with peppermint and a poultice to draw the heat from her chest and forehead, Kat took them into Darling. Resting the poultice on her forehead and placing the tincture by her bed, Kat left her to sleep off the fever whilst she went back downstairs.

It took two more days until the fever broke and Kat was able to start feeding Darling's weakened body. She had just come in from the garden, having picked some of the summer harvest to put into a broth, when the shop bell tinkled. Chastising herself for forgetting to bolt the door, she wiped her hands clean of soil.

A smartly dressed man whom she did not recognise was waiting at the counter. He greeted her with an accent that suggested he was not local.

Smiling broadly, she greeted him. "Welcome sir. How can I be of assistance?"

The man looked nervous and there was an air of impatience about him. "Where's the Apothecary? It is a matter of great importance that I speak with him immediately."

Folding her arms across her chest, Kat took her place behind the counter. "You are looking at *her,* Sir."

Aghast, he tried to look over her shoulder. "Where's your husband?" he demanded, noting the nakedness of her wedding finger. Kat had removed the ring before work and had forgotten to put it back on. His gaze shifted back to her face, as though he instantly had the sum of her. He took a step back. "I see."

Kat felt her heart thud in her chest. People could be quick to judge, to form ideas and she resented the fact that a woman's skills with plants and herbs should be considered any different to a man's. "You are in the best apothecary shop for miles, perhaps even the county," she said haughtily. "It is my grandmother's trade and I work with her. We look after many of the Winchester gentry: the Verneys, Chudleighs and Sturges, to name but a few. Even the local Physics prefer to use us for medicaments." Kat kept her expression stern, her gaze holding his with unwavering confidence.

"Of course, I do not doubt it." he said, clearing his throat. "I have been told that this is the place to come. It is a matter of urgency." He handed her a roll of parchment and she gestured for him to wait whilst she spread it across the counter. Amongst a list of many items was a list of ingredients and she recognised them straight away.

"These are the ingredients for serious cramping." She tapped her nail on the list. "Is this for a man, or a woman?"

"That need not be any business of yours," he snapped. "Just concern yourself with fetching the supplies."

"Well, you see, Sir, it is my concern. If it is for a woman and she is with child, some of these ingredients would risk harming the unborn babe. If, however, they are for a man and they are needed for what I suspect is ailing him, then the recipe, as it stands, could do with a small adjustment to assist with the pain. It is by no means a cure, but it will offer better respite for a stone."

The man was beginning to lose his patience, looking back into the street, aware that he was taking far more time than was clearly expected of him. "We do not need your opinions, girl. The instruction on what is to be dispensed has been provided by a learned physician who has been using a trusted London Apothecary for years. It is just ill fortune that he is not with us here in Winchester. Kindly find the ingredients listed and dispense the medicine as you have been instructed."

Smarting from his abrasive manner, Kat pressed her lips together tightly as she found the necessities from the many jars on her shelves before flinging back the curtain to the dispensary. "Very well. A cupful, four times a day. Mind to chase each dose with honey, lest the taste be too foul to swallow."

He grunted in retort as she busied herself with making up the medicine before dipping her quill and writing out the amount that was owed. Important people always wanted a written record of what had been spent.

There was a pause as he grumbled something and handed her a small pouch of money. "You can keep what is left from that. I do not have the time to be waiting any longer. There are important matters happening here in Winchester. Any perversion of the court of justice will not be taken lightly."

"Justice?" Kat hadn't meant to speak so loudly, but the word echoed as warning in her head.

Her tone took him by surprise. "Yes. Justice," he confirmed. "Good day to you, Miss." Not wanting for any more disruption to his errand, he didn't hesitate in turning and hurrying away.

Kat felt the hairs on the nape of her neck prickle. She knew that the time had come. The judge the spirit world had warned her of had arrived in Winchester. The assizes must have opened but she had been too caught up with looking after Darling and the shop to realise. She hadn't even managed to take her washing down to any of the women at the river. Her skin prickled and her eyes clouded over as she drifted back into her mind's eye and saw the vision of Lady Alice Lisle asleep in her cell, too old and exhausted to pay much attention to the cruel hands that were pulling her to her feet, forcing her to move out of the dreadful place that had become her home. In her head she heard the clatter of a carter's wheels against the cobbles and her flesh and bone protested against the discomfort of the hard, wooden joins of the cart pressing into her. In spite of the heat, a chill breeze seemed to whip up and Kat moved over to the door to look out into the street. Everything appeared normal. A cat was stretching lazily in the sunshine, a flustered looking woman hurried past carrying an angry baby who was hungry for his milk, and Mr Kirkford, a tailor from the top of town, was carrying a bundle of material.

Merlin appeared from around the corner. Bending at the knee, she stooped to welcome him home with a hug and then smoothed his fur.

It was just as she was shutting the shop for the day, that Mistress Hemingway rounded the corner of the street. Kat groaned inwardly as she realised that she had been seen. It was evident that the woman was keen to strike up conversation.

"Oh Kateryn, have you heard the news?" she asked, breathless with excitement. "A dreadful business." Her cheeks were rosy and her eyes wide, suggesting that the business was anything but dreadful to her mind, but that she needed to give whatever it was the appropriate label.

"Heard?" Kat smiled politely, hoping that she could bring the conversation to a swift close.

"About the trial that is being brought to the assizes tomorrow, the one with the gentlewoman, Alice Lisle?"

"Tomorrow, you say?" Kat repeated what she had been told, but her stomach was churning as she thought again of the old woman's suffering. She already knew about the trial, of the verdict that would be reached and the sentence that would come to pass.

Mistress Hemingway made a great show of rolling her eyes and gave a sharp click of her tongue. "Where have you been hiding, Kateryn? Everyone knows that it is tomorrow. Only this afternoon they brought her here from Fisherton." She gave Kat a look that demonstrated the horror of the situation. "My husband was repairing a clock for Henry Dawley over at Lainston this morning. He told me that Henry Dawley has been empanelled for the jury."

"Jury?" Kat's heart was beginning to hammer, her blood rushing in her ears.

She looked at her as though she was stupid. Her tone was brimming with impatience. "Yes! The jury panel that has been summoned for tomorrow's trial; the one involving the first of the rebels who have been captured. It is the Lord Chief Justice Jeffreys who the woman will stand trial in front of." Licking her lips, she seemed to relish the juicy gossip that she was able to impart to ignorant ears. "Rumour has it that he is the harshest of all of them. By all accounts, he has a face of stone and a heart to match. Still, it is a dreadful crime. The worst to be committed: treason." She leaned forward, lowering her voice, as though even saying the word 'treason' could somehow incriminate her. Then she pulled back, straightened herself up and bid Kat a good day as she spotted somebody else further up the street to share her news with.

Kat stepped back inside, closing the door and leaning against it.

The judge is coming. She thought of those words, still hanging in the atmosphere around her. They echoed in Kat's head, goading her and she saw a face: straight and prominent nose, dark eyes and a firm jaw that was framed by the immaculate arrangement of curls from a judge's headpiece.

"God have mercy on you all," Kat found herself whispering and she drew a breath, steadying herself.

Back in the kitchen, she poured herself some small ale and sank down into a chair at the table. She thought about the news that Mistress Hemingway had so gleefully imparted and of the man who had come for a remedy. She wondered what would be going through the mind of Alice Lisle. No doubt there would be plenty of onlookers at her trial. Kat would not go. She had never considered the assizes to be a source of entertainment. From her years growing up in Winchester, she recalled how there was always a different atmosphere in the streets when the court was opened in the Great Hall and the county's felons were trialled and sentenced. Kat had never been one to enjoy the desperate plight of those handed sentences that mostly led to the gibbet. For many though, they would flock to see the grisly demise of wrongdoers and lawbreakers.

Stoking the embers of the fire, she added more dry bracken to encourage the flame so that it would heat the broth she was going to prepare. Darling looked so thin that Kat prayed she could keep it down. As she chopped the vegetables to add to the broth, her mind drifted back to the dreams she had experienced of Alice Lisle. The sooner the trial in Winchester was over, the better, Kat thought. She could not cope with the idea of any more visions of that nature, and the fact that she had no idea what she was meant to do about it all. If she was meant to stop her impending death, she wondered how that was even possible. What good could the granddaughter of an Apothecary do?

The following day, there was little improvement in Darling's condition and she had started to complain of pains in her chest again. Kat wanted to send for a doctor but Darling refused, insisting that it was just the summer cold getting to her in old age. Darling had never liked men intruding on her space, even doctors. She said that she trusted none of them, that some considered it their duty to unburden parishes from old women with no husband to speak of. Kat's concern for Darling's ill health was too great though. Finding some parchment, she took the quill and inkpot from the shop into the kitchen and sat down to write a letter to her mother. Then she found the hiding place that she and Darling used for money and took out a coin. She would find a trustworthy young lad to see to it that the note reached her parents.

Just as she was slipping on her outdoors shoes, the man who had visited the day before burst through the door.

"What can I do for you today?" Kat asked tersely, not bothering to hide her displeasure at being reacquainted.

The man turned and his demeanour was nervous. "We need you up at the Great Hall. You said you knew a better remedy for the cramping. It is for the Lord Chief Justice Jeffreys. He has instructed me to advise you properly on what the remedy is intended for. His physic has diagnosed stones but, under the circumstances, Lord Jeffreys has requested that you dispense exactly as you usually would." He gave her an accusing glance before continuing. "The tincture you supplied yesterday has done nothing to ease the pain. There is no need to impress on you the importance of today's trial. You will be doing your service to the King by making the appropriate remedy. Bring it up there as soon as it is ready and request to speak with me: Mr Giles." There was no offer of payment, no courteous note of thanks in advance for her efforts. Kat was simply expected to oblige the demand that had been made of her. Satisfied that he had made clear his requirements, the man turned and left.

Kat stared after him, wishing that she had the means to refuse. Heeding his warning about perverting the course of justice she reluctantly reached for the pestle and mortar.

Taking some milk thistle, she added it to willow bark and then gathered the rest of the ingredients. Angrily, she crushed the ingredients together. What made men like Mr Giles think that they could treat people like herself with such disrespect, voicing their ill-mannered demands?

Audrey arrived for work and Kat asked her to bring a pitcher of cider through from the kitchen. She poured some into a bottle before adding the mixture of crushed herbs and roots. Then she stoppered it and shook it hard before asking Audrey to go and stay by Darling's bedside until her return. "She must not be left alone for long," she advised and the girl nodded obediently.

Taking off the necklace that Darling had given her, Kat went to find a safe place to put it. The importance of the assizes would have attracted many to the Great Hall and the streets would be open for opportunists and nimble-fingered vagrants. A lone woman was easy pickings.

In her chamber, she kissed the stone and hooked the chain over the candlestick atop the small chest of drawers where Darling kept her best linen. As she went to leave, she felt compelled to turn back. A shadow was dancing over the face of the obsidian pendant. She held her breath, trying to decipher whether it was a trick of the light. Taking a few steps closer, she picked it up, cradling it in the palm of her hand. This was no trick of the light. Kat gasped.

There he was, as clear as day, in the polished surface of the stone, staring back at her. "Gideon!" she cried out.

He was standing but he looked dishevelled and worn out. He appeared a broken man, dirty and in pain. The image became larger, more real and she watched him sit and reach down to rub his feet. They were sore. She could smell the tang of leather and the sweat of horses. Gideon was in a stabling yard. A shadow crossed over him and he looked up. The sky was flame red, just as she had imagined it had been wherever he was earlier that morning. Kat looked harder, trying to make out the expression on his face. It was pained but curious. Then she saw another: a woman who was perhaps just a little younger than Kat's years. Her dark hair was worn high with white ribbons, she had skin like cream and eyes as dark as night. The woman was smiling and there was mischief in her eyes. She was holding something, offering it to Gideon. Kat watched as he gladly took it from her, and she noticed how the woman's fingers lingered, grazing his far longer than they should have. When the woman's eyes locked with Gideon's, Kat felt something ugly twist deep inside her.

The image faded to black, leaving the stone inanimate again, leaving her wondering if she had seen him at all. She looked harder but he had gone.

CHAPTER SIX

I am not just tired, I am exhausted. And I am hungry, hot and sore. Slowly, painfully, I climb down from the hayloft and reach for one of the water pails. At one point during the night it rained hard and so water fresh from the heavens is plentiful. I think of the torrents pouring down across the moors amongst all those bodies, so many of them, and I close my eyes, trying to blot out the horror that I have witnessed in recent days. Had I known…

The same thought whirls around in my brain, like the ever-spinning wheel of an overturned carriage. Overcome with nausea, I grip the rung of the ladder to steady myself. The sun is blazing this morning. I can feel its heat already. Lifting the bucket, I throw it over myself without a care for the clothes that I am in. The water is refreshing and it drips from my hair, over my shoulders, beads of it trickling like tears over my chest. I shake my head, waiting for the water to cool my body and then I sit down on a stool so that I can rest and take in the new dawn.

I shut my eyes, savouring the peace before the place starts to wake. A shadow crosses over my face and my eyelids flutter open. A young woman. Beautiful. Everything about her is soft, delicate and pristine. She is smiling at me and I notice how her eyes follow the droplets of water as they course over my still burning skin. "Here," she says and holds out a cup filled with milk.

I take it from her and our fingers touch. She keeps hers there for long enough to suggest flirtation. I withdraw my hand as I think of home again. This woman's attentions are nothing new. Girls from wealthy homes always make playful eyes at the footmen. The taller, broader, more handsome, the better. I am no fool. I know that it is all harmless, that there is no meaning to it. And yet, I cannot still my beating heart. The touch of a woman's hand has stirred a fire inside me. It is a sensation that I thought I would never enjoy again. She smiles and there is a wicked twinkle to it because she knows what power her beauty has over a man.

My mind shows me another face, the lips puckered in disapproval. Shame adds even more heat to my cheeks. I have done nothing wrong, but I feel as though I have. I feel as though I am being watched.

CHAPTER SEVEN

Ruth's head was swimming and she could see nothing but murky ripples in front of her. Although she was still sitting upright at the table, she realised that her eyes must be shut. Had she been dreaming? It had been as though she had been in another place and time, caught in a dream. In that dream, somebody had been knocking against a door. As her senses began to clear, Ruth noticed that she could still hear the knocking. The noise echoed through her head, growing louder. As she attempted to flicker her eyelids open, she realised that they had never been closed. The air in front of her was clearing – past back to present. Draped from her fingers was the necklace, its shiny black stone reflecting a face. It was not her own. With a horrified gasp, Ruth dropped it on to the table.

"Yoo-hoo, Ruth. Are you alright in there, dear?" The knocking sounded out again and Ruth was suddenly aware of Mrs Tibbs from down the road peering in at her through the window.

Pushing her chair back, she stood up abruptly and gripped the edge of the table for support.

"Ruth?" Mrs Tibbs called and tapped at the windowpane.

Regaining her composure, Ruth went through into the conservatory so that she could unlock the door. She wondered how long Mrs Tibbs had been watching her for.

"Good heavens, Ruth dear," she said, shaking off her umbrella. "Are you alright? Away with the fairies you were."

She turned to look back at the table. A cold cup of coffee was next to the discarded necklace. Making the excuse of a lack of sleep, she offered a tea or coffee.

"I really shouldn't, dear." Mrs Tibbs gave the answer she always did as she pulled up a chair and made herself comfortable. "I was only stopping by briefly as I'm on my way over to Zoe's to do the clean." She studied Ruth's face and frowned. "Are you sure there's nothing wrong? You look ever so peaky."

With an apologetic smile, Ruth went to boil the kettle. "Not at all. Like you said, I was just away with the fairies and thinking about a few things."

"I suppose it is such a busy time of year." She took off her coat and hung it over the back of the chair. "Tea please, if you're sure it isn't too much trouble, dear," she added. "Just the usual way please – milky with two sugars." She eyed Ruth's untouched cup of coffee suspiciously but clearly thought better than to mention it. Then her eyes rested on the necklace. "Oh, I say. That's very pretty. Was it a gift?" She went to pick it up, but Ruth was too quick for her, swiping it away from her grasp.

"A client left it," Ruth replied in a hurry. "I should put it somewhere safe, until I get it back to him." She tucked the necklace into the pocket of her kimono dressing gown.

Nodding, Mrs Tibbs waited as Ruth warmed a mince pie to accompany the tea. "Popped by for some of your fancy magic did he, dear?" she asked, referencing Ruth's Tarot work. Mrs Tibbs always referred to it as 'fancy magic'. Ruth knew that as a regular church-goer she didn't really approve of the work she did, merely tolerated it.

"Something like that," she answered and served everything up before returning to her seat.

Mrs Tibbs dabbed at some crumbs on the corner of her mouth. "Zoe had mentioned that you and Grayson are off to Somerset for Christmas, to see Tim. I wondered if you would like me to pop in and feed Meg whilst you're gone?" Tim was Ruth's younger brother. He lived with his boyfriend, Max, in a beautiful barn renovation in a quaint Somerset village. Even when Casimir had been living at home, Grayson and Ruth had taken it in turns with Tim and Max to host Christmas. Grayson had always complained when it was their turn to visit Tim. He hated the 'bleak landscape' and always moaned that it was 'too far from civilisation'. None of Grayson's family bothered with get-togethers over Christmas. They were not a close family and Ruth's tradition with Tim had always been alien to him. To Grayson's mind it would be far more preferable to be holed away in a penthouse apartment in London over Christmas, with easy access to bars that stayed open and food that they didn't have to cook themselves. On the contrary, Ruth loved it. They would take long walks over crystalline heathland or through woodlands filled with ancient oaks and then they would return to the house for mulled wine, stollen and roasted chestnuts before finishing any last minute gift wrapping.

Grateful for the offer, Ruth nodded. "That would be wonderful, if you don't mind?" She knew that Mrs Tibbs liked nothing more than to be busy and she had a dreadful soft spot for Meg, often bringing a little cream to add to the milk saucer, or some fresh pieces of chicken or fish.

Putting down her teacup, Mrs Tibbs wiped her hands on a piece of kitchen roll and reached down to Meg who had curled happily by her feet. "Of course I don't mind." She scooped up the cat and began stroking her tabby fur. Meg looked less than impressed at being disturbed. "I would love to do it." Bringing the cat to her face, she made a kissing noise. "I expect you'll enjoy some turkey and stuffing over Christmas, sweetie."

Ruth grinned. Meg would not miss her at all with Mrs Tibbs popping in. "When do you go?" she asked as she returned the cat to the spot by her feet.

"Next week," Ruth replied, suddenly realising how terribly disorganised she was. She had barely made a dent in her Christmas shopping. "I'll give you the key."

"Wonderful," Mrs Tibbs said, before her face dropped. "Unless Cas is coming back home at all? I suppose you won't need me then?"

Ruth shook her head sadly. It would be the first Christmas that Casimir would be elsewhere. "Cas called to say that he will be spending this year in Germany. He's met a lovely young lady, so I gather. I'm sure we will meet her soon enough."

Mrs Tibbs couldn't hide how pleased she was to be getting Meg all to herself. "That's just lovely for him, Ruth dear. Very exciting. Anyway, I'll drop by in the next day or two and you can go over the instructions with me. I do like to get it right." She pushed back her chair. "I shan't keep you any longer. I expect there is carnage next door." Shaking her head, she added: "Those boys run rings around poor Zoe and I don't know how she does it with such a big job."

"She is an everyday superwoman," Ruth agreed.

"Just as well Paul works from home most days, I suppose," Mrs Tibbs added, referring to Zoe's husband. "It's all so different to my day. My husband wouldn't have had the first clue about the kids, God rest his soul." Her eyes glazed over for a moment as she recalled some distant memories, then she was back to her fussing. "Would you like me to pop by and do anything over here once I have finished at Zoe's? You really don't seem yourself today." She looked around the kitchen and Ruth realised with embarrassment that it really was rather a mess.

"No really, I'm fine. Thank you. Pop over any time to go through the instructions for Meg." She winked at her and said, "I'll get those iced gingerbread biscuits you like and make a pot with the proper tea leaves, not just a bag."

"Don't go to any effort just for me. As long as it's hot, wet and sugary, I'm happy," she said as Ruth showed her to the front door. "I'll see you soon then, dear," she called back as she headed down the pathway.

Ruth checked the time and swore under her breath. There was barely enough time to get ready for her afternoon shift at work. Cleaning the kitchen would have to wait until much later. Closing the door, she hurried upstairs to take a shower.

CHAPTER EIGHT

Leaden rainclouds scudded across the sky overhead as Jeremy rounded the heath at the top of Stockbridge Downs. Behind him he could hear the excited whinny of horses, free to graze. Rex was in his element, sniffing at every hedgerow and the pitted ground as they walked. The low, early morning mist would soon be washed away by the downpour that threatened as he felt the first few splashes of rain on his forehead.

Lost in thought, he trudged on, in no hurry to get back to the lonely cottage with the stifling atmosphere. He checked his watch. There was a long time to wait until he could meet Ruth Meadows again. It was just fortunate that he had the distraction of walking Rex as it would hopefully keep his mind off the strange occurrences in the house.

He planned to pop in to the university prior to meeting Ruth in town. That way he could drop off some of the tedious paperwork he had been required to complete prior to starting in his new lecturing role. It was beyond him why everything couldn't be handled digitally these days.

Nothing untoward had happened in the house the night before and he took solace in that. Maybe the ghost was scared of dogs? He might be an appalling guard dog when it came to watching out for living, breathing intruders, but he was showing his worth at keeping the supernatural ones at bay, so far at least. Jeremy shuddered at the thought of Rex leaving. Lisa and Roy would be due back in just a couple of days. With Christmas fast approaching, it would be a lonely week in a country that he had only just started to settle into. Reminding himself that the isolation would give him time to work on tracing back the origins of the necklace, he thought of the family tree he had been researching and his mood darkened, just as it did each time he thought about the real reason why he was doing it.

Rex bounded back to him with a bark of excitement, temporarily prising him from his state of melancholy. Jeremy took a gulp of the fresh winter air as he thought about the ghost again. He had never seen anything remotely paranormal before. It didn't sit comfortably with him. He preferred his history on the pages of a book, trapped behind the glass encasements of museums or on fine storytelling displays in sites of national heritage, not hiding in the shadows of his remote home. Another feeling of loneliness engulfed him and he quietly berated himself. Hadn't that been what he had wanted? Nobody asking him questions, prying into his personal life, digging around for information on what had happened before?

The rain began to fall harder. Soon it would be thrashing its way across the Downs. Icy droplets fell from his lashes and mingled with the tears that had begun to fall. He hadn't even realised that he was crying. That was how the emotion had been taking him: the waves of sickness, the sharp blades of guilt cutting into him and then the tears. In a wild moment of anger, he wondered if *she* had brought this restless spirit to his door as a way to avenge him for what he had done, what had happened when-

"Stop it!" Jeremy brought his hands to his ears to shut out the thoughts that nearly always dominated his mind during his waking hours. To the casual observer, he probably appeared mad: a man hurrying through the rain, hands over his ears, with only a huge dog for company. In his haste to close down his thoughts, he had dropped the lead. "Shit!"

Up ahead, Rex was running carefree. If he caught sight of a fox, a deer, even a horse or cow, he would likely give chase and in spite of his nine years he was still a fast dog. "Reeeeeeeeeex!" Jeremy yelled above the thrash of rain and was relieved to see the faint, grey figure jerk to a stop. He called again and took the whistle to his mouth. Almost bowling him over, the dog ran for him, leaping to one side at the last minute. "Good boy! Good boy." Jeremy praised him and reached for a treat in his pocket before retrieving the lead and securing it to the dog's collar. "Let's get you home."

After bundling Rex into the back of his Defender, he checked the time and wondered how the psychic woman, Ruth, was feeling about their imminent meeting. He recalled the accusation in her voice the night before on the phone and cringed. It was a small mercy he had left the necklace with her. He needed to know what she had seen. It would do no good having somebody like her jumping to conclusions about things, talking to people, picking away at a scab he just wanted to heal over. No, he could not let that happen.

******

The admin office Ruth worked in was decked with a gaudy clash of colour. Green, red, gold, pink and blue pieces of tinsel snaked around computer screens and desks and draped from the ceiling. There was a buzz of excitement that the holidays would be beginning in a few short hours. Students flitted back and forth in a flurry of last minute panic to get assignments handed in, their bleary-eyed expressions the result of extended parties, late night work to get everything completed on time and, most likely, a frenzied mixture of both.

Ruth was in the middle of finishing off a letter that was due to be sent out to staff, when somebody approached the front desk. She sighed inwardly, expecting to smell the tell-tale stale odour of sweat and too much beer from the night before. Students were always flustered and stressed at this time of year: stressed about assignments, stressed about living off the last drips of cash or overdraft and stressed about the journey home to their parents. Plastering on her most accommodating and patient smile, she looked up and almost fell off her chair.

"I thought it was you." The familiar masculine twang took her completely by surprise. Dressed in a dark cable knit jumper and jeans and looking far more relaxed than he had the day before, was Jeremy.

"What are you doing here?" The question came across as accusing and not at all how she had intended. No matter what reservations she had about the man, she reminded herself that she was at work and needed to remain professional. "Sorry, what I meant to say was that I didn't expect to see you here." In the back of her mind, she couldn't help worry that he had found out where she worked and had come to pester her for the necklace or beg her not to say anything about what she had seen. So near to closing, there was nobody else left in the office. Her mind raced. What if he knew that she had witnessed some foul play from the reading and he had come to shut her up? Her hand hovered over the phone on her desk.

"I could say the same," he said with a friendly smile. He certainly didn't look like a man who may be hiding some dreadful, macabre secret.

"Are you a student? I've not seen you before." Ruth couldn't hide the suspicion in her tone.

"My name should be on an envelope here." He leaned over the desk, looking amidst the paperwork. "Jez Franklyn, the new Professor of Early Modern History. I believe I need to hand in some of these forms and that you have a welcome pack for me to pick up?"

"Jez?" Ruth was momentarily confused by the trendy abbreviation of his name before the penny dropped.

He laughed. "I much prefer Jeremy, but I usually find the younger students listen more if you've got a cool name."

Nodding, Ruth had to agree. He did look decidedly cooler as 'Jez'. "Wait there a moment, I have everything you need over here." She found the appropriate out-tray and picked up the brown envelope containing the glossy package that was filled with information about the campus, staff handbook and all the other paraphernalia that she could not imagine any sane and busy person having the time to comb through. "There you go."

He took the package and leaned against the counter. "So, what are *you* doing here? If you don't mind me asking."

Letting her hands fall to her sides with an audible slapping noise, Ruth shrugged. "Day job. It was supposed to fill the gap after my son got older, although Grayson always says it's a waste of time."

"Grayson?"

"My husband," Ruth explained and thought she noticed Jeremy's face drop.

"Oh, I see," he said and avoided her gaze. "I wouldn't say that any job is a waste of time, although I suppose it isn't quite as exciting as the evening job you have."

Ruth chuckled bashfully, "I suppose it's not." She did not bother to explain that Grayson was even more scathing of that particular career choice. Husband bashing wasn't exactly the most attractive trait in any woman. Keen to change the subject, she bent to retrieve her bag from beneath the desk. "As you're here, you may as well take this." Ruth pulled out a parcel of tissue paper. Unable to abide touching it again, she had wrapped the necklace before leaving the house.

Thanking her, Jeremy reached into his pocket for his wallet, a sheepish look on his face as he searched for the money he owed. "I'm not sure I've got the cash on me right now. Can you direct me to an ATM on campus?"

Shaking her head, Ruth held up her hands. "Please don't worry about it. I think I scared you away."

"No, I shouldn't have just run off. I've never done anything like that before, so I just didn't know what to expect and I have to admit, it was a little unnerving seeing you like that. I suppose it's second nature for a medium though?" He scratched the back of his head awkwardly.

"That doesn't usually happen." Ruth was quick to reassure him that she wasn't some kind of lunatic 'self-proclaimed' psychic who played up to the role. Standing in front of the desk, he appeared completely normal and - nice. She decided to broach the subject of what she had seen during the reading. "I saw a woman during the reading," she said suddenly. "One who is no longer with us."

Something sparked in his eyes and he looked around shiftily. His reaction put her on edge again. Leaning across the counter and keeping his voice low, he asked, "What did she look like?"

"Long hair, auburn, I think. Pretty. She was scared of something." She paused and watched how his Adam's apple bounced up and down in his throat as he swallowed. "I think she drowned," she added in a whisper.

"Oh." His tone was deadpan, giving nothing away.

"Does it make any sense to you?" Ruth asked, wondering if she was in danger of provoking him.

He shook his head but his eyes told her otherwise. "What about this?" he asked, waving the small package containing the necklace. "Did you get anything from it?"

"Can you tell me who it belongs to?" Ruth challenged.

Jeremy shrugged before looking away. "Your guess is as good as mine. I think it's old. Really old." His expression was haunted. "I was hoping you could tell me a little more about its history."

Ruth raised her eyebrows. "Isn't that your job?"

Colour flushed his skin and he gave a nervous chuckle. "I can do the academic bit; work on dating it; give a brief summary of the purpose it would have likely served in history but I can't do the really interesting part. I can't get any more insight into the lady who might have owned it as there are no distinct markings that give any clue." He shrugged. "I suppose that means that she was an ordinary woman, somebody who was nothing of any particular note."

"Ordinary does not necessarily mean she was nothing of note," Ruth snapped, feeling the hairs bristle on the back of her neck. She did not know why the remark stung so much, but it did.

The colour in Jeremy's cheeks deepened. "I didn't mean to suggest that social status would have made the original owner any less important. It's just that history tends to only document the rich, the dastardly villains and those with an extraordinary tale to tell."

Ruth knew all of this and felt a pang of guilt for being so quick to bite.

The awkward moment was broken by Jeremy's revelation. "I think I may have seen the original owner of the necklace. I was hoping you might have seen her too."

"Where?" He had piqued Ruth's interest. Neither of them needed to state the obvious fact that he was referring to a dead woman.

Scanning the length of the corridor, Jeremy appeared nervous. "I don't think I can really say too much about it here. Perhaps I could explain somewhere other than work?"

Another student interrupted their conversation and after Ruth had finished dealing with the query thrown at her, she gave Jeremy a sympathetic smile. "How about we still have that meeting for coffee later?" She had already managed to read between the lines. The man was experiencing something paranormal and he was completely reeling from the whole experience. Who else could he confide in over something like that? Most people would laugh it off or think the whole story was an utter fabrication. "I can't guarantee that I've got any of the answers that you need, but I can listen with an open mind if it helps?"

"It'll help." Looking as though a weight had slipped a little from his shoulders, Jeremy slotted the brown envelope he was holding underneath his arm before adding, "And then you can tell me that I've lost the plot."

******

Town was crowded. People were weighed down with assorted bags of Christmas shopping, bumping into one another or closely dodging each other. A school choir had set up by the Buttercross in the centre of town, angelic voices giving their version of various Christmas carols. Pleased parents and cooing relatives had gathered to watch. Above them, the Christmas lights lit up the High Street in a festive array of blue, white and gold orbs.

The air was particularly chilly and Ruth snuggled her face into her scarf as she walked past the choir and through the short walkway leading to The Square, where the coffee shop-cum-bistro was located.

As she neared the agreed venue, Ruth found herself dazzled by the tiny twinkling lights that lit a spectacular curtain of jasmine draped over the fascia. It was her favourite place to have coffee or lunch and she instantly felt herself relax as the gentleman behind the bar greeted her warmly. The feeling that she was doing something sordid and wrong began to creep up on her. Usually, she would take lunch with Grayson or meet Zoe there. Now she was meeting a handsome stranger. Gabbling that she was meeting a client, she headed up the stairs and into a little mirrored alcove that was mercifully empty. Scrabbling inside her bag for her mobile, she went to find the number that Jeremy had called her from the night before, wondering whether she should just call the whole meeting off.

"Nice place." He appeared from behind her, looking particularly dapper in a navy trench coat and mustard checked scarf.

Ruth opened her mouth to speak but only managed to stammer a greeting of sorts. It was preposterous to be feeling so guilty. She was doing nothing wrong. Her behaviour did not go unnoticed. "Is everything alright?" he asked with concern.

Taking her coat off, Ruth took a breath. It was a simple meeting with a client, she reminded herself. Plenty of people met on business. "Just a little panicked seeing everyone looking so organised with their Christmas shopping, that's all," she retorted as she took her seat.

He laughed and joined her by sitting opposite. "I'm pleased to say that I'm going to be a grumpy old recluse this year. No panic buying to worry about for me."

"Lucky you." Ruth picked up a menu and eyeballed the cocktail list. "How about a Christmas tipple whilst we talk?" she suggested. "You seemed a little shaken earlier. It might take the edge off."

They each settled on a gingerbread Martini and then fell into conversation that skirted around the subject Jeremy had wanted to confide. Ruth was glad of it though. It felt good to have a conversation with somebody other than her friends.

Jeremy had moved from Auckland to the UK a couple of months earlier and had found the lecturer post in Winchester. They spoke about working life on the campus, about the wonderful history attached to the city and of the great locations that he planned to visit. He was working on a personal research project for somebody, tracing back their family history and there were roots in England that he had already dated back to the eighteenth century. They had almost drained their drinks by the time Ruth broached the subject of the Tarot reading.

A shadow crossed Jeremy's face. "Shame we're both driving, I could have done with another one of these," he said, tapping his fingertip on the side of the glass.

"Just blurt it out," Ruth suggested, her voice kind and patient. "You're talking to somebody who sees the past, present and future through pictures on cards for goodness sake, nothing you say is going to sound at all strange to me."

Jeremy inhaled deeply. "Okay then." Tipping his head back, he threw the last of his drink down his throat and set the glass down on the table. "Somebody left me this necklace. I had no idea about it before it was bequeathed to me." He drifted for a moment, considering whether to divulge any further information but appeared to decide against it. "It looks like it dates back to the seventeenth century." He went on to explain how people had used obsidian gemstones for scrying, particularly when backed onto silver.

When Ruth nodded, indicating that she knew the history linking certain gemstones to witchcraft, he hurried the story along. "I've been waking up to noises that appear to be linked to the necklace." He paused and began tearing the corner of a napkin, shredding it into tiny pieces. "I've seen her a couple of times now, but only ever in the mirror. I can see her standing there, this woman, but only ever as a reflection. When I look into the room, there's nobody to be seen. It's getting to the point of ridiculous. I'm a grown man and I'm terrified of going to bed."

"Have you seen her in daylight yet?"

Shaking his head, he pushed the pile of papery green napkin confetti to one side. "I'm not hanging around long enough I suppose. Or maybe she only comes out at night." He turned his eyes from the napkin shreds to Ruth. "Tell me your thoughts? Do you think she is a ghost, or some sort of imprint in time? Is she bringing some sort of message? I mean, why me?"

Ruth noticed that his hand was trembling slightly and she reached out to still it. "Is there a message you're hoping for, Jeremy?" Their eyes locked and he pulled his hand away quickly, leaving her feeling awkward.

"The only thing I'm hoping for is that she'll go away and leave me alone."

"She could just be attached to the necklace. That's all. You probably shouldn't take her presence so personally. I appreciate that it must be disconcerting though."

He gave her an incredulous look. "Disconcerting? Jeez, the woman scared me shitless!"

The pair of them looked at each other, his statement hanging in the air between them, and they both laughed.

Jeremy shook his head. "Sorry, excuse the language. I'm not behaving like much of a gent, am I?"

Ruth waved a dismissive hand. "Don't worry, you're quite safe. I've heard far worse." She leaned across the table. "The good news is that I'm pretty confident that she's haunting the necklace rather than haunting you. I get the impression that she is attached to it."

He looked up, his eyes gleaming with curiosity. "What makes you think that?"

Ruth thought about what she had seen the night before and the trance she had fallen into in the kitchen that morning. The details were too blurry to remember, but she was certain that it had to do with the woman. "Last night, I saw something too and then I fell into some kind of reverie this morning. I don't really remember much of it, but I know it was something to do with her."

"Shit!" He swore again and turned to call a passing waiter. "Can we get more drinks please? A strong coffee for me. What would you like?"

Ruth ordered a matcha tea and the waiter disappeared, leaving them to finish talking.

"So, do you think you could try doing something directly with the necklace?" Jeremy asked, fishing it out of his pocket and placing it on the table between them.

Instinctively, Ruth recoiled. "No. Not here. Put it back in your pocket." She suddenly didn't want to see it or be near it. The necklace filled her with a sense of despair and she could sense the darkness surrounding it. Even without touching it she could tell that it had once been used for very deep magic, something far more advanced than she could even dream of. "Bring it over tomorrow afternoon," she at last conceded.

******

Jeremy had been sitting in front of his laptop for over two hours. Rex had adopted his usual position, sprawled across Jeremy's feet. The screensaver kicked in and he realised he had drifted into other thoughts again. Reprimanding himself for losing focus, he hit the space bar. The words on the screen were blurred. He rubbed his eyes. Each of the little boxes depicting the details for each member of the family tree had taken him back to the earlier part of the eighteenth century so far. He considered the idea that the necklace could have once belonged to any of the women but he suspected that it dated further back in the family than he had so far traced. There were no untimely deaths that suggested any of the women had been trialled for witchcraft, although he imagined that if they had, it would have been earlier than the eighteenth century. Drumming his fingers on the edge of the laptop, he wondered if he would end up tracing it back to the original owner being from the era of the famous Witchfinder General, Matthew Hopkins. So far, he was drawing blanks.

The family tree had started as a casual project, something that they had been supposed to finish together. Just the two of them. Nothing had been finished though. Not really. Now he was left doing it alone. It was guilt that had originally spurred him on to pick it up again after he had moved to the UK – guilt and of course, a curious fear about the woman he had seen. Tears blurred his vision and he pinched the bridge of his nose.

Picking up a pen and his notebook, Jeremy tried not to allow his mind to wander down the dangerous labyrinth of questions that he could not answer. He jotted down the name of the man who he had managed to find himself stuck on, then he noted the date and place of death. The records kept confusing him. Whilst the records from the later years of this man's life were detailed and clear, it was becoming impossible to track his birth. Chewing the end of the pen, Jeremy stared for a long time at the many names that appeared on the screen, all of which were possible links. The date of the gentleman's death was 1732. He must have been of an ample age for the time due to all of his children and their various birth dates, but there were no records that matched a man by the same name to the year of his birth in the area. The lack of records suggested that he was not from wealthy roots but one of his sons was of considerable note, being a well-connected lawyer. From what Jeremy had been able to decipher, that son had had been the only child in the family to have received an education. It must have been a good one too as he had gone on to have a son of his own who, it appeared, had played a part in the Bridgwater Treaty, a document that had significantly influenced the abolition of slavery.

Stifling a yawn, he saved down his page on the laptop and turned it off before glancing over at the bookcase. He had slipped the necklace behind a book the moment that he had returned from town and he wondered if it would bring the spectral figure back.

Tiredness was ebbing away at him, causing his head to loll forward now and again, but he was reluctant to go to bed. It was always at night that the woman appeared. Even though he didn't fancy seeing the apparition in the mirror again, he needed proof that she really existed and that he was not going mad. Flicking on the television, he decided to keep it on in the background. Watching something would hopefully help him keep awake and if she appeared again, he had his phone next to him so that he could photograph her. Tucking the necklace behind the books was an experiment. The bookshelf was not in sight of the mirror, so that would mean that to get to the chain, the spirit would need to be fully absorbed in the actual room.

On the television screen there was an onslaught of gunshot and a huge explosion. He glanced down at the dog who seemed non-plussed. The film he had put on was reaching its dramatic climax, but it did not have his attention. Jeremy's thoughts wandered back to what Ruth had said about seeing the spirit of the woman at her house too. It was no coincidence that it had happened whilst the necklace had been in Ruth's possession.

During their conversation in the bistro, they had started sharing small pieces of information about their lives and what had brought them to that very point of meeting. He couldn't deny that he found her attractive, but it wasn't just physical attraction; there was something about her that appealed to his deeper nature. When he had explained about his interest in British history, particularly the seventeenth century, she had been genuinely intrigued and asked so many questions. Most people bored quite quickly when it came to his passion for history. In spite of her very English roots, Cathy had always become so bored. The thought struck him hard and he bit down on his lip. Cathy. She was permanently there, waiting in the wings of his mind, with that sad smile that she had always worn so well; the smile that he had fallen for. Shutting his eyes, he stopped himself. The pain was embedded so deeply. Cathy.

Guilt and grief made his bottom lip tremble. Pushing the feelings aside, he forced his thoughts back to the present and refocused on the conversation he had shared with Ruth on their way to the carpark: "The single life eh?" she had teased when he had gone onto explain that he had moved to the UK to live a bachelor's life. "Fast cars and fast women, you mean?"

"Hardly," he had joked. "I drive a twenty-five year old vehicle and the only female to step foot over my threshold is evidently a ghost."

They had laughed at that and he had felt the beat of his heart drum a bit harder in his chest. Then he had stopped, reminding himself that she had a husband and he had his own commitments. Even if things were different for her, they were not for him. His heart belonged to another.

The film ended and Jeremy's eyelids fell heavily, his head tipping backwards. His body ached with fatigue and he grabbed a cushion, plumping it before placing it beneath his head and lying back.

He woke to the sound of static from the television screen. Rex had moved to his beanbag on the floor and was fast asleep. Picking up the remote, he flicked it off. The room was still aglow with light streaming in from the kitchen. Strange, he thought, how light could make a place appear less disconcerting.

When he was sitting upright, his gaze wandered to the mirror. It reflected the worn, brown arm of the old chesterfield sofa and the guitar that he had decoratively hung on the wall. Beneath it was a nest of oak tables and a half empty mug of coffee. There was no sign of the ethereal image he had seen reflected on previous nights, but the air around him felt cold. Wasn't a temperature dip supposed to be a sign that something supernatural was in the room?

The sound of old pipes clanging into life caught him by surprise and he jumped before reminding himself that the house was old and draughty. It got cold quickly in the cottage and the storage heaters were often battling to keep it warm.

Flicking back his wrist, he checked his watch. It was almost two in the morning. Staying up any longer wasn't going to do him any good whatsoever. Stretching, he stood and took one final look in the mirror before taking the discarded coffee mug through to the kitchen.

As he crossed the threshold separating the lounge from the kitchen, an unexpected thud caught him off guard. The cup he had been holding fell to the floor, smashing to pieces. A brown stream of liquid seeped into the cracks between the flagstones but Jeremy was too alarmed to take much notice of the mess. Slowly, he turned. The lounge looked darker, as though a film of murky air had drifted in and was blurring everything. Instinctively, he turned his attention to the mirror. Nothing out of the ordinary was reflected in its shiny surface.

Lifting his hand, he leaned against the doorframe, staring into the dimly lit room, looking for signs of disruption. Rex was awake and sitting upright. He was staring at the mirror above the fireplace.

Jeremy glanced from the mirror to the bookcase and noticed the gap between the books. The hardback book he had tucked the necklace behind was lying on the floor, the pages open. With a whimper, Rex retreated from the sitting room, tail between legs.

Pivoting, Jeremy scanned the whole room, adrenalin pumping. It was empty and the heat was returning swiftly as the heaters pumped away furiously. On the shelf, the necklace was still there. It hadn't been moved. Shaken, he put the book back and flipped out the light, hurrying up to his bedroom.

Turning over his underwear drawer, he found the earplugs he reserved for noisy planes. After brushing his teeth, he pushed them into his ears. Blocking out any noise would hopefully keep him from waking to any more unnatural disturbances. Pulling back the thick duvet, he slipped into bed and reached for the lamp before hesitating, fingers poised to turn it off. Perhaps he would leave it on for the night - just this once.

******

"You look as though you could do with a stiff drink." The following afternoon, Ruth greeted Jeremy with a curious smile. The comfortable interior of her house was a welcome refuge from the bitter nip of winter air. He could tell the small details and finishing touches were her doing. Just like her, the décor had a very Bohemian and other worldly style to it. As she led him through into her lounge, he noticed that she had decorated a small Norwegian spruce. Pine needles and oranges stuck with cloves mingled together creating a spicy, festive scent.

"Just a rough night," Jeremy replied as she ushered for him to sit down.

"Your nocturnal visitor?" she asked, heading into the kitchen. The busy clatter of spoons and china suggested she was preparing a hot drink.

He picking up a frayed piece of tinsel that had fallen to the floor. "Yep." As she appeared in the doorway holding a jar of coffee, he gave an ironic chuckle. "You would think I'd be pleased to have a beautiful woman wake me up in the dead of night. Maybe I'm just an ungrateful moron." In spite of his attempt to make light of the situation, he couldn't shake the unease that he had felt creeping over him all day. It was getting under his skin, permeating his bones, flowing through his veins.

"She's beautiful then, this ghost of yours?" She shook the coffee jar at him and raised her eyebrows.

"Coffee would be great, thanks. Yes, she is, I suppose. You should know that though, having seen her for yourself."

"It was dark and I didn't hang around long enough to see the full profile. Mind you, I should imagine a beautiful woman visiting in the dead of night is not quite the same when it's a malevolent spirit."

"Do you think it's a malign presence then?" The thought hadn't occurred to him before. It wasn't particularly appealing to think that something of a sinister nature was prowling around his rather isolated cottage.

The sound of a kettle being switched on to boil preceded the sound of a biscuit tin being opened and then Ruth appeared again, an apologetic look upon her face. "I didn't mean that. Sorry, it wasn't a particularly tactful thing to say."

"Did you sense something malevolent? When you did the reading?"

Shaking her head, Ruth set down the tray she was carrying. She looked particularly ethereal in a long floaty turquoise dress that set off her eyes. The style suited her. "I didn't feel anything like that." She gestured at the sugar bowl and Jeremy shook his head.

Plunging the coffee pot and pouring, she handed him a cup and saucer before joining him on the sofa. "But I did sense a dreadful despair and I felt as though I was drowning. Then I heard a man's voice."

"So do you think there's more than one spirit?" Jeremy asked, his concerns escalating.

"I really don't know. Maybe we can get some more answers today."

Taking a sip of his coffee, he hoped his nerves would settle. "So where do you want to do this?" he asked. "In here? The back room again? Your kitchen?"

"You make it sound so ominous," she remarked with a cheeky twinkle in her eye and then looked away, aware of how flirtatious she had sounded.

He hesitated to answer and it heightened the awkwardness. The comment had been full of flirtatious wit and he had liked it, a little too much. He could not allow himself to get swept into anything like that though. Not now and not with a married woman.

Embarrassed, she cleared her throat and asked to hold the jewellery. "We may as well do it in here," she said in a much more officious tone and held out her hand. "I've not read jewellery before. Not seriously anyway. I'm not sure if anything will come of it."

"I appreciate this," Jeremy said as he placed the necklace into her palm. He felt nervous again but reminded himself that it did not really belong to him. It would not be his thoughts and memories that Ruth would be tapping into and he could stop her at any moment.

Taking a deep breath, Ruth sat back in the sofa and tried to relax. "You just need to give me a minute or two. I need to focus and breathe." Her eyelids fluttered closed as she began to inhale and slowly exhale in one long, fine breath. After a short while, with the twinkling of the fairy lights from the Christmas tree and the warmth of the house, the whole scene seemed hypnotic. Jeremy felt a sense of peace and calm fall over him and his shoulders dropped as he waited. All the tension he had been feeling from his sleepless nights seemed to roll off him in waves. This woman was good. Was she doing this on purpose? She had mentioned that she was a healer.

"Who are you?" The words tripped from her lips, light and airy, almost musical. "Who are you?" she breathed again.

"What can you see?" he asked her but she didn't respond. Instead, he noticed that her expression had changed from one of serenity to something harder. "Ruth?" Instinct made him edge away from her.

Suddenly, her eyes snapped open and she was staring straight ahead. "Winchester," she said and her voice was distant. "I see Winchester. Up at the Westgate. What do you want?" Her gaze was locked on something that Jeremy was unable to see. The hairs on his arms bristled and he noticed that she had started to tremble. Sweat was beading on her forehead. "It's so hot. This dress, the material is so thick." She clawed at her collarbone and neck with her free hand.

"Maybe this isn't such a good idea," Jeremy pointed out, standing up and moving in front of her. "Maybe you should just stop there."

Ruth did not appear to hear him, or see him. She unfurled her fingers, revealing the necklace. Jeremy sucked in his breath. The stone was glowing a molten shade of red. He reached out to take it from her but Ruth began hooking the chain over her neck. She appeared vexed. "I don't recall taking this off." Her voice sounded different, detached from the room that she was sitting in. The glowing pendant slipped beneath the material of her dress and her eyes rolled backwards.

"Ruth!" he shouted, rushing towards her. It was too late. Her head was tilting backwards and she was slipping away from him. "What's happening?" He caught her by the shoulder and tried to shake her back to her senses. "Look at me. You need to look at me!"

CHAPTER NINE

Kat was staring at the imposing grey stone of the city's Westgate. Somebody's hand was resting on her shoulder and she could hear a voice: "Look at me. You need to look at me!" The voice belonged to a man but it sounded distorted, as though he was shouting at her through a tunnel.

The hand slipped from Kat's shoulder and she whirled around, almost knocking into a woman carrying a crying, red faced child, several more clinging to her skirts to keep up. "Take a care, now!" The woman sidestepped as she snapped at Kat, cross that she had almost collided with her. "Stick close," she warned the children who were following her like a little row of ducklings, "people are too busy dallying and hurrying for the front row of this afternoon's assizes to watch out for other folk." She shot Kat a look of irritation before hurrying on up the hill, instructing the children to pick up their pace.

Kat turned, confused and disorientated as she looked ahead of her. Was she hearing things? The voice had sounded familiar and at first, she had thought it to belong to Gideon. But that was merely wishful thinking.

Frowning, she looked around. Why was she at the Westgate? Panic began to take over as she realised that she couldn't remember. Her mind felt cloudy and she stopped, taking a moment to gather her senses.

All around her, daily business was already beginning to slow. Above the general noise on the street, she could hear snippets of conversation about the impending trial, evidently to be the last one of the day. Her memory returned with such force that she almost cried out. She was taking the medicine to Mr Giles, up at the Great Hall, where the assizes court was always held. She was meant to hurry.

Shaking her head, she wondered if the heat was getting to her as she continued to climb the gentle incline that stretched towards the arch of the Westgate.

From the debtors' prison, she could hear the shouts of prisoners. Kat's chest tightened. She knew what it was like inside those drab, crowded cells. The stink and darkness of Fisherton, where Alice Lisle had been held, was still burned into the forefront of her mind. She wondered what kind of state she would be in when she arrived at the Great Hall for her trial.

If Alice Lisle pleaded not guilty, she would be made to stand in front of a jury. Mistress Hemingway had said that Henry Dawley of Lainston Manor would be on the panel. The Dawley family were one of the wealthiest in

Hampshire. Kat had met Henry Dawley once, when she had still been a young girl. Following a hunting accident, the Dawley's physician had sent for Darling to assist with the treatment. Afterwards, Henry Dawley had come to the shop, to pay a special visit and give his deepest thanks for all Darling had done. He had appeared a good man, of a kind disposition. If he were to be sworn, surely he would not find an old woman guilty of such a dreadful crime?

At the Westgate, she caught the eye of a gate guard who was quick to demand her business. Head high, she explained her purpose. He nodded and she felt suddenly afraid. She had no desire to meet the infamous Lord Jeffreys. His fearsome reputation preceded him in newssheets and in talk on the streets. Taking a steadying breath, she reminded herself that Mr Giles had instructed her to ask for him, not the Lord Chief Justice.

Clutching the handle of the basket that she had slipped the phial into, Kat hoped that somebody would simply take the bottle from her and send her on her way. She didn't even care for payment. She just wanted to leave, to get back to her grandmother and the quiet of their house.

The Great Hall loomed ahead of her; the shade of its brickwork striking a dull harmony with the clouds beginning to scud overhead. Expecting somebody to come and take the goods from her, she paused to stare at the foreboding doors that led into where the assizes were being held. A jackdaw landed on the step outside. It pecked fruitlessly at the ground and then cocked its head, regarding her with shiny black eyes. Kat looked at it, feeling as though the bird had her locked in its gaze: a silent challenge of who dared look away first.

Somebody took hold of her by the sleeve and she gasped with shock. Claiming its victory, the jackdaw took off with a rambunctious caw. A burly looking man was trying to hurry her along. Once again she explained her business, feeling as though she was being treated with the disdain and lack of respect usually saved for those facing trial. There was a tension in the air. People were anxious. They all felt it. The country was on the brink of significant change. The rebels had risen again, although this time there was no leader amongst them like Cromwell had been. Having faced the executioner as a coward who had begged the King for his life, the man whom they had fought for was dead. She knew the old stories of how it had been back then, the hope that Cromwell's rule had brought to families like her husband's. There were many like them, whose hearts still beat for times before Kat had even been born, when the monarchy had been stripped of its power and King Charles had lost his head.

Gideon had worked for noble families who had stories to share of their experience of the Royal Court. These were stories of how the court had been during the reign of Charles II, the King's brother, when the court had been magnificently opulent. Such tales Gideon had heard; even Kat had been awestruck. For a man like Gideon, so easily impressed by great fortune and luxury, his loyalties had easily turned from those of his puritan upbringing.

"Make haste then, Miss!" Startled, Kat was jolted forward by the impatient instruction of the man in front of her as he motioned for her to follow him to the back of the court.

She was to go up the stairs and wait outside the room where the jury gathered to decide their verdict. Kat had never been in this part of the Great Hall before and she could not help but feel herself getting caught up in the atmosphere. People always gathered for the assizes but, as she looked out of the smart line of mullioned windows onto the crowds below, she sensed anticipation and excitement far greater than she had ever known before. This was no ordinary case and people wanted to watch.

Footsteps approached the other side of the door. Mr Giles greeted her by unhooking the basket from her arm. He barely stopped to listen to the instruction she gave. It did not matter so much though. She had written it all down, although whether anyone would stop to read it was another matter entirely. The door was slammed shut again and Kat was given the signal that she could leave. Taking a few steps down towards the doors leading to the Great Hall, Kat paused. A part of her was curious to stay and watch.

The great doors were opened and nobody asked of her business as she walked through to join those who had already jostled their way in to watch the previous cases during the course of the day. Being slight of build, Kat was able to duck and weave her way through to a position nearer the front.

Excited chatter filled the court as they waited for what was to be the crescendo of the month's assizes. The sound of heavy feet descending the staircase brought the chatter to a mere murmur and a line of stern looking men appeared. These were the judges. There were four of them, each one as austere-looking as the next. As they each took their places in court, she noticed that the fifth chair, the one reserved for the Lord Chief Justice, remained empty. Everyone fell to a hush as another set of footsteps could be heard as an ominous echo reverberating from the walls and high ceiling.

The large silhouette of a man appeared in the doorway and Kat took a sharp intake of breath. He paused, his dark eyes sweeping the room before he crossed the threshold. His stride was deliberately slow and his steps heavy. The rectangular white wings of his neck collar were a powerful contrast to the black of his gown and scarlet robe. Shadows in the room obscured the clarity of his features and Kat felt the hairs on her arms and nape of her neck prickle. This must be him. This must be the Lord Chief Justice Jeffreys.

His presence and command tightened the tension in the Great Hall. Unable to look away, Kat stared, transfixed by his presence. At the head of the court, he took his seat with the Crown Counsel, clearing his throat as he did so. In front of him was a flask that he swigged from, the deep red stain above his top lip giving away that it was wine. Now that his face was in plain view, she could see that the whites of his eyes were bloodshot and set into a complexion that was also reddened, she suspected, by the amount of wine he consumed. His expression was hard and cold, devoid of anything human and she could not help but marvel at how he was more monster than man.

A nervous sweat began to gather on her forehead and under her arms. Silence engulfed the room as Alice Lisle was brought forward, treated with the disdain and roughness of any ordinary prisoner. Kat stifled a gasp. She was as she had seen her during the vision: tired and pale, the skin beneath her chin loose and lines etched deeply into her face. As the indictment was read out and a man by her side repeated it for the benefit of her old, failing ears, she looked a pitiful and forlorn figure.

"How sayst thou Alice Lisle, art thou guilty of the high treason contained in this indictment, or not guilty?"

There was a pause as the court waited for her answer. When she spoke, the confidence in her voice defied her frail form. "Not guilty."

Kat closed her eyes, images and words rushing through her mind. It was all unfolding just as she had seen it. Above the clatter of noise in her head, the jury panel was summoned and sworn and Lady Alice selected twelve of the men.

By virtue of her age and health, she was allowed to sit. With a silent respect, Kat noticed how the old woman did not so much as flinch when the indictment was explained in plainer terms to the jury and the prosecution opened its case, providing evidence that a John Hicks, one of the men whom she was accused of harbouring, had played an active part in the treasonous rebellion led by the Duke of Monmouth.

As the trial progressed and the very little patience of the Lord Chief Justice Jeffreys rapidly thinned, Kat could not help but pay attention. She noticed how on more than one occasion a tremor rippled through the jury when he raised his voice to a bellow.

When a man by the name of James Dunne was brought to the bar, accused of showing the traitors to the sanctuary of Lady Alice's home, Judge Jeffreys did nothing to hide his disdain. Kat willed the man, Dunne, to say something of credibility, but with all of his dithering and stumbling over the events that he was questioned about, he did nothing to be of any help to the poor woman.

Cringing inwardly, Kat flinched at the boom of the judge's voice. "Ay, you blockhead!" he shouted, his face colouring with anger. "Is that not a plain question?!"

The court shuddered and a candle was pushed beneath the quaking man's nose, lighting up the fear on his pockmarked face as he attempted to explain that he was cluttered of all his senses.

Kat saw the derisive curl of Lord Jeffreys' top lip as he regarded the man in front of him. Motivated by his impatience and rage, he delivered yet another disparaging summary of what a lying villain the man named James Dunne had proved himself to be.

The place was suddenly thick with silence. Everybody was waiting for what would happen next. The hall seemed to grow hotter and Kat looked up at the overbearing arches of the windows. With the clouds shielding the late afternoon sun, there was nothing to lift the sullen atmosphere.

The room was filled with a murmur of surprise when Lady Alice spoke out, and the court fell into further hush. "I hope I shall not be condemned without being heard?" Holding her head high, she gave Judge Jeffreys a withering glare.

Sitting in his position above the court, the expression on his face was unmistakable. Alice Lisle had caught him off guard, but only for a moment. The hard look returned and he offered the same caustic expression previously reserved for James Dunne. The colour in his cheeks deepened as he digested her impudence. "No, God forbid," he retorted with a sneer. "That was the practice in your husband's time, but God be thanked that it is not so now; the King's courts of law never condemn without hearing."

Somebody near to Kat whispered something about Lady Alice's late husband as she opened her mouth to retort but no sound came out. What could she possibly say in return? The statement was like a sharpened sword, its tip pointing directly to the travesty and outrage for which her late regicide husband was responsible. It was not fair. Kat wanted to protest but all she could do was swallow back the whimper that caught in her throat as she saw the look of defeat cross Lady Alice's face. With those words, Judge Jeffreys had said it all. This was vengeance. Guilty or not, Alice Lisle would pay dearly for her husband's actions. Looking around the courtroom, Kat could see that others shared her opinion on the injustice of this case. It would not be a fair trial, that much was obvious, but nobody would challenge it. How could they? Speaking out would suggest disloyalty to the King and where would that lead? She sat on her hands, stifling the instinctive urge to stand and shout out how very wrong it all was.

Without further ado, the next witness was called.

Time passed painfully slowly. Voices boomed. Men made futile attempts to defend their actions as they were called to the stand and all the while Kat noticed how it was as though Lady Alice had given up all hope, with her head lolling to one side as she struggled to keep her eyes open. Every now and again, the man by her side would nudge her in an attempt to keep her alert, but the old lady was too exhausted. Fisherton had taken her spirit and it seemed as though Judge Jeffreys intended on taking her life too.

When at last the defendant was called to speak, she made good her case, articulating herself well. For the Crown Counsel, who were sitting high and righteous in their seats, her defence fell upon deaf ears. Kat glanced over at the jury: twelve men, a sea of stern faces, all well practised in giving nothing of their thoughts away.

The case was summarised and the steely gaze of Judge Jeffreys rested on the jury as he warned them to think carefully upon their verdict. Kat was appalled. Was nobody else outraged by the undertone of threat in his voice? She glared at him and then at the men whose verdict would be responsible for the fate of Lady Alice Lisle. Surely, they could not think that the feeble figure in front of them was guilty of treason?

If she felt any terror, the old woman gave nothing away. In spite of her obvious exhaustion, she remained quietly dignified. There was no glimmer of sympathy upon the judge's face even though it was most apparent that her prison cell had already brought her nearer to death's door. Was that not enough for this bloodthirsty judge and his vengeful King?

It was all too much for Kat. Pushing her way through the closely packed bodies, she blindly found her way outside. Bursting through the last of the masses, she gulped at the dry air. People were talking, voicing their opinions in low voices but the words mingled into a terrible buzzing noise. Her legs felt weak and her head was pounding. Sickened and horrified by what she had just witnessed, she turned and ran, refusing to slow until she reached home.

******

Darling had left her bed and was sitting at the table in the kitchen. A figure appeared in the doorway beside her.

"Mother?" Kat swiftly became a bundle of nerves. The last time she had seen her mother had been when she had denounced her place in the family, giving up any rights to her dowry by insisting that she would still wed Gideon without the blessing of her parents. Whilst her father had told her that she would never be welcome in the family home again, Kat's mother had watched. She had not said a word to defend her daughter and, as Kat had left, her expression had remained hard.

"Kateryn." With a tight smile, Kat's mother curtly acknowledged her presence before turning her attention back to Darling. "You did not mention that she is working here."

"You did not think to ask," Darling responded and she sounded exhausted.

"If you visited grandmother more often, you would know very well that I am working in the shop." She did not admit to the fact that she was living there too, her marital home under threat of being taken from her.

Kat's mother shot a reproachful glare in Darling's direction.

"What does it matter?" Darling asked and her patience was wearing thin. "The problems you share between you should not be mine to shoulder too. If there is to be any trouble, then I ask that you take it outside of my home." She pressed her head into her hands.

Hurrying over to her, Kat's mother put her arms around Darling's shoulders. "Mother, you look so pale. Let me help you back to bed."

Shrugging her off, Darling shook her head. "I will surely die of boredom if I have to spend any more time in that room!" Turning her head to address Kat, she looked her up and down. "You should talk to one another. It makes no sense for three generations to be torn apart by one man."

Standing rigidly, Kat's mother folded her arms across her chest. "It is not Gideon Fox who ruined this family, it is the decision Kateryn made to wed him." She turned her nose up in distaste: "A mere footman from a family of peasants!"

"It should not have been a decision that I was forced to make!" Kat countered, stepping forward. "We married for love. I do not care for family titles. Why should it matter? We make our own way."

"Every woman has her duty, Kateryn. You should be no different. Marriage is not about love. You are a selfish girl and you have broken your father's heart. Love is a fool's reason for marrying, as I see you have found out." Her words stung. As Kat recoiled, her mother snorted with disgust. "Oh yes, the news has made it to me; the troubles you are having so early in this marriage of *love*. Now he has abandoned you. I could have warned you he would. Your childish fancies about love have left you with no dowry and no husband."

"He has not abandoned me! He has taken a new post with a different employer and he says that it will bring us a better fortune."

"Please don't argue. Not now," Darling pleaded and Kat rushed to her side. She was shaking and her breathing had quickened. Together, Kat and her mother took her back to bed.

By the time they returned to the kitchen and Darling was resting again, the air had settled between them. "She took the turn at the beginning of the week," Kat explained. "Our knowledge is not sufficient for this type of ailment but she refuses to see anyone else."

"Your father has sent for our physic. We use the same man as the Stewkley family. He should be here by nightfall." Her mother's earlier hardness had softened and Kat saw the fear on her face as the earlier tensions between them fell away. "Oh Kateryn, what if it is too late?"

Kat poured three cups of wine and added some spices. Then she held a poker over the fire until the tip was glowing. The ruby liquid hissed as she plunged the fiery end into each cup. "Grandmother is a strong woman, the strongest I know. This will help soothe and clear her chest. It will bring her some rest too, at least until the physic arrives." She put one of the cups in front of her mother. "Take this, it will help you too."

When she returned, her mother was pouring another cup for herself, although she did not bother with the spice or heat. The strain showed in her face. "How did we allow it to come to this, Kateryn?"

"Men," she replied after a mouthful of the warm and spicy liquid. "Darling says that you were different before you married father, that he gave you airs and graces."

Taking another drink, her mother gave her a stern glare. "Does she indeed? She is a fine one to talk." She stood up and went to look out of the window, into the garden behind the house. "You've heard about the case they have brought to the assizes, then?"

Nodding, Kat explained that the reason why she had not been at home with Darling was because she had been dispensing a remedy at the Great Hall. With renewed interest, Kat's mother looked at her. "Do you think she is guilty?"

"She is the same age as Darling. It would have been a lot of trouble to go to for an elderly widow who has no need for money or political gain."

"Wise words. They will give her a handsome fine and send her on her way, I shouldn't wonder."

Recalling the terrible smell of faggots and the certainty of the verdict in her mind's eye, Kat shook her head. "Not likely. The Lord Chief Justice Jeffreys was formidable." Chewing on her fingernails, she wondered again what she was supposed to do with the knowledge of what would happen to Alice Lisle. Was it a warning of some sort, demonstrating the lack of mercy that would be shown? Kat could not think what it could have to do with her. Once the trial was over, the King's legal procession would leave Winchester and she could return to her troubled life.

******

The following day, there was a sombre mood in the streets of Winchester. After much deliberation the previous day, the verdict had been passed as 'guilty'.

Kat chose to stay away when Lady Alice Lisle was delivered her sentence. She wanted no part in seeing a woman of her grandmother's years suffer for giving weary travellers shelter and food. To Kat's mind, the very fact that Lady Alice had a distant association with the man, John Hickes, was reason enough for her not to have turned them away. Her only crime had been an act of kindness, but here she was being sentenced for treason.

Holding a parcel of meat, Kat was hurrying home when she narrowly missed colliding with somebody.

"Mind your step!"

Startled, Kat lifted her head to see Mistress Hemingway standing in front of her. A young girl, loaded down with several items, was struggling to keep pace with her stride. "I hear that you were at the assizes court yesterday," she commented as she beamed with curiosity.

Smiling politely, Kat nodded. She did not wish to speak of it.

"I heard that you were running an errand for the Lord Chief Justice Jeffreys!" Mistress Hemingway went on to exclaim and her words were spiked with envy. Kat realised that this fact was obviously making its way around the gossip circles. "Were you bringing him something for his pain? They say he is terribly ailed."

Kat shrugged. "I am sure that you understand I am not obliged to divulge the business of my customers."

Mistress Hemingway pulled back and pursed her lips. "Of course not. I would not ask you to provide such details." Embarrassed, she turned her line of enquiry back to the case. "I expect that you have already heard of the sentencing this morning?"

"No, I have not. My grandmother is sick and I have been taking care of her." Kat went to sidestep out of the way. "You must excuse me, Mistress Hemingway, as I am in a hurry to return home to her. I have left Audrey alone in the shop. I am sure I shall hear all about it from the customers today." She attempted to move on but Mistress Hemingway blocked her path.

"No need to wait to hear the news. I have it all on good authority from…"

Her voice was drowned out by Kat's racing thoughts. She did not need Mistress Hemingway to share the latest news with her. Alice Lisle was to be handed the sentence reserved for a traitor of common blood and she had no doubt that by the end of the day the whole of Winchester would witness an old woman burned at the stake.

Mistress Hemingway frowned as she noticed how Kat's attention had waned. "Are you feeling well?" She took a cautious step backwards. "Perhaps you have caught your grandmother's ailment? Did you even hear what I said?"

"I am quite well, thank you," Kat snapped, impatient to leave. "I am just a little distracted with remembering everything that I need."

A look of relief crossed Mistress Hemingway's face before she returned to the story. "It is quite an unexpected turn of events. Do you not agree?" Her tone was peppered with vexation at Kat's evident lack of reaction.

"When is it to take place, the burning?" Kat asked, deciding that she would stay well away from the public spectacle that it would no doubt be.

"Burning?" Mistress Hemingway put a hand to her chest, weakened by the very thought. "You really haven't been listening, have you? The Lord Chief Justice had a change of heart."

Kat's interest piqued and for a moment, she was sure she had misheard. "What do you mean?"

"I heard from Mistress Poulter, who heard from Mistress Beadon, whose son is posted up at the Great Hall, that at first he sentenced her to be burned at the stake this very afternoon. But Mistress Beadon's son said that the Lord Chief Justice agreed to a letter being written to the King, requesting a reprieve." She leaned closer, her otherwise, joyless face beaming from sharing the news with someone who did not yet know it. "In fact, it is said that it was the Lord Chief Justice who suggested that Lady Lisle write to the King. He told her to ask that her sentence might be reconsidered. He even provided the means for her to write the letter there and then." She raised her eyebrows and waited for Kat's reaction.

Kat was speechless. Did this mean that Alice Lisle would be pardoned, that she would not die after-all?

"It is just as well for him," Mistress Hemingway continued. "People were up in arms yesterday, saying that he had bullied the jury. Burning a woman of her standing this very afternoon would have caused an outcry."

"What changed his mind?" Kat asked, wondering if there was perhaps more to this feared man than met the eye.

Mistress Hemingway simply shrugged. "What does it matter? It would be a horror for the woman to burn. Who knows if it will do any good, but evidently she looked half dead at the trial yesterday - could hardly keep her eyes open. Of course, you would know that." She waited for Kat to elaborate on what she had witnessed in the Great Hall the day before.

Kat recalled only too well how exhausted and ill Alice Lisle had appeared in the bleakness of the Great Hall, but she was not prepared to add more detail to Mistress Hemingway's stories. She was saved by another of the gossips approaching: "If you want my thoughts on it," the approaching woman said, pleased to be contributing her opinion, "I hope she receives a pardon from King James and can be returned to her family, where she can die at peace, warm in her bed." She clicked her tongue with disapproval. "Should never have come to court this one," she concluded.

Nervous of being overheard by an eavesdropper, Mistress Hemingway motioned for her to lower her voice. The consequences of being considered on the side of the rebels could be dire. Everyone knew it. Words were easy to misconstrue or twist and if repeated to the wrong ears, trouble would be made.

The woman was quick to defend herself. "I'm only stating what everyone else is saying. Walk past any of the taverns and you'll hear for yourself. They're saying that the woman's trial is a matter of revenge, that it is the King seeking his vengeance for the execution of his father during Cromwell's war."

The pair got lost in the conversation and neither noticed when Kat excused herself, leaving them to swap opinions and speculation at the expense of another woman's downfall.

******

Days passed and Darling regained some of her strength. Kat's mother dropped by each morning and they nursed Darling together, putting their differences aside.

On the first day of September, Kat answered the door to her mother who brought more news of the trial. Lady Alice Lisle had received her reply from King James that very morning. He had given her a reprieve but she would not live. The King had agreed to a more lenient penalty reserved for those of noble standing; the following morning, Alice Lisle would meet the henchman's axe.

In the privacy of her chamber, Kat wept for Lady Alice and for her family. She could not imagine what pain they were suffering. Even though the bridges were not fully repaired between Kat and her own mother, when they were saying their goodbyes later that day, she reached for her hands. To her surprise, her mother did not pull away and unspent tears made her eyes sparkle.

The news had affected Kat far more than she had expected. She wished that Gideon was with her and that things were as they had once been. Before all their troubles had started, he would have laughed at her for being so sensitive to affairs that did not concern her and then he would have held her, kissing away her tears.

Merlin found Kat in the shop. She was sitting on a stool, watching the darkness of night creep in. He placed a soft paw on her knee and nudged her. Smoothing his fur, she told him he was a good dog and that she would miss him when Gideon eventually returned home. Then she put on her outdoors shoes and walked with him.

Passing the Buttercross, she looked at the statue depicting the Blessed Virgin and Saints, and decided that on her way home she would walk past the cathedral and say a prayer.

The route took her past the imposing building on the corner where she had sensed Alice Lisle would sleep her final night. She stopped to gaze up at it again. The building's oak beams loomed above the street and the familiar sense of dread rippled through her body. Then something caught her eye. Through a dimly lit window at the top of the building, she noticed a grey shadow waver behind the thin pane of glass. Squinting, Kat looked harder. The shadow became clearer. It was a woman and she was looking down onto the street. Her gaze rested on Kat and their eyes locked.

She recognised the hooded eyes, the sad, drawn face. Lady Alice Lisle. So that *was* where they were holding her. They stared at one another for some time, neither woman moving. Kat wondered about Judge Jeffreys and his fearsome reputation, quietly speculating over what had convinced him to allow the old woman to ask for a reprieve. She wondered if he was aware of the anger that he had stirred within Winchester and whether he would pray for the soul of Lady Alice Lisle? Would he feel any hint of emotion when the henchman's blade glinted in the morning sunlight?

Someone nudged past her, catching her off balance. When she looked back at the window, Alice Lisle had gone.

CHAPTER TEN

Somebody was shaking her. Ruth opened her eyes with a groan, aware of a searing heat in her chest. The pain jolted her upright and she began clawing at the chain around her neck. "Get it off!" she cried as she tugged wildly at it. She was aware of gentle hands helping her. Jeremy.

Carefully, he unclasped the chain and helped her sit back again. As the pain subsided, Ruth began recollecting fragments of memory. She had seen things, spoken to people, breathed the air of a different place and time. It was just that everything was swiftly blurring, none of it making any sense.

"How did you do that?" Jeremy asked as she shuffled into a more dignified position.

"Do what?" Ruth rubbed at the spot on her chest where the pendant had been resting.

"What you just did. For a minute there, I thought you were going to have some sort of fit, but it was as though your eyes had rolled all the way back and you were talking, only it wasn't you." Visibly shaken, he plonked down beside her. "You're the real deal, aren't you?"

Swallowing a lump in her throat, Ruth asked him what it was he had expected to happen.

Shrugging, Jeremy rolled the stone between thumb and forefinger. "I didn't know what to expect, if I'm honest." Sighing, he tucked the chain back into the pocket of his jeans and sighed. "Not this."

"Me neither," Ruth confessed and tried to stand up but the blood in her veins hadn't finished the rushed ascent to her head.

"Here, let me help." Within moments Jeremy was jumping up and effortlessly supporting her weight.

On her feet, she felt more grounded but he kept a hold of her, propping her up until satisfied that she was okay. "How long was I out for?"

Jeremy scratched the back of his head. "Five or ten minutes. I was too busy panicking to remember to time you."

Managing a weak laugh, Ruth focused on supporting herself without any assistance. "Are you sure you should be walking about so quickly?" he asked.

She raised an eyebrow. "Why? Was it that bad?"

He gave her a sympathetic smile. "Worse."

Cringing at what he must have seen, Ruth suggested they go into the conservatory, away from the central heating.

"I'll get you a glass of water," Jeremy offered and she didn't argue.

It was cooler in the conservatory but snug with the soft glow of lights and thick throws over the chairs and sofas. A wintry wind thrashed at the windows. Handing her a glass, Jeremy took the seat next to hers. "When you first went under you said a whole lot of things. It didn't entirely make sense but there were a few parts that I pulled out of it. You mentioned the assizes and the Great Hall."

"The Great Hall in Winchester town centre?"

Nodding, he took another gulp of coffee. "You were afraid to go in there. It was as though you knew something that you shouldn't. You said that you were running an errand."

"What kind of errand?"

Shaking his head, Jeremy set his mug back down on a coaster. "The rest made no sense. You were terrified though – terrified and full of despair. It was a rollercoaster of misery."

"Oh." Ruth looked out into the garden. The spindly limbs of once vibrant shrubs and trees reached upwards to a monochrome sky. It looked as bleak as she felt. "Can I keep hold of the necklace?"

The question appeared to take him by surprise. She didn't blame him. It hadn't been something she had planned on asking. He frowned with concern. "Are you sure?"

Nodding, she gazed up at the clouds bruising the late afternoon sky. "I can probably get a little more from it."

Reluctantly he handed it over. "You'll call if anything happens though?"

A feeling of impatience thrust itself upon her. She needed the necklace and it was more than mere curiosity. It was a deep-seated need, as though it was pulling her towards it. She stood up abruptly, hinting that it was time for him to leave. "Don't worry, I'll call you the minute I get any answers to any of this."

Jeremy was stung. "I meant if anything happens to you, Ruth." His expression changed. "What time will your husband be home?"

"He won't be home. Not tonight." She was unable to keep the bitterness from her tone. Grayson hadn't even replied to her earlier text. She knew from experience that he wouldn't bother to contact her, even to check in and say goodnight.

"Do you think it is a good idea to keep the necklace here when you're on your own?"

"What difference is it being here to being at your house? You're alone too," Ruth pointed out before she sighed and shook her head. "Sorry. I didn't mean to be so snappy. I think this whole thing has messed a little with my head."

He nodded in understanding. "I'm not surprised. But you don't have to-"

"I want to, Jeremy. There's a story here and it needs to come out. I'm just shocked that I've been able to read it at all, to connect with this spirit, or whatever entity she may be. It really isn't the sort of thing my work has ever stretched to. I had no idea I was even capable of anything like it." She omitted to confess to her worries prior to meeting him, the fear that she was a fraud and a fake.

He was quiet for a moment before making the suggestion. "Ruth, do you think you're well enough to take a trip into town?"

"What for?"

"I want to take you to the Great Hall, to see if you feel anything there." He bit down on his bottom lip, rethinking his suggestion. "I don't want to suggest anything inappropriate, especially if your husband would get upset. It's easy to misconstrue things."

A wild sense of adventure took hold and Ruth was quick to respond. "My husband is off gallivanting with clients. He couldn't care less about what I'm doing. He is taking care of his business and I'm taking care of mine." She stood to go and fetch her coat. "Let's go before it closes."

The car journey into Winchester was quiet. Following Ruth disclosing the obvious rift she had with Grayson, neither spoke. She felt embarrassed and awkward. It had not been her intention to share so much. The outburst made her realise just how much resentment she was harbouring. It wasn't even that his actions hurt any longer. She just hated feeling like a worn-out old piece of furniture, pushed to the side of the room and covered with a blanket so nobody had to look at how tired and neglected it had become. That was what hurt.

As they pulled onto the road that eventually led down to the Great Hall, Ruth tried to forget about Grayson and instead started piecing together the scramble of images that had fragmented in her mind from the events earlier in the afternoon.

In all of her experience of Tarot and healing, she had never witnessed anything quite like it. Any recent worries about being a fraud were well behind her now, but the alternative was unsettling.

They approached from the top of the city, passing by the law courts and the place where the assizes had been held. Splashes of rain began to freckle the windscreen and the wipers arced across the glass with a squeak. Jeremy took the corner that led to the multi-storey car park. "Are you sure you're okay to do this?" he asked, noting how quiet she had become.

Giving him a reassuring smile, Ruth nodded and opened the car door.

Darkness was already falling fast as the city clock chimed four times. The lights of Winchester twinkled proudly, lighting up the Great Hall as they crossed the road. Ruth admired the neat rows of uniform grey stone, built around centuries of history.

"You know that this is one of the best surviving aisled halls from the thirteenth century?" Jeremy's passion for his subject was obvious as he began to explain about the history of the building. "It used to be part of the original castle here, in William the Conqueror's time." They followed the flagstone pathway until the building was looming over them. "Of course," he continued, "you almost lost the whole thing during the Civil War. Cromwell ordered it to be completely demolished..."

The sound of Jeremy's voice trailed off as Ruth put one foot in front of the other. A part of her brain was informing her that she had been here long before, that she was simply retracing *her* steps....

She had been carrying a basket containing a decoction. It had been an important errand, one that had set her on edge. She had been shaking, nervous that they would start asking questions of her that she couldn't answer. There had been some terrible piece of knowledge that she had been holding on to as well. It had been a secret that she could impart to nobody and it was about what a necklace had shown her: the obsidian necklace.

Suddenly, the idea of venturing into the Great Hall did not feel so appealing. Just before they reached the main entrance, Ruth stopped walking. This wasn't the right way in. It certainly wasn't the entrance she had used before.

Beside her, Jeremy was still chatting away, something about Sir Walter Raleigh. She didn't care. He was talking about an event that had taken place long before the time she remembered standing in this Hall. That had been the first time she had seen him in person – the man who would change the country, ruin families and soak the countryside with blood.

Blindly, she followed Jeremy as he led the way inside and chatted to the friendly woman on the counter. They didn't have to pay. The woman either knew him or had fallen for his unmistakable charm. She gestured for them to go through. Nowhere was off limits to them. Jeremy was clearly a revered guest. "They're opening up the Sally Ports for me next month. They run under the city. There is supposed to be a huge network of these tunnels as they were used for times when the castle was under siege."

Ruth tried to appear excited by what he was saying but she was struggling to free herself from the pull of an entirely different time. The memories from that time were slotting into place like a hideous jigsaw.

"Ruth?"

She turned and smiled again, but he had already guessed that something was wrong. The woman who had greeted them was watching, so he pulled her by the arm and led her further down the gallery. "You're seeing stuff, aren't you?"

"I'm fine. Really, I am. Just a bit jaded." Her eyes darted around with uncertainty, taking in the red staircase that was cordoned off by a rope. "Can we go up?"

Lifting the rope, Jeremy gestured for her to go first. "We can go anywhere. Historian's rights."

Taking the steps as quickly as she could, Ruth opened the door on the left. "This is where the jurors convened after Lady Alice's trial," she commented as they marched through a room with a long table running through the centre. When they reached the door at the far end, she hesitated, her hand hovering on the handle. "This is it. This is the room I was told to wait outside." Swinging her arm to point to the staircase that led back down to the Great Hall, she continued allowing the memory to unravel: "And down there was where I first heard him, where I saw him for the very first time."

"Who?"

Ruth shook her head. The memory was there but it was hiding in the crevices of her mind. It was a memory that felt alien and intrusive. "It's all coming through in dribs and drabs. Can we move on? I might pick up more."

He didn't push her for more information as they continued to walk. Their footsteps echoed those she had heard in the past and she recalled that somebody had marched through the room to take something from her. It had been a basket. Her fingers closed around the handle of the door. Someone who had struck terror in her heart had been behind the door of this room. The handle turned in Ruth's hand and she pushed, but the door jarred in the lock.

"Will you be needing access beyond this point? Only, we've locked up now we're approaching closing and we don't usually let visitors up here anyway." The woman from the front desk had appeared, looking smart and knowledgeable in her navy suit with her badge.

"Do you want to go in there?" Jeremy asked.

The question struck a chord of fear. "No!" Ruth turned to address the woman. "We won't be needing any further access, thank you for asking."

Bewildered by her sudden change of heart, Jeremy didn't say anything but he followed her to the door at the end of the room and down the stairs.

"Feel free to take a look in the aisled hall." The woman was gesturing towards the building's main attraction. "The Gothic archways over the marble pillars are truly magnificent. Jeremy can point out all the history to you." She winked at Jeremy, as though conspiring with him over something and Ruth noticed the sudden flush in his cheeks.

"She thinks I've brought you here on a date," he said through gritted teeth when the guide was out of earshot.

"As far as dates go, it wouldn't be a bad one," she replied and instantly regretted it. In spite of how abandoned Grayson so often made her feel, she was not a cheat.

"I can think of better ones," he said with a chuckle. "But whilst we're here…." He held out his arm so that he could lead the way in to the hall.

Being empty, the room looked huge. It hadn't appeared that way before, during Kat's time, when she had seen the old woman falling asleep at the bar, the quivering witness, James Dunne, and the crowds of people fighting their way through to get a better view.

Ruth's legs wobbled and she thought she might be sick. This is where it had happened. This is where they had found the old woman guilty. It was the place where the sentence that would make history had been given. Searching her brain for more, Ruth whimpered with frustration as she failed to find the missing pieces of memory. The room began to spin and she could hear voices: a hushed murmur of whispers seeping from the walls and then the sound of heavy footsteps.

"This is where it all began," she said and she clawed at Jeremy's arm as she felt the presence of somebody else begin to take hold. "This is where it all began falling apart. Everything." She clutched at him, emotion taking over her senses. "He could have stopped at a handful of men. That would have been enough. News spreads. People were afraid enough as it was. Lessons had been learned. But it didn't stop. He didn't stop and I became lost in it all."

A wind had picked up and Ruth could hear it howling in her ears. She felt as though a force was trying to suck her back through time, to the point where she had been standing in the hall, when it had been used as a courtroom.

"Okay. I think it's time to go." Jeremy's voice jarred her back into the present. He began to guide her away so that they were hurrying from the hall and back down the red-carpeted gallery to the front desk. She put up no protest.

On the wall to her left, gold lacquered rectangles framed important drawings and portraits. They whizzed by in a blur, one after the other. She was desperate for the smell of fresh air, the sound of people going about their business, the purr of car engines or the impatient honk of horns.

"Almost there," Jeremy said calmly as they neared the doors that would lead them out into the festively lit city again, but Ruth stopped abruptly in front of one of the gilded frames.

All of her breath had caught in her throat and she was aware of a strange gargling noise. Words were trying to prise their way out as she stared at the face on the framed canvas: soft, plump lips, dark eyes, the unblemished pale skin framed by a rich waterfall of dark brown curls that rested against a cloak of the richest scarlet. "That's him," she whispered. "That is the man who we all soon came to know as The Hanging Judge."

CHAPTER ELEVEN

Jeremy had insisted on taking Ruth home the moment they had stepped outside the Great Hall. She hadn't the strength to protest.

Back at Jeremy's house, she was curled up on the sofa beneath a blanket that he had given her, trying to hide the fact that she was shivering. Rex had joined them and was licking Ruth's hand.

"He obviously likes you," Jeremy commented warmly.

"More likely it's the cat that he can smell." Ruth withdrew her hand so that she could smooth the dog's fur.

Jeremy was ridden with guilt. "I should never have taken you there. Not so soon after what happened."

"Don't blame yourself. It was me who insisted I was fine." She smiled wanly at him. "At least we have an answer now. We know that the woman lived during the reign of King James II, that it must have related to the assizes from then."

"That's only part of the answer," Jeremy reminded her. "The bloody assizes, as they are now known, impacted a lot of lives and families. They were far-reaching across the West Country but the message they sent changed everything for King James. Four years after all that happened, there was little love lost for him down here during the Glorious Revolution, when William of Orange took the crown."

"I'm not surprised. The whole thing sounds so macabre." Ruth retorted, recalling everything that Jeremy had told her about that period of history when they had been driving home. "I really can't believe that the King would have supported such a massacre."

"Supported it? He demanded it, although he claimed not to have been aware of quite how bloody the assizes became. It sounds dreadful to us but back then capital punishment was commonplace and the grisly penalty for high treason was nothing out of the ordinary. Back then people were hanged for stealing. Still," he added, "the sentences dished out by Judge Jeffreys were famed to have been overly harsh. Particularly in the case of Lady Alice Lisle." His gaze rested on Ruth's face. "You mentioned her name when we were in the Great Hall. In fact, Alice's name was cleared several years later."

"Pah." Ruth spat out her disgust. "Too late by then." Her mind had opened up, allowing her to glimpse back over the images that she had seen when holding the necklace. "I just don't understand what our spirit lady wants us to do about it. Do you think that Kateryn was possibly related to Alice Lisle?"

Jeremy shook his head. "Kateryn Fox is a commoner's name. Alice was from a long line of noble blood. Her husband was responsible for the execution of Charles the First, by the way."

"I know," Ruth said miserably as snippets of conversation she had witnessed regarding the trial came back to her.

"Not all of those who were convicted were executed, of course. Some were sold as slaves and sent to the West Indies. Quite a handsome profit was fetched for the prisoners who were sold into slavery."

"It's so sad," Ruth commented. "Mind you, rather that than the alternative."

"Not really. Most people have no concept of how appalling slaves were treated on the plantations. Those who were convicted prisoners were expected to be worked to death long before their sentence ended." He gave a grimace. "Not only that but the ships they were transported on were cramped and squalid. They risked catching disease such as smallpox or being thrown overboard to the sharks."

Clamping a hand over her mouth, Ruth gasped. "That's awful."

Lost in thought, Jeremy made a sound of agreement before adding: "I imagine that many died even before the formal pardon in 1689."

"That's tragic."

He sank back into the sofa and crossed one leg over his knee. "It is, but it's also thought that the experiences of men who did manage to return very likely influenced the first petition to parliament for the abolition of slavery. Don't forget that these men will have experienced and witnessed the appalling cruelty of the trans-Atlantic slave trade and how enslaved African people were treated. It was a town called Bridgwater that introduced the first petition which later resulted in a combined effort that eventually put an end to British involvement in that kind of trade." Noting Ruth's look of bewilderment, he continued. "Men from and near to Bridgwater were transported to the plantations for their part in the rebellion. Somerset was a very rebellious county and a lot of the convicted rebels were from the likes of Taunton, Bridgwater and all the surrounding villages and hamlets."

Fascinated, Ruth nodded. "I feel rather ashamed that you know more about the history of my own country than I do."

He shrugged. "It's not just my job, it's a general interest too. Plus, some of the family tree research I've been doing has led me to research that area a little more."

"Oh?"

Looking pleased with himself, Jeremy grabbed his laptop from the side table and opened it. "The person who I'm doing this for would be pleased to know that one of her ancestors appears to be linked to the Bridgwater petition of 1785. He was a respected lawyer with a lot of political connections, it would seem." He rubbed his chin as he stared at the screen. "It's strange though as I can't work it any further back than his grandfather and I'd expect to be able to trace further back for a family with the sort of wealth that gave a person the education and connections that this man clearly had."

His gaze became distant. "She would probably also be pleased to know that her lineage is such an enigma."

"Is this lady a client of yours? I hadn't realised you could pay somebody to research your family tree. It's a good idea, I suppose."

Uncomfortable, Jeremy looked away. "Not a client, no. It's a personal thing." All of his body language implied that he no longer wanted to talk about it and Ruth could sense the emotion there. The distant look and the hint of a smile at the corners of his mouth should have been hint enough; this was for somebody special in his life.

An unexpected feeling of disappointment rippled through her. "Oh, I see."

He switched off the laptop and seemed suddenly distracted, making Ruth feel like she was outstaying her welcome. Overcome with fatigue, her shoulders felt heavy. "I think I've had enough excitement for one day. Time to go home and have a long, hot soak followed by an early night."

"Of course." Jeremy was up on his feet, ready to drive her home. Disgruntled by Ruth's sudden decision to leave, Rex skulked off to the kitchen and could be heard nudging his dinner bowl. "I'll drive you back. Are you sure you'll be okay on your own tonight?"

Ruth couldn't remember the last time Grayson had asked her if she would be 'okay' alone. "I'll be fine," she said, feeling the miserable sensation of loneliness expand as she took in the homely surroundings of Jeremy's cottage. It was idyllic, in the midst of countryside with a garden full of wildlife and nothing but open space stretching beyond the front of it and woodland behind it. She imagined how he might be later that night, hunched over his laptop, combing through history for the special woman he was doing such a big personal favour for. Whoever it was had captured his heart.

******

After her bath, Ruth pulled on an oversized jumper and a pair of joggers before making her way down to the kitchen. She was half way through preparing a mackerel salad when there was a knock at the door.

"Fancy a partner in wine?" Zoe, her neighbour and best friend, breezed through whilst waving a bottle in front of her. All Ruth fancied was an early night, but there was such a hopeful look on her friend's face that she felt unkind turning her down.

"Sounds great." She gestured for Zoe to go through to the kitchen. With three children and a busy career, Zoe was often in need of a little respite for an hour or two come the end of the week. Plonking the wine on the table, she noted the untouched mackerel salad. "Sorry, I hadn't realised I would be interrupting your dinner."

Ruth moved the plate to one side. "You're not. Truth be told, I'm not overly hungry. Just peckish." After tipping the salad into a container and putting it in the fridge, she pulled out some pitta and hummus and found an unopened bag of tortilla chips.

Helping herself to the wine glasses, Zoe unscrewed the bottle she was holding and began to pour. "Is everything okay?" She eyed Ruth carefully as she pushed a glass across to her.

"Of course it is." Ruth felt her voice rise in protest and the look on Zoe's face told her that her tone was far too defensive.

Without taking a sip, Zoe put her wine glass back down and frowned. "Come on, Ruth. It's me you're talking to now. You don't have to keep anything to yourself."

Ruth's heart began to pound and she felt her face and neck grow hot. Had Zoe seen Jeremy and jumped to the wrong conclusion? "It's nothing. It really isn't anything at all."

Zoe was shaking her head in disapproval. "I knew it. I bloody well knew it." She took a large glug of wine and Ruth was taken aback by the anger on her face. Ruth's heart sank as she realised that Zoe must have decided that she had started some sort of illicit relationship with Jeremy. All the jokes about 'Mr X' and then the fact that he had visited her house again. Had she also seen them lost in deep conversation together in the coffee shop the day before? Ruth and Grayson had been friends with Zoe and Paul for years but she had always assumed that it was her relationship with Zoe that was the stronger, that the alliances would always lie with her if they were to ever find out just how rocky things were with her marriage. Now she was being accused of an affair.

"Zoe, it really isn't what you think," she began to protest, but her emotions got the better of her and the strain of everything she had experienced with the necklace and Jeremy broke her reserve. Putting her hands to her face, she prepared herself to relay everything that had gone on over the last two days. "Oh Zoe, something *has* happened and never in a million years would I have thought I'd be telling you something like this but-"

"The bloody bastard!" Zoe's outburst took her by surprise. "And at Christmas too." She took another swig of her drink. "I've always kept it zipped about Grayson and the way he treats you, but this time he's gone too far. So, what did he say? You look truly drained, Ruth." Offering Ruth her hand, Zoe's eyes were sparkling with emotion. "I'm so sorry."

Her jaw slack, Ruth stared back at her, unable to think of a suitable response. She suddenly felt cold and clammy. The feeling that had been a heavy weight in the pit of her stomach began to grow, permeating the rest of her body. Her mouth felt dry and she tried to swallow but found herself choking back tears. She knew what was coming. In fact, she had known for a long time but for self-preservation, or maybe because she had just not wanted to face the truth, she had swept it all under the carpet. "Tell me what you know," she said flatly and Zoe flinched.

"Hardly anything, Ruth. And the only reason why I do have any idea about it is because he swore Paul to secrecy."

"Paul?!" Ruth was shocked. "What exactly has he said to Paul?"

Zoe swallowed and Ruth thought she had never seen her friend look so worried. "Ruthie, he didn't confide in Paul. Paul caught him, confronted him."

"What do you mean 'caught him'?" Ruth hadn't realised how much it would hurt when the truth was finally out and it took her by surprise.

"Oh." Zoe opened her mouth to say something more but quickly shut it again. It had clearly dawned on her that Ruth knew nothing.

"You need to tell me everything," Ruth said slowly and firmly and Zoe dropped her head on to her hands. "Do not miss out a single detail."

"I'm so sorry, Ruth. I thought you knew. He told Paul that you weren't stupid, that you had known everything and that he wouldn't be with you for Christmas as the two of you needed some space. Given that he left with that case yesterday, I just thought that-"

Her temper boiling, Ruth rubbed the stem of the wine glass. "When did he tell Paul this?"

Zoe looked as though she might cry. "Earlier this evening. Paul bumped into him after work. It was… awkward evidently, but Grayson had been quite outright about the whole thing."

"Was he with another woman?" Ruth felt a strange hollow feeling as though her emotions were being carved from her body.

The look that Zoe gave her said it all.

Ruth laughed, although none of it was at all amusing. "Let me guess, bobbed hair, lips inflated as though she has been stung several hundred times and decked out like a Christmas tree on the jewellery front?"

Surprised, Zoe agreed with the description. "You know who she is then?"

Feeling the hot sting of tears, Ruth dashed them away before they could fall. "I've known for about a year now, I suppose. It's just that…" She was unable to finish before the sob broke off her words.

Zoe was over by her side, putting her arm around her shoulders. "I'm so sorry, Ruth. Paul was adamant that Grayson had told you. And the size of the case he left with. It looked like he was going on holiday for weeks."

"He hasn't said a thing," Ruth sobbed and picked up her phone from the table. "He's not even had the decency to call me or answer any of my messages." She looked up. "He can't have just left without saying anything though. I mean, he's been a total arse for the past few years and even worse this last one, but he would surely not sink that low?"

Zoe cringed. "Have you checked his wardrobe?"

Pushing back her chair, Ruth marched through the corridor and up the stairs to the bedroom, flinging open Grayson's wardrobe. The sound of empty coat hangers knocking together reverberated through the room. He had stripped out most of his belongings. Turning to the bedside table, Ruth pulled the drawer out with such force that the whole thing came out in her hands. Aside from a few old pairs of socks and the watch that she had bought him for his fortieth eight years earlier, it was bare.

Dropping the drawer onto the bed, Ruth crumpled to the floor. "How could I have been so stupid? Why did I never confront him over this?" She thought of all the signs: the late meetings, the business trips that she was suddenly no longer invited to, the way Paul had smartened up considerably the year before. He had done it all for *her*. "Veda Watkins," Ruth said sourly. "That's her name. She and her husband invested in the business two years ago. I've met her a few times at business dinners. Veda is supposed to be a 'silent partner'." She gave an ironic laugh, although there was no mirth in it. "She's done a great job of playing that role hasn't she? Taken it quite literally. I wonder what her husband thinks, if he even knows that is."

Handing her a tissue from the dresser, Zoe joined her on the floor. "You should call him."

The thought was tempting but Ruth shook her head. "What and ruin his Christmas too? If he doesn't know already, he'll find out but it should be his wife that tells him, not somebody else. That's the most unbearable way of all, being the last to know. I must look so bloody stupid." Her voice cracked again and Zoe drew her into a fierce hug.

"Not at all. You're not the stupid one here!" The emotion caught in Zoe's voice as she saw how upset Ruth was. "I'm so sorry. I really thought you knew, otherwise I'd never have broken the news the way that I did. You're such a good person, you don't deserve any of this."

The tears flowed for a while and Ruth allowed herself to fall into the friendly embrace, but it offered little comfort for the gaping hole that she was left with. She realised that far more than any love lost, it was the betrayal that made her feel less of a woman. Ruth couldn't recall the last time that Grayson had looked at her with any emotion. If she was perfectly honest with herself, she could not remember the last time that she had looked at him that way either. The chemistry had long fizzled out on both sides. It had started with them living as companions but the friendship wasn't enough. Unlike Grayson though, she had not looked elsewhere. Ruth had always known it was coming but the news Zoe had brought made it so final. A terrible thought crashed into her mind - Cas, blissfully unaware and in Germany. How would she tell him? What could she possibly say?

"She's not a patch on you. That's what Paul said after he saw them together." Zoe kept up the fiercely loyal words meant to provide comfort.

With a weak smile, Ruth pulled away from the hug and dabbed at her eyes with the tissue before blowing her nose. "Thanks," she said and pulled her knees to her chest. "I'm not even that bothered about her. Truth be told, Grayson and I were done a long time ago, but it still dents the ego and makes you wonder what you did that was so terribly wrong."

"You did nothing wrong. Don't ever blame yourself! There's nothing wrong with you whatsoever. Look over there." Zoe pointed in the direction of the mirrors in the large fitted wardrobe. "That's a beautiful and strong woman reflected back at you. It will be his loss. You'll see."

As she stared at the dishevelled woman in the mirror, hair tumbling in all directions and a puffy, red face, she didn't think she could see anything deserving of the description, 'beautiful and strong'. Her voice cracked again. "I don't feel it though. What a mess."

Zoe took her back downstairs and handed her the glass of wine she had poured as she began to explain all the ways in which Ruth had demonstrated her strength of character. "You've stood by that man for years, through thick and thin. You left a great career that you loved to bring up your son and you have silently and stoically carried all this emotional baggage from a marriage that has been falling apart at the seams for years. Yet you still find the strength to help other people with their problems. Look at how you help people with those readings and the healing that you do, and you don't always charge. Ruth, you have a heart of gold. Never forget that. Never doubt it."

They took their wine into the lounge and Ruth gulped it back, trying to allow Zoe's words to reassure her. It was impossible not to think about what

Grayson was doing. She imagined him together with Veda Watkins, drinking champagne and laughing, the pair of them so pleased with themselves.

"Will you stay here for Christmas now?" Zoe asked. "There is always room at our table for you. You know that."

"Thanks, Zoe." Ruth sniffed and reached out to touch a bauble. It was one that they had let Cas choose as a young boy. A small bell tinkled as it bobbed up and down, the sound lonely and sad. "You're a great friend, and I really appreciate the offer, but I'm still going to go and stay with Tim. It'll be a breath of fresh air not having to listen to Grayson whinge the whole way there." She meant it and the thought lifted her spirits a little. There were a lot of things that might be slightly easier without Grayson criticising from the side lines.

Zoe smiled. "Well, the offer's there should you change your mind." She noted Ruth's almost drained glass. "I'll get you another."

"No, I should really be going to bed. It's been a long day and I'm feeling shattered." Ruth gave her an apologetic look. "Sorry to be boring, especially when you brought this over."

"Not at all." Zoe was on her feet and taking Ruth's glass from her. "I'll put the wine in the fridge. You get an early night. It's the right thing to sleep on it."

After apologising to Zoe for being such a party pooper, Ruth finished tidying everything away and called for Meg who followed her sleepily upstairs.

Her heart still heavy, Ruth snapped out the lights. The moment her head hit the pillow, she felt her eyelids weighing heavily and the welcome hood of sleep slipping over her. At the end of the bed, Meg had nestled into her usual spot, curled up in a fluffy, tabby ball. Neither stirred when the door to the bedroom nudged open a notch.

It was Meg who opened her eyes first. Something had drifted across the room, although to the casual observer, nothing appeared out of place. The cat was on all fours, back arched and mouth open, a slow hiss escaping her. A shadow drifted past the mirror, disappearing as quickly as it had come.

With a meow of terror, Meg jumped onto the floor and squeezed through the gap in the door. Behind her, it gently closed, leaving Ruth sleeping and alone with whatever had entered the room. She stirred as the curls around her head lifted gently, exposing her ear. Then the drawer of her dresser was jarred open inch by inch. The glint of moonlight penetrating the thin fabric of the voile curtains was reflected in a shiny black surface. Slowly sliding from its resting place, a long silver chain shimmied over the drawer's edge.

Ruth slept on, unaware that the necklace had dropped onto the floor of her room, the obsidian charm glowing.

Downstairs, the cat flap shook violently as Meg made swift her departure and the baubles on the Christmas tree knocked gently together. As she slept, Ruth's breath gathered in the air above her in silvery, chilly puffs. Beneath her eyelids, her eyes moved rapidly back and forth. Her lips parted as though she was saying something.

Ricocheting through the house was the sound of monotonous hammering. It could have been old pipes or beams settling, but the house wasn't particularly old. The hammering grew louder, penetrating her dreams. Sitting up in bed, her eyes opened but her mind was still pooling in the dreams that come with a deep sleep, Ruth brought her hands to her head, moaning and wishing for the relentless din to cease…

CHAPTER TWELVE

Kat pressed her hands to her ears, wishing that the noise would stop. She was walking through a narrow street that ran parallel with the main route through Winchester when she had become aware of the sound of iron striking against wood. In her hand, she was clasping the pendant. It had been pulsing against her chest like a tiny beating heart and she had felt compelled to pull it from beneath her clothes and gaze into the shiny, mirrored surface. Darling's words played through her mind: *'The obsidian stone can show you future, past and present, Kateryn. It will speak to you when it is time.'*

"Show me," Kat had whispered to it and she had not needed to wait for long. The surface rippled from black to grey to green and then to a beautiful shade of gold, the colour of a buttery sunset. As it cleared, the image began to take form. It was the image of a woman. Her head was resting upon a luxurious bolster, the golden curls spread across it. The bolster was a far cry from the hard thing that Kat was accustomed to. Kat recognised the woman at once. This was the spirit woman who she had seen in Darling's chamber. She looked so peaceful and serene. "Come to me," she whispered. "Come and show me what has become of my Gideon."

The banging noises from town persisted, breaking her concentration. The stone faded back to black as though it had done its job. "Don't go!" Kat whimpered. "Please don't go." She shook the stone and struck it in frustration against the stonework of a house, but once again, it was inanimate.

Slipping the pendant back into place, she picked up her skirts and ran. As she rounded the corner, she realised that her path was taking her to the place where Alice Lisle was being held. The hammering grew louder and Kat realised that it must be the men working on the scaffolding that would host Alice Lisle's execution. She wondered if Judge Jeffreys could hear the abominable noise from his lodgings or whether he had already left Winchester.

Rounding the corner that opened out onto where Alice Lisle was prisoner, Kat's breath caught in her throat. A crowd had gathered and they too were staring at the same sight. It seemed that the judge had presented another twist to the ugly, dark side he was rumoured to have. She imagined the malevolent smile spreading slowly on his face as he had given instructions for the cruel position of where the scaffolding was to be erected. Every bang would reverberate through the old woman's bones as she lived out her final night in that room.

Merlin was by Kat's side growling a warning and she was not surprised; everything felt wrong and dark. A sense of foreboding was clinging to the air. Hurrying back to the shop, she ran straight up to Darling's chamber.

The air in the house was close and acrid. Darling's fever had returned. Kat rushed to her side. She was somewhere between sleep and consciousness.

Without hesitation, Kat ran downstairs to make up a poultice and something to cool her from the inside. All the while she could hear the incessant hammering of slats and posts as they were constructed for a public execution.

Pressing the poultice to Darling's forehead, she propped her up so that she could drink the decoction of peppermint. It brought her some respite and her breathing steadied.

Bringing more candles, Kat lit them. Then she set about making a bed for herself on the floor. She would not leave her grandmother's side until the fever broke. Holding her hand, she sat in silent companionship with her and the night wore on.

Kat's head was tipping forward, her eyelids struggling to remain open, when Darling spoke: "I saw Gideon!" The words coiled into the night air, hanging wraithlike above the bed.

Alert, Kat leaned towards her. "Where? Tell me where I can find him!"

Darling slipped back into senseless rambling, muttering about the things that troubled her. Amidst the noise from outside, her thoughts tumbled out in a messy, fevered jumble.

"Oh, that sound!" Darling cried out, writhing with agony. "Will it never end?"

Hushing her, Kat smoothed down Darling's damp hair and dabbed away the sweat. Darling's moans continued until, at last, the hammering of the scaffolding stopped. Then, with her tongue thick in her mouth, she spoke Gideon's name again: "You will find what you seek," she said. "You will find Gideon." At that, her throat constricted with pain and Kat pressed the poultice to her chest, drawing out the heat.

"Where can I find him?" Kat pressed, impatient to glean more information. "Where will I find Gideon?"

Shaking her head, Darling began to cry.

Frustrated, Kat took her by the shoulders, shaking her to wake up. "Do you see him? Tell me where he is?"

In her grasp, Darling had become limp and weak. Panicked, Kat tried to bring her round but it was as though she had given up. Then her eyelids snapped open, revealing only the whites of her eyes. She rasped for breath and clawed at the air. Frightened, Kat tried to soothe her, but her arms thrashed and her legs kicked. Then, slowly, she began to turn her head, her voice suddenly strong. "Take a care my girl, or you will have blood on your hands."

The words were an echo of those the strange market trader had spoken and Kat's skin crawled. "What do you mean?"

"When the time comes, you will hold great power and influence over Gideon's fate, Kateryn. Hard times lie ahead and there will be darkness that surrounds you, but to save him, you must follow the righteous path."

With a feeble cry, her head fell back and her sleep was instantly deep. "Darling!" Kat tried to wake her, but her consciousness was lost. She had no choice but to lie on the floor next to her and wait for the fever to break.

When the first shards of sunlight pierced the cracks in the shutters, Darling's eyes fluttered open. Kat reached for her hand but it was cold. She rubbed it, feeling the nodules of knitted bones. "Is it a new day?" Darling sounded so feeble.

Kat nodded, trying not to cry at the sight of how weak and vulnerable her grandmother had become.

"I know that I told you I saw Gideon." The fever had left her and Kat could see the pain in Darling's eyes. She gestured for Kat to give her some of the small ale that was on the table next to the guttering candles. Most of the liquid spilled down her chin and onto her shift as she attempted to raise her head enough to drink.

"You need to tell me where I can find him, so that I can bring him home," Kat pleaded.

"You can never bring him home, Kateryn." In spite of her physical weakness, her tone was hard.

Kat looked into her face with searching eyes, trying to make sense of it all. "You told me last night that I can save him but that I must follow the righteous path. What does that mean?"

"It means you never lose sight of who you are, not who you become. And it means that you must never take him back as your husband. Never look upon him as your husband again! You have no husband."

Her bottom lip quivering, Kat did not understand. "But Gideon *is* my husband. How can you ask that of me?"

Lifting her head, Darling begged her to listen: "It is my dying wish, Kateryn. You must promise me that you will not look upon him as your husband again."

A surge of anger filled her. "What has mother been saying? Filling your ears with poison, I should not wonder. Is that what this is all about?"

"Not-your-mother." She broke into a fit of coughing and Kat helped prop her up against the bolster. The fit led her into a state of breathlessness. She could speak no more and Kat knew that it would be detrimental to make her try.

Clasping a hand to her mouth, she felt her shoulders shake. What had Gideon done? Who was he with? Had he betrayed her? She recalled what the obsidian stone had shown her. The fine angles of the beautiful young woman's face ran through her mind and she recalled the look she had given Gideon, the way her fingers had stroked his. Kat wanted to be sick. She and Gideon had married for love. Husbands who married for love did not allow other women to warm their beds.

Another dreadful wheezing noise emanated from Darling's chest and Kat jumped up to open the shutters to let some air into the stale room. Then she returned to the bedside. The frail grip of Darling's fingers curled around her own. Tears pricked at her eyeballs as she thought of the long hot summers they had spent together when she had been growing up: Darling showing her all the different plants and flowers, demonstrating how to extract the good parts – and the bad; memories of sitting in front of the fire together, learning to sew; arguing over remedies in the shop; laughing over mindless gossip and long talks over a warming posset.

As she watched her, Kat noticed how the black of Darling's iris appeared to become smaller, leaving only the stormy grey. "You will promise me, won't you, Kateryn?" Formed through dry lips, her words were barely audible.

Kat reached for the cup by her bedside again, but Darling batted it away. It rolled across the floor, liquid running between the cracks. "Promise me that you will take that wedding ring off and never return it to your finger. You must hide it and forget about it."

"But you told me to follow the righteous path," Kat protested bringing her hand protectively to her wedding finger. "That is not a righteous thing to do."

Darling was vehement. "It is the thing that must be done! Now promise me!"

"I promise," she whispered and placed a kiss on her cheek.

The sound of a gathering crowd could be heard from outside, reminding her that it was the day Lady Alice Lisle would face her executioner. She moved to close the shutters but Darling stopped her. "Don't," she said. "Keep them open so that I might hear the birds sing as they welcome a new day."

Swallowing a lump in her throat, Kat dropped to her knees so that she could be by Darling's head. The smell of lavender lingered with sweat and illness. There was a fluttering sound and she turned to see a robin had hopped onto the window ledge. Its scarlet chest puffed outwards before it cocked its head to one side. He opened his beak and chirruped a series of notes. Darling turned to look at him and smiled. Then she looked back at Kat.

In the heart of Winchester, a roar from the crowd rang out. The sound rang through the air like the melancholy knelling of a bell. It was followed swiftly by silence. The robin took flight and disappeared into the distance. Kat closed her eyes. The silence told her that Lady Alice Lisle was now a martyr.

Her attempt to hold back her tears was becoming futile. She pressed her palm to Darling's forehead. It felt cold. "Let me fetch you a fresh poultice. I shall warm it over the fire and make a caudle with ginger."

Darling went to protest, but no sound came from her lips. Kat felt her grasp tighten around her hand. "No. Stay here with me awhile." Her lips twitched as she drew them into a small smile and closed her eyes.

Fatigue and sadness overwhelming her, Kat rested her head on Darling's chest, hearing the rattle of her breath. It was strangely comforting, the feeling of being so close. Tears clustered like tiny silver balls on the tips of Kat's lashes until they splashed onto her grandmother's shift, seeping through the material to her skin. She wondered if they felt comforting to Darling and if the weight of her head resting on her chest would bring back memories of happier times when youth had been on her side.

There was an eerie stillness to the streets outside. Even the chatter of birds and crickets had ceased. Winchester was in mourning.

As Darling's breathing slowed, Kat felt her own breath fall into sync. She allowed her eyes to close as she navigated the deep rivers of her memory. The hypnotic rhythm of their breathing was the only sound to be heard in the room. Dust motes danced in the light above them as the sun rose higher. Everything was peaceful.

The rhythm stopped, pulling Kat into a state of wakefulness. She waited for the continued gentle rise and fall of her grandmother's chest. None came.

Sitting up, she pushed back a lock of silvery white hair that had strayed onto Darling's forehead. There was no flicker on her face. Kat pressed her fingers to Darling's neck but found no pulsing beneath. Pressing harder, she was certain that she must have missed something. Nothing.

Pushing herself from the bed, she scrabbled around the top of the dresser, knocking over ointments and bottles of tonics as she looked for the pretty handheld mirror. Resting it beneath Darling's nose, she waited for it to steam over at the slightest breath. Nothing.

Sinking onto the stool by the dresser, Kat continued holding the mirror. The reflection of her grandmother's unmoving body was behind her. She waited, watching it carefully, certain she would see a glimmer of movement, something to suggest that there was still life within the shell of skin and bone.

Taking a sobering breath, she held back the sob that was rising in the back of her throat. Then she fetched some rags to soak up the spillage from the bottles. Sinking to her knees, Kat pressed the rags to the pool of liquid, watching the material darken. Then she looked back at Darling, scrutinising the position of her hands, her head, the line of her lips, trying to decipher whether there had been any fraction of change whilst her attention had been diverted. A hand slipped from the bed, dangling inches from Kat's face and she fell back, banging her head against the dresser. Pulling her knees to her chest, Kat drew her gaze up Darling's arm and to her face. Her lips were already outlined blue.

The sob that Kat had been fighting found its way out of her mouth with startling force. Unabated tears fell over her cheeks as her anguish flowed out. The morning wore on, with no customers or visitors. Kat was alone with her grief.

CHAPTER THIRTEEN

It was the grief that woke her. The unrelenting stab of sorrow twisted her stomach. She felt hollow and lost. Never had she felt such dark despair.

Ruth touched her cheek and felt the wet warmth of freshly shed tears. Her shoulders were shaking and the taste of bile had risen in her throat. As she looked around the shadowy room, the feeling began to slowly ebb and she was brought back to her own time.

Something shiny on the floor by the dresser caught her eye. It was a stone. In the moonlight she could see the open drawer. To her surprise, she did not feel frightened.

Getting out of bed, she picked up the necklace and took it downstairs. The surface was still very mirror-like. It was the most curious object she had ever seen, the way it reacted to different light.

Casting her mind back to when she had gone to bed, she tried to recall whether she had opened the drawer and taken the necklace out. She couldn't remember doing so but the glass of wine and heavy fatigue had dulled her recollection. Licking her lips, she realised how parched she felt and filled the kettle to make a cup of chamomile tea.

Nursing the tea, she went into the lounge, flipped on the Christmas tree lights and curled up on the sofa. "Who are you?" she asked the empty room but there was no answer. She shut her eyes, feeling the hangover of her dream. With a sense of gloom, she knew that it was not over. Somebody was lurking in the shadows of the house, waiting for her eyelids to become heavy again. She could sense it and Ruth knew that this would be the time when she was at her most vulnerable. It was the time between sleeping and waking, where things from other planes could reach her.

The pleasantly cosy tick of the clock on the mantelpiece warmed the room, lulling her into a false sense of security. Almost half two in the morning. Ruth tried to focus on the present: the sound of that clock ticking through time, the twinkle of fairy lights and the gaudy colours of the baubles that were hanging from the tree. Ruth fought the weight of tiredness that was threatening. Her head dropped forward and she forced herself back awake.

Behind the door of the room, she thought she could hear the press of a foot against a floorboard. "Move on," she said. "Take your woes and move on from here." Her voice was sleepy, the words dulled and slurred. "Please go."

Tiredness was winning and her head fell forward just as her empty cup fell into her lap.

A shadow stretched across the floor as the air around Ruth began to haze. In her hand, she felt something cold and in her sleep Ruth noted how her palms were sweating. "Stop!" she cried and then again: "Stop!"

CHAPTER FOURTEEN

The door handle felt blissfully cool against the prickle of sweat on her palms. She began to push down. "Stop!" she screamed, but the voice that came out sounded strangled and unfamiliar. She tried to swallow but her throat was dry and her tongue felt cumbersome in her mouth. Hands were pulling at her, roughly pinning her in place against the uncomfortable threadbare seat of the carriage. Kat felt the thick haze of sleep drift away from her as reality hit.

"You've had a nightmare, Mistress Fox."

The thick drapes covering the stagecoach windows made the light dim, but Kat could still make out the man in front of her. It was Mr Giles.

He had arrived at the shop when the sun was setting and he had not stopped knocking until Kat had answered. Her mother had been with her at the time, making arrangements for Darling's burial.

"What is it that you want?" Kat had asked him bitterly.

Upon seeing her red rimmed eyes, he had cleared his throat nervously. "May I come in?"

Without saying a word, Kat had held open the door for him and watched him go through. "Your service is required." He avoided looking at her face, her obvious distress making him uncomfortable.

"You can leave your order with me and it will be dispensed in the morning," Kat replied flatly. She wanted him out. "The shop is closed."

Clearing his throat again, Mr Giles walked over to the counter. "There will be no need for you to go to any work tonight. The judges are now in Salisbury. Their work is done in Winchester."

"Then why are you still here?" A sense of unease had started creeping over Kat's shoulders and crawling up her neck.

"I have been sent to fetch you. You will need to bring everything you need to keep Lord Jeffreys in as good health as he can be, whilst the assizes run through the month." He reached into his pocket and pulled out a ledger. "You will be paid of course."

Kat shook her head. "I am afraid I cannot accept the offer. My grandmother has-"

There was no need for her to finish. If it was possible, Mr Giles looked all the more awkward. "Oh, I see." He turned his attention to the ledger and dropped it on the counter top. "My condolences."

Holding open the door for him to leave, Kat gave him a tight smile. "Your condolences are appreciated, Mr Giles. It has been a long day and there is a lot to arrange."

"Of course, but you do understand that the coach will be with you at first light. There is little time to waste."

"I do not think you understand, Mr Giles. I said I am unable to accept your offer." She marched over to the ledger and thrust it back to him.

When he had spoken, his voice had been low but commanding. "No, I do not think that you understand, Mistress Fox. This is no offer. This is your duty to the King." He gently pushed the book into her chest before walking past her to the door.

"A coach will arrive for you at first light." Taking a piece of parchment from his pocket, he had then placed it on the chair by the door. A crisp, neat fold ensured the wording on it remained hidden.

When he had left, Kat's mother had joined her, standing over her shoulder as she unfolded the piece of parchment. Numbers had been neatly written across the page. It was to be the payment for her time. Kat had gasped. This was far more money than the apothecary shop made in several months. "You will take it, won't you?" Her mother was quick to grab the opportunity.

Spinning around to face her, Kat had been outraged. "And leave before we bury Darling?"

"You heard him. You have little choice, Kateryn."

"I won't do it. How can they force me?"

Snatching the parchment from her hands, her mother strode over to the counter. "If you refuse, it will be as good as suggesting your allegiance with the rebels." Her expression had iced over. "This family has suffered enough from your foolish decisions, Kateryn. Do not defy the wishes of those who work for our monarch. Your grandmother would not wish for it."

"But what about the shop? And what about Merlin?" Kat had protested, determined to find a reason that would mean she could stay.

"I am here to keep an eye on the shop and I can take the hound. Your father and I will take care of things."

"And how can I not say goodbye to her?"

"How can you not go with them?" Her mother had glowered at her, challenging her to argue back if she dared. She was right of course; Darling had warned her to follow the righteous path and, in God's eyes, doing her duty by the King was just that. When she had climbed the steps of the stagecoach, after the jars, bottles and phials that she needed had been placed in the travelling trunk, her heart had been heavy.

In the small space between them, Mr Giles looked at her with sympathy. She did not want his pity. He was responsible for all of it.

Turning her head to prevent him seeing the emotion on her face, she wondered whether they had yet moved Darling's body to her mother's house. It was not right that she wouldn't be there for the funeral.

As the wheels of the coach clattered against the ground beneath them, Mr Giles twitched the black drape and peered out nervously. Kat knew the reason for his nerves. The countryside would be thick with traitors in hiding. Even with the King's soldiers posted to weed out any likely suspects, they were not safe.

Mr Giles had told her that they were heading for Dorchester. Her stomach had fluttered with panic when he had said it. She knew people in Dorchester. It was where Gideon had grown up and they had called it home for the first year of their marriage. The people of Dorchester were loudly opposed to the fiercely Catholic King James. What would happen if somebody recognised her and gave away her connections? She had allowed Mr Giles to continue with his assumption that she was a spinster who had spent her whole life with her grandmother in Winchester. Kat felt her stomach lurch and then twist. "We need to stop."

"Impossible." Mr Giles glared at her. "The countryside is overrun with rebels. After we left the coaching inn, I informed the coachman that we are to not stop for any reason."

The rich, green pastureland of Dorset flanked the old Roman road. Fine showers of shale sprayed against the coach as the horses gathered even more speed. Kat clutched at the seat. Clearly the driver was determined to reach their destination as quickly as possible.

Sheep were out to graze and the land was dotted with folk gleaning what they could of a late summer harvest. At this time of year there were usually many more in those fields. The impact of the rebellion showed in those numbers. So many men had been taken, either by the rebel army or the King's army. Kat let the curtain drop over the view and leaned back against the seat.

When the horses began to slow in pace, Kat looked out again. She could see the familiar mismatched roofs of Dorchester, some tiled, some thatched. The inconsistent roofline was an unpleasant reminder of the town's dreadful misfortunes with fire over the years. A sense of foreboding overcame her as she recalled the High Priestess's warning. The people of Dorchester were yet to see far worse hardships than fire. As she silently contemplated the messages she had been shown so far, she found herself mouthing the High Priestess's words: 'The judge is coming. God have mercy on you all.'

The horses drew to a halt next to the church of St Peter. Its place in town was a prominent one. A shout of caution from the road was swiftly followed by the carriage jerking back into motion as a gruff voice instructed the horses to move on so that they were forced hard to the left before stopping again. Kat strained to listen to the heavy sound of wooden wheels that were navigating the cobbled street. The noise was getting louder and closer and Mr Giles shifted across the seat opposite and joined her in looking out the window.

Several carters carrying scores of men passed by. The passengers were dirty, their faces streaked with muck and their clothing dishevelled to rags. Kat stared into the sea of faces that all appeared to blur into one. Then she recognised the cobalt blue eyes of Joseph Speed, the shoemaker from Colyton. When she and Gideon had lived in Dorchester, it had been Joseph Speed who had kept Gideon in his boots for his job as a footman. Joseph had ensured they were comfortable and well-heeled for his job. He was a kindly man who had a good and unblemished reputation. Kat remembered him well. It had been a journey to travel to Joseph but one that Gideon had always insisted was worthwhile enough to make. Kat had always accompanied him and had enjoyed pleasant exchange with his wife who had always been very accommodating.

For a moment, their eyes locked and Kat felt as though her heart had stopped beating. Soldiers were riding behind them, ensuring no man was to jump to his freedom, for these were prisoners. These were the rebels whom Mr Giles had spoken of with such disdain.

Reaching for the door handle, Kat swung open the carriage door and before she could apply much thought to her actions, she was jumping to the street. Somebody shouted at her, but she was lost in the horror that she had seen in Joseph Speed's eyes. There were many more like him, their vague expressions and the heavy slump of their shoulders making plain their defeat. The nagging fear that Gideon had somehow become caught up in it all began eating away at her again. Joining other onlookers, she watched, trying to pick out Gideon's striking copper hair and green eyes from the crowd of dishevelled, dirty and disheartened faces. There were more faces she recognised but none of them were Gideon. There was their old neighbour, John Ratchett, Bill Davies, the most talented weaver in the county and his youngest son, Tom. Kat felt her stomach plunge. The last time she had seen Tom Davies, she had scolded him for causing mischief. His face now appeared far older than his years. Kat tried to recall his exact age. He could not be much older than thirteen. How could anybody throw a child as young as Tom into that cart of men?

Running forward, Kat called to them but somebody was pulling at her arm with surprising force. Mr Giles was holding her back, keeping her from running into the path of the prisoner carts. "Have you lost your senses, woman? You were almost under the wheels of those carts."

Feeling her legs wobble beneath her weight, Kat turned, a terrible lump in her throat. Around her neck the necklace throbbed impatiently as images flashed through her mind. It was showing her their fate. "They journey to their death," she said and she did not recognise her voice. It did not sound like her own.

Mr Giles tugged at her arm, impatient to lead her away. "They will be given the opportunity of a fair trial," he said coldly. "It is more than they deserve."

The carts rolled away towards the County gaol. Shaking herself free of his grasp, Kat stared in horror. A late afternoon haze had fallen silently and discreetly over Dorchester so that the air between her and the church seemed to ripple. Then she saw the impossible. Men from those carts were standing in front of her as a bloody mass of apparitions, heads lolling, mouths pulled into permanent silent screams. Behind them was a figure, broad and brutal in appearance. An axe blade glinted in the sunlight.

She wanted it to stop. Clutching at her head, she willed the terrible vision to disappear but there were more of them, each one lining up in front of her; a failed and shamed army of dead traitors. Kat tried to run but her legs would not move. Then rough hands were pulling her away from it all. A blissful screen of blackness fell in front of her and Kat's head rolled back.

******

Kat stirred to the sound of arguing between a man and a woman. She was lying across a seat in a room that smelled old and smoky. In spite of the window behind her, the room did not benefit from much light. A stout-looking woman was lighting candles. The acrid stench of fat spitting and melting at the base of the candle wicks accosted Kat's nose. "Must you light those things?" the male voice asked and there was a cough.

"We save the beeswax candles for the guest chambers and dining hall, Mr Giles." The woman's accent was Dorsetshire through and through, reminding Kat of where she was. She watched the ebb and flare of flame whilst recalling the carts that had been filled with men. Then she remembered that Joseph Speed, the Colyton shoemaker, had been amongst them. The hollowed out features of his once bright and cheery face burned in her mind and an involuntary pained moan escaped her lips. Mr Giles hurried over, carrying a wide necked bottle.

Kat felt her eyelids flicker shut again. The energy required to keep them open was too much. Feeling the cool lip of the bottle graze her nostrils, she recognised the smell of hartshorn. With a cough, her stomach muscles spasmed and her heart pounded hard.

"Not too much, Mr Giles! You could do her a mischief!" Kat opened her eyes in time to see the woman march over to snatch the bottle away. Her meaty arms were then underneath Kat's head, attempting to prop her up.

"Are you well, Mistress Fox?" Mr Giles sounded full of concern.

"No need to rush her. Took a nasty turn, this one did."

"That will be all, Mary." The stern note had returned to his voice as Mr Giles dismissed her. He did not see the glowering look upon Mary's face as she told him that she would be in the kitchen ensuring that a sufficient meal would be served upon the arrival of the important guests.

Her head clearing, Kat used her elbows to prop herself against the curved arm of the seat. "Careful now." Mr Giles was rushing over to her once more, worry lines etched into his forehead. "Do you recall what happened?"

Kat shook her head. How could she tell him all that she had seen? How could she say that she knew the fate of those men before they were to even stand trial? She would be branded a witch. "I am afraid I do not travel well, Mr Giles."

He was impatient again, pacing towards the window and looking out. "So I see. You are well now though. That is what matters." Rubbing his hands together, he gave her a hopeful smile. "Do you think you are well enough to check the inventory of items from your shop? I took the liberty of requesting that they place it all in the room you will have for your work. It is rather small, I am afraid. Nevertheless, it will serve quite well for the job."

"I am to start straight away?"

"When the physician arrives. He is travelling with Lord Jeffreys from Salisbury. I should think he will instruct you after examining Lord Jeffreys." Mr Giles walked over to a writing desk and began sorting through it. "Perhaps you will see if there is anything Mary can get you from the kitchen and I am sure one of the servants will show you to your chamber." Pulling up a chair, he sat down and inspected an inkpot before leafing through some documents.

Kat drew a breath, intending on asking if she could be given the means to write to her mother and ensure all was well after the funeral, but Mr Giles appeared lost in his work and her presence was no longer acknowledged.

It was late when the legal conclave arrived and they were taken straight to dine. There was much fuss in the house and Kat retreated to her chamber to escape the noise. She had been put at the top of the house with the other servants, although mercifully given her own accommodation. A stab of homesickness pierced through her as she looked out of the window and over the tightly packed rooftops, silvery grey beneath the moonlight. Memories of happier, simpler times were here in this town for Kat. Her eyes followed the uneven rows of thatch and tile. Gideon's parents would be sleeping beneath one of those roofs. She wondered if they had heard from him.

The physician's instructions arrived late. There was to be no chance of a full night of rest for Kat. In the makeshift stillroom that had been prepared for her, she held a candle to the list. She would have to work in the dark to prepare what was needed for morning. The remainder she could finish the following day. The physician had glared at her with mistrust when he had given her his instruction. He was a spindly man with thin lips and a sharp nose that hardened his cold reserve. To dispense some of what he expected, she would need to run errands. It seemed preposterous that so much could be required for one man but she did not dare question any of it.

Once she had finished her work, she fell into bed exhausted. In her fist she held the obsidian stone. As she slept, she dreamed of a journey beneath the relentless heat of the sun, of rutted roads and of countryside overflowing with men, some on horses but most on foot. She could smell the danger and hear the anxious shouts.

Then she could see the sharp point of a church spire, a dark shape shimmying up to the top of it. The sun dazzled her eyes but as the man on the spire turned to address those on the ground beneath him, a cloud passed overhead offering her a clearer view of his face. This was the dead Duke. He looked so pleased and proud at the top of that spire, clueless as to the fate that was waiting for him.

Somebody was throwing orders at her. She was suddenly the important one, revered for the power in her legs, her agility. Sweaty palms were slapping her on the back as words of encouragement were given, but a sense of dread was beginning to crawl over her skin. This was a mistake. She knew that she had no place there, that she was there for the wrong reasons.

Nightfall and she was marching, the muffled sound of thousands of feet challenged only by the odd snort of a horse, or nervous whisper. The crescent moon and low hanging mist were good signs. It meant that God was on their side. These messages of reassurance gave her no comfort though and the foreboding that she had felt earlier was growing with every step. It was dark enough to fall away, to hope not to be seen and make good her escape. Before she could think on it further, a hand was shoving at her and a hard, authoritative voice telling her that they had reached the stretch of water that they must cross. She was to go first and the rest of them to follow. On the instruction, she would be required to run and speed would be of the essence.

The water was suddenly waist deep. Kat held up her arms, determined to keep the bundle of dry clothing above her head. She breathed hard as the chill of the water permeated her bones, but she remained disciplined. There was to be no noise, no cursing, no coughing, no splashing – their lives and victory depended on it. Struggling to recall the detailed instructions she had been given earlier, she tried to remember who would be positioned where and what she was to do.

Then she was out and swiftly removing the waterlogged clothing, hastily replacing it with the bundle that had been kept dry and taking the dry boots that had been handed to her. It was difficult to change in the dark marshland, but the raw desire for survival kept her going. Somebody was by her side, giving her the final instruction as the rest of the men began to cross in droves. It was all on her now and a new feeling began to overtake the fear – a concoction of determination, excitement and pride. The future was near, she could smell it, taste it, almost see the inside of the Royal Court that she had been promised would be within her reach. In her dream, Kat felt the renewed courage that came with the glory of being considered a hero. She could feel the impatient sensation in her legs and arms; she wanted to run, needed to run. Her legs began to move and she was doing it, she was beginning to run the race of her life.

It was quite sudden: the hot crack of the gun ripping through the darkness, followed by the silhouettes of birds bursting from trees, their wings flapping against the low hung crescent moon. Shouts came from all directions. Above them, the steady bang of drums. As soon as she heard it, she knew that it was over.

Her thoughts raced from foolish optimism to despair and she continued to run, but she no longer knew where she was running to. Disorientated, she thought of the glittering promises in dark inns that were now hanging like shadows in her memory, and she wondered how she had been so stupid. This was not her place, not her time. There would be no honour this night. She could smell water and wet earth but above all, fear.

Kat felt her legs moving faster, her feet picking up speed so that they barely glanced over the ground beneath them as she headed into a dark abyss that seemed to welcome her with its large gaping mouth. There was confusion and chaos and she felt as though she was falling. As sweat poured from her, she wondered if she was in the pit of hell? Then, through the darkness, she could see a wink of light.

CHAPTER FIFTEEN

The terrible burning has gone but I am parched and my tongue feels thick and cumbersome in my mouth. I feel my eyelids flutter open, only for them to close again at the brightness of the light. I am in a chamber far finer than any I have stayed in before. A breeze ruffles my hair and I moan. I long to drink. Somebody thrusts something into my hand. A cup. I struggle to sit up. Hands help me. I drink deep, the liquid spilling over the sides of my mouth. When I am done, I open my eyes again and look.

Her dark eyes are wide and staring at me with such intensity. I have seen this face before. I recognise the full lips, the creamy skin and the dark hair full of fine silken ribbons.

I am suddenly aware of my nakedness beneath the sheets. I have been stripped and there is a bowl of water with rags on the side. She sees my gaze rest on the bowl, notes my expression and is quick to explain that one of the servants had stripped me when I was brought inside. It does not make me feel any better. She asks me my name and I refuse to answer. I feel vulnerable, violated. I do not know who any of these people are. I ask for Lord Granville but she can only shake her head. She says that he has had to continue his journey without me but that I can stay whilst I regain my strength. She looks pleased at this and I wonder if her family know that she is in here with me. I suspect that they do not.

"Three weeks," she says in her melodious voice when I ask her how long I have been here. "The fever broke last night." Wringing out one of the rags, she brings it to me and dabs my head and face. She brings her lips to my ear so that I can feel the tickle of her breath on my skin. "You will not know the news," she whispers and she does not wait for me to enquire as to what news she is referring to. "The Duke of Monmouth lost his head."

My guts twist at that and she must see the panic as she smiles kindly. "They say that the King is sending the most formidable of his judges to lead the assizes, that it will be his wrath that the rebels face." Holding the rag above me, she does not seem to notice that the water is steadily dripping from it onto my chest and soaking the bed around me. She is lost in the morbid excitement of it all. She brings the cloth to my chest and rubs as she tells me in her melodious voice that her name is Honoria.

Back home, I think, this water would have been scented with lavender, rose petals or some other sweet-smelling plant that can soothe and heal. Honoria does not possess these skills though. She is a woman quite content with being kept and it is unlikely she will ever need to live any other way.

"Are you hungry?" she asks and I nod, so she leaves the room and momentarily, I hear the efficient tinkle of a hand bell.

I am well fed and watered, like a pampered lapdog. Only the servants and Honoria visit me. She keeps me company for as much of the day as she can and I see her slip one of the servants something, whispering to them.

In the far corner of the room is a copper tub. Several buckets are needed to fill it even a quarter full and they keep coming. I am given a wash ball and clothes that must have once belonged to a man of the house. It occurs to me that I do not even know who the owner of the house is and this fills me with a sense of panic.

Dutifully, I wash and I scrub, pushing aside all the terrible thoughts that sit on the periphery of my mind. I try to enjoy the sensation of the water on my skin, the splash and drip of it with every slight move I make, but it is hopeless; I will never be rid of the memory of that muddy, cold water from the rhynes – its unearthly chill and marshy smell.

Outside, the sun is setting. I think of her, my wife. Then I see her in a deep pocket of my imagination. She is full of reproach, full of questions, full of rage. Something has changed in her. I see a power that I have never seen before and she is beautiful with it, but dangerous. My eyes snap open and I realise that I must have fallen asleep. Sunlight has been replaced by moonlight and the room is almost in darkness.

I step out of the bath and fumble around to ready myself for bed. I am stronger now but tired. My eyelids are heavy again. It is as though I have been given a small piece of heaven, sleeping in this wonderfully soft bed, in this richly decorated chamber.

I fall asleep. Only in my dreams do I sense the figure that steps into my room, just before dawn.

CHAPTER SIXTEEN

With the exception of some of the servants starting their long day, all was quiet when Kat descended the staircase leading to the kitchen area. It was first light and she had woken to the sound of crying only to realise that her face was wet with tears. She had dreamed so vividly of Gideon.

There was to be a sermon at the church that morning, but she needed to escape the oppressive, suffocating atmosphere of the house first. Aside from stray animals nosing for scraps, the streets were quiet. With soldiers posted in the town, Kat imagined that the townsfolk were less keen to be out. She had overheard the servants in the house talking. They said that people were being arrested for crimes they had not even realised they were committing; things they had said in support of the rebellion, or any small action that might link them to it. The stories lingered around the dark corridors of the lodgings, a sinister warning of what could happen to anyone who stepped a foot wrong. It was a relief to escape.

Beneath the pink hues of sunrise, Kat hurried down the street, her stride filled with purpose. The little stone cottage they had once shared, still young and naïve to the tribulations of love, overlooked the mills at Fordington. There were plenty of hedgerow berries, wild roots and herbs nearby and so Kat picked as she walked, placing them in her basket.

The thatch of her old cottage gleamed gold against the rising sun. Quietly approaching it, lest she disturbed whoever might be residing there, she noted the door that had once been there was gone. On closer inspection, she could see that the windows were also bare, the woollen curtains ragged or ripped away and she wondered what had happened to the last tenants that it should have been left in such disarray.

The foliage on the tiny piece of land out the front was overgrown and in desperate need for somebody to cut it back a little. Kat walked to where the door had once been and looked down at the shards of wood. It had been broken with force. Crossing the threshold, she went into the kitchen where she and Gideon had once shared stories and their deepest thoughts late into the night. The table was on its side, pots lay in pieces on the floor, the cast iron cauldron had been tipped over, its contents long since dried into the flagstones and nibbled by rodents. Herbs that would have been hung from the beams to dry out over the summer had been torn down. The whole place had been destroyed.

Hurrying around the wall that separated the main living area from the chamber, she saw that two chairs had been overturned and the bed broken in several places.

Beneath her feet was ash from the fireplace, as though scattered by the force of a terrible gale blowing down the chimney. It had been a long, balmy summer though, so that could not be the reason for the dreadful mess.

The place had been ransacked and there was no need to question who had done such a thing. "The King's soldiers," she muttered as she returned to the kitchen area. "They must have come looking for men when they called the muster-roll."

As she stooped to pick up the shattered fragments of a broken clay pot, a cold tongue of dread glided over her neck as she wondered what had become of the people who had been living in the cottage.

Behind the wall at the back of the kitchen was the storeroom. Kat went in and knelt on the floor next to a half full sack of grain. Rodents had nibbled through the sacking, creating a banquet across the floor. Kat could hear them scuttling about, alerted to her presence, hiding in the nooks and crannies until she was gone. She crouched to inspect the far corner of the little room and felt for the loose stone. It took a little work to dislodge it but what had been hidden there remained. The latest residents had obviously remained oblivious to its presence. Kat pulled out the copper scrying bowl that her grandmother had given to her. She had never dared use it and had forgotten all about it when they had returned to Winchester. When Kat had been a child, Darling had shown her how to scry. She had shown her lots of things in the certainty that one day she might embrace the gift of divination. It had never seemed possible until now. The thought of doing it for herself was terrifying but the bowl felt right in her hands. Her arms tingled with an unfamiliar power and an insatiable desire to harness more of it crept up on her. A feeling so intense washed over her and she dropped the dish. The frantic scratch of retreating tiny clawed feet followed the sound of the dish crashing to the floor. As quickly as it had come, the feeling left her. Taking a moment to regain her sense of calm, she rested against the uneven surface of the wall and shut her eyes.

Kat took several breaths and held onto the last. The crunch of boots could be heard on the path outside. With haste she tucked the little dish into her basket, covering it with her cloth. Then she returned the stone and hurried back into the kitchen. If the owners were returning, she did not want to appear as though she was stealing anything. She wondered whether she would have time to make a run for it out the door but that was a hopeless plan as she would certainly be seen. The best thing to do would be to smile and explain that she had noticed the damaged door upon passing and had simply entered the cottage to ensure that nobody had been hurt. She reached the table just as the barrel of a musket appeared in the doorway. It pushed aside the debris that cluttered the entrance. A young man with a clean-shaven face greeted her with surprise. He had not expected to find her there. Another man, this one older, appeared by his side. Soldiers. They both stared at her. The younger turned to his acquaintance, waiting for direction.

The older one stepped forward, his cold, hard eyes the colour of wintry seawater. "Where's your husband hiding then?" he grunted, barging his way in.

"I am alone." Kat remained behind the table, keeping her distance.

"That's what they all say," he sneered and instructed the other to start searching. "This place was deserted before now." He stomped around towards the storeroom and she heard him spilling the remaining contents of the grains.

"This is not my home. I was walking and saw the door had been broken, so I came in. I thought somebody might be hurt."

The man glanced at her wedding finger and narrowed his eyes. "You know the people who live here?"

Kat shook her head.

His eyes narrowed as he regarded her with suspicion. "You don't speak like them around these parts. What's your business here?"

"As I told you, I was walking."

Having finished searching the grain store, the other soldier was poking around the sleeping area. He emerged shaking his head to indicate that there was no sign of anyone else. "Walking?" the older man asked. "A likely story." Lifting his gun, he motioned for her to sit down.

Kat obediently followed his order.

"Check the garden and I'll stay here with this one." He looked about the kitchen, noting the basket that she had been carrying and the herb bundles she had collected and then his gaze moved to her chest. With despair, Kat realised the necklace must have slipped from the collar of her dress. Roughly reaching for it, the man clutched it in his fist tightly so that the chain rubbed at her neck. "What's this then?" The stone glinted red as it caught the sun that was seeping through the window. As though it had burned him, he dropped it and took a cautious step back. "A cunning woman," he said and his voice was a low growl. Kat hoped that this man was superstitious enough to make swift his exit but instead his thick lips broke into a sinister smile, revealing crooked discoloured teeth. "They won't mind so much then, what happens to a woman like you."

Shrinking away from him, Kat tried to explain that she was travelling with Lord Jeffreys, but her voice fell on deaf ears. The man was too intent on making cruel fun for himself to hear any of it.

"So, you're alone here, you say. No husband or family to speak of?" He reached for her thigh with his hand and squeezed it hard, causing her to wince. Something wicked flashed across his face as he took obvious pleasure from seeing her discomfort. "The women around here are desperate to please. It's almost too easy," he said as he got to his feet and drew his musket in the pretence that he intended to shoot her. "Never met one of your kind before." There was no fear in his eyes, no concern that her skills with the herbs meant that she could curse him for any wrongdoing, but she wondered if that was because he did not intend on leaving her alive.

Kat swallowed back a whimper of fear and the soldier gave a cruel laugh. Then, holding the butt of his gun, he pointed it downwards. The cold metal pressed at her legs before lifting her skirts to reveal the bare flesh beneath.

"All clear." The younger soldier returned and on seeing Kat in the chair, her skirts now lifted to above her thighs, he licked his lips.

Horror washed over her. These men had done this before. It had become routine. Before she knew what was happening, they had hauled her from the seat and the front of her dress was ripped. She could smell the sweat on them, rancid and days old. "Get off me!" she shouted but that only served to be to her detriment. Taking a fistful of her hair, the younger began dragging her from the kitchen to the bedchamber. "No man in her life to discipline her," he said and pushed her hard against the wall so that she screamed out.

Terrified, Kat tried to turn to face her adversaries but they were too strong, too accomplished at what they intended to do. She began kicking behind her and there was a satisfactory cry of pain as her boot caught a shin. Taken off guard, the younger man doubled over, enabling her to turn and kick him hard in the groin. Behind him, the other had already undone the buckle of his trousers, rendering him unable to reach her swiftly enough. It gave Kat the precious time she needed to try to escape but the men were still too quick. A burly hand grabbed at her wrist pulling her back as they began barking threats, telling her what they intended to do.

The roughened skin of the older man's palm encircled her jaw. With thumb and forefinger, he pressed hard so that she was unable to form words. A burning pain shot through her as he slammed her against the wall again, her shoulder taking the force of impact.

As her vision blurred, Kat noticed a shadow in the doorway. Another man had joined them. She squeezed her eyes shut in a bid to blot out what was happening. There were shouts and she prayed it would be over soon, that they would not maim her or take her life.

The unforgiving grip around her jaw suddenly dropped and she held her breath, waiting for what dreadful atrocity was to come next. Her head was spinning. She could hear voices but she couldn't decipher what they were saying. Then somebody was calling her name.

"Can you hear me, Mistress Fox? Mistress Fox?" The voice was familiar and Kat opened her eyes to see two more soldiers rounding up the rogues who had attacked her, leading them away.

Eyes that gleamed like well-polished buttons stared at her. Kat recognised the face at once: the square line of his jaw and how his left cheek dimpled with certain expressions.

"Mr Giles!" In spite of the terrible ache in her jaw, she wanted to laugh with relief at the sight of this awkward looking man who had saved her from the hands of the two brutes.

"You're safe now. They will be dealt with harshly for their actions." Fury and concern coloured his face and his gaze fell to the rip at the front of her dress. Hurrying to find a blanket to wrap her in, he then turned to the soldiers with whom he had arrived and instructed them on where to take the other two, warning them how seriously such a slur against the royal army's reputation would be taken if word was to get out.

"They intended to rape me and Lord knows what else." Kat was shaking, but even in the state that Mr Giles had found her, she knew that the men would simply be warned. There would be no punishment. They could not afford news of that nature tarnishing the campaign's reputation.

"They did not though. Did they?" Mr Giles asked and Kat flinched as he touched her shoulder.

"They meant to!" she countered. "Had you not turned up, they would have done far worse."

"But they did not?" he asked again, much more firmly.

"No. You stopped them."

Satisfied with her answer, he nodded. "Can you walk?"

She told him that she could and propping her up, they made the walk back to the lodgings. "Hold on to me should you need to," he said. For such a slight man, he was strong.

As they walked the road that ran east to west through the town, he began to reprimand her. "Just as well your escape from the house was reported to me. Why did you leave and what is it that you were doing?"

"Why should I not?" she answered defiantly. "I am not one of your prisoners, am I?"

"Mistress Fox, need I remind you of the danger you put yourself in and the precious time you have wasted this morning? Now please be gracious enough to answer my question. What is it that you were doing walking all that way out there with no word to anyone?"

"I only went to gather some more roots and herbs. I noticed the stream on our way in and the hedgerow that ran alongside it. I wanted to see if I could collect some more supplies before starting work for the day. Mine will not last forever."

"It is a dangerous place for a woman to be out alone. There could be rebels hiding. You saw the likes of them being brought in by the carters yesterday. They are little more than savages."

Swallowing back an angry retort, Kat did not like the way he referred to men who had once been her neighbours, but she could not give away that she had once lived there. "I had not realised the danger I was in."

"So it would seem," he replied and they walked in silence the rest of the way. They entered the lodgings through the stabling yard and when they were inside, he took her straight to the parlour room. "We cannot have scandal ruining the important work that is being done here," he warned her as he helped her sit down.

Kat knew that it would be futile to protest, to tell him that those men had done it before, and worse. She did not tell him about their boasts. There was no point. He wanted for no trouble and she had already made plenty.

Mary shot Kat a wary look as she took in her bedraggled appearance. "Whatever happened here?" Kat lifted her hand to her jaw. She could feel the bruise coming out already.

"Nothing a little soap, water and dash of brandy wine won't fix," Mr Giles answered as he opened the shuttered windows to let some light in.

Doing as he asked, Mary left a water dish on the table along with a wash ball, clean rags and brandy wine. Kat took the rags and dipped them in the water, attempting with difficulty to slip beneath her clothing to press against her shoulder. "Can I be of assistance, Mistress Fox?" Mr Giles went to take the rags from her.

"I am quite alright, thank you," she insisted, persevering with the impossible task in hand and wincing at the pain.

"You are in pain. Should I fetch Mary to help?"

"No!" Kat didn't want Mary's rough hands nursing her wounds. She was a cumbersome and ham-fisted woman and the look upon her face had showed no sign of sympathy for Kat's misfortune, only the inconvenience it had brought.

"Then here, let me help." Mr Giles was softly spoken. There was a gentle kindness to him as he carefully and respectfully found a way of applying the cool, damp material to her skin without compromising Kat's dignity. He dabbed at it and then reached for another. He smelled of lemon balm and rosemary. It was a pleasant contrast to the sweat of the soldiers. "There is only a little blood," he commented as he worked. "A graze. But I think it will bruise. What would you usually use to take down the swelling and bruising?" he asked as he gently dabbed.

"Powdered mummy," Kat answered facetiously.

"Ah." Mr Giles paused. "A simple ingredient then." There was a moment's pause before they looked at one another and laughed, breaking the tension in the air between them.

Kat started again, her tone softer. "At home, I would soak a joint of meat in ale and smoke it. Then I would apply it to the area."

"Very well. We shall ask Mary to do that and you shall have your remedy." He left the rag against her skin. It felt pleasantly cool and soft. Then he brought his hand to her face, touching it very gently so that he could study the area of her jaw where the soldier's cruel fingers had pressed and pinched. "May I?" he asked as his fingertips gently grazed her cheek. The sensation was pleasant, the touch almost intimate.

"Yes," she whispered, unable to find her voice and their eyes locked for a moment.

"You will live." He stepped back abruptly, a flush spotting his cheeks as he nervously cleared his throat. "You should take more care in the future. There are too many men who hate the puritans. If they mistake you as being from these parts and that you are alone, they will believe that they can do as they please, that their position as the King's soldiers protects them. You must stay within these walls."

Anger and fear exploded inside her and she stood up, ignoring the jarring pain in her shoulder. "And become just another prisoner? How can you demand that of me?"

He gave her a grim smile. "I do not demand it, Mistress Fox. I ask it. It would be a great tragedy if the world was to lose a woman like you."

That had been the same turn of phrase the soldier had used: a woman like you. Whereas the soldier had meant it in a disparaging way, Mr Giles had said it with great respect. The compliment gave her cause to blush and she cast her eyes to the ground.

There was another nervous cough from Mr Giles. "We should be on our way to church," he said in a hurry, breaking the awkward silence that had built between them. "It would not do to be late."

******

As the sun burned high over the rooftops of Dorchester, its heat was uncomfortable and prickly. It was just behind the church opposite the lodgings that Kat saw a familiar face. Bridget – the wife of Gideon's brother, Robert. Her first instinct was to slip back into the shadowy street. What good reason could she give for being in this part of the country with no husband and no obvious purpose?

Bridget walked past her, shoulders slumped forwards and face heavy, every step burdened by an invisible weight. Her children were nowhere to be seen, which was strange in itself. The sight of her tugged at Kat's heart. How she wanted to call out Bridget's name, throw her arms around her shoulders and tell her everything. Shame stopped her though. Gideon's family had been as furious as hers. He had changed and they had blamed Kat for it. They had warned him not to marry higher than he should, had told him his ambition would lead to certain misery, but he had ignored it, had told them Kat was different, that they were in love. How could she tell them that he was now missing, that they had argued so dreadfully before it had happened and that all their troubles had stemmed from his stubborn determination to give Kat the life that he believed she deserved?

Bridget stopped, her hunched form unravelling somewhat and then she turned. "Kat?" It was as though she did not dare believe what she was seeing. "Is that really you?"

Panicked, Kat considered running, pulling her hood over her head and walking by as though she did not recognise her. But there was such woe in Bridget's large eyes that she could not ignore her.

"It is you, isn't it?" She stumbled into the narrow street, reaching out to touch Kat on the arm.

"Oh, Bridget." Overcome with emotion, Kat put a hand to her mouth. They hugged and Kat sniffed back the tears that suddenly threatened.

Pulling back from their embrace, Bridget paled. "Is it Gideon? Is he...?" She looked around, conscious of being watched by the many soldiers posted around the town.

Kat shook her head. "Gideon is not with me and he is not in Dorchester."

Bridget was confused. "Then why? How?"

Kat did not know how to answer. Dorchester was suffering. Husbands, lovers, sons and brothers were imprisoned and awaiting trial with the judge whose reputation was already whispered about, and here she was travelling with him, keeping his ailments at bay with her work. They would hate her for it. "You have to understand that I had no choice," she said at last.

The look on Bridget's face demonstrated that she was no wiser and Kat sighed. "They took me from the apothecary in Winchester, said it was my duty to the King."

Recoiling, Bridget gasped. "You have come with Judge Jeffreys?"

"Not willingly."

"But you are with them, with *him*?"

"Yes, I am," Kat replied in a low voice.

Bridget shook her head in disbelief. "But where is Gideon? What did he have to say about this?"

"He is away on business and I do not know what to do with myself for the worry it has brought me."

Bridget's expression darkened. "You are worried because your husband is travelling on business? What about the families of the men they are holding here? Spare a thought for them. They say that he is a monster, this Judge."

"He is just a man." Kat hated herself for jumping to his defence, but it was all she could think of to say.

Bridget gripped her arm, her face close. "What is he like? Is he really so ghastly? Do you think he will give a fair trial?"

Recalling his pointed statement to Lady Alice Lisle and the sentence he so easily served her, Kat hesitated before giving her answer. "I cannot say. He says that he is here to bring justice to the King."

Crumpling before her, Bridget's knees appeared to buckle beneath her weight and Kat caught her by the elbow, helping to keep her on her feet. "I am sorry," she said and as her eyes filled up, Kat guided her to sit on a nearby wall. Between sobs she spoke. "I have just been to the prison." She looked straight into Kat's face. In that moment she looked so much older. "Robert is there."

"Robert?" Kat swallowed but her mouth was so dry that it forced her to cough. "He is to be trialled at the assizes?"

Nodding her head, Bridget folded into more tears. "Yes, for his part in the rebellion. It has been so dreadful. I begged him not to go but he would not listen. There were such celebrations when the Duke arrived on the shores of Lyme Regis and marched through. There was the promise of a better life under a new King; the rightful King, they said. They were all so certain and the Duke looked so handsome and brave." The tears fell over her cheeks, already puffy from crying. "There were so many men here who thought the same, who were prepared to fight for a new King. When I saw Robert this morning, he appeared to be such a very different man to the one who left."

Silence clung to the air between them as Bridget's sobs continued and Kat tried to comfort her with an embrace. "How was he?" she asked at last, her mouth dry and her words thick.

"Broken. I barely recognised him. As good as lost his mind, he has, but he said that they told him to plead guilty. A guilty plea may bring a reprieve, so they said." Her shoulders shook as she spoke.

"Then he must plead guilty," Kat insisted as she recalled the outcome of the late Lady Alice Lisle's plea of 'not guilty'.

Bridget was aghast. "No! I told him not to be a fool."

"He would be a fool to plead anything but; I have seen how the judge was in Winchester."

Bridget collapsed into more tears and Kat draped an arm around her shoulders. "He has made his point already in Winchester. He cannot condemn all of these men. Who will work the lands for the noblemen? Who will pay the taxes? It is not in the King's interest to sentence them all." Even as she said it, she knew she was wrong. The spirit world had shown her the countryside awash with blood, the men whose heads were on pikes and the death of an elderly lady. Truth be told, she thought that there was little hope for any of those being held in Dorchester.

Calming somewhat, Bridget nodded but the sadness did not leave her face. "There are so many of them, Kat. You should see some of them. Their hands have been burned to stumps and they have been tortured to the brink of death by the King's men. Some will not survive another night. And then there is the woman who is being held here."

Kat did not know who Bridget was referring to.

"The whole town speaks of her." Bridget recounted what she knew of a school mistress by the name of Blake who was being held alongside the rebels. "From Taunton, they say. She made a flag for the Duke of Monmouth and had her pupils present it to him. I have heard she has smallpox, that she may not face the Judge at all."

Reflecting quietly on this, Kat thought it may well be a small mercy for the woman if she was to die in the dank, dark place she was being held.

"Will you come with me tomorrow? To the assizes court?" Bridget asked and Kat's heart sank.

She struggled to deliver the answer that she knew she had to give. "Bridget, I cannot."

"Whyever not? Robert is family, as am I!"

Kat imagined the consequences of being seen with Bridget as Robert emerged for his trial. People would talk and the gossip would land back with the servants and, in turn, the five judges and Mr Giles. They had whipped a man in Salisbury for a silly throwaway comment that suggested his support for the rebellion. Kat could not risk it. Bridget could surely understand that? "I am in service to Lord Jeffreys. If anyone from the house was to see-"

Jumping to her feet, Bridget turned on her, sparks in her eyes. "But Robert is family! Who are these people to you?"

"Please Bridget, you do not understand!" Kat reached out to stop her but Bridget was running and she would not stop. "Bridget!"

No good could come of chasing after her. Kat realised she would have to leave her. It would be too dangerous to do otherwise. All she could do was pray for Robert and hope that Judge Jeffreys would be true to his word, that those who pleaded guilty would be shown some mercy. Sadly, she returned to the lodgings.

For the rest of the day Kat worked with a heavy heart. The pain in her shoulder had dulled to insignificance compared with what she knew Bridget and Gideon's family would be experiencing with Robert in prison. It was hard to focus, hard to prepare anything with hands that would not stop trembling.

The stillroom she had been appointed was where the servants would usually eat, so it was furnished with a hearth and a large table of scrubbed wood. It was not what Kat would have hoped for but the lodgings lacked a proper stillroom. Jars, phials and pots from the apothecary had been lined up at one end of the large wooden table and the room already smelled of crushed roots and herbs. Approaching footsteps made Kat turn to see Mary Althrop appear in the arched entrance. Her face was pink from the heat of the kitchen. "The meal for the judges is to be served." She eyed Kat's work critically, visibly baulking at the mess. Mary was evidently a much neater worker. "I have been told that you have the medicine he must take before he eats."

"Yes, I have made this." Kat filled a cup with the elixir wine she had been making and handed it to Mary. "The whole cup must be drained before eating. You will remember to give the instructions?"

Mary responded with a glare before marching off with the cup. There was an animosity towards Kat that she had noticed and it was not just because she had taken over the room that they were supposed to eat in. Her position in the house was something between servant and guest. Nobody quite knew her place, but special privileges such as her own chamber had been bestowed upon her and her position had not been planned. Nobody had been expecting the judge's apothecary to be a female and certainly not one so young and attractive. She was a mysterious imposition and Kat could tell that Mary thought her to be trouble. The chatter of servants carried through from the kitchen area and she felt so very alone. When she was finished with her work, she passed by the dining room where she could hear the boom of the five judges as they laughed about the townsfolk, making light of people who they viewed as poorly educated and unimportant. Even the servants whom the legal party had brought with them from London considered themselves superior to the poor folk of Dorset. It was as though they had forgotten or dismissed the fact that these people were terrified and grieving for those men who had been returned, some so very different to how they had been when they had marched with the Duke's army.

In her hand she held a remedy that would calm the relentless, uncomfortable pulsing in her head. She intended to find Mr Giles, to ensure that her service was no longer required before she retired to bed.

"Ah, Mistress Fox, there you are." Mr Giles looked harassed as he held open the door to the drawing room and beckoned for her to enter. He asked her if she had the inventory of medicaments that she had been asked to prepare and she presented it to him. She had been careful to price everything just as her grandmother would have done. There would be no small favours for these pompous men.

As he was running his eyes over the inventory of medicaments, there was a knock on the door. His presence was required with the judges. A matter of importance and urgency that needed clearing up. Mr Giles appeared flustered, stumbling over his words before he left Kat alone in the room. "I will not be long. You will remain here until I return."

Sconces lit the room and a tall candelabra had been placed by a writing desk. A chair had been left at an angle at the front of the desk, as though somebody had been sitting there. Wandering over to it, she could see a crow feather quill resting in an inkpot and some parchment. Tracing her fingers over the smooth walnut surface of the desk, she remembered what it had been like to live in a house with beautiful furniture and fine tapestries. Her father had a desk much like this one. As her fingers brushed the parchment, it drifted to the floor. When she stooped to pick it up, her eyes trained to the fine writing across the page and she held it closer to the candlelight. With a gasp, she realised that she was reading instructions for the disposal of the prisoners. The lettering was quite beautiful to look at but the words on the page chilled her. This was an order for gallows to be erected in the most public place and for faggots to burn the bowels of the prisoners, as well as a furnace and cauldron to boil heads and quarters, with half a bushel of salt required for each traitor and finally, tar, spears and poles. Had Bridget not said that the prisoners had been told that there was the chance of mercy for those who pleaded guilty?

As she read on, her blood froze in her veins. There were spaces ready for the numbers to be applied. Was that what Mr Giles was meeting with Lord Jeffreys about? Had they already decided how many men should face the penalty for treason, regardless of the trial? With a cry of horror, she dropped the parchment back to the desk. Mr Giles must have prepared this order. How had he not winced and flinched and retched as he had written those words?

Backing away from the desk, Kat thought of her brother-in-law, Robert. She thought of the men who she had seen arrive with the carters: Joseph Speed, John Ratchett and young Tom, the son of Bill Davies. Was this the fate that awaited them? Then she thought of Gideon and she found herself falling back into a large armchair, the air suddenly too close and nausea rising.

Mr Giles returned to the room and his eyes were heavy with a burden known only to him as he glanced at Kat and then at the desk. "Your service is much appreciated," he said sombrely. "Have you eaten? I will have Mary bring you some supper."

"I have no appetite," Kat retorted, anger and disgust getting the better of her. "I may not support the rebels, but I have a heart, Mr Giles. Do you think the women whose loved ones face trial will sleep tonight? Do you suppose that they should sleep ever again?"

The sharpness of her tongue caught him off guard. Mr Giles did not say a word but walked solemnly back to his chair. "Those men are not halfwits." He picked up the quill and poured himself another drink. "None were forced to choose the side they pledged their allegiance to. All of them had a purpose: to murder and slay so that they could put a pretender onto the throne. Every man knows the consequences of high treason. Besides, Lord Jeffreys is willing to show mercy to those who confess." He turned back to his letter, the crow feather quill poised above the inkpot, ready to finish the macabre orders with numbers still to be filled. The feather glistened jet black in his hand and it was like an ominous shadow. "Should your appetite return, you will find Mary in the kitchen. Your services are dismissed, as are your opinions, Mistress Fox." Mr Giles did not turn to address her but simply returned the fine nib to the parchment and began to scratch across it.

Kat turned the door handle and paused. "It is most fitting, Mr Giles, that the quill you use to craft your words is one from the plumage of the bird commonly associated with death."

As she opened the door, she did not see or hear the quill drop to the desk, nor the ragged breath drawn by Mr Giles as he read back over his words with moist eyes.

CHAPTER SEVENTEEN

'You okay? Anything go bump in the night?' The sparky ping of Jeremy's text startled Ruth. Earlier that morning she had woken up on the sofa with a stiff neck and a full bladder after achieving what felt like only an hour worth of sleep.

Nursing her second cup of tea, she was considering what she should do about Grayson when Jeremy's text arrived. She wanted to confront him in person but did not want the humiliation of coming face to face with him and Veda together. The message from Jeremy was a welcome distraction. Poised to reply, she wondered how to respond. Plenty had gone bump in the night, starting with her marriage. She wanted to feel the hot sting of tears fill her eyes when she thought about it but no emotion would come. Her whole body felt numb and she wondered if aside from her pride she was even upset? Putting the phone aside she decided to wait until her mind was a little more together before speaking with Jeremy.

Picking up a stray magazine, she turned the pages, looking for a different sort of distraction before giving up and grabbing her phone again.

Jeremy answered on the third ring. "Good news or bad news?"

Ruth hesitated. There was no point mentioning anything to do with Grayson. The last thing she wanted was to involve a stranger and worse, a client. "Depends whether you consider something 'going bump' is a good or bad thing?" She tried to keep her tone light.

"Oh, I see." There was a pause and she could hear his laboured breathing amongst the rush of wind against the mouthpiece of the phone. It sounded like he was outside. "Are you okay, or is that a stupid question?"

"It's a perfectly valid question," Ruth replied and found herself smiling. Just hearing the genuine concern in Jeremy's voice made her feel better. "Aside from a lack of sleep, I'm fine."

The sound of a dog barking came through the phone and Jeremy whistled. "Sorry, I've taken Rex out for a stomp over the Downs before Lisa and Roy get back. It's good exercise and I have to admit that I'm going to miss him. The house won't be the same without him plodding around."

"I bet. He's a lovely dog."

"Lazy around the house but full of energy out here." There was a pause and it sounded like he was putting the dog back on the lead. "So, when are you going to tell me what happened last night?"

Ruth sighed and wandered into the lounge, drawing back the curtains to reveal a very grey day. "She was here. I found the necklace on the bedroom floor, but I know that I put it in the drawer before I went to bed."

"I should never have left that damn necklace with you. I'm so sorry, Ruth." He paused for breath and she imagined him ascending the large sweeping hills that led to the heathland of the Downs.

"I wanted to keep hold of it. Don't blame yourself. Who better to take care of it than a psychic?" Ruth thought back to how she had felt during the night, sitting on the sofa, trying her hardest to stay awake. There had been a presence in the house. She had felt it before being pulled back into her dreams of centuries past. "This is going to sound ridiculous but I think that I have a connection with the spirit's mortal self."

There was a pause. "You mean her ghost is coming to you?"

"No, I mean that I am connected to Kateryn during a period of her life, when she was actually living it. I think I'm being drawn into her time."

Jeremy didn't respond and she could imagine him shaking his head, the forked frown lines appearing between his eyes. "Are you suggesting time travel?"

Ruth wasn't sure and thought carefully before answering. "I think I'm experiencing an astral projection of sorts, into her time. Is that time travel?"

When he didn't answer, she continued her explanation. "I'm not doing it of my own free will. I feel like I'm being dragged there, quite literally. I think she is using the necklace to bring me to her." Drawing a breath, she realised how preposterous it all sounded and expected him to tell her that she barking mad.

His reaction took her by surprise. "Shit, Ruth, this is amazing! You do realise what you're saying?"

"If you can make sense of it, then please do enlighten me." She had walked over to the mantelpiece above the fire and was rearranging the pictures, turning those of her and Grayson face down.

"If what you're saying is true, you're getting a first-hand view of history."

The 'if' was a slap in the face. She couldn't blame him for thinking that she was making it all up or imagining it. "Look, I realise how ridiculous it sounds and, let's face it, I suppose I am suggesting what the law of physics suggests is currently impossible, but I really do think that I am being spirited into the past."

Jeremy was quick to plaster over his careless turn of phrase. "I didn't mean that you might be spinning me a yarn. Sorry if it came across like that."

Fatigue hitting her, Ruth sank onto the sofa. "I wouldn't blame you if you did think that. I question it too as soon as I say it loud. It's a first for me, but that's not to say it isn't happening."

He swore several times. "In my wildest dreams, I couldn't have imagined this happening. I thought it was something to do with her, that she was punishing me for-" He stopped short, the almost revelation mingling with wind and static.

"Who do you mean, Jeremy? Punishing you for what?" That feeling of unease about whatever it was that he was keeping from her began to bother Ruth again.

There was a sigh. "Can we meet? It might make things a little easier. We can have a bite to eat somewhere, my treat. I owe you, especially given that it's me who has brought all of this on your doorstep and I didn't even pay for the reading."

Ruth began to protest but he interrupted. "Please say yes. It's hard talking over the phone and in spite of what you say, I do owe you."

Reasoning with herself that there was certainly nothing better she would be doing that evening, Ruth agreed.

"Good. Meet me at seven at the front of the cathedral, by the mulled wine stand?"

"Okay." The line was disconnected and Ruth realised that she was nervous. Was it because he was keeping something from her or because she felt strangely excited about going out with a handsome stranger for a meal?

Taking her cup to the sink, Ruth called for Meg but she was nowhere to be seen and her food bowl was untouched. After hunting around the house and garden for the cat, Ruth dressed and knocked for Zoe, to find out whether Meg had ventured over there.

The moment she had stepped into Zoe's large and modern house, the impending excitement of Christmas hit her. Zoe's three boys were running around, laughing as they chased each other from room to room. From the snug, she could hear a Christmas film playing. Fancy tinsel had been wrapped around the banister and fairy lights twinkled in the kitchen. It was a far cry from Ruth's modest Christmas tree and she felt the weight of her sadness grow as she remembered all the effort she had gone to at Christmas when Cas had been growing up. He wouldn't even be home for Christmas this year and Ruth could not help but wonder if things would have been different if she and Grayson had a happier marriage. Damn him! Ruth realised that her fists were tightly clenched. He had taken the zeal from her over the years and now what was left? She was an empty shell of her former self, slowly hollowed out over the years by what had become a loveless marriage.

Sensing her pain, Zoe gave her arm a squeeze. "Great to have you over here, Ruth. Did you manage to get any sleep last night?"

"A bit," Ruth replied and smiled over at Paul who was making a pot of coffee.

Changing the subject, in an attempt to brighten Ruth's mood, Zoe nodded over towards an impressive looking Christmas cake. "Paul has just applied the final touches. Can we tempt you with a slice?" Zoe picked up a knife, eager to get stuck in, but Paul was having none of it.

"Easy tiger, this is a masterpiece and I'd like it on display for at least five minutes before you start hacking away at it." He moved the cake away and lifted the coffee pot. "Coffee?"

Ruth laughed at the pleasant banter between the pair of them. "Just a glass of water, thanks." She followed Zoe into the lounge and watched her open the door of the wood burner to throw another log in. Dusting off her hands, she pointed at a plate of iced gingerbread on the coffee table. "More of Paul's handiwork there. Help yourself."

"My goodness, he has been busy." The biscuits looked delicious but Ruth wasn't even tempted. The prospect of meeting Jeremy for dinner that evening had made her a bundle of nerves.

Zoe took a biscuit for herself and dunked it into her coffee. "A glass of water and nil by mouth. You're not yourself, Ruthie. I'm not surprised, of course." Her attractive features folded into a scowl. "Not after what that total arse has done. You can't starve yourself though."

"I'll be fine. I just need a bit of time to get my head around the whole thing. If you don't mind, I'd rather not talk about Grayson."

Zoe set her cup down. "Of course, I understand completely. But you do know you can come to me for anything. Paul's absolutely on your side too."

"Thanks." Ruth sipped at her water. "Meg hasn't passed by on her adventures, has she?"

"No, I've not seen her at all. Has she gone MIA?"

"It seems she pulled a moonlight flit and hasn't come back since. She hasn't touched her breakfast and she didn't come pestering me for a morning cuddle. That's not like her."

Curling up on the sofa, Zoe called out to Paul, asking him if he'd seen Meg at all. Paul appeared in the doorway wiping his hands on a towel. "Not seen her, no. Want me to ask the boys?"

"Yes, do that and tell them to keep an eye out," Zoe said before turning back to face Ruth. "Don't worry too much about her. Cats do this all the time. She won't have gone far. I'm sure."

"I'd just like her back before I go to stay with Tim. Mrs Tibbs said she would look after her but I won't go until I know she's back safe and sound. I wanted to leave tomorrow. I don't think I can face staying here much longer after everything that has happened."

"That's understandable. Will you call him?"

"Already tried. I doubt I'll see him again before Christmas and I'm not even sure that I want to."

Giving her a look of sympathy, Zoe rested the remainder of her biscuit on her saucer. "You know you can pop over here tonight and we'll shut ourselves away from the rabble and just have a proper heart to heart."

"Thanks Zoe, I appreciate it. As it happens though, I'm going out tonight." No sooner than she had said it, Ruth felt a wave of guilt, as though it were she who was doing wrong by Grayson.

"Oh? Anyone I know?" She lifted her coffee cup to her mouth and took a sip as she waited for Ruth's answer.

"Mr X."

Almost spitting out her drink, Zoe's eyes widened. "The guy who I saw walking down your path yesterday?"

Ruth nodded and tried to ignore the flutter in her stomach.

"Well good on you. You certainly don't waste time." She leaned forward and lowered her voice. "Mr X is hot!"

Aghast, Ruth was quick to deny the romance Zoe had assumed was blooming. "It's not like that at all and his name is Jeremy, by the way! Besides, I'm quite sure he has a girlfriend, or at least a woman he's romantically attached to. This dinner is strictly professional." Ruth flipped her curls over shoulder and tried to ignore the look of scrutiny Zoe was giving her. "It's all very strange though..." Relieved to have the opportunity to change the subject from her failed marriage, she told Zoe all about the necklace that Jeremy had brought to her. As she proceeded to share the events that had led to the dinner arrangement, she made sure to gloss over the particularly peculiar parts. Zoe was used to her supernatural stories but these just seemed too far-fetched.

"How many of your other clients have you agreed to dinner with?" Determined not to give up on her line of inquiry, Zoe raised her eyebrows.

"Don't start trying to read any more into this than the plain and simple fact that we are working on a complicated case. Honestly Zoe, I've never experienced anything like this before." Ruth hoped that the inexplicable guilt she felt for looking forward to the dinner wasn't written all over her face. "We're trying to get to the bottom of where the necklace originally came from. Evidently it is a family heirloom of sorts, but this is where the mystery love interest comes in. He's very closed off about who gave it to him. He says that it dates back to the seventeenth century and was likely to have had pagan use."

"Sounds fascinating." Zoe turned to check that Paul wasn't in earshot and leaned forward, "You have to admit that this Jeremy is an absolute dish. The dinner invite couldn't have come at a better time. Anyway, this isn't a sudden thing with Grayson. You've been unhappy for a long time."

"You really need to stop this, Zoe!" Exasperated, Ruth gave her friend a pleading look. She could not have this getting out as being anything other than the innocent arrangement that it was. "Like I said, it's purely professional."

Seeing the distress on her face, Zoe apologised. "You're right. Sorry, that was out of order. I won't keep going on. I just want for you to be happy."

"I know and in time things will get better. A real Mr X will come along and sweep me off my feet, I'm sure. Just not yet though. You won't tell Paul about the dinner, will you? I don't want him jumping to the wrong conclusions."

Zoe mimed pulling a zipper across her lips. "I promise."

To Ruth's relief, the conversation was interrupted by Archie, Zoe's eldest. "Mum, Mrs Tibbs is here."

Zoe craned her neck to try and look behind him. "Well show her through, love. Where is she?"

"At the door."

"Oh Archie, don't tell me you've just left her standing there in the cold?" Flashing Ruth a look that said, 'Kids!', she got up to go and greet Mrs Tibbs.

Zoe returned to the room with a happy grin on her face. "Looks like Meg fancied a change of scene."

Mrs Tibbs followed her through, cradling Meg in her arms. The cat was lapping up the attention and almost drooling as she purred. "Morning, Ruth dear. When there was no reply at your house, I thought you might be here. Found this one tapping away at my back door first thing. Poor thing was frozen half to death. I fed her some leftovers from the chicken last night. I hope you don't mind?"

Hurrying over to give Meg a tickle behind the ears, Ruth breathed a sigh of relief. "Thank you, Mrs Tibbs and of course I don't mind. She must have bolted during the night. I came over here looking for her as she never misses a meal."

"Poor love," Mrs Tibbs said, "I wonder if it was fireworks? I do wish folk would stop with all that at random times of year. In my day, it was fireworks on Guy Fawkes night only. And what about all these whizzes and bangs they have now too? It's all really very unnecessary." She went to hand Meg over to

Ruth, but the cat arched her back and hissed before making a swipe and catching the back of Ruth's hand.

"Oh!" It was all that she could say as she felt the hot sting of Meg's claws.

Struggling to keep hold of the cat, Mrs Tibbs tried to soothe her but she jumped from her arms and ran behind the sofa.

"What's got into that cat?" Zoe exclaimed as she tried to coax Meg from her hiding place.

"It's the necklace," Ruth answered as she and Mrs Tibbs each took a turn at trying to encourage the frightened animal out from behind the sofa. "I told you Zoe, it's haunted. There's your proof."

Muttering a string of expletives, Zoe caught herself and looked around, checking to ensure her children weren't in earshot. Mrs Tibbs was far too distracted to have noticed the swearing or anything that Ruth had said.

"Perhaps it's better that you keep hold of her for the time being, Mrs Tibbs," Ruth suggested. "Something is obviously upsetting her and I don't want to risk her running away, especially before I leave for Somerset."

Mrs Tibbs looked delighted but reluctantly gave Ruth the opportunity to change her mind. "If you're sure, dear? I know how much you love her."

"And I know how much she loves you. I'm leaving tomorrow anyway and I know she will be in safe hands with you. I'll bring you a good supply of food and all of her things."

"Of course, dear." Mrs Tibbs had managed to scoop Meg up. "She will be well looked after, don't you fret about that. You just enjoy your Christmas." She glanced down at Ruth's hand and the stream of blood that was beginning to fork its way over her skin. "I'd get some antiseptic on that and a plaster." She turned to Zoe. "Don't worry about me. I can see myself out. Just see to it that Ruth here is patched up. I'll see you the day after tomorrow, Zoe, for the pre-Christmas clean."

As Zoe located the first aid kit, she turned to Ruth. "You will let me know when you're back tonight, won't you?"

"Yes, mum," Ruth joked but she appreciated her friend's concern. "And I'll pop over tomorrow before I leave." They finished cleaning up Ruth's hand and then said their goodbyes.

******

The cathedral was spectacularly lit in a haze of pink and purple and she could hear a carol service from inside. "Beautiful, isn't it?" The pleasant twang of Jeremy's voice made her turn. Smiling, he handed her a mulled wine.

Thanking him, Ruth took it and suggested they take a walk around the market. The rich smell of roasting chestnuts, spices and street food scented the air and they laughed together as they watched people tackling the ice-rink in the centre of it all. "I knew that Winchester was renowned to be a beautiful city, but I hadn't realised that I'd be blown away by it. There's so much heritage, so much history that's been protected and nurtured here. The buildings, the features in town, just the very feel of it… I love it all!" Jeremy exclaimed as they weaved their way through the crowds, looping around the little market stalls until they were in front of the entrance to the cathedral again.

Ruth laughed, unable to help herself being swept away with his enthusiasm. "I've never thought too much about all the history here, until I met you that is," she admitted and drank the last of her mulled wine, enjoying the rich spiciness as it warmed her palate.

"It's amazing really. This is why I love Britain. It's so full of history."

"You need to go to York."

"For the history?" he asked as they walked back towards the main high street.

"It's supposed to be the most haunted city in England."

"It's history I'm interested in, not ghosts," he reminded her, relieving her of her cup and tossing it into a recycle bin.

"I know," she replied with a smile and she wrapped her arms around herself to keep warm. "But don't you agree that where there are lots of ghosts, there must be an abundance of history?"

He thought for a moment and then nodded. "I hadn't thought of it like that, but you're right." The starbursts around his eyes deepened as he smiled. "I like the way you do that."

"Do what?"

"Make me consider things from a different angle. I've never met anyone who has managed to do that before." He fell silent and the moment turned awkward.

Feeling her neck and face grow hot, Ruth looked ahead and pointed. "Over there," she said, desperate to change the subject, "that's the street that The Eclipse pub sits on."

"Ah, the place where Dame Alice Lisle was executed," he said and he looked relieved that the conversation had so swiftly changed. "She was the last woman to be beheaded by judicial sentence in England, you know." So as not to be overheard by passers-by, he lowered his voice. "Do you feel okay here? No strange sensations from that necklace? No weird thoughts triggering?"

Grateful for his concern, Ruth shook her head. "Not a thing. But it is strange as I can envisage it all as if it's an old memory." They looked down the street as they passed by the pub.

"What was it like?" Jeremy asked. "Seeing it all in person, I mean?"

"I only remember snippets," Ruth replied. "I don't think Kat actually witnessed the beheading of Alice Lisle. I can only recall that she knew it had happened. I think she was with her grandmother at the time. She was dying."

"Oh, I see." He sounded disappointed and Ruth frowned.

"I don't think I could have coped if she had been there and I had witnessed it. What a dreadful thing to see happen."

"But back then it was usual for an execution to bring lots of spectators." Jeremy rubbed his chin. "No different to you or I watching a gory horror film on television."

Shuddering, Ruth wrinkled up her nose. "It's completely different! Horror films aren't real. Those sorts of things were. It's bloody awful and barbaric!"

With a shrug, Jeremy led the way as they walked through the arch that took them on to the High Street. "It's history."

Ruth had no response to that one and each of them lost in their own private thoughts, they took their table in the restaurant.

After the waitress had poured the wine, it was all Ruth could do not to glug it back to take the edge off her nerves. It wasn't just being out with another man, but the memory of what had happened the night before. "So can you tell me a bit more about what happened last night?" Jeremy broke the silence and his gaze penetrated hers.

Nodding, Ruth took a breath and recounted all that she had experienced. "The thing is," she confided, referring to the way that the dreams and visions were taking hold, "I've not ever had this happen before and I'm not sure that I'm altogether okay with it."

He wore a look of concern as he lifted his glass. "You need to tell me everything, Ruth. It's my fault that this is happening to you. If I hadn't come to your doorstep-"

"No!" Ruth was quick to snap. It wasn't fair that he was taking the burden of responsibility on his shoulders. "It's not your fault and if you keep blaming yourself, I'm not going to share anything more with you."

"Woah!" Jeremy leaned back in his chair. "I guess I've been told! It's just that I feel so guilty for involving you."

"It's my job," Ruth added quietly as the starters were brought over. It wasn't until they had finished their first course that Ruth broached the real reason why Jeremy had arranged the reading with her. "So, I just have to come out with it." After her last mouthful of fish, she set down her knife and fork. "I don't think you've been entirely truthful with me."

Jeremy stiffened and visibly paled. So, there was something that he was hiding from her. She recalled the reading and how that final card had brought on the sensation of drowning. It hadn't been connected to Kat, but an entirely different woman and Ruth had felt her presence attached to the necklace too. When she had turned that card, she had sensed that Jeremy was somehow connected to the drowning woman. He had been there when she had lost her life. The sensation and vision came hurtling back to her at breakneck speed: The wild foaming waves, the moment her head had dipped beneath them, submerged into what she knew would become a murky grave. The vision whirred through her mind as she witnessed how the woman's survival instinct had struggled against the water filling her lungs. Her brain told her she needed to swim upwards but something had been holding her down, stopping her from breaking through the foaming blue. Somebody had asked for forgiveness at that point, their voice an eerie echo against the thrash of the waves. The more she thought about it, the more positive she was that it had been Jeremy's voice she had heard. He had been there when it had happened. He had seen it happen and worse, he had been involved.

He had noticed the distant look on her face and the worry lines on his deepened. "Ruth?" He reached out to touch her across the table but she recoiled.

"Something happened, didn't it?" Ruth glared at him, challenging him to deny it. When he said nothing, she pressed him further. "It's not the origin of the necklace that your mind was questioning when you came to me, was it? That was just an excuse."

"What did you see?" His voice was quiet and she noticed his bottom lip tremble.

"It's not so much what I saw, but what I felt." The sensation was still there, in the back of her mind, fighting its way past everything that she had experienced with Kat. This was another spirit trying to get through, a soul who she could sense had only recently departed its mortal shell. The gentle hum of happy voices and clatter of cutlery began to fade away and Ruth was aware of a heat by her right shoulder. Somebody was with them. She eyed Jeremy carefully, trying to assess whether he had noticed but he was looking down at his plate. There was no denying the shame painted on what she could see of his face and something else too: deep pain.

The heat behind her intensified and she turned to see the air moving. This wasn't Kateryn Fox, it was another woman. Ruth closed her eyes, tried to focus on the name. "Who was Cathy?" she asked just as the waitress returned to clear their plates.

Jeremy's chair shot back and heads turned. He looked around, his face panic stricken. "Excuse me please," he said, before heading in the direction of the toilets.

The main course had arrived by the time he returned and he looked worse than he had before he had left. People were staring again and Ruth wanted to tell them to mind their own business. The presence behind her shoulder had long disappeared but a scent lingered: white lilies and musk.

Unable to hide her curiosity, the waitress hovered for longer than needed as she brought everything to their table. Ruth could tell that she was hoping to get a hint of whatever had caused Jeremy's dramatic exit to the toilet, but he kept his eyes on the food in front of him, avoiding Ruth's gaze.

Thanking the waitress for the food and telling her for the second time that there really wasn't anything more that they required, Ruth waited until she was out of earshot before speaking. "She was here."

Although her voice was barely audible, Jeremy's head snapped up. "What?"

"Cathy was here," Ruth confirmed.

His mouth quivered and his eyes sparked. Was that fear, guilt or sadness in them? Maybe it was all three? Ruth knew what she had to say. "There was no animosity to her presence. No anger. She gave me a message for you, Jeremy. She said: 'I do'."

Placing a wad of notes on the table, Jeremy got up again. "I'm sorry. I have to leave." His words were choked by emotion. Whatever secret he was harbouring, the feelings were still raw and the guilt was plain on his face. Whatever was running through his head pained him physically. Ruth could see that clearly. She watched as he left the restaurant and once again, heads turned in her direction. They probably thought that she and Jeremy had fallen out over something and she wondered if perhaps they had? Mortified, Ruth asked for the bill, apologised to the amused looking waitress and made her exit.

CHAPTER EIGHTEEN

The taxi took a painfully long time to bump down the unmade track back to the farm estate. Paying his fare, Jeremy hurried across the puddled courtyard and jammed his key into the lock. For the whole journey he had been holding back the emotion that was threatening to spill over.

Inside the house it was still mercifully warm. It felt empty without Rex, though. Roy and Lisa had returned and collected him just before he had gone to meet Ruth. Without him padding about the place with the lazy look in his eyes, everything felt hollow. Jeremy reached for a heavy crystal cut glass and filled it with a generous measure of whisky before slugging it back, the amber liquid was blissfully sweet as it burned his throat. Breathing deeply, he steeled himself before draining the rest.

Picking up the bottle, he wandered into the lounge and slumped into a chair before pouring another. On the coffee table was the box that contained the unopened document that had arrived along with some of the storage boxes earlier that day; the name on the front had been scribed in a fine tip and the ink was so old that he was surprised it had survived the test of time. The letter had been intended for Cathy but she clearly never got around to opening it – or couldn't bring herself to. Things had been tough when the solicitor had got in touch. Jeremy and Cathy had barely been speaking. She had looked at him with such resentment at times and then she had been really sweet to him again. It had been a rollercoaster of emotion and he supposed she had known what his reaction would have been if he had seen the deliciously tempting unbroken wax seal that was holding together the crisp parchment. This was a valuable artefact, possibly more so than the necklace. Breaking the seal would cause damage. There were ways of reading letters like this. Still, the fact that it bore her name and the year it was to be delivered to her unnerved him. The hand that had written it would be long gone; flesh rotted to bone. Lifting the lid of the box, he carefully picked up the parchment and brought it to his nose, inhaling the earthy odour. For a moment, he considered opening it. No, he was not ready for that. Instead, he put the box on the bookshelf and thought again about the message that Ruth had told him was from Cathy: 'I do.'

It was the answer to the question he had silently asked when he had gone for the reading. Now he had the answer, it felt as though all the blood was draining from his head and seeping out from the soles of his feet. There was no sense of relief, no respite from the stabbing sensation of guilt. For a long time, he stared into the space in front of him and then his gaze fell upon the bookshelf once again. Behind the box was a small, neat row of books. One particular spine caught his eye. That particular book had belonged to *her*. It had been a firm favourite. He had seen her read it several times. It held its place on his bookshelf for posterity rather than anything that was of interest to him. The black, purple and scarlet of the cover reminded him of an angry bruise but it also reminded him of the day that life had been turned upside down. It had been a Sunday and she had been reading the book. They had been stuck indoors all weekend and he had asked her if she was going to join him on a walk. As had become usual, she had been miserable and snappy. It had seemed that she was always angry with him for everything he said and did. That had been the day he had snapped back:

"If you're not going to tell me what your problem really is, couldn't you at least just feign a smile, pretend that nothing is wrong, rather than being an utter bitch all the time?"

It had been a hot day, too hot. Jeremy had never fared well in the heat. That, and her mood swings, had been a recipe for disaster. A red mist clouding his vision, he had snatched the book from her hands, secretly pleased at the look of shock on her face. He had thrown it on the floor, stamped on it, told her that it was that kind of shit that was changing her, making her hate men. The shock on her face had dissolved into bubbles of anger. How dare he? How dare he be so aggressive? That accusation had made him laugh, although it was a laugh filled with irony rather than humour. He had reminded her how she had made him her doormat for the past few months, how he was not going to put up with it any longer. They had called each other names, got personal. He had asked her if she had developed some disease that had eaten away all the good parts of her personality and turned her into a complete bitch.

As he recalled the painful memory, Jeremy choked back a sob and squeezed his eyes shut.

They had both been angry and frustrated. She had said far worse to him but that did not excuse it. He recalled how her pretty face had twisted into something ugly and full of hatred. It had incensed him, driven him to the brink of getting personal to get back at her. He had wanted her to hurt as much as he had been hurting.

In a moment of fury, she had lunged for him, her small fists pounding into his stomach. He had yelled at her to stop. She hadn't stopped. She had kept going, letting all of her pent-up frustrations out. Coughing and wheezing, he had grabbed her by the wrists, forcing her to stop before she did any more damage. Then she had screamed the words that would change things forever.

Dinner with Ruth, the reading – it had brought it all back to him. With a cry of anguish, Jeremy threw his glass at the wall. It splintered into tiny pieces, the sound ricocheting around the room. What had Ruth seen? What was she holding back from saying to him?

Angrily, he dashed at the tears that were leaking from his eyes. He had been stupid to engage a medium. Pushing himself up from the sofa, he went to look in the mirror over the mantel, careful to avoid the shards of glass beneath his feet. Putting his hands to his face, he pulled down at the skin on his cheeks, applying pressure as he did so. He knew exactly why he had continued to stay in touch with Ruth Meadows. The necklace had been a convenient distraction of course. His real motives had been something entirely different. Now she had seen something that he had wanted to keep hidden and he couldn't help but want to find out what it was that she thought she knew. It was like picking at a scab; the more that peeled away, the more it hurt but it was impossible to resist.

Ruth Meadows had glimpsed into the darkness of his past and she was quickly putting two and two together. Finding his mobile in his coat pocket, he called the taxi back. He could not allow her to continue drawing any more conclusions about what had happened in his past.

CHAPTER NINETEEN

Ruth was shaking. The whole incident in the restaurant with Jeremy had left her embarrassed and self-conscious. Even when he had been at his worst, Grayson had never publicly humiliated her like that.

Kicking off her shoes, she looked at her reflection in the mirror. Tiny flecks of snow had settled in her hair. She gave the image staring back at her a sympathetic smile. "Silly, deluded woman," she said sadly as she considered her dented ego. Jeremy's swift and dramatic departure had made her realise that she had invested in some stupid notion that going out with a man for dinner was going to give her a sense of validation, make her feel feminine and wanted again. Disgusted with herself, she grabbed a tissue from the decorative box on the hall table and dabbed at her eyes. It served her right. She had gone out with a man who was not only clearly already romantically involved with another woman but had some sinister connection to a dead one.

Balling up the tissue, Ruth threw it into the bin to the side of the console table. It shouldn't be a surprise that she had found somebody like him; wasn't that what people did when they were emotionally vulnerable - attract the worst possible type? After years of feeling like a spare part, she had been craving companionable male company. The casual flirtatious comments with Jeremy, the additional attention she had spent on her appearance that evening, it had all been a dead giveaway. Zoe had seen it all and Ruth had denied it.

Feeling even more foolish, she stepped into her slippers and made her way into the lounge. She had to pull herself together. There was something dark about Jeremy. Something was lurking in his past. Feeling hurt and upset by the fact that he had walked out on her in a restaurant was just ridiculous. She should consider it a lucky escape.

Drumming her fingers against the arm of the chair she had perched on, Ruth thought about the necklace. Would he want it back? It was clearly valuable. Worry began to hover on the periphery of her mind. She felt an irrational possessiveness over it. It had only just found her. She needed to hold it in her palm again, feel the familiar, cool smoothness of the pendant.

Hurrying upstairs, she opened the drawer. It was exactly as she had left it. The chain was coiled over the top of the pendant stone like a silver serpent guarding treasure. Holding her breath, Ruth lifted it. Even touching it made her feel closer to Kat. The moment she had crossed the threshold of her bedroom, she had been able to feel the power emanating from the stone. Was that Kat's power or the necklace? Bringing it to her lips, she whispered: "Speak to me, Kat. Are you here with me now?"

Ruth wasn't sure what to expect but the house remained silent and the obsidian inanimate. Of course, she knew that this was not the way to invoke the spirit world. They would not just arrive on demand – not unless they were devious, miscreant souls.

Tucking the necklace back into its place in the drawer, she sighed, but then she stopped and held her breath. Something had changed in the atmosphere. Her gaze rested on the door. She had pushed it shut upon entering the bedroom so she could see nothing of the landing beyond it but she could have sworn she had seen a movement in the gap at the bottom. The murmur of a shifting floorboard from outside the room caught her attention and Ruth berated herself for trying to invoke Kateryn's spirit. She had heard of hitchhikers from the other realm, those who stalked the layer between the mortal and immortal, biding their time to pounce. This was the danger of sudden invocations like the Ouija board or seances. Ruth had avoided them for her whole psychic career and she had no idea how to reverse summoning a bad entity. In front of her, she thought she could see the handle of the door twitch a fraction.

Frantically, she searched the room for a talisman, anything that she could use to protect herself. There wasn't even an incense stick. The handle jarred and she noticed how the air was rent with a sense of desperation. She could sense death, betrayal and darkness. The presence was suffocating and she could feel ethereal fingers jabbing at her skull, trying to permeate the bone.

Pressing her palm to the panel of the door, she focused on creating a barrier. Under no circumstances could she let it into her mind. This was a dark soul. In life it had seen horror, had fallen on the wrong path. In death, it had repented, but it was too late.

Stepping back again, Ruth whimpered. "Please, Kateryn, if you are here, stop this. Don't let the negative energy through. I am only a channel for Kateryn," she cried out fruitlessly. "I can only be a channel for the Godly, for those with pure intentions."

The door handle continued to jar violently and she thought she heard a breathless whispering. "You are not welcome here!" she called, trying to sound brave, but her voice betrayed her. The fingers continued to dig and poke, feeling for a crack in her armour. Ruth knew that this was not a spirit who had entered the afterlife naturally; this was the spirit of another. It wanted to show her the guilt that it carried, to lay its sins bare for her to see, but Ruth did not want to know.

She began to back away from the rattling door. Her mind was whirling and it felt as though a thousand cogs were fruitlessly spinning as she attempted to think of a solution to get rid of whatever was behind the door, but Ruth didn't have the experience.

Three short sharp bangs were followed by the house being thrust into silence. The atmosphere lifted immediately and everything was still once again. Holding her breath, Ruth waited, ears keen. She tiptoed across the room and gently pressed her ear against the wooden panelling. The three bangs sounded out again and she realised that it was somebody at her front door.

CHAPTER TWENTY

Jeremy had been the last person who she had expected to see on her doorstep. His brown hair was peppered with the flurry of snowflakes that had been falling and he was shivering. Full of apologies, he insisted that he needed to explain things to her.

The irony of her dilemma was not on lost her: Remain alone in the house with a potentially malevolent spirit, or let in a man whom she suspected could be responsible for another woman's death. Under the circumstances, the latter option held marginally more appeal.

Glowering at him, she opened the door wider and sidestepped so that he could enter the house. They did not speak before they were both in the kitchen. Standing at opposite ends, Ruth deliberately declined to offer him a seat or any form of hospitality. Leaning against the kitchen counter, she folded her arms across her chest and Jeremy began pacing, his anxiety obvious. Instinctively, her hand hovered over her phone which was charging just behind her. His eyes rested on it.

"You're scared of me?" Jeremy's question was brimming with incredulity.

"You haven't done much to give me a reason to trust you," Ruth replied and she grasped her phone, holding it with the clear threat that she would not hesitate to use it if necessary. "Go on then, tell me what it is you so urgently need to share."

He pressed a hand to his forehead and groaned. "I know that I've behaved like a complete idiot, but it's complicated."

"Simplify it then. Tell me whatever it is that you came all this way to say and then we can move on."

He looked at her with doleful eyes and she noticed how heavily burdened he was. Taking a breath, he eyed her cautiously. "What is it that you *think* you know about me, Ruth?"

She didn't like the way he framed that question and her reply was curt. "I only know what the cards showed me."

"Is she here now? Is Cathy here?" There was urgency in his tone. It wasn't from panic, but a much deeper emotion. This was pain.

Ruth shut her eyes, took several deep breaths and waited for the strange static that she had felt in the air when they had been in the restaurant. "Nothing."

For a while, neither spoke. Jeremy dropped his head into his hands, pinching the bridge of his nose with thumb and forefinger. Whatever was on his mind was difficult for him to impart.

"We could try the cards again?" Ruth suggested in a quiet voice. Even as she said it, she could not quite believe what she was offering to do when, less than half an hour earlier, she had been certain that her tinkering had invited in some malevolent force. It seemed as though it was the only way to get the truth out of him and to find the closure that he so obviously needed.

Struggling to hold back tears, he appeared much smaller, more vulnerable. He did not fit the image of a cold-blooded murderer. "Do you think that will work?"

Ruth gestured for him to follow her to the room where she kept her Tarot deck. "If we don't try, we will never know." After flipping on the lights, she found the matches she kept on the sideboard and proceeded to light several candles. "Candles make for a better opportunity of contact. Flame, water, earth, any of these elements help," Ruth explained. Once she was done, she turned out the main light and gently shook the cards free of the green silk cloth.

Knowing that she was looking to connect with Cathy gave her a focus. It would be easier to keep Kateryn Fox and whatever darkness had accompanied her at bay whilst Ruth concentrated on the woman who had once been in Jeremy's life.

She watched as, with trepidation, Jeremy pulled up a chair. He could not keep his hands still for nerves.

"You need to verbalise your question, Jeremy," she instructed, glaring at him as she passed him the deck.

With cumbersome fingers he shuffled the cards before sliding them back across the table.

"Ask it now," Ruth said and she was surprised at how commanding her tone had become.

He looked at her with shining eyes. "Cathy?" he asked, his voice cracking as Ruth dealt a three-card spread: Past, present and future. "Cathy, I want to know if you forgive me?"

As she turned the first card, Ruth looked up, her senses alert. Why was he seeking forgiveness? What dreadful thing had he done? The questions began racing through her head and she tasted the bitterness of fear in her mouth. "The High Priestess," she whispered. "Reversed."

He stared at her, waiting for her to explain its meaning.

Ruth focused hard before saying anymore. At last, the words came to her: "Somebody has a secret, a terrible, dark secret."

******

Jeremy's mind raced back to the day that he had confronted Cathy. She had been so angry, so wild, so lost.

As he watched Ruth turn over the first card and listened to her speak about what went before him, he turned his mind back to his life in New Zealand. He remembered it all so vividly…

Cathy's wrists had felt so small and fragile in his hands but her eyes had burned into his as the words had tumbled from her mouth:

A tumour. The unbearable headaches, mood swings, forgetting things; all of it had been down to that. Too deep to operate.

As he had felt the weight of her crumple in his hold, he had also felt their world caving in. He hadn't let go of her that night, pressing her close to him, breathing in her familiar scent, feeling the beat of her heart against his chest, the warmth of her breath tickling his skin and trying not to wonder - when would be the last time that he would hold her in his arms?

She had said three months, possibly four, and if they were lucky, maybe even six. They had only been blessed with two.

Jeremy dropped his head into his palms and swallowed down the grief as the gnawing guilt returned. He didn't raise his head when Ruth's tone changed. She was speaking as though she was Cathy, reliving the stark horror of waking up to a searing agony, her sight in one eye stolen overnight. She had declined the care that would have left her drugged and persistently lethargic.

"I want to see the sun rise from the wrong side," she had told him. "I want to sit up all night and watch it come up over the horizon of the ocean, burning the sky pink and orange." So they had packed up the camper and had driven through the night, taking the Waikare Forest route to Russell. After they had arrived, they had sat in front of the van with croissants, fruit and a bottle of champagne, ready to watch the sun begin its ascent over the misted, foaming sea.

Cathy had clinked his glass and downed her champagne. "Easy," he had warned, "you know you shouldn't really be drinking this stuff."

"I'm dying, Jeremy." Her voice had been as cold and steely as the water that stretched beyond them. "I think that qualifies me to be allowed to drink whatever I want." Then she had held her glass out for another and quietly, he had obliged.

The memory hit him with full force. It was morbidly beautiful, the sort that he could get lost in but never dared to for fear of being unable to find his way out. Shaking his head to free himself from the image of Cathy, the wildness in her eyes, the way her untamed hair had fallen so carefree around her shoulders, framing her gaunt face, he looked across the table at Ruth. Tears were streaming silently down her cheeks and her eyes were closed.

Just as he began wondering whether Ruth was seeing things through his eyes or through Cathy's, her lids snapped open. The blue of her iris had muddied to a hazel and she flicked her tongue over her lips to speak, just as Cathy had always done. "It's the most beautiful sight I've ever seen," she said and Jeremy recognised those words. Ruth's voice had taken on the same soft twang as Cathy's. The way she had said it had been exactly as Cathy had on that day at Russell, when they had watched the sunrise from the 'wrong side'. He swallowed hard, recalling how she had turned to him, hazel eyes full of determination:

"I don't want to see another whitewashed wall, or smell any more detergent or sick, or the stench of medication and bedpans. Jeremy, I want this to be the last thing that I see before I go."

He hadn't known how to answer, so he had simply drawn her into his arms, wishing he could take all the fear and the agony away. All the while, he had been painfully aware that in a few hours they were supposed to be back in the hospital, that they couldn't put it off forever. They didn't have 'forever', he had reminded himself and he had held her tighter.

As though sensing his thoughts, Cathy had shifted in his embrace. In that moment, she had no longer felt so small and fragile. They had kissed and it had been deliciously long but full of melancholy. Jeremy had refilled his own glass and as he had drained it, he had felt the weight of both physical and mental exhaustion on his body. They had stretched out on the rocky alcove, the beginnings of a hot day breathing warmth on their skin, and Jeremy had shut his eyes, savouring the feeling of Cathy resting her head on his chest.

It had been the first perfect sleep in a long while. Nature had been their bed and for a blissful hour or so Jeremy had succumbed to the empty nothingness that sleep had brought. The sound of gulls had pulled him from the sanctuary of his rest and the first thing he had been aware of was the fact that the weight had lifted from his chest and his arms were empty.

Cathy had left his side. Beside him was the upturned bottle of champagne. They had packed another in the icebox though. Turning in the direction of the camper van, he expected to see Cathy bringing out the next one, laughing as she popped the cork. Then he had noticed the keys on the rock. Next to them something had been glinting in the orange hue of sunlight: Cathy's necklace. It had been the one that she had always worn and never taken off. She had once told him that it was a family heirloom.

"Stop, Ruth. Please stop." Jeremy opened his eyes as he choked out his plea. He had been unaware that he had even shut them.

Ruth did not move, but her cheeks were damp from tears that were still falling.

"Ruth, you need to stop this now," he said, his tone raised. He did not want to show her any more of that day. He did not want to see it all over again, face the reason for the shame and guilt that had haunted him ever since. He did not want anyone to know what he had done.

It was too late. The smell of sea salt pervaded the room and with it, the sound of water lapping at the rocks, accompanied by another sound. "Cathy!" he cried out, but just as it had been on that morning, she did not reply:

His heart had begun beating so wildly that he could feel and hear the blood pounding through his eardrums. A cocktail of anger and fear bubbled up inside him as he looked out towards the horizon, through the rapidly clearing mist.

Cathy was almost knee deep in water, wading out. "What about sharks, Cath? It's not a good idea!" He had called out to her, wishing that she would just stop with this crazy desire to be at one with nature for her last days.

She had not stopped, had not even hesitated. Nor had she turned to look back at him.

In the distance were the smooth, curved silhouettes of a school of dolphins as they broke the water's surface with a series of graceful leaps. He had wondered if Cathy had seen them too and was attempting to check something else off her bucket list. She had loved dolphins and had always wanted to swim with them in the wild.

Jeremy had run to the water's edge. "Cathy!" As he had called out to her, he had seen the weight of the rocks in her coat pockets, just before they had dipped beneath the surface. Then Cathy was partly swimming, partly propelling herself forward, by bouncing from the seabed with as much strength as she could muster.

Splashing and sliding, Jeremy waded in after her, but she made no attempt to slow down. She was beyond her depth. He had seen how her physical instincts had kicked in and how she had begun to splutter and gasp for air. She had not called out to him for help, though. As the awful scene had unfolded, Jeremy recalled what she had said to him earlier on the beach: "I want this to be the last thing that I see before I go."

Waist deep, he had stopped. "Forgive me." His sobbed words had been carried away by the thrash of waves and he had watched as the water swell had completely swallowed her. The darkness of her head could be seen faintly beneath the surface as the waves rolled towards the rocks. He might have been able to reach her if he had rushed swiftly forward, had started swimming, but he had done neither of those things. Instead, he had watched as the majesty of the ocean had welcomed Cathy into her watery grave.

The dolphins in the distance had disappeared and the morning sea mist had melted away beneath a glorious sun. Another day had started spectacularly, just as Cathy had taken her final gulp of salty, sea air.

They had dragged her body that evening. The weight of the cluster of rocks in her pockets had been no match for the pull of the undercurrent. Her body had been dragged to the cruel jagged edges of the rocks.

Jeremy had given his statement. He had said that they had fallen asleep, that he had been too late when he had woken up. He had not said that instead of trying to reach her, he had decided letting her go was the best way to save her. He had kept hold of that secret and locked it away in his mind: the image of her in her final moments, part swimming, part leaping into nature's wild and deadly embrace.

Ruth's house was calm again, the air clear. She was staring at him and her eyes had returned to their unique shade of blue. "That's what Cathy wanted," she whispered as she reached out and took his hands in hers. "She is so grateful that you had listened to what she had said, that you read between the lines and let her go." Ruth squeezed gently. "She said that there is nothing to forgive."

Unable to hold back the sob expelled from his body, Jeremy let the tears flow freely as relief and grief ebbed through him. "Is she still here?"

Ruth shook her head. The reading had drained her and left her shaken. "No, I can't feel her here any longer. She just wanted you to know." She paused. There was something else and he waited for her to tell him.

Ruth took a breath and she appeared perplexed. "There was one other thing," she started saying and paused to rub her head. She suddenly looked exhausted. "Cathy said that you have to break the seal." She paused, bewildered by the message that she was passing on. It held no meaning to Ruth. "She said that if you do not break the seal, everything will be altered."

For a few moments Jeremy was confused. "Break the seal?"

"Ask her what she means," he said but Ruth was shaking her head.

"She's gone."

They sat in silence and Jeremy chewed on his fingernails until Ruth got up to go and put the kettle on.

He looked out the window and could see that the snow was beginning to settle beneath the glow of the streetlamps at the bottom of the driveway. Why was Cathy speaking in riddles? What did she mean by 'break the seal'? He was still stewing over it when Ruth appeared carrying two mugs of tea.

"I'm sorry for your loss," she said quietly, handing him one of the mugs.

He took the mug and set it down. The lump in his throat was too prominent to drink anything. "Thanks."

"Did you understand her message?"

He shook his head.

"I suppose that sometimes the spirit world can become confused and the messages they send can scramble." She sighed and took a sip of tea. "It's probably the reason why people like me exist, to decode the more cryptic messages between the dead and the living."

"It's Cathy's family tree that I'm researching," he said quietly, his voice still a little shaky. "It was her necklace."

"I see." Ruth didn't appear surprised and Jeremy assumed she had already worked that part out.

The memories leading up to Cathy's death were still raw and it was as though somebody had ripped a plaster off a wound, picking it until it opened again. Then he remembered the letter that he had found in the storage boxes. He thought of the ruby red wax seal. Was that what Cathy's message had been referring to? It seemed obvious when he thought about it. "The mystery isn't over," he said at last. "I know you're due to go away for Christmas but do you think we could pick it all up when you're back? I'll pay you for your time, of course. I just think that there is something more to this, that there's a deeper link between Cathy and Kat." He paused and was on the brink of telling Ruth about the letter when her phone rang.

Her face paled as she looked at the screen. "I'm so sorry, but I need to get this."

Checking his watch, Jeremy smiled. "I really should be going. I'll call a cab. Don't rush that call."

As Ruth hurried off, he found the taxi number and called for the cab. They told him one was in the area and it would only be five minutes. Looking down the hallway, he considered shouting out a goodbye but decided against it. Something told him that he wouldn't see Ruth again before she left for Somerset. It was late to be receiving a call from anyone and he knew that she was having marital problems, although she had not divulged any great detail. He wondered if the call was from her wayward husband. Putting on his coat and shoes he opened the front door and went out in to the snow.

CHAPTER TWENTY ONE

Blinking in disbelief at her phone screen, Ruth hurried into the privacy of the conservatory before answering. "It's rather late for the obligatory call to your wife." She did not bother to disguise the bitter edge of her tone.

Ruth could hear the hum of a train in the background and the signal was dipping slightly. "Are you up?"

"About to go to bed, actually." She knew that she should confront him but she wanted to give him the chance to do the right thing and provide her with an explanation as to where he had been and who he had been with.

"It's just that the train is due in at five past and I don't know if I have a key."

So, he was on his way home. At least he hadn't had the audacity to ask her for a lift. "I'll leave the door unlocked."

"Will you be up when I get back?"

"I can wait. I assume it's just you catching the taxi from the station?" The question was loaded but he didn't appear to be fazed.

"Of course it is. I'll see you in about twenty-five minutes."

Putting the phone down, Ruth went to pour herself a glass of wine. It was all she could think of to take the edge off. When she heard the front door open, she was already pouring her second glass. The sound of Grayson plonking down his case and stamping the snow off his shoes travelled down the corridor and into the kitchen. He walked in looking smart but tired and washed his hands at the sink. "One there for me?" he asked, glancing at the wine glass in front of Ruth.

"Grab a glass from the cupboard and help yourself."

He took a seat on the other side of the table and she noticed that he didn't have his phone glued to his hand for once. Pushing the wine bottle towards him, she watched him pour a large glass and then take a glug. "What? No kiss or declarations of how much you have missed me?"

"Oh come on, Ruth. Don't be like that."

Irritation tweaked at her nerves and she glared at him. "Be like what? I don't think it's too much for a wife to ask of her husband. It's a quick kiss, a bit of affection. Especially after you haven't called or texted the whole time you've been away."

He took another swig of his wine, a look of annoyance crossing his face. "And since when did that start to bother you? We never talk when I'm away."

"We never talk," Ruth shot back.

Taking his wine into the living room, he shook his head. "Don't be so high maintenance, Ruth. I have enough of that to deal with from my clients. The last thing I need is for my wife to add to the load."

Furious, Ruth followed him through. "Maybe I'm sick and tired of being a doormat, Grayson. You come and go as you please, you barely acknowledge me and you certainly don't treat me like your wife, more like an employee who lives with you."

"Where is all this coming from? I work hard so that you get to live comfortably in a nice house in a lovely village. I supported you when you gave up your career. You don't want for anything. All I ask in return is for a bit of space to wind down after a busy trip away."

"I gave up my law career to bring up our son, in case you have forgotten. And I do work. I have two jobs. I don't sit on my laurels, Grayson. And I don't think I'm asking for anything unreasonable. I just want to be acknowledged, to be loved, to be more important to you than Veda bloody Watkins."

That stopped him. Placing down his wine glass, he narrowed his eyes, his face flushing. "Is that what this is about? You're jealous now?"

"Have I got reason to be?" She hovered on the threshold between the kitchen and living room, waiting for him to deny it, hoping that what Paul had seen had all been a huge misunderstanding and that Grayson wasn't making a fool of her.

His shoulders sagged and he looked away. "I had been intending on waiting until after Christmas. I didn't want to ruin things for you."

It was like being punched in the chest. "So it's true then? You're not even making any effort to deny it. You were planning on sitting at the Christmas dinner table with all of us pretending that we're still happy families."

He scoffed and stood up. "We've been far from that for a long time, Ruth. You have to admit it. We're hardly love's young dream."

Hurt by his indifference, Ruth felt her eyes fill with tears. "What did I ever do to you? I gave up everything for you."

"No. You gave it up for Cas. You just said that yourself."

Years of pent-up rage spilling over, Ruth found herself shouting. "Stop it! Just stop! Accept some responsibility for what you have done, Grayson. Stop trying to throw this on me."

"I'm not the only one who allowed this marriage to sour. Don't dare put all of this on me. You stopped being my wife a long time ago, Ruth."

"No. You stopped noticing me a long time ago. You haven't even noticed that I'm wearing a dress and make up right now! Don't you want to know where I have been, who I have been with?" She knew she was coming across as petulant and spiteful but the hurt and anger were spurring her on. "I'd happily tell you, but the truth is you wouldn't care if I'd been out with ten different men tonight, would you?"

Giving her a look of disgust, he brushed past her and reached for the coat he had slung over the back of the chair in the kitchen.

"Where are you going?" she demanded.

He whirled around. "Anywhere that gets me far enough away from you, from this shambles of a marriage." He picked up the keys to the four by four. "To think that I had decided against staying away, to at least come back and spend some time together, to keep things dignified."

"That's my car you're taking," she commented, choosing to ignore the outrageously unfair statement he had just made.

His retort was deadpan. "Mine is rear wheel drive. It doesn't handle the snow well and there's a lot forecast overnight."

"What about Somerset?" she asked, already knowing the answer.

"Please do give my apologies to your darling brother and Max. I'm sure I'll be sorely missed." His reply was full of sarcasm.

"You know it will be too risky for me to drive your car all that way in heavy snow. Stay here and I'll give you a lift to the station in the morning if you're going back to London."

"I'm not staying."

"Then you're not taking my car." She held her hand out for the keys.

Ignoring her, he picked up his bags. "I think you'll find both cars are registered in my name, darling. I'll take whichever one I please."

"But how do you suppose I'll get to Tim's tomorrow?"

On his way out the door he shrugged. "Not my problem, Ruth." He didn't wait for a reply and she was left in the hallway, mouth open in shock. The tears came suddenly, her body shaking. He had always had a hard side that lacked empathy, but he had never been so mean and cold.

Sleep had been surprisingly easy. After the initial shock of Grayson leaving, Ruth had felt a strange sense of release. There would be no barbed comments designed as 'jokes' on the journey to her brother's house; no more listening to his snoring and being sworn at if she dared ask him to turn over; no more derisive looks that made her feel ugly and worthless; no more scornful questioning of everything she said or did and no more feeling invisible, unheard, unimportant. It didn't matter that it was only over Christmas, the point was that she was free.

A wet layer of muddy slush lined Ruth's driveway. Tim had already been on the phone, insisting that he would drive out and pick her up rather than attempting to drive Grayson's sports car and that she must not let a bit of snow thwart their plans for Christmas. He had been unable to hide his relief that Grayson would not be accompanying her and doing his usual sulking and moaning about being 'stuck in the middle of nowhere'.

In true 'Tim' fashion, he had asked if there was a companion who she could bring to make up the numbers and add to the Christmas spirit. She had laughed it off, but it made her heart feel heavy. The feeling of being free of Grayson was of course, a double-edged sword.

"Leaving already?" Zoe appeared from around the hedge that divided their houses. She had no doubt spotted Ruth from the vantage point of her upstairs study. Looking dazzlingly festive in a black and gold poncho top that had been slung over a black polo neck, her dark tight curls were still damp from her morning shower. "Not that I blame you of course," she added, looking fretfully at the heavy-bellied clouds overhead. "I had rather hoped the snow might keep you here. It would have been great to have you over on Christmas Day. We could have knocked back champagne and slagged off Grayson into the small hours." Noting the look that Ruth shot her, she apologised. "Sorry, I know that's not your style. But I'm just so cross on your behalf. If he comes back whilst you're away, I'll be straight over. He won't get away with this, Ruthie. Paul is on the warpath too."

"He did come home last night."

Zoe looked shocked. "What?! Did you speak to him? Did he admit to anything?"

"In a way," Ruth answered. "He didn't deny it when I confronted him. It all ended in a row. I got a few things off my chest and he said a few things too."

"He should have been grovelling, not entertaining an argument," Zoe spat the words out with disgust. She peered over Ruth's shoulder. "What's he doing now?"

"He went back to London. Took my car and left me the one that is hopeless in any kind of dusting, let alone the snowstorm that's been forecast."

"Oh crikey." Zoe glanced at the garage where the little sports car was tucked away. "Any chance you'll change your mind and stay here instead? I mean it when I say you're always welcome."

"Actually, I was rather hoping you would give me a lift to the station."

Disappointed, Zoe folded her arms across her chest as she shivered against the bitter air. "Absolutely I'll take you to the station, but are you sure you won't stay? Keep an old friend company, save me from the in-laws?"

Ruth gave Zoe an apologetic smile as she went to fetch her luggage and the gift that she had for her. "Sorry, making a dash for it before the railway line madness starts. You know how it is in this country when a bit of snow starts to fall." She frowned. "You won't say anything to anyone about Grayson, will you?"

Aghast, Zoe shook her head. "Of course not. Neither of us would do that. I know that it was us who broke the news to you, but you must know that we are both on your side and here to support you."

"Thanks, I know that and I appreciate it."

As they hugged, the sound of tyres crunching through snowfall approached and Jeremy's Defender pulled up onto the driveway.

Raising her eyebrows, Zoe gave a knowing smile. "Looks like you might not need my services after all. The knight in shining armour has just arrived." She gave Jeremy a wave before going back inside.

He lowered the window. "Everything alright when I left you last night? Sorry I didn't say goodbye. I thought it best I leave you to it."

"Everything was fine," she replied but the look on her face was not at all convincing. "Want a quick coffee? I'm just finishing packing as I'm catching the train in an hour."

"You're not driving down?"

Rolling her eyes, Ruth gestured for him to follow her indoors. "Long story."

They sipped their coffee in the conservatory with the heaters on. Ruth explained what had happened and he didn't appear at all surprised. "I could tell there was trouble in paradise when that call came through."

Ruth gave a snort. "I'd hardly call it paradise. Not for a long while I'm afraid." She looked out the window. The snow had started falling in thicker clumps and the garden was quickly becoming a blanket of white. "Anyway, enough of my problems, what about you? What do you have planned for Christmas?"

"Beans on toast, a bottle of cheap champagne and a cheesy film."

"Wow! Pushing the boat out then?" They both laughed and Ruth felt suddenly reckless. "Why don't you come with me? Tim and Max are desperate for another person to join us. They love a good party."

Jeremy looked hesitant. "It's a tempting offer but I'll be quite happy with the beans and champagne. I might even drink it from a flute rather than a mug."

"Sounds idyllic," she joked but she was embarrassed by the rebuff. It was too forward after what she had just told him about Grayson and had likely given the wrong impression. Flicking her wrist, she checked her watch. "I should really get going. Can't afford to miss this train and risk any delays."

After saying her goodbyes to Zoe, she hopped into the Defender next to Jeremy and they headed to the station. Insisting that he help her with her luggage, Jeremy parked up and accompanied her to the platform just as the announcement chimed out the delay. "I'll wait with you," he offered and suggested they sit in the café.

"You don't have to." Ruth was still feeling the sting of the embarrassing rejection of her innocent invitation to join her for Christmas.

Reaching for her arm, he gave it a squeeze. The gesture took her by surprise. "I'd like to."

They sat in the little café to the side of the station, chatting about anything and everything until the voice over the tannoy announced that the train was in fact cancelled. Ruth felt crestfallen. She hadn't realised how much she had been looking forward to arriving at Tim's and just getting away from the disaster that her life had become. "Looks like I'll be quaffing champagne with Zoe after all," she said, trying to sound upbeat and like she wasn't at all bothered.

"Is it too late to accept your earlier offer?"

"What?"

"If it still stands that is," he added with a bashful smile. "The Defender might be a few years old but it's the ideal set of wheels for all weather. Besides, it's the perfect excuse to get away and have a bit of an adventure. Truth be told I wasn't entirely comfortable about being so far away from you with the mystery surrounding the necklace unresolved."

"It would be great to have you join us, Jeremy. The offer was never retracted."

He grinned and looked genuinely excited. "In that case, give me ten minutes back at the cottage to pack my things and we'll be on our way."

When they crossed the Somerset border, a heavier flurry of snow had begun to fall and the traffic had slowed considerably. Jeremy needed to stop for petrol before they hit the country roads, so they pulled into a garage at a large supermarket. After taking the opportunity to grab some sandwiches for lunch, as well as stocking up on wine and champagne for the Christmas table, they sat in the car and ate before continuing the rest of the journey.

Jeremy peeled back the film on his sandwich carton. "I was up early this morning as I wanted to do a bit of research on our spectral friend."

"And?"

"I couldn't find anything that documented a Kateryn Fox in Winchester or Dorchester. What did you say her husband's name was?"

"Gideon. I think she wants me to help her find him. She has doubts about his business trip and is worried that he was somehow caught up in the Monmouth Rebellion."

Jeremy looked thoughtful. "We should be able to find a record of those trialled online, and failing that there are the archives. There's still a lot more for me to research on Cathy's family too and as we know that the necklace belonged to this Kateryn Fox, I'm assuming that I'm going to find her which means I might well find her husband, Gideon. I packed the laptop so I can put a bit of late-night work in." His eyes dimmed and he frowned. "The thing I can't quite fathom out from this family tree is that I keep hitting a dead end with this guy who died in 1732 and things just don't seem to be adding up.

"He had four sons but one seems to have been well educated in law and extremely well connected - very strange for somebody who is from a family with no hint of wealth."

"What makes you come to that conclusion?" Ruth took a bite of her sandwich.

"Because that son was a lawyer who also went on to have a son who appears to be directly connected to the Bridport Treaty, a very influential political campaign that lobbied for the eventual abolition of slavery. To have become that respected and influential, he would have needed to move in the right circles and have had some sort of wealthy background. But there is no record of his father's birth or his mother's, which suggests to me that this was a family of little money. It gets far more difficult to trace back those family trees with little or no wealth due to the lack of records."

"And where does Kat fit into all this? If the necklace has been passed down through Cathy's ancestors, she must surely feature somewhere and that might help us with what happened to Gideon."

Jeremy shook his head. "That's just it. I still can't trace any further back than 1732 and there's no mention of a Kateryn Fox within the family, or any surname 'Fox'."

"Do you think the necklace somehow ended up in Cathy's lineage some other way then?"

Tapping the edge of the steering wheel, he looked pensive. "Possibly. Foul play, passed into different hands when Kateryn Fox was on her deathbed, or it could have been something she lost and somebody else found it."

Ruth felt despondent. "So, it's pretty much like looking for a needle in a haystack then?"

"I haven't given up yet and I think there's still a lot we can do to try and find out what happened to Gideon and whether he really was caught up in the rebellion. A good start would be to view the complete list of names of those held, executed and transported. It's not just as simple as looking them up on the internet. Much better to get directly to the source and so it's pretty convenient we're headed to Somerset. Taunton's Somerset Heritage Centre has an archive of the documentation we'll need. I just need to get a reading card."

"How do you go about doing that?"

"I've got all the ID I need. Fortunately, I've been living in the country long enough to have clocked up a couple of utility bills. If an e-copy isn't enough, I'm sure I can get Lisa and Roy to let themselves into the cottage and post me something."

It meant nothing to Ruth, but she nodded and smiled. If it helped Kat, she was happy to follow his lead. "I just want to help her," she said, "but I really don't understand why after all the generations that necklace has passed through, it's me, or us, that she's reaching out to."

"Why do you think most of your clients come to you?" Jeremy asked.

Shrugging, Ruth looked out of the window into the busy car park. "Lots of reasons. Loneliness, comfort, peace of mind…" She turned her head towards him and added: "And some are looking for forgiveness."

He bristled at that and closed his sandwich box leaving the crusts. "Pass me your rubbish," he said, changing the subject. "I'll take everything out to the bin and then we should get on our way."

Ruth handed it over and swigged at her water as she watched him find a bin. She bit down on her bottom lip, feeling guilty. She had touched a nerve.

When they were back on the road, Ruth dared to broach it again. "How are you feeling – about everything?"

His jaw tightened for a moment and he paused before answering. "Better now I have peace of mind that Cathy's okay." He took a sharp breath as he bit back on his emotion. "But even though she said there's nothing to forgive, I'll probably never forgive myself."

Ruth didn't know how to respond without getting too deep and she could tell that he needed to keep those feelings inside, digest them, take time to turn them over and find peace within himself. She had given him all the answers he needed. That was all she could do.

He gripped the steering wheel so that his knuckles whitened. "Sorry, I'm not so good with emotion. Always considered myself to be a tough guy, not a soft centred wimp."

"There's nothing soft centred about admitting how you feel. It's one of the first steps towards healing," Ruth answered and they continued the journey in companionable silence as the Defender battled its way through the swiftly falling snow.

CHAPTER TWENTY TWO

The barn conversion was nestled on a lesser-travelled country road that stemmed from the main one running through the village of Barrington. Against the thin, watery light of a wintry afternoon, the twinkling of the barn lights was a welcome sight.

As Jeremy tackled the cases, Ruth grabbed shopping.

"Ruthie!" Tim trudged over to help unburden them from their luggage.

"This is Jeremy. Jeremy, meet Tim," Ruth rested the icebox and shopping bags in the snow and reminded him of the text she had sent earlier to let him know that Jeremy would be coming. "I hope you don't mind. You did say to bring a companion."

Tim appeared delighted. "Mind? We're delighted! I'm so glad you came. No offence to my sister, but it's not quite the party with only three of us, is it?"

"Great to meet you, Tim." Jeremy rested the cases on the snow to extend a handshake.

"Aussie?" Tim asked, picking up on the accent when they made their introductions.

"New Zealand, but I'll forgive you," Jeremy joked and the pair entered into immediate conversation as the three of them traipsed through the snow to the house.

Tim's partner, Max, was standing over the stove in an open plan kitchen and dining area. He looked the quintessential domestic chef wearing a navy and white striped apron and holding a spoon. The rich smell of cooking laced the air. "Smells great!" Ruth exclaimed as she dumped the shopping bag onto one end of the central island. She lifted out a good bottle of Malbec. "Should go well with this."

"Come here, you!" Max opened his arms and she fell into his huge embrace as he planted a wine-soaked kiss onto her forehead. "We've just cracked one open with the cooking but it looks marvellous."

"I see you're still working out then," Ruth commented, playfully squeezing his bicep. Max was famed for his annual Ironman events. If there was anything competitive he could enter, he would.

"Of course," he said and flexed his muscles. "I need these for all this cooking that your brother gets me doing." Max looked over her shoulder to see Tim and Jeremy dumping the cases at the bottom of the staircase. "You must be Jeremy. Good to have you here." He marched over and gave Jeremy a friendly slap on the back whilst Tim busied himself with finding two more wine glasses.

"Why don't you both get settled in your rooms and we'll get the drinks poured?" Tim suggested brightly. "I thought we'd give Jeremy the bedroom in the eaves, if that's okay?"

"Sounds great," Jeremy responded as Ruth showed him upstairs.

They took the stairs that led to the top floor and Jeremy let out a low whistle. A beautiful four poster bed luxuriously decorated with coverings the shade of duck egg blue was the central focus. The off-white furniture surrounding it gave a French neoclassical style to it. Off to one side was a spacious bathroom with a large walk-in monsoon shower and a marble step that led to a bath in front of a huge window. "If this is the spare bedroom, what does the master room look like?" Jeremy returned to the bedroom, pressed down on the mattress appreciatively and then looked out the window at the rolling, white glazed countryside.

"I'm sure you'll get the full tour later. Tim is extremely proud of the place. It was a wreck when they bought it. Got it for a steal. Tim and Max run a company that develops high end, luxury retirement properties, so they have all the right contacts."

"The retirement properties must be something else."

Ruth joined him over by the window. The snow was falling so heavily that the landscape almost blended into the sky. "The prices are something else too," she added with a chuckle. "Not something I'll be able to afford as a single divorcee, juggling two part-time jobs."

"Are you worried?" Jeremy asked as he stroked the voile curtain.

Shaking her head, Ruth wrinkled her nose. "The mortgage on the house is pretty much paid off. Regardless of whether we sell it or Grayson buys me out, there'll be enough for me to settle into a small terraced cottage with a rambling garden somewhere and become a crazy cat lady."

"You have it all planned then?"

"Isn't that what happens to a woman of my age? Washed up and put back on the shelf as a tired old has-been?" She had meant to come across as jovial, but the truth was that it was a niggling concern in the back of her mind.

"Pah!" Jeremy waved a dismissive hand. "I hate it when people go on about age. What's that got to do with anything? You're an intelligent, kind and beautiful woman. I really don't think you'll have anything to worry about." He looked her up and down with a critical eye. "Besides, you can only be in your thirties; life is just beginning."

Blushing, Ruth smiled gratefully. "You're very generous to say all that. Add a good decade on and you have the truth of it. Thank you though."

With a shrug, Jeremy looked back out at the view from the window. "It's fact, not a bunch of words intended to appease you, Ruth."

She liked how candid he was. "It's strange, because today I feel rather liberated. It occurred to me that I won't have to think about anybody else when I go to the supermarket; there's nobody else to tidy up after and no more pants and socks left within a metre of the washing basket. Plus, I can go out for dinner with other people without feeling guilty."

Their eyes locked and Jeremy was suddenly awkward. He scratched the back of his head. "I am so sorry about last night. I owe you big time over that." He paused and she could tell that he was thinking carefully about how to frame whatever he had to say next. "Would you brave doing it again with me? Properly this time though. If nothing else, it will take your mind off everything that has happened. Friends are so important during times like these."

She smiled and nodded.

"Great. I could do with a friend over here. I had thought I'd want to be all broody and lonely after Cathy, but I'm beginning to appreciate that having company will be far better. It's what gets you through it all, you know."

"My choice next time then," she said brightly, ignoring the feeling of rejection that the word 'friend' had given her. It had to be rebound feelings that she was experiencing as a result of the constant but very final rejection she had experienced with Grayson. Waggling a finger, she joked: "But pull a stunt like last night and you'll have a whole bottle of wine thrown over you."

"Come on you two. What are you doing up there? Drinks are served and canapés ready." Tim could be heard ascending the staircase impatiently.

"Ten minutes," Ruth called back. "I just want to freshen up."

Twenty minutes later, when she emerged with her hair still wet from the shower and dressed in jeans with a chunky knit cardigan thrown over a camisole, everyone was waiting. Tim had laid out an assortment of nibbles and, having abandoned his work as chef, Max was languishing in front of the fire, glass in hand and engaged in conversation with Jeremy.

Taking a wine glass from Tim, Ruth followed him into the seating area. "At last!" Max exclaimed and gave Jeremy a nudge. "These two are just as bad as one another with timekeeping. It clearly runs in the family."

Ruth swatted him playfully. "Ignore Max. He's a world champion wind-up merchant."

Max gave her a wink and then raised his glass. "Great to see you again, Ruthie. To family, new friends and a bloody good Christmas!"

Jeremy took a hearty swig. "Good stuff."

"You're supposed to savour it, or my darling brother will go quite mad!" Ruth pointed out with a laugh. Everything was a matter of perfection for Tim, right down to the style of glass that a drink was served in.

Plonking himself back onto the sofa, Max roared with laughter. "That's what I like to see, somebody else up for a party. Top him up, Timothy!"

They all settled and relaxed so easily into conversation, that it was as though both Tim and Max had known Jeremy forever. Ruth and Jeremy shared the story of how they had met but did not divulge all the details. They kept it brief, explaining that Jeremy had gone for a Tarot reading and that Ruth was helping him with some research for a family tree. The necklace remained undiscussed.

It was long after seven before they sat down to eat and Ruth had tossed all of her troubles aside thanks to the jovial discussion and laughter that they all enjoyed. Tactfully, both Tim and Max were careful to avoid any conversation about Grayson, in the knowledge that Ruth would just need some space from thinking about any of it. She always marvelled at how, no matter how infrequently they met up, the sibling connection that she and Tim shared never seemed to falter. The night ended on a high and Ruth knew that it was time for bed, lest she feel the effects of too much wine the following day.

As she closed the blinds in her room, she thought of the necklace tucked away in a pocket of her suitcase. She could not feel any presence and began to ponder as to whether the entity she had connected with had remained in Winchester. The sense of peace and relief that washed over her was almost dizzying. She had not realised quite how drained she had become over the last few days. Arriving at the barn had been a tonic. The spirited conversations and laughter over dinner and drinks had relaxed her. Even Jeremy had looked as though all of his burdens had lifted. Removing the clothes from her case, she pulled the zip and put it in the bottom of the wardrobe. It was best the necklace remained out of sight, at least for the time being.

Her head hit the pillow and the combination of both wine and fatigue pulled her into a deep, undisturbed slumber.

It was early when she woke. The house was still dark and nobody was up. Slipping into a pair of joggers and a long sleeved top, she went downstairs to make a coffee.

Curling up on the sofa, she sat in the warm glow of lamplight for a long time, thinking about Grayson, thinking about Cas and what she should say to him. She doubted Grayson would take on the responsibility of explanation.

Finding her phone, she sent Cas a text, wishing him well and asking him to let her know a good time for a call. She would leave breaking the news to him until after Christmas, maybe even after New Year, although she wasn't sure how upset he would be. The differences and distance between Ruth and Grayson had been obvious to their son. He had once told them both that things would be far better, far more normal if they split up. It had been after a weekend visit earlier that year. There had been no arguments, no unkind words, just silence. Cas had said it had been like living with two ghosts. He had said it had always been that way, for as long as he could remember. That statement had twisted so hard in Ruth's gut. She had wondered what damage her empty, loveless marriage had done to their son. Both she and Grayson had been in denial of course, but Ruth had seen the burden of her own guilt reflected on her husband's face. Maybe that had been the turning point for Grayson? Still, she thought bitterly, it would have been better that he had sat down with her and had a conversation rather than running off with Veda Watkins. It wouldn't have ended in a row. With the exception of their last encounter, they never argued. Not any longer. That was the problem, though. There was no passion left. Cas had seen that and he had called it out. Blinking back tears, Ruth picked up her coffee before realising it was no longer hot. A shadow flitted against the wall, startling her.

"Morning. Do you always get up this early on a day off?" Jeremy had emerged showered and dressed, making Ruth feel suddenly self-conscious about how dishevelled she must appear.

With a shrug, she stood up and went to tip away her coffee. "I'm a morning person. Always have been. You appear to be too."

"Hey," Jeremy said softly, reaching out to touch her shoulder, "you've been crying."

Rinsing her mug, she tried to gloss it over. "It's nothing. Just a bit emotional. It all catches up, doesn't it? And I'm having a guilt trip for our son. Poor Cas. Goodness knows how I'm going to tell him." She felt the tears brim up again and dashed them away.

Jeremy leaned against the island counter. "You have nothing to feel guilty about, Ruth. You've been the glue that has held your family together all these years. You're the one who sacrificed everything to give Cas the best childhood. Don't beat yourself up."

His words were comforting and Ruth managed a nod and a smile. "Thanks. I'll try not to." Dropping her hands to her side, she sniffed. "I look a complete mess. I should really go and take a shower."

"I like the 'just got out of bed' look." Jeremy gave her a cheeky grin and his eyes lingered in a way that utterly conflicted with the 'friend' statement he had made the evening before.

She wondered if he was teasing her. "You're a terrible flirt but you know how to cheer a girl up."

"How about I work out how to use that complicated coffee machine whilst you take your shower?" He tapped the coffee pod carousel so that it began to spin.

"Sounds good."

Even when Ruth had dressed, there was still no sign of Tim and Max. It didn't surprise her. She knew how much her brother loved a lie in. "I've got something to show you," Jeremy said and reached for his phone. "I asked a contact of mine who works tirelessly on the history of Winchester to do a bit of digging for us. He's found our ghost."

Perching on a barstool next to Jeremy, Ruth listened as he relayed everything his contact had found.

"It seems that he has found a Kateryn who may well be our lady."

"How? Where?"

"You told me that you thought she was from a reasonably comfortable background in Winchester before she married. I've assumed from the things you have said that she is relatively young: early twenties, if not younger. And we know that the year she is making contact with you from is 1685, during the Bloody Assizes."

"Go on."

"I asked him to pull all the birth records he could find for a Kateryn, born in any of the Winchester parishes between 1660 and 1670, and to then check the family names against the hearth tax register."

Ruth tucked a loose piece of hair behind her ear and frowned. "Why the hearth tax register?"

"Because the number of hearths registered gives a good indication of how wealthy a family was. We don't want anyone too wealthy, like the Dawley family at Lainston, but we want those of the sort of wealth akin to a merchant, or a profession of that ilk."

Nodding, Ruth raised her eyebrows. "Clever."

Tapping the side of his head, he winked. "See, not just a pretty face." He looked back down at his phone screen and continued. "So, he shortlisted a couple and I've tried to put two and two together."

"And?"

"A Kateryn Ann was born into the Verny family on 15th April 1663. The Verny family certainly fit the bracket of middling wealth. Charles Verny is recorded as having paid tax for eight hearths so we have focused on the Verny family tree. Kateryn was the middle of three. Looks like the youngest didn't survive beyond early childhood, leaving just Kateryn and her older brother,

John." He glanced up at Ruth, waiting for any sense of recognition or memory to trigger.

"I don't remember any mention of an older brother."

Unfazed, Jeremy continued. "The thing that stopped me was that it does look like she married but there is no mention of the family she married into."

Curling a leg beneath her bottom, Ruth leaned on the polished white of the quartz island counter. "Interesting. Go on."

"There is no record of her death either, but the lifespan of every other family member is recorded. Her brother John married a woman by the name of Emmott and they had four children. He died in 1728. All four children went on to marry and have children of their own. You have quite a rich source of data here to make a family tree so it's strange that there is nothing more on Kateryn. It's as though she just disappeared."

"Why does that make you think that she married?"

"On its own it doesn't, but you mentioned that your Kateryn had a husband and that as a result of her family disapproving of the marriage she lost her dowry. I should imagine that, in the long run, they lost all ties."

"And there are no other records?"

Shaking his head, Jeremy put the phone down. "None."

"So how can you be so sure this is her?"

"Because we have a record of her grandmother. Died 2nd September 1685. Same day as Lady Alice Lisle was executed."

"Darling!" Ruth gripped the edge of her stool as her head began to spin. A wave of emotion washed over her, rocking her senses. She took a deep, sobering breath. "So, we have our lady, Kateryn Verny. Can we do anything more to trace her as Kateryn Fox, or perhaps through Gideon's name? They lived in Winchester, but I recall that Gideon was from Dorchester and that they lived for a while there too. So surely they would be listed on the hearth tax in either of those places?"

"Sadly, the records aren't always easy to find, particularly in the latter part of the century. A lot of the tax was collected privately back then, which created some discrepancies."

"Oh." Ruth's shoulders slumped with disappointment as she tried to remember everything that she had seen through Kat's eyes. "What about Gideon's family? Would that give us any clues?"

Giving her an apologetic look, he shrugged. "We could try but I wouldn't hold out much hope. You mentioned that Gideon was a footman who craved a more luxurious lifestyle, that he came from a poor background and his ambition for wealth caused arguments between him and Kateryn. So, it could very well be the case that his family were too poor to be included on the register."

Impatience bubbled away inside her and she grabbed him by the arm as the memory of Kat's emotions spilled into her thoughts. "We need to check the archives you spoke about yesterday, the ones that list the prisoners. I have to find out what happened to him. I have to find out if he-"

There was a bang from upstairs and they both looked up. It broke the spell that Ruth had found herself falling under. "Tim and Max must be up," she said and jumped off the barstool before going to the fridge. "I'll make a start on breakfast." She pulled out several eggs and tried to shake off the sensation that made her feel as though something was trying to penetrate her skin and claw its way back into her mind. "Scrambled, fried, boiled or poached?" Her voice was too bright as she attempted to disguise the feelings that had engulfed her only moments earlier.

Jeremy's expression darkened. "You feel her again, don't you?"

Finding a large bowl and tapping the eggs on the edge, Ruth refused to answer.

"Where's the necklace?" he asked, his tone suddenly curt.

"It's locked away." She did not bother to say where. "Scrambled it is then." Ruth continued to busy herself with the cooking, as though their conversation had never happened. "I always think there's something quite festive about scrambled eggs with smoked salmon. I noticed Max saved some salmon from last night. Would you mind checking the fridge?"

"You're changing the subject," Jeremy said tersely.

"I know and I'm sorry. I just don't want her to get to me here and you're right, I could feel her. She's using me and she has such power. I don't even think she realises it." She tapped the last egg against the side of the bowl, neatly splitting the shell in two. The sound of Max and Tim descending the staircase made her lower her voice. "Let's talk about it later, when my brother isn't in earshot. He'll only fret if he knows what's been going on."

******

The remainder of the morning was spent at a leisurely pace. After lunch, Tim and Max suggested they all go for a walk around the village and then stop at the pub but the fatigue of losing so much sleep in the nights leading up to arriving in Somerset, Ruth decided she would take the time to have a nap instead.

When the front door had closed, she went upstairs to her room and strolled over to the window. More snow was falling and settling on the fields at the rear of the house to create what would be a powdery finish befitting the front of a Christmas card. Crossing her arms over her chest, Ruth shivered. Since breakfast, she had been sensing that Kat had been attempting to reach her. It had been exhausting trying to stop her, but at last, the feeling of invisible fingers clawing for her brain had gone and she was alone again.

Climbing onto the bed, Ruth felt a heavy curtain of tiredness engulf her. A power nap was all that she needed to feel revived. Shutting her eyes, it was easy to give in to the thrall of sleep. It did not last though. The house was quiet but not peaceful. Ruth's eyes snapped open and she sat up, aware that she had broken out in a cold sweat. Shadows flitted in the corridor and she could tell that she was no longer alone. "Leave this place," she called out, her voice trembling. "There is nothing for you here. You need to leave!" Even as she said it, she knew that the words were futile against the presence. This was not a spirit. This was Kateryn, from hundreds of years ago, drifting through time to take her by the hand and drag Ruth back with her.

Pressing her palm to her chest, Ruth could feel the rapid build of her heart rate and… something else. The coolness of the stone pressed against her skin and she looked down, horror unwinding itself slowly. How was this even possible? She had not taken the necklace from its hiding place in her suitcase. Had she been sleepwalking? It had never happened before, but she supposed it was a plausible explanation.

Fumbling for the clasp of the chain, her fingers worked fruitlessly at unhooking it. Why had she ever decided to bring the damned thing with her? The question struck her as she thought of the pendant resting against the skin of her cleavage like a glinting, wicked, all-seeing eye. That eye belonged to a witch. She was certain of that now. Kateryn Fox had known things. In life she had held a certain power. Her grandmother had been a cunning woman too. She had warned Kateryn of the dark side of their power, but bad things had happened to Kat. Ruth felt a dreadful certainty that darkness had beckoned and enshrouded Kateryn. She had witnessed a change in her.

The familiar surge of emotion hit her: anger, grief and a deep-seated thirst for vengeance. Somebody had wronged her. During her life, Kateryn Fox had been a woman scorned by men. The thoughts began rushing through her head and she could feel Kat's presence and the time that she had lived. It was dangerously close to overlapping with her own time. Only a thin veil was hanging in the air between them.

Somewhere in the deep roots of her consciousness, she could see the obsidian stone; a kaleidoscope of green, purple and blue were blurring the edges, fighting their way to the central point, merging together until they formed an oval. "Stop!" she screamed, but it was too late; her vision had become obscured by the stone. The colourful oval began moving in and out of focus.

She needed to get out of the house. Stumbling for the bedroom door, she tripped. A figure was at the top of the staircase. It was the figure of a woman, kneeling. There was no subservience in the position, though. Power emanated from her and it was a power that the woman knew very well was her gift.

Ruth opened her mouth to speak and when she did, her voice sounded alien and protracted, as though an echo from another time. “Speak to me, Kateryn,” she said, “tell me what it is that you want.”

CHAPTER TWENTY THREE

They had all left the lodgings long before Kat stirred from her sleep. It had been a deep, dreamless sleep where she had been swallowed by the sanctuary of nothing. Upon waking she had felt dazed, confused as to where she was until the beams above her head and the tightly cramped room had reminded her.

Aside from Mary sweeping the grates, the big house on High West Street was nothing but an ugly, hollow shell. Kat was in the stillroom when Mary strode in, red faced and out of breath. It was a nuisance that there was no door to separate her workspace from Mary's, who obviously thought that she had the right to wander wherever she pleased.

Mary pointed out that the court proceedings had started early: "A lot of 'em to get through," she said and her mouth puckered with distaste as she went on to inform her of the sheer number awaiting their fate in the town's prison. Kat did not know whether Mary's sympathies lay with Judge Jeffreys or the rebels. Mary was a widow twice over, with no sons or brothers to worry about. She was a hard woman with a frosty edge, but Kat could not imagine that she was the type of woman to wish ill upon her neighbours and friends.

Robert, Gideon's brother, would be amongst those men standing trial in front of the formidable judge. If Gideon knew… She shut her eyes and gripped the table edge. In spite of the distance that had grown between them, Gideon had still thought fondly of his brother. It would destroy him if anything were to happen to Robert.

Kat thought of how she had refused Bridget's request to stand by her side at court and she felt deep shame. Then she thought of Gideon's parents, and she wished that she could go and stand beside them all to show her solidarity. Kat knew that to do so would be foolish. What would become of her if Lord Jeffreys or any of the other judges were to find out that she was married into a family of traitors and that her husband was missing? The sinister words inked across the letter that Mr Giles had been writing drifted to the forefront of her mind. She recalled the cold instruction on how the town must prepare for the disposal of the traitors. She thought of Lady Alice Lisle - noble, old and dignified to the end, walking out onto the scaffold to a death that nobody in Winchester had thought she deserved. If any of these men with their stern faces and smart robes were to think that Kat was somehow involved with any of the traitors too, there would be no exceptions, no turning a blind eye.

Her appetite gone, she dropped the loaf that she had taken to break her fast and returned to the privacy of her chamber where she could not be seen or heard by Mary.

Unclasping the necklace and sinking to her knees, she held it in front of her. Its power was growing, along with her sense of urgency and fear. She could feel its strength surging through her body as she held it in the palm of her hand. It made her feel different, powerful.

"Show me," she said, over and over as she watched the ebony stone glint in the shafts of light streaming through the window. There was a noise from the corner of the room, much like a whisper. Raising the stone to her lips, she kissed it and asked again: "Bring me the High Priestess."

The air in front of the window began to move and the shape of a woman emerged. Holding her breath, she waited, preparing to bolt as the shape slowly took substance. Long tendrils of hair glimmered coppery blonde in the sunlight, framing an almond shaped face. It was the spirit woman who Kat believed to be a High Priestess from the other realm.

"Speak to me, Kateryn. Tell me what it is that you want." The woman's voice drifted across the room like fine gossamer dancing on a breeze.

Disconcerted by the fact that this spirit had spoken her name, Kat almost dropped the necklace. Regaining her composure, she reminded herself that she had summoned her. Her very presence was the result of Kat's power. Gaining confidence, she slowly raised herself to her feet. "I want you to help me," she commanded steadily. "I need you to show me where he is. Show me my Gideon." Her hands trembled as she spoke because she knew the risk of abusing such power. The consequences could turn on her three-fold. This was desperation, though. She was unable to shake the terrible, sick feeling she had when she thought of what she had seen of Gideon and what she knew of his brother, Robert.

"Show me where he is," Kat implored her, ignoring the protests that she could hear in her head. "Where is Gideon Fox?"

The woman's face crumpled helplessly and she shook her head.

Blood pulsed hard and fast through Kat's veins. "What do you know?" she demanded and she rushed towards the figure, reaching for her shoulders. Even beneath the strange, thick, red woollen garment that she was wearing, the woman was so delicate in appearance that Kat thought she might snap her if she was to get hold of her. She retracted her arms and stopped, choking back the fury, frustration and fear.

A look of sincere regret and sorrow shadowed the beautiful face. "I am sorry, Kateryn. I cannot help you. You need to stop seeking me."

Kat opened her mouth to protest, swallowing a mouthful of stale air, but the figure was fading much faster than it had appeared. She swiped at the spot where the woman had been standing and her hands clawed uselessly through the empty space in front of her.

"No, I will never stop!" she cried out. "Where is Gideon?"

There was no reply.

Dropping the necklace, despair weighed heavily upon her and with a frustrated cry she pounded the floor with her fists. Through her sobs, she thought of Darling and wished that she were still with her, offering advice and comfort. Kat closed her eyes and recalled how the sweet, purple fragrance of lavender had scented Darling's hair and skin. The thought calmed her, gave clarity to her thoughts. She needed to get out of the house with its endless dark corridors and heavy wooden doors.

Even outside, the atmosphere was stifling. Kat could feel the misery that was suspended above Dorchester as one large, billowing, invisible cloud. Three hundred and thirty-seven men, Mary had said. That was how many were to stand trial at the Dorchester assizes. They had been promised to be shown mercy if they were to confess their guilt, but she knew that soon, like Winchester, the town would echo with the bangs and thuds of a gallows being erected and they would all smell the thick, acrid stench of the pitch. Her stomach turned even at the thought of it.

Soldiers outside the house eyed her warily and her heart quickened as she approached them. Instinct warned her to turn around and take a different route, but she did not want to appear guilty of anything. The shorter man's expression suggested that he recognised her, although she did not know him. Resting his hand on his musket, he watched her through narrowed eyes.

As she passed, she heard one of them spit on the path that she had crossed. These men knew who she was, that she was in service to Lord Jeffreys, making remedies and concoctions to aid his health. They thought her a witch.

Kat turned to look back at them and they both looked away. They were afraid of her and she supposed that they should be. It was the prickle in her fingertips, the blood that was still rushing through her veins that worried her; because in that moment, Kat realised that it pleased her to be feared. The soldiers whom she had encountered only days before had so easily ripped at her clothes and beaten her. Had it not been for Mr Giles, they would have raped and murdered her without a second thought. Now Kat was the one with power. She supposed that she *could* do them harm, if she so wished. She knew the plants and roots that could be used to end the suffering of one who was so ailed that it would be considered a kindness. If a woman whose husband was cruel wanted Kat to slip her a poison that would not point to foul play, it could be done. Now that she could summon the spirit world at her own will, she realised that her capabilities made her even more powerful than the Lord Chief Justice Jeffreys.

With a shiver, she pushed the dangerous thought aside and soon found a crowd cloistered around the place where the prisoners were standing trial, in the red hung court.

People spilled from court onto the streets, and the hum of voices rose and fell as news was shared. There were gasps and whimpered protests, shouts of disagreement and cries of horror as the men inside each took their turn to stand at the bar and plead guilty or not guilty. She stood on her tiptoes and heard the name Robert Fox. The murmur of voices dipped to silence as they waited to hear what Robert would say.

Bridget would be in there, waiting to hear his plea, to hear the charge that was being brought against her husband.

Pulling the hood of her cloak over her head, Kat nudged her way through the crowd, ignoring the angry looks and indignant hisses. Taking advantage of her size, she twisted and ducked, slipping through the sea of bodies until she was inside the building that housed the courtroom. There were more people on the stairs leading up to the room and Kat managed to climb past them. At the top, she noticed Bridget immediately. She was wearing a clean dress and her white cap was straight and neat. This was her effort to make a good show for her husband, demonstrate that their family was a respectable one. Bridget did not see Kat. Her eyes were focused only on Robert who looked painfully thin and dirty as he stood at one end of a line of men in front of Judge Jeffreys and his counsel.

"Robert Fox, how do you plead?" The question was asked of him again and Kat could see that he was struggling. Bridget had told her that the men had been assured a plea of guilty would bring them the chance of mercy. Robert's limbs trembled and she could see how torn he was, unable to decide which plea gave him the greatest chance of survival. The court waited in silence and she saw Judge Jeffreys shift in his seat and reach for the bottle that contained the tincture she had prepared. He winced and took a deep swig. His face was flushed from both heat and irritation. Springing the upper half of his body forward, he slammed his free hand down hard. "It is not such a difficult question, man! Guilty or not guilty, how do you plead?"

From his place in line, Robert's face twitched nervously and his eyes darted to the side as though to search for Bridget, or another familiar face, before thinking better of it. "Guilty, my Lord," he replied, his voice gravelly and low.

Above the flurry of voices that followed, was Bridget's: "No, Robert! Why?"

The sound of the clerk's gavel striking the wooden surface of his desk ricocheted from the walls. From his position in front of the scarlet swathes of cloth hanging in the courtroom, Judge Jeffreys glared with threatening eyes. His lips glistened from the draught that he had swigged. The court hushed and Bridget's sobs were muffled as she pressed her head into another woman's shoulder – a friend who had been by her side throughout the trial, showing the solidarity that Kat had not.

Keen to press on, the clerk moved to the last convict in Robert's line, calling his name and asking for his plea. Once again the room erupted with voices, only this time it was more muted. People were waiting to hear what would be said next.

Lord Jeffreys licked his lips. There was a glint in his eye that Kat did not care for as his glare travelled along the line of men in front of him. It was as if he was giving them one more chance to impart more information. With the rest of the spectators, Kat waited, wondering whom these men might name in a final effort to save their mortal selves. The room was silent and Kat held her breath. Nobody said a word.

Lord Jeffreys leaned further into the highbacked chair as though distancing himself from the crowd of expectant faces. For a moment, Kat wondered if his resolve was about to falter as he gave another uncomfortable groan. When he spoke, he addressed all of the men in front of him, advising them that their guilty plea would bring with it a sentence of the harshest order. He allowed a half smile to play on his lips but it did not reach his eyes, which were hollow and black. Then he informed them that, at the King's pleasure, they would be taken back to the place from where they had come, ready to be drawn upon a hurdle to the place of execution where they would be hanged by the neck and cut down to see their entrails and members severed from their bodies and burned in front of them.

Kat's head was spinning. The words were spiked as they danced wickedly in the muggy air of the courtroom. She did not want to think of it, but he took such delight in imparting their fate so colourfully that she was unable to do anything but. Their heads would be taken and their bodies divided into four parts before being disposed of.

Near to her, there was a retching noise. A man with a limp was leading a woman from the court, warning her to remain calm. Robert did not flinch. He held his head high and kept his gaze on Judge Jeffreys, his expression silently challenging him for going back on his word that pleading guilty would bring mercy. The judge caught his gaze and held it. Neither wanted to be the first to break away.

"Do not make it worse for yourself, Robert," Kat whispered, for she knew how this man dealt with those who crossed him or his King. Above their upset, Kat could hear the voices of those keen to be seen condemning the actions of the rebels. They tossed around words like 'scoundrels', 'rogues' and 'devils', careless as to whose ears they would fall upon. Their numbers were few in comparison to those who remained loyal to the men on trial.

Judge Jeffreys said nothing more to address the prisoners but flicked his wrist, gesturing for them to be taken away.

Heavy chains clanked between their legs as the men were led away, and Kat's gaze travelled across the room until it rested on a man on the other side. Quietly, he was watching the scene unfold in front of him, his eyes heavy with a burden known only to him. Mr Giles. He appeared drawn and pallid, as though it were he who had just received the ghastly sentence. Before looking down at his hands, his eyes locked with Kat's. Those hands had been responsible for the instructions that would now be with the mayor. By his hand, the people of Dorchester would soon hear the chilling sound of iron clattering against wood. Those who had pleaded 'not guilty' and not acquitted would be first. Their demise was to be on display for all of Dorchester to witness. Kat had missed who those men were as they had already been marched away before she had arrived at court. It had not escaped her attention, however, that within the dishevelled lines of those pleading guilty alongside Robert, there had been no sign of the bright blue eyes that belonged to Joseph Speed, the kindly cobbler from Colyton.

People left the courtroom in a huge surge of sweaty flesh. Kat was pulled and pushed as elbows and limbs prodded her body. Women were crying, people were shouting. Kat thought that there could be no way of Lord Jeffreys or any of his Crown Counsel escaping the wrath of an angry mob. People felt betrayed. It appeared that many of those men had been told to confess for the opportunity of some sort of reprieve. Soldiers were standing ready to control the crowd. In Winchester, the life of a woman none of the ordinary folk had known had been taken. Here it was the lives of brothers, sons, husbands, friends and neighbours. When she was outside again, Kat saw the lonely figure of Joseph Speed's wife and she rushed toward her.

"Mistress Speed!" She touched the woman's shoulder and she turned. Her face looked hollow, as though all of her spirit had been sucked away. There were no tears for Mistress Speed left to cry, or perhaps the news had not yet sunk in.

Her bottom lip quivered as she looked Kat up and down. With time and grief, she did not seem to recognise her. "It is a dark day that has been brought to Dorchester by a dark King and his dark servant." Her gaze wandered behind Kat and rested on the women comforting one another or calming those close to hysteria. "The Devil has come to this town," she warned, "and may those who walk with him burn in Hell." At that she turned and walked away.

Kat searched the crowd for Bridget but she had disappeared and so she walked up the incline, past the church and towards the house that Bridget shared with Robert and their three children. With every step, Kat worried for her friend. What would become of Bridget now that she would soon be the widow of a traitor, and a poor one at that? She would become a burden upon the parish, with three young mouths to feed. How would she pay the rent? Bridget was young and pretty, so there was time enough to marry again, but Kat doubted there was much that Robert had been able to leave to her.

Bridget's house was small but neatly kept. It was nestled between several other houses. The chimney was smoking and Kat could smell cooking. If it had not been for the sight of Bridget crumpled in her sister's arms whilst her young children looked upon them, confusion and fear on their little faces, everything would have appeared ordinary. Kat stepped into the open doorway. "Bridget?" Recognition lighting up his eyes, little Walter called out her name as he ran towards her to show her a flower that he had picked that morning. Bridget's mother reached for the child and scooped him up, shooting Kat a look of scorn. "How is she?" Kat asked, unable to find the right words.

Bridget's mother pursed her lips as she perched Walter on her ample hip. "How do you think she is?"

"I'm sorry, I…" Kat stammered, taken aback by the frosty tone. "What about Robert's parents? I did not see them in the courtroom."

"Been too busy with yer new life to visit, have you? Thomas can't get nowhere much these days and Sarah spends all her time caring for him, but she ain't the same either. You broke both their hearts when you ran off with their boy, Gideon. What with poor Robert, now…" She put Walter down so that she could round on Kat. "You never cared enough to come before, so don't come back here now, with yer false pretences that you do, Kateryn Fox. Ain't nothing you have ever done for that family other than bring 'em grief. And now you bring shame too."

Shocked, Kat opened her mouth to protest, to deny the accusations being thrown at her, but Bridget's mother was quick to interrupt. "Don't go giving me that look. We all know. We've all seen you over at the Judge's lodgings, and Mary Althrop has told us too; said you give him yer potions to relieve his pain. So go back to your monstrous master, cos none of us want you here."

"That's enough, mother!" Bridget's sister shouted and one of the children started to cry, setting the other off too.

But Bridget's mother was only just beginning her attack. She narrowed her eyes and took another threatening step towards Kat. "And where is that husband of yours now? Deserted us all the right time, didn't he? Hidden away by that pompous family of yours, I shouldn't wonder. Leaving the rest of us to rot. Where was he when his brother was fighting for their father and forefathers? You turned him, made him full of ambition well beyond his reach when he should have been out there with Robert. If Gideon had fought by his brother's side, Robert might have had half a chance to escape and my daughter would not be in this pitiful state."

"Mother, stop!" Bridget was dabbing at her eyes with her apron, her young face shadowed with grief. "Show some respect."

"Show some respect for Mistress Laarrdy Dah, here? To even suggest that when Robert is-" She stopped, unable to finish what she had started to say. They all loved Robert dearly.

"Not for her," Bridget said, giving Kat a look of pure contempt. "Show some respect for Robert. He would not want for this. He was a good man. An honest man."

Kat moved closer to where Bridget was sitting, desperate to take her in her arms and offer her some level of comfort. "Oh Bridget, I am so sorry."

"Get out." Glowering, Bridget pressed her fists into the table to stand up. "How could you work for *him*, Kat? How could you do it?"

Her cheeks flared with colour as she felt the full impact of her shame. Why could they not see that it was not her choosing? "You must understand, Bridget. I have no choice."

"We all have a choice, Kateryn," Bridget said coldly and from behind her, the eldest started to weep. "It won't end here and that makes you worse than him. That monster's health is in your hands and you keep him well enough so that he can use the law to murder good men like my husband, your own brother-in-law."

Kat wanted to argue her innocence but she had no words.

"Leave!" Bridget shrieked, pounding the table so that everything on it rattled wildly. "Leave, leave, leave!"

Pivoting on the ball of her foot, Kat turned and fled from the little house, tears flowing. Bridget and her mother were right. She had betrayed them all.

Kat did not stop running until she reached the millstream. When she and Gideon had lived in Dorchester, the millstream and the surrounding wilderness had been her peaceful place. It was where the wilder roots and plants grew, those of a rarer variety that could be used in decoctions and remedies.

Swans floated gracefully downstream, observing her cautiously as she walked the riverbank. The shadows of tree limbs crossed her path and she looked up to see the ripe yellow plum fruit that she would have once used to make into a jam for Gideon. She dashed a hand across her cheeks but the tears had dried, leaving only a tight fist of anger clenching the pit of her stomach.

The sky had changed and rainclouds were scudding across it, the low light of the sun turning the ragged edges silver. Picking some meadowsweet and water mint, she tried to take her mind off the awful situation she had found herself in. The meadowsweet would help sweeten the flavour of the mead and the water mint would do well as a soothing remedy for the ailments Lord Jeffreys suffered. Amongst the creamy meadowsweet, her gaze fell on the pale clusters of the plant that was growing alongside it.

Kat knew what this was. The plant was seeding but she only needed the roots. Wrapping her apron around her hand, she was careful not to let it touch her skin as she worked carefully to dislodge it. Then she turned to make her way back to the lodgings, her heart pounding hard against her ribcage. If somebody were to stop and search her, there would be a serious penalty to pay. To be found carrying this plant would demonstrate ill intent and certainly have her condemned as a cunning woman.

Onward she marched, her expression sombre as a drumroll of thunder shook the darkening skies. She could hear the noise from the prison where hundreds of unfortunate men like Robert were being held, but all she could think about was the hemlock, tucked away in the pocket of her apron.

CHAPTER TWENTY FOUR

Ruth remembered it all with distinct clarity - the view of Dorchester, the audible grief of the townsfolk, the oppressive atmosphere of the lodgings on High West Street, the scent of the trees and marshy dampness along the river and how it had felt to find and pick the hemlock. Swallowing back a wave of nausea, she ran to the bathroom to splash her face with cold water.

Steadying herself by gripping the edge of the sink, she thought about how absurd the very idea was, but it had happened. She still had no recollection of how she had come to be wearing the pendant chain. Ruth stared at her reflection in the bathroom mirror, looking at the stone and noticing that the surface was innocuously dull again. It was a portal of sorts, providing a gateway between past and present, and Kat was using it to summon Ruth whenever she pleased.

No longer relishing the idea of being alone in the barn, Ruth hurried downstairs. Finding some paracetamol in the medicine cupboard, she popped the casing to release two tablets and gulped them down with a small glass of water before putting on her coat. She would send Tim a text, find out where they were and let them know that she would be joining them after all. As she returned to the main living area, she noticed the large clock on the wall and frowned. Almost three hours had passed since she had gone upstairs. It did not seem possible. Picking up her phone, she illuminated the screen, but there was no discrepancy between the time on that and the wall clock.

Alerted by a car on the driveway, Ruth opened the door to see Tim's car swinging into its space and all three men sharing some light hearted conversation as they stepped out. "Feeling any better?" Jeremy asked brightly as she relieved him of one of the bags he was carrying.

Feigning a carefree smile, Ruth nodded.

"Anyone else in dire need of a cup of tea and slice of Christmas cake?" Tim called out as he put a carton of milk into the fridge. Already he was reaching for the tin and instructing Max to get the guest tea set out before anybody had a chance to answer.

Ruth glanced at Jeremy and gave a wry smile. "I suppose that means we will all be having tea and cake."

With everything meticulously prepared, Tim brought over a glazed porcelain tea-set. It was balanced on top of a tray. "We missed you at lunch sis, but Jeremy here has kept us well entertained." He kissed her cheek and whispered in her ear: "He's a keeper."

Embarrassed, Ruth pulled away but Jeremy was too busy asking Max about something to have noticed. "It's not like that," she hissed, and Tim raised his brow in a way that suggested he thought otherwise.

"Hey, how about we take Jeremy to see the Museum of Somerset tomorrow?" Max suggested as he reached for a slice of cake.

"In Taunton?" Ruth asked, thinking that it might be a nice idea to soak up some of the festive atmosphere there.

"Why not? It's only a half hour away and it will give us a chance to pick up any last minute bits."

They all agreed that it seemed like a good idea and one that they could co-ordinate with Jeremy's trip to the South West Heritage Centre. After draining his tea, Max said he would sort out somewhere for dinner afterwards.

It wasn't until later that evening, when Max and Tim had retired to bed early, that Ruth told Jeremy about what had happened whilst she had been alone. In spite of Tim's protests, they were finishing the clearing up.

Jeremy looked worried. "Why didn't you say something before?"

As she finished wiping the last of the mats, Ruth shrugged. "It's hardly something I was likely to announce in front of my brother and Max."

"I guess not. You're okay though, aren't you?"

"Yes, but she's getting better at this. I'd tucked the necklace away in the wardrobe, but when I woke up it was around my neck." The hairs on her arms had raised at the very thought of it. "The only explanation I have is that she somehow did that."

Responding to the look of bewilderment on Jeremy's face, Ruth continued. "I told you that it was as though I was moving through time, to her time, in 1685. What I didn't tell you was what happened the night we had dinner together, after I had returned home."

Taking a seat in one of the dining chairs, Jeremy looked at her intensely. "Go on."

"I sensed something – a presence. I had tried to communicate with Kat using the necklace and something was suddenly there, in the house with me. It was right before you knocked. The presence felt suffocating, evil, full of malice. I thought it was another spirit at first, one that I'd inadvertently opened the door to." She took a breath and Jeremy waited patiently for her to continue.

"Anyway, after what happened this afternoon, I'm not so sure that the presence was that of another spirit. I think it was Kateryn Fox."

"What makes you say that?"

"Because when I saw her this afternoon, there was something different about her. I managed to get away from the hold she had over me but I somehow hijacked her mind and I willingly stayed with her. I followed her to the court in Dorchester and then onto a river. I could see all the dark thoughts running through her mind. She found hemlock dropwort. She picked it and that was when I woke up."

Shaking his head, Jeremy's brow knitted together. "I don't follow."

"Hemlock is an ancient and well-known poison. She picked it with the intent of using it. I could even see who she intended to use it on and how."

"Geez! Are you sure about this?"

Ruth nodded. "She was consumed with hurt and hatred and all of her anger was directed at Judge Jeffreys. She had convinced herself that she had more power than he did, by virtue of the fact that his health and, ultimately his life, were in her hands."

As he digested the insight she was sharing with him, Jeremy scratched the back of his neck. "But she can't have used it. For his part in leading the Bloody Assizes, George Jeffreys was leveraged to Lord Chancellor and he lived for almost another four years. It was the kidney failure that killed him in the end, when he was held in the Tower of London, after Mary and William of Orange overthrew James."

"Doesn't mean she didn't attempt it. What if she got caught? What if Kat tried to murder him and she was executed for it?"

"Not possible. Something like that would have made history. They would have made an example of her."

Frustrated, Ruth raked her fingers through her curls. "But the feeling I am beginning to sense from her is exactly the same as the one I sensed coming from the spirit I felt on the other side of my bedroom door, in Winchester."

The argument was going nowhere and Jeremy looked exasperated. "All I'm saying is that she can't have been caught trying to commit a crime as sinister as murder."

Ruth let out a heavy sigh. "You're right, but even so, the more she witnesses of these awful events, the more time she spends with the men who were responsible for ruining the lives of so many, I see something hard and cruel unfolding in her. I have to admit, I'm scared."

Jeremy hesitated before speaking and started picking at a thread on the edge of his sleeve. He was embarrassed, awkward. "Ruth, you said yourself that you've lost sleep. How much of this do you think could be dreams mixed with reality?"

The question floored her and Ruth felt as though she had been winded. "Are you serious?"

By the look on his face, he was and it brought all of the trust they had built crashing down. Had nothing that they had experienced together felt authentic to him? How long had he been having these doubts about her integrity? "Why would you ask me that? Why would you doubt me?"

"I'm not doubting you, Ruth. I'm just-"

Ruth couldn't help it; the comment had embarrassed her as well as flaring her frustration and temper. It was hard enough accepting and admitting what was happening to her, but to be disbelieved, dismissed even, it was too much. "I think we should end this conversation right now. There's no point going over it. I'm tired and I'm sure you are." She breezed past him, indignation hardening her expression.

"Ruth, please wait. I want to talk."

"I don't," she answered huffily. "I'm off to bed. I'll see you in the morning." She didn't turn to look at him as she headed up the stairs. In the last few days her resilience had diminished considerably and she knew that if she was to catch the look on his face, it would bring her to her knees. Only when she was in the privacy of her room did she sink to the floor and weep.

CHAPTER TWENTY FIVE

It was either very late, or very early. Outside, an almost full moon was suspended against an inky canvas. Its light spilled through the skylights in the roof of the barn, elongating shadows and making them dance ominously. Everyone in the house was asleep. Nobody stirred, not even when the strange glow in one of the bedrooms began to burn brighter and stronger; first a dull yellow, then pulsing into orange and soon becoming a fiery orb of red. As the glow bloomed, the silhouette of a woman appeared. She was looking down at something, reaching out, summoning the presence of another…

At the top of the house, Jeremy tried to call out in his sleep. Something was wrong with Ruth. He could sense it. In his dreams, he could see the careful, calculated footsteps of a tall spindly woman. She was reaching out, her intention being to take hold of Ruth. Unable to find his voice and unable to move, Jeremy's eyes flickered open momentarily but the lull of sleep and of the nightmare he was enduring pulled him back.

Then he was in a dark place, beneath the crash and thrash of waves, fighting for breath as he struggled to see through the mad swirl of water. Hands clawed at his kicking legs and beneath him he could see Cathy's face. Her mouth was opening and closing, as though screaming something at him. He needed to surface, to find Ruth and bring her back but Cathy would not let go.

As Jeremy's nightmare unfolded, Ruth slept on. A burning red light brandished her pale skin and one hand fell down the side of the bed. It was enough for the thing that was snaking out of the shadows to reach out and touch. Deep in her conscience Ruth knew that she was not alone, but the force that was with her was too strong to resist.

CHAPTER TWENTY SIX

Kat had crept from the window of her chamber out onto the rooftop. Had it not been for the ebbing daylight, the vantage point would have offered her a spectacular view across the top of the other houses and out onto the surrounding outcrops of land. As the last of the sun bled out across the sky, its red bloom was a fitting end to a day that had been for revenge. Only two days earlier, thirty men had pleaded not guilty and just one acquitted. The rest had been promised that they would be made an example of for all of Dorchester to see. So far there had only been time for twelve of them to suffer at the orders that had been given in the letter she had found Mr Giles writing.

Grimacing, Kat recalled the events that had unfolded earlier that day, when the town had witnessed the dreadful sound of one of those men begging for his life on Gallows Hill. As far as she knew, he had been the only one to beg for mercy but Kat reckoned that the tortured cries of those men would echo through the streets of Dorchester forever and that the noise would always be shackled to a far corner of her mind.

The Lord Chief Justice Jeffreys had deemed it appropriate to attend the execution, accompanied by the bloodthirsty crowds who never tired of such macabre entertainment, and by those who offered solidarity to the men in their final, terrifying moments. Kat had not even been near the place when she had heard those cries. She dared not imagine what horror those who had witnessed it had seen.

Robert's sentence was to be carried out at a later date, so it would seem. It was no longer safe for Kat to be alone outside of the house. Those who remembered her, who knew of her ties with the Fox family, would now also know that she was working for the wicked, heartless judge who had made twelve women widows and their children fatherless. They were angry. They wanted somebody to blame, somebody to hit out at. Grief could be a dangerous weapon and fear an even deadlier one. She thought of the hemlock tucked away beneath her bed, now wrapped in pale blue cloth.

She had not yet found the courage to dispatch it as she had intended, but the dizzying thought struck her again as she recalled Bridget's words: *That monster's health is in your hands.* If the health of Lord Jeffreys was in her hands, did that mean that she could change things, that by virtue of her position she could decide his fate?

The thought sent a strangely delicious tingle through her body and she felt heat in her fingertips. It made her stronger and she knew that she could easily summon the High Priestess again. Darling had always told her that the best times to harness her gift had been at dawn and dusk, when the power of the moon and sun were at their best: Dark giving birth to light; light being swallowed by dark.

Kat took the knife and looked up at the still rising moon. It was a blood moon and she knew instinctively that it was the right time. She needed to create a deeper connection with the High Priestess. She would not let her slip away again. The older, darker ways needed flesh and blood. Closing her eyes, she drew the blade swiftly over her palm and winced at the pain. She watched as three drops of blood rippled the water in the bowl that she had placed in front of her. "Hear me, High Priestess," she said in a low voice, "I offer my flesh and my blood in return for the answers I seek." The wind whispered around her and she waited for answers, but there were none. Wincing with pain she squeezed her palm tightly, forcing more blood. "I give you my blood in return for my Gideon. I beseech you to give me the answers I seek." Even as she did it, the warnings Darling had given echoed in her head. Dark magic seeks retribution three-fold. One must always be prepared for sacrifices that are required. Ignoring the distant recollection of those warnings, she dipped the obsidian pendant into the dish and watched the spectacular swirl of colour. The dusky silhouette of the rooftops began to fade and soon she could hear the gentle rise and fall of breath. Then she could see her – the High Priestess who went by the name of Ruth. For some time, she observed the sleeping woman. The bed she was lying on looked as soft as a cloud and her body was hidden beneath sheets as white as snow. "Forever joined in blood," she whispered.

The woman groaned and her eyes flickered open.

A sudden wind picked up and Kat was back on the rooftops, her hair whipping about her face. She could no longer see the High Priestess, but she could still feel her presence. It was as though she had brought her with her, away from the peaceful softness of the chamber and into the harsh, brutal reality of Kat's own world.

Moving through the house with a stealth that she had become well accustomed to, Kat kept to the shadows for fear of bumping into one of the judges, especially Lord Jeffreys. All she needed to do was find something to bind her hand with and stem the flow of blood.

Upon her arrival at the lodgings, she had asked Mary to arrange for a clean bundle of rags to be delivered to the stillroom. A stock of clean rags was a necessary part of her work and could be used for wrapping any small wounds.

There would be no questions as to why she had wrapped her hand. Cuts were a common occurrence for the hands of an apothecary. She needed to wrap the wound and then focus on grounding herself properly. Every part of her body was tingling and it felt as though something was squirming around inside her. It was a dizzying sensation and she thought she must look wild, the remnants of deep magic marking her in some way. If she could just get to the stillroom without anybody seeing her…

A protracted growl that sounded more beast than man travelled the length of the narrow corridor. Shadows flickered amidst the sconces and Kat heard the heavy tread of heeled boots.

Pressing herself against the wall, she willed the sound to grow more distant, to disappear down another passage or into a room. Darkness seemed to permeate the corridor as the noise became more prominent. It was the sound of a throat being cleared, or perhaps a grimace of pain. The cool sweep of fine cloth brushed against her and she held her breath as the cloak swelled behind the purposeful stride of its owner. He had not noticed her, this overbearing figure of a man, but she waited quietly, watching and noting his intoxicated swagger. Kat silently willed him to disappear into the gloom, grateful for the distance that each step he took put between them. The figure stopped. It did not turn straight away.

Slowly, he turned his head and Kat stiffened. The dimly lit corridor offered limited visibility and so his face was shadowed, but she could feel the inferno of his gaze fall upon her. He took a step forward and then another, so that they were only inches apart. Towering over her, he brought his face to the top of her head and she could feel his breath tickling her skin. He inhaled deeply, taking in the scent of her and when he pulled back, he was close enough for her to see his face lit only by candlelight.

He was smiling with amusement, for he was the cat cornering the mouse. Kat pressed her back harder to the wall and, noting her fear, his grin broadened. She could smell the wine on his breath. As she stared back at him, she did not dare drop her gaze. Mistress Speed had described him as the devil and Kat thought how very apt that description was as he towered over her, eyes as black as night and cheeks as scarlet as the red hung court room that he ruled in.

"What do you do here? Work in the kitchens? Make up the chambers? Empty the pots full of piss?" He laughed at what he believed was his wit and the laughter soon erupted into a coughing fit that made him clutch his side.

She waited until he had regained what composure he had before answering him. "I am the apothecary, my Lord."

"You are what?" He appeared taken aback for a moment as he sized her up. "But you are a woman."

"You have a keen eye," she answered dryly.

He stepped backwards to appraise her. "Ah yes, I remember now. We brought the Winchester apothecary with us. They said it was a woman." He sniffed and rubbed his chin thoughtfully. "So, you are the a-p-o-t-h-e-c-a-r-y." He rolled the word around on his tongue, allowing the lilt of his accent to make it sound as though he was mocking.

Leaning toward her again, he put his lips to her ear as he pressed up against her. "They did not say how pretty the Judge's Apothecary is."

Kat did not like the tone to his voice, the way he was staking a claim on her. "You may think differently with a sober mind and in the light of day. These corridors are dark and you are merry with wine," she said quickly, shrinking from the touch of him.

Tipping his head back, he gave a belly laugh. "Oh! It is like that, is it? You have a quick tongue. But do not forget that it is the wine that has been laced with your remedies that I have been drinking. Perhaps it is a potion that it was laced with, if it is true that you are not so pleasing on the eye? Perhaps you are in fact, the Judge's Witch?"

Her stomach turned uncomfortably at his words "I am no witch, my Lord."

Ignoring her protest, he sniffed the air. "What it must be to be a woman, even a cunning one." He reached for a lock of her hair and the gesture bordered on intimate.

Horrified, Kat realised that she had forgotten to put her cap back on. His fingers gently wound their way around the strands that tumbled over her shoulders towards her breasts. His words were slurred when he spoke, the sentiment of them shocking her. "What must it be like to sit back and watch from a safe distance as men destroy one another, tearing each other apart, killing one another in the name of politics?"

She did not know how to answer that, although she did not think he was asking her the question. Frozen to the spot, she was aware of how vulnerable she suddenly was. This man had the power to end life in the most brutal of ways and all in the name of the King. He was perhaps the most powerful and feared man in the country and now she was at his mercy. For a moment, she feared he was going to do something terrible to her, but his hand suddenly dropped and he stumbled backwards so that the darkness of the corridor was swallowing his features again.

"There are times when men must kill one another to save themselves." In spite of the intoxicated slur of his speech, there was no disguising the morose edge. "It is a sad fact, a necessary evil that a woman could never understand."

In the shadows, she could see him drop his head so that his chin rested on his chest. This was not the same man whom she had seen in court, full of angry bravado and clever, cruel wit. He was afraid too. Kat felt an unexpected turn of empathy as she realised that this was simply a man bound to his duty for fear of losing his own life.

The soft click of a door opening broke the spell and he appeared to regain his composure. From further down the corridor, Mr Giles addressed Lord Jeffreys and, as though their encounter had never happened, Lord Jeffreys walked away.

******

Early the next morning Kat bumped into Mary who was bleary eyed and foul of temper. Like Kat, she appeared to be reluctantly in service to the men who had come to serve justice on behalf of the King. It was a way to make ends meet for Mary and it had no doubt been impressed on her that it was her duty. The servants who had been brought with the judge and his Crown Counsel appeared more concerned with the much humbler environment that they were expected to work in, than the reason why they were there. Kat had noticed how they looked down their noses at Mary with her strong Dorsetshire accent, their disdain clearly adding to the burden that was already upon her shoulders.

With a grunt and a grumble about something or other, Mary bustled past and disappeared from the kitchen, leaving Kat alone. There was no collusion between them, no familiar ground sought. Mary would be well aware of what they were saying about Kat in the town and had likely contributed to those opinions. To Mary, it most probably appeared as though Kat did have a choice about whom she worked for, that she was no better than the servants who had been brought along with the legal party.

In her hand, Kat was carrying the scrying dish that she had used the night before. Throwing the contents into the flame, she listened to the hiss of protest as the water hit the ashes.

The image hit her with such startling clarity that she cried out and fell into a chair.

Gideon.

So, the magic she had invoked was doing its work. The High Priestess must be showing her where she could find her husband.

Gideon's face was tired, the lines too deep for a man of his age.

Nervously, Kat looked around. Mary had gone and nobody was about, she was alone in the kitchen. "Gideon?" she whispered, searching the flames for further clues. "Where are you?"

He was oblivious to her presence and she could see that he was in a bed, sleeping. It was difficult to make out the room, but the view showed her a door and it was opening. A shadow appeared in the crack. It hovered for a moment and Gideon's slumber appeared undisturbed. Kat's heart pounded. There was something very wrong. Was he in danger? She wanted to cry out, to warn him, tell him to wake up, but she knew that would be futile. The fire hissed and spat as the flames grew wilder, revealing more....

CHAPTER TWENTY SEVEN

I hear the tread of a floorboard. It is the same one as has disturbed me the past few nights. The soft squeak stirs me from my nightmare. I see him on the moors, the life that has barely even started bleeding from him. He was the son of a farmer whose constant intoxication had been the ruin of them. Four years my junior, he was full of misplaced ambition. I think how terrible it is that when his heart finally stops beating and he takes his final, choked breath, there will be nobody to miss him, nobody to mourn his departed soul. I go to call out his name but I cannot remember it. For every second that passes that I fail to remember it, the life drains from him. My mind races and I hear a voice:

Remember his name and you can give him a second chance at life. You must remember his name.

I do not know who this voice belongs to but it whispers at me again and again. His name is important and it floats in the hidden crevices of my mind, amidst the shadowy corners with the horrors that are too awful to unearth. I scream at him to get up and pull on his arm, trying to hoist him over my shoulder but now the blood spills from his mouth. The wound to his stomach is too deep to be anything other than fatal and so I drop him against the wet, muddy ground. Then I run.

There is another creak as the intruder takes another step, pulling me from the sharpened clutches of the nightmare. This is not the first time this intruder has come. On other occasions, I was too tired, too lost in sleep to be brought to my senses. The same sense of vulnerability takes hold. I am outraged, yet complemented. This time I will catch the culprit. I know exactly who it is.

The cloaked figure hesitates before tiptoeing over the threshold and gently pulling the door closed. The slightness of build and graceful walk gives away that this is a woman. She comes to my bedside and does as she has done for the past few nights, standing above me, unaware that my eyelids have flickered open enough to see.

I wait and my hand is taken, the same words are whispered: a prayer to God to keep me safe and to keep me here in this house that has become my golden cage. They say I must wait, that I am still too weak to make the journey back to Dorchester and that Lord Granville will return for me. They are fools if they believe that. He is a wicked man, full of deceit and betrayal. I have doubts that he will make good on his promise to return from wherever it is he has gone.

I wonder how long has passed since I last spoke with this woman. She leans closer to me now and I can feel her breath on my exposed chest, rising to my neck and then to my lips. I can smell the scent of roses on her. Honoria.

Dawn is breaking and the sun is beginning to burn through the clouds outside my window. My eyes open fully, but she does not notice. Hers are closed. In a moment she will back away silently and it will be as though she had never been there. I wait and I wonder if she can hear the frantic thump of my heart. I refuse to give in to the temptation and I wonder if this is perhaps a test of sorts? I see her lips part, she is about to say something and an untamed urgency in me is unleashed. I lift my head and press my lips to hers. Hard.

Honoria lets out a moan of surprise and her eyes open. I let my head drop back against the pillow and whisper an apology. Now I am terrified that she will scream, shout out my crime. But she does not.

She throws herself on to me and we are kissing. I pull her head closer to mine and allow myself to be entirely absorbed in the sensation. I am not thinking of her though. I am not thinking of my wife either. I can think only of the view of that damned battlefield. I kiss her so hard, as though her lips can draw out all of the nightmares that I know will continue to haunt me to the end of my days. It is not enough. I want to forget. I want to be lost in something. Then I cry out in frustration and push her away from me. I will never be lost in anything again because they will always find me, those unearthly cries of men, defeated, shamed and tortured. And I will never forget that I left them there to save myself.

CHAPTER TWENTY EIGHT

"What are you doing?" The accusing, hard voice belonging to Mary echoed through the kitchen and Kat realised that she was kneeling on the floor, almost touching the flame.

Righting herself, she stood quickly. "My hands were cold. They can get stiff in the mornings, particularly now the weather is beginning to cool." The image from the flame continued to burn in her head as she thought of how the woman had pushed back her hood and leaned towards Gideon's face, her lips almost grazing his. She had not seen the rest. The flames had distorted the view too much and then Mary had interrupted, but the heavy feeling in her chest told her that it was not entirely innocent on her husband's part. Where was he? Who was he with and why?

Mary eyed her with suspicion but she said nothing. The awkward moment was broken when a young boy hurried through with a shovel. Ushering Kat out of the way, Mary instructed him to use the glowing embers from the kitchen hearth to get the fire going again in the dining room. The boy dutifully nodded and got on with his task, heeding her harsh warnings to take a care not to drop any of it.

Taking herself away from Mary's mistrusting stares, Kat started to make her way to her stillroom. From the dining room she could hear the careful scrape of the shovel against the hearth as the young boy attempted to get the fire going. A sudden clatter shook the house and the shrill scream that followed curdled Kat's blood. The house was filled with the sound of footsteps. If anybody had still been sleeping, they would surely be awake now?

Hurrying into the main section of the house, Kat could hear stunted cries followed by a sharp intake of breath. She did not move until the boy was brought out, crying and trembling. Neither of the women supporting him appeared angry. Their expressions were gaunt and they spoke in hushed voices, soothing him, imploring him not to make a fuss.

The dining room was empty again. With trepidation, Kat walked towards the door. Glowing embers had settled dangerously near the rush matting and she was quick to stamp them out. As she did so, something caught the corner of her eye. She did not want to turn her head to take a second look, but it was as though an invisible force was pulling her to the windows that faced the church opposite.

Between the lead latticework of the glass pane, she saw a patchwork picture of early morning mist, coiling and wraithlike as it worked its way through the macabre scene on the street. Kat's feet moved of their own accord, one in front of the other, closer and closer until her breath steamed the windowpanes.

Staring back at her through glazed eyes that were filled with the horror of his final moments was Joseph Speed, the cobbler from Colyton.

It had been said that the men from Gallows Hill would be dispatched across the town but Kat had not imagined it would be in such close proximity. She felt her stomach convulse and her body shake as she recalled the vision that had struck her outside the church on the day of her arrival. This was no vision. This was real.

Mary had joined her in the dining room. The emotion on her face was an ugly concoction of horror, fear, disgust and grief. There was a rattling noise coming from Mary's throat as her mind processed what was in front of her. Aside from the head of Joseph Speed, it was impossible to decipher who the other body parts belonged to but Mary would have known many of the men standing trial, for Mary had lived in Dorchester all of her life. She clasped a hand to her mouth, stifling the cry that was threatening to tear its way from her throat. Kat reached for her, supported her by the elbow. Mary leaned on her as her body trembled. For the first time since arriving at the lodgings, the two women stood together, united by the atrocity that the Devil judge had inflicted upon the town.

Leading Mary to the kitchen, Kat heated some ale and poured her some. "You will be alright, Mary?"

Ashen, Mary nodded. "Just a shock, is all." She took the ale and gulped it back. "Never expected to see any of it. Not so close. Not so-" Her voice cracked. She could not finish.

"I do not know why they had to bring the remains here, to that very spot?" Kat was outraged, but Mary looked at her as though she was stupid for asking such a question.

"What better place to leave them than for the pleasure of the Lord Chief Justice Jeffreys? It is his work, his reason for being here."

Reeling from what Mary was suggesting, Kat pressed a hand to her mouth. "Are you suggesting that those men were dispatched outside at the instruction of Lord Jeffreys?"

"That is exactly what happened," Mary said and drank more of the ale before asking for another.

Kat poured another and one for herself and then she left the kitchen with the intention of going to the privacy of her chamber at the top of the house, far enough away from what was on the street.

On the first floor she came to an abrupt halt as she found herself face to face with Mr Giles. "Ah, Mistress Fox," he exclaimed and his voice sounded surprisingly normal. "There appears to be much commotion downstairs and it has disturbed everyone on a very important morning. We are due another extremely busy day at the assizes and that sort of noise will not do."

Kat studied his face, wondering how he could be so unaffected by what had been erected outside the house. "Have you not seen?" she asked, unable to keep the tremble from her voice.

Opening his mouth to answer, his gaze flickered towards the closed door of the chamber belonging to Lord Jeffreys. He gave a solemn nod of his head. "They will serve as example to all who have ill intentions towards our rightful King." He looked away, unable to hold her unforgiving glare.

She wanted to remind him that he had been the one to order all of it, that it had been the ugly pointed tip of the crow's quill that he had held in his hand that had scratched out the fate of those unfortunate men. Kat noted him swallow hard as he considered what to say next. "Lord Jeffreys wishes for more of your decoction to be added to his drink today. He says it helps ease the burden of the pain in court."

"I made quite enough yesterday. It can do no good to take too much," she replied flatly, but there was to be no argument.

"Take it to his room, Mistress Fox," he replied through gritted teeth. "He has insisted that it must be you who takes it to him."

By the time Kat returned with the prepared drink, Mr Giles had retreated back into the shadows of the house. She hesitated outside the chamber belonging to Lord Jeffreys before raising her hand in readiness to knock.

From behind the door, she heard several sharp intakes of breath and then the bang of a fist against furniture. Nervously, she tapped on the door and waited, hoping she would be told to leave the drink outside, but the gruff response instructed her to enter.

Keeping her gaze low, she opened the door and stepped into the room, her cheeks burning at the memory of their encounter the night before. She wondered if he would remember and hoped that he had been too intoxicated to recall any of it.

Waiting for him to acknowledge her presence, she looked around, noting the size of the chamber. To the centre was a large bed, pushed against the wall. Green velvet curtains that had been hung from the oak frame were still to be tied back, so they obscured her view of the other side.

To the far side of the room was a hearth. Either side of it were two chairs covered in a green brocade that had become worn with age. Between them was a table with the remnants of cheese, bread and wine still to be cleared from the evening before.

Lord Jeffreys was not visible and she suspected he was on the other side of the bed, hidden by the curtain. She hoped that he was not still in his bed, in his night garments. The thought of it struck her with disgust. Why had he insisted that she bring the drink to him? Any of the other servants could have done so. Clearing her throat to remind him of her presence, Kat noticed a shape casting a shadow on the floor at the foot of the bed. She edged around the bed, bringing herself closer and then she could see him. His back was turned and his shoulders arched as he hunched over the top of a chair, gripping the high back.

"I have brought your decoction, as requested," she said and he stiffened at the sound of her voice.

"Come. Leave it over here." His breathing was shallow, as though he was struggling to take air.

"Should I fetch for the physic, my Lord?" Kat asked as he coughed into a handkerchief but he shook his head vigorously and gestured for her to put the drink down beside him.

Carefully, she set it down before casting him a sidelong glance. Even with the limited visibility in the shuttered room, misted by the smoky haze of candles, she noted the white of his knuckles as he continued to grip the back of the chair. He said nothing more and she turned to leave.

"Stay," he commanded and her heart sank. Backing away, she put as much distance between them as was possible without appearing frightened or offensive. He straightened, no longer requiring the support that the chair had been providing. The change was sudden, unnatural. He turned to look towards the window. Upon closer inspection Kat noticed that, although not yet turned back, the shutters appeared to have been disturbed, as though somebody had opened them and pushed them back together in a hurry. "Have you looked out on the morning yet?" he enquired in a pleasant tone that did not suit him, He moved the chair that he had been leaning against and gestured for Kat to join him.

"There was still a low mist when I rose," she replied, trying to read the thoughts behind his dark eyes.

"Let us hope that it has lifted then," he said and moved closer to her so that she could see the bloodshot redness of his eyes. Small ale laced with honey would have been a far better choice for his morning drink rather than what she had been instructed to bring. With an impatient snap of his head, he turned to the door. "Where are those servants? I advised that I would be breaking my fast in my chamber this morning and still nobody has come. This will not do!" His agitation was making him pace and more than anything Kat wanted to leave.

"Open the shutters," he instructed her quietly and he noted her hesitation with an intolerant growl before raising his voice. "Open them."

Kat did not want to do it. She knew what she would see in the street below. Reluctantly, she walked over, feeling the rough of the wood at her fingertips.

"Well go on," His agitation growing, Lord Jeffreys advanced several paces towards her.

Holding her breath and keeping her gaze tilted upwards, Kat folded back the shutters. There was a thud as she heard the weight of Lord Jeffreys fall into the chair. "A glorious morning indeed," he said, but there was no conviction to his words.

Careful not to look out, Kat turned to face him, pleased that she could keep her back to the dreadful sight outside. "Indeed it is, Lord Jeffreys," she agreed.

He was staring past her, a strange smile plastered on his face. It was more of a leer than a smile, as though invisible hands were pulling the corners of his mouth upwards. "Fetch me the wine."

Kat obeyed the order, pouring it into a cup for him. Snatching it from her, he drank deeply, draining it in one go. Not even for one moment did he avert his gaze from the view below the window. Throwing the cup to the floor, he stood up abruptly and took her hand in his. "Come, join me in seeing what justice looks like."

"I am quite alright here," Kat insisted. "Let me fetch you another cup of wine."

His grip tightened and he dragged her towards the casement window. "Look!" he demanded and took her roughly by the shoulders. "Look out on to the street."

"I do not want to," Kat replied, her voice shaking.

"You will look!" His voice echoed about the room. "What do you see?"

Kat was unable to answer as she looked at the bloody mess of body parts that had once belonged to good and honest men she had once known; all unrecognisable but for the empty, glassy glare of Joseph Speed.

"Do you see God's fury?" He shook her and bowed his head so that his mouth was by her ear. "Do you see justice?"

Aghast, Kat did not know how to answer.

"Tell me that you understand now, woman. Tell me that what you see down there is justice." He pressed his mouth to her ear, his stale breath hot. "If you truly understand, you will know that this is what the King expects, what the country needs to maintain order and respect." He paced angrily across to the flask of wine and then thrust it to his lips, gulping it back. "That," he said, pointing with his free hand, "is my job, my responsibility to the Crown."

Wiping his mouth with his sleeve, he sat down heavily. Then he laughed and it was the laugh of a madman. "I shall need to capture it, of course. In here." He tapped at the side of his head. "Just as an artist captures the masterpiece he paints. And I shall write to the King and to Lord Sunderland, including every last colourful detail."

He shifted his gaze so that it rested on her but she did not flinch. "You are not upset?" He sounded almost disappointed and Kat thought how wrong she had been to have felt even a morsel of empathy for him the night before. He was indeed proving himself to be the monster that people described him to be.

"The country will be better off for being rid of these sorts of scoundrels," he continued, his face contorting with disgust. "Most women do not have the constitution to see traitors brought to justice. You though…" He tilted his head to his shoulder, observing her with a look of intrigue. "There is something different about you."

Kat did not know if this was an intended compliment but she knew that she had to speak up. Darling would not have allowed him to sully the memory of those men any longer. She would have stood up for the people who had once been her neighbours, friends – and family. "These men had families, wives and children, all left behind to grieve, to somehow survive." As she spoke, she felt her fear succumbing to anger. "I have learned that the man whose head is now on a pike was called Joseph Speed, a shoemaker from Colyton. I happened upon his wife yesterday, after the trial."

Lord Jeffreys brought his fist down hard so that it pummelled the arm of the chair. "Her tears mean nothing. She should not have married a man who planned treason. I could have her whipped for it, show the town the consequences for anyone who dares grieve the end of traitors." He glowered at Kat, the suggestion that he could have her whipped too was burning in his eyes.

"She is a woman. She has no opinion on the rebellion. That is for the minds of men," Kat countered, terrified that he would come good on his threat. "Her grief is for the loss of a husband, not a man who was foolish enough to join such a dreadful campaign." She chose her words carefully. "She told me that her husband had a smile for everyone and always a coin to spare for those poorer than him, even if it meant they would go with less food on their table. It was his way, so she said. You are right, of course. The country will be better off for being rid of that sort of scoundrel."

Rage was boiling within him. Kat could see it and instantly she regretted saying too much. Such talk was likely to land her at the bar in front of him, so that he could judge and punish her however he saw most fitting.

He stood up, the height of him slowly unfurling until he was towering above her. When he spoke, his voice was level and the maddened look had been replaced by pure malice. "You have said enough and I implore you to say no more. Your work can still be done with the scold's bridle firmly in place. I am certain Mr Giles can seek one out." He attempted a smile to convey his apparent enjoyment of bringing back such a cruel punishment for her loose tongue, but she could see that he did not intend it, that his mind was already occupied with other thoughts. He walked back to the window to look out in quiet contemplation. "You may now leave me to continue my enjoyment of capturing how well justice has been served."

When Kat was back in her chamber, pressing her head against the cool of the wooden door panelling, she realised that her time in that chamber with Lord Jeffreys had brought a moment of clarity. In spite of his cruel bravado, she had seen the hesitation in his face, the way he had needed to harden his own constitution to look out of the window. He could not do it alone. And he too was afraid. He was afraid of King James. He was afraid of the consequences if he did not succeed in demonstrating that retribution had been brought to the crown. The coldness of his manner and brutality of his words belonged to the monster that he needed to be, not the man who he was. When he had touched her, Kat had seen a hidden part of him. It had been quite unexpected and she knew that this was the gift that had been her grandmother's legacy:

Lord Jeffreys believed that, by looking upon those wretched men for long enough and repeating that the blood and grief brought upon them and their loved ones was simply 'justice', he could create an impervious shell.

******

The house was sombre in its atmosphere. Nobody said a word as they carried out their chores. Not one word was uttered about the horror propped outside the house like a macabre sculpture.

There was a fuss when the judges were set to leave for the red hung courtroom once again. Kat could hear a heated discussion between Mr Giles and another man as they considered the best route for the Crown Counsel to take. "The streets are not safe. You have heard the mobs."

"What, and we are to move about like rodents, underground?" Mr Giles asked, his tone incredulous. "What if they are to break through and find their way in? We will be cornered."

"There can be no other way," the man retorted urgently. Kat had seen him only briefly to know that he was a soldier with authority.

"There are the rooftops," Mr Giles suggested and Kat paused. The rooftop was her quiet place. It had been a peaceful and private place to invoke the spirit of the High Priestess. She did not want these men trampling all over what little sanctuary she had.

"We take the passage," the man said firmly, asserting whatever authority he had over Mr Giles. "My men have their posts on the streets. The mobs will not breach any entrance to get near the Crown Counsel."

Kat moved in the direction of the voices, silently following the flurry of activity as they went downstairs. The heavy clang of keys and bolts reverberated through the house as the entrance way to a dark passage was revealed.

In the glow of candlelight, the judges were ushered down the stone staircase, into the gaping mouth that smelled of damp and rats. Armed soldiers led the way and Kat hurried past the young servant who was to wait for the instruction to seal it off once again. She fled down the steps and watched as the procession walked further into the gloom, two judges in front and three at the back. The heavy step of their boots resounded against the cold, wet stone. Behind them, their robes billowed together as one, swelling like the crest of a gigantic, blood-red wave.

Kat watched until they disappeared into the blackness and she hurried back up the steps, escaping the violent chill of underground. As the bolts were shunted back into place, she wondered how many more families would be broken and ruined by the time those bolts were released once again.

CHAPTER TWENTY NINE

The days that followed drew Kat deeper into misery. She had seen no more of Gideon but the memory of the woman hovering over him, her lips dangerously close to his, taunted her.

Darkness seemed to swamp the house, seeping through the corridors and up the winding stairs. The house revolved around the whims and tempers of Lord Jeffreys. He was like an unearthly demon, rarely seen, but always heard: footsteps, shouts, things breaking.

Everyone in the house crept about. Everyone was afraid. Each day in the stillroom, Kat reminded herself that she had the power to end it, to turn him off. Often her fingers hovered over the pale blue cloth wrapped around the hemlock and the knife in her hand shook as she thought about how quickly she could do it, what she could slip it into. But each time, she stalled and returned the deadly parcel to its hiding place. To end a life would change everything and she could not find the courage to face an eternity of damnation.

An early onslaught of rain brought an earthy smell to the air on the day when the Dorchester assizes were drawing near to a close.

Lord Jeffreys and his fellow judges had already made their way to court, picking their way across the rooftops of Dorchester. It had finally been agreed that it was no longer safe for any of them to travel through the passageways beneath the town. Emotions were running high and people had travelled from neighbouring towns for the trials. They were all full of loathing for the Lord Chief Justice Jeffreys and his fellow judges.

The sound of people gathering and raised voices from the streets disturbed the silence in the house. Soldiers were outside, attempting to bring order to the ensuing chaos.

Hurrying to the dining room, Kat was soon joined by others. Mary Althrop looked grimly down onto the street, careful to avoid looking at those who had already paid dearly. "It's that boy from Weymouth," she said and shook her head sadly. "William Wiseman."

Everyone knew about William Wiseman. Only fourteen years old, the rumours surrounding young William had worked their way up and down Dorchester and into the staff quarters of the lodgings on High West Street. They said that he had a mind so keen and sharp that he could challenge even the country's most educated men. When the Duke of Monmouth had landed, young William had been asked to read the proclamation. In recent days, he had appeared before judge and jury and he had been shaking like a leaf. It was no surprise; what went on in the red hung courtroom had become common knowledge, and the rumours of the Lord Chief Justice Jeffreys, with his soulless eyes and menacing smile as he delivered sentences, were enough to make any man quake.

The court had fallen silent as they had waited for the judge to state his decision on how best to address William's crime. The room had erupted when the judge had spoken. Young William had been sentenced to a whipping through all of the market towns of Dorsetshire.

"But he suffered his sentence yesterday," Kat said to Mary, stretching her neck to look through the gathering crowd.

Mary shook her head, her expression lugubrious. "A man came by yesterday, told the Lord Chief Justice that the gaoler delivering the whipping went easy on the lad."

"Nonsense!" Kat challenged and she pressed her palm against the thin pane of glass. "I heard the poor boy cry out."

"As did all of us." A young lad from the stabling yard agreed with Kat. "But Jane says she overheard Lord Jeffreys speaking of it with his visitor." He pushed a timid looking girl forwards, telling her to repeat what she had heard.

The girl looked frightened as she prepared to speak. People were standing trial for careless words. They all knew it was dangerous to speak ill of the King's campaign.

"Go on then. Say what you heard. It is only repeating fact." Kat encouraged, trying to keep the sense of impatience she was feeling from her tone.

Turning her head, the girl checked who was in earshot and then kept her voice low. "A man came here last night. He said that the leniency of the whipping would reflect poorly on Lord Jeffreys." She hesitated, glancing at the stable lad, then Mary and Kat.

The boy nudged her. "And the rest."

"I heard them saying that it would suggest that he had sympathies for the Presbyterians." She tilted her head and looked down at the ground. "And I heard Lord Jeffreys say that the boy must be whipped again today, that it is to be done as it should have been."

Kat shook her head in disbelief. "They can't. A whipping two days straight, the boy will surely die? There will be an uproar."

Stepping aside, Mary averted her gaze from the street. "They will do it if that's what the Lord Chief Justice Jeffreys wants," she said dolefully.

Sickened, Kat continued her protest. "But what if he dies?"

Mary simply shrugged. "What's another life, now?"

******

Kat had returned to the stillroom after the news that William Wiseman was to repeat his punishment. Nobody had disturbed her and she had remained there without breaking her fast.

The unmistakable crack of the gaoler's whip had started shortly afterwards and the poor boy did not take the punishment quietly. Soon he would be too exhausted, too pained to cry out and there would be no soothing poultice for the split, raw flesh, no kind arms to hold him and comfort him. Kat doubted he would last the night.

Everything on the table in front of her was lined up ready to prepare a sleeping draught for Lord Jeffreys. It had been out all morning but she had not lifted a finger to even make a start. Instead, she had been staring at the hemlock again, searching for the conviction inside her to drop it into her pestle and mortar so that it could be crushed. By nightfall he could have consumed it and daybreak he would be cold.

"What are you doing?" The voice was an echo but very real. With a gasp, Kat raised her head and a haze of sunlight pouring through the small window momentarily blinded her. As her vision cleared she could make out a shape amidst the dust motes dancing in the iridescent beams. Then she heard his voice again – Gideon's.

Stumbling backwards, she drew a shocked breath. He asked the question once again, accusation in his voice. The shape taking form in front of her had become two and Kat realised that she was watching Gideon and somebody else. The question had not been directed at her.

"Gideon?" Reaching out for him, she walked over to the brilliant shafts of light, her skin caressed by the warmth of it. Almost at once she could feel his skin against her own. Shutting her eyes, Kat allowed herself to fall forward into the space in front of her until she was no longer in Dorchester, but somewhere else.

Then she felt the urgent press of Gideon's lips against her own and, desperate to feel her passion and lust returned, she responded. There was no feeling there though. Gideon's lips were cold and his eyes devoid of emotion. She tried harder, eager to please him, to feel loved but there was no love. It was as though she was kissing a hard shell….

"What are you doing?" I ask because, in spite of the fact that I have already pushed the woman away from me, she has returned. Now she is pressing herself again on me, bewitching me into thinking that she is my wife. I see Kat's face. Confused, enchanted, I kiss back, but this cannot be real. "What are you doing?" I ask again, between hot and urgent kisses.

She does not reply with words, only by offering herself to me with a renewed vigour and my body responds. My hand cups the curve of her breast as I continue to kiss her with a fevered passion that is nothing to do with lust or love, but something else entirely. Then I stop abruptly, turning my head away and pushing her from me once more. This is not my wife. I do not love her. I am not attracted to her. I simply have a burning desire to feel some level of emotion. But there is nothing. It is as though my beating heart was torn from my chest on those moors and left with the men laid to waste on them - left with HIM, the one whose name I fail to remember but whose pale, unblinking eyes glint back at me in the moonlight.

The rising sun outside offers more light in the room and she sees my cold, hard gaze. There is nothing left inside me now except for the hellish horror of the journey that brought me here.

She looks hurt by the rejection, but then something changes in her. She leans over me, her eyes burning with the embarrassment and shame of being turned down. This is a spoiled, arrogant girl full of self-importance; a girl not accustomed to being spurned. She brings her lips close to my ear and whispers that I should leave. When she draws away again, there is a hint of bitter satisfaction on her face. It makes the blood in my veins run cold. Without hesitation, I throw back the sheets.

The day is going to be a bright one. Only a year ago, I would have enjoyed watching the sparkle of sunlight make the windows glint, the warmth of it baking my face. Not today. Today I pray for clouds and rain, anything that will assist me. I pull on my boots and skirt around the edge of the building, careful to avoid the stabling area. Ahead of me is the edge of a wood. I know it leads to the moors eventually, but it offers the benefit of cover. Holding my breath, I scan my surroundings. The stable yard is animated with noise. That is where they are. If I do not run now, I never will. Overhead, buzzards are circling. I look at them and swallow but my throat is dry. She always says that buzzards are a sign, a bad portent. In this case, she is right. I know exactly why they are circling. With a burst of energy, my feet take me, faster and faster.

My goal is to reach the enclave of trees ahead. The gentle breeze feels as though it is suddenly rushing at me, hindering my speed. I want to cry out in frustration but I do not. I just keep running and keeping my eyes focused. My mind starts to frantically work out the distance ahead, the time it will take to get there at my speed. It feels as though time is slowing, that I'm running through mud. But soon I am closer and I see an opening; it is a wide, welcoming dark gap between the foliage. I cry out as I race to it, ready to embrace the darkness and that is when I hear the thundering of hooves.

Blood rushes through my veins, pounding at my temples as I exert myself. I dare not look back for that will be my undoing. The silver-grey bark of the trees is suddenly close. With an almighty effort, I burst into the welcome shadow of the woods. Twigs crack noisily beneath my feet and the ground is less forgiving. I know that I could find myself ensnared in a trap meant for rabbits or foxes, but that is the risk I must take. The magnificent trunks of these trees will slow those pursuing me but I need a plan of where to run to. Hiding will do no good if they release the hounds, but why would they bother for a man like me? I am of no importance. It will soon be fruitless to maintain the chase for a commoner. Fear keeps me going and I am not tiring. Deeper and deeper, I run into the woodland without a care for the thorns or low hanging branches that whip and scratch at my face. The horse hooves become more distant and I hear shouts. I think they might be calling off the chase, but I do not allow that knowledge to hamper my pace. I run on, my body adapting to the new rhythm required to navigate this tricky terrain with upturned roots and fallen logs. Then I see a glimmer of light. I run towards it and my lungs are burning. It is like a beacon of hope. Perhaps there will be a barn or an isolated farmhouse that I can take shelter in and catch my breath.

I near the light, soon bursting through a bundle of low hanging vines and into the open space beyond. My vision is startled by the contrast of shadow to bright sky. It takes a few moments for my eyes to adjust as I continue to run and the ground becomes sludgy beneath my feet. At last, I see a rhyne and I grin as I remember how the horses had struggled with such an obstacle. I'll need to be careful but crossing it will give me more time. I look left to right. The rhyne is long and eventually meets the river. I must not be too hasty. It is impossible to say how deep it runs. I am slowed considerably by the marshland now and the water and mud threaten to take my boots if I am too slow or too quick. It reaches my shins, my thighs and soon I am waist deep, wading through. I am grateful for the warm day as I will need to find somewhere to strip and dry my clothes for fear of catching another fever. I will need my strength and for my mind to remain sharp. Home is many miles away, but I can do it. I know I can do it.

Suddenly there is nothing but water beneath me and my head is submerged as I kick wildly. This is how men drown. I have seen it before, not so long ago. They panic and they flail their arms whilst thrashing their feet. The water and mud pull them under. This is not my time though. Water is in my mouth and I want to cough, to thrash about even more, but I do not. I think of her, summoning the beauty of her to the forefront of my mind.

She is standing in front of me. The early evening sun bounces from her hair and makes her skin luminescent. She is smiling and holding a basket of herbs. I can see earth beneath her fingernails from where she has been tending to the garden.

I surface whilst coughing and gasping for air, swimming as best I can. I wish that I had not thought of her like that, why my mind had to bring that particular memory back. Reluctant for the memory to progress any further, I try to freeze that moment and think only of her looking so beautiful and serene with the rushing sound of the nearby mill wheel ploughing through the river. My toes kick at the mud bed but I am careful not to sink into it and then the water is shallower. I claw at the long grass, pulling myself through. When at last the land is firmer beneath my feet, I look for shelter, somewhere to stop and rest awhile. I am certain that I am no longer being chased. There are bodies here though, of men and horses. I see them as ominous dark shapes scattered across the landscape, giving away the recent events and I close my eyes, but she is there again, in front of me – still smiling.

And I am drunk, imagining her standing there in the gardens of a manor house rather than the poky square of land that belongs to our dreary humble cottage, squeezed between others like it. The dreams that Lord Granville have given me are loose on my tongue. They tumble out, incoherent, boyish and full of fancy. Her smile fades at the sight and sound of me and I see the worry. She is so perceptive, so clever. Far more intelligent than most of those men whose company I clamour for with Lord Granville. She calls me a fool and I raise my hand. The rest is a blur. All I see is the basket lying on the ground, herbs scattered at her feet. It was the last time I saw her smile.

I trudge on, guilt burdening my progress as I step over the fallen men, just as I had stepped over those fallen herbs. Then I see the barn. It is the shelter I need, just to catch my breath and dry out. My feet are running again, faster and faster. The barn is a blur and I realise that it is because I am crying. I am crying for fear, for guilt, for remorse. I am crying for her.

The smell of old straw is welcome against the stench of death and marshland and I do not slow until I near the entrance. In my haste I do not see the figures flanking the sides of the barn and I do not hear the tread of their footsteps until it is too late and I am pinned to the ground.

CHAPTER THIRTY

"Late night?" Tim was spraying the kitchen surfaces when Ruth emerged.

"Not really, just a bad sleep." She pushed her hair out of her face and Tim put down the spray and the cloth, making it obvious he had something important he wanted to discuss.

"What happened last night? Between you and Jeremy, I mean?"

Ruth's heart sank. Had he heard their disagreement? She hadn't thought they had been particularly loud. "Nothing," she replied with a casual shrug.

"Funny, that's just what he said before he left for the archives this morning. But both of you have exactly the same funk about you." He pulled up a stool and gestured for her to sit down next to him. "Come on. Spill."

Ruth swatted his arm. "Don't start the big-little brother routine." It was a longstanding joke that Tim, although the youngest by two years, had always been hotly defensive of Ruth, even when they had been growing up.

"Why not? I'm allowed to be concerned for my sister, aren't I? There's no shame if you have any sort of romantic involvement, you know."

Pressing her hands to her head, Ruth groaned. "What is it with you and Zoe? She's been just the same about all of this. We're just friends."

"Don't give me the 'just friends' line. There's enough electricity between you to light up the Christmas decorations throughout the whole village! Besides, even if you are only friends, those rugged good looks and that body cannot have escaped your attention."

"Looks aren't everything you know." Ruth was defensive. The last thing she needed was Tim playing matchmaker. "Besides, I'm still married."

With a snort of disgust, he went to grab a carton of orange juice from the fridge. "Marriage didn't stop Grayson, did it? You deserve a bit of happiness, Ruth."

"Happiness will come," she replied as he handed her a glass. "First, I'm just finding 'me' again."

Taking the hint, Tim did not bring up the subject anymore. "You're going to have to get a shift on. If we're to meet up at the museum, we'll need to leave in the next forty-five minutes."

Their timing for meeting one another was impeccable. Tim pulled into a space just as Jeremy swung in beside him. Ruth was happy to let Tim and Max do all the talking as she hung back, quietly reflecting on the disagreement she and Jeremy had experienced the night before. It felt awkward and she didn't want to just act as though none of it had happened. That felt insincere. It was easier not to say anything at all.

"I don't suppose you've been to Taunton before, have you?" Max asked him as they followed the footpath from the car park that took them towards the town centre. He looked extremely pleased with himself for coming up with the idea.

"Not before this morning," Jeremy answered, "but I know a fair bit about its history." He pointed at the grand looking castle that appeared in front of them as they crossed the road. "One of the many castle projects of Henry de Blois, in fact," He turned to Ruth. "So, there's your link to Winchester."

Giving him a polite nod of acknowledgement, Ruth smiled. In spite of how uncomfortable she felt, she didn't want to appear rude or huffy.

Jeremy was far too distracted by the site of historical interest to notice that Ruth was quieter than usual. He elaborated on his knowledge: "De Blois was responsible for Wolvesey Castle, Winchester Palace and some of the final stages of Winchester Cathedral. He wasn't just a bishop, you know, he was a man with a fine architectural mind. Not really my era, but fascinating all the same. I find British history extraordinary. It's very different to the history of my homeland. Both countries with their own historical curiosities in their own right, but I suppose the grass always looked greener on the other side of the pond, and so I chose to study the British early modern period at university. Taunton Castle's role as an Assizes court and prison is closer to my era."

"We'll have our own personal tour guide. This will be great!" Max exclaimed and Tim rolled his eyes before sidling up next to Ruth.

"Well how about you two bores take a history tour whilst Ruthie and I do a spot of shopping?" He hooked his arm through hers. "What do you say to buying a few Christmas treats for ourselves?"

It sounded like a great way to alleviate the uncomfortable situation she found herself in, but Ruth couldn't help feeling a little disappointed. Jeremy had really turned her head towards history. "We've booked tickets though, Tim."

"So what? It's free entry. Nobody loses out."

Ruth had been looking forward to the tour and wanted to spend a little more time in Jeremy's company. "Couldn't we join them for a short while and then go off? That way we get the best of both worlds."

Rubbing his hands together, Max was full of enthusiasm. "Sounds great, Ruth." He flicked his wrist and checked his watch. "Come on, I'd like a good hour here. Lots to see."

Snow still blanketed the ground but the approach to the castle had cleared a little beneath the busy footfall of shoppers, sightseers and those seeking some fun on the enchanting-looking ice rink on Castle Green.

The castle walls, a great mosaic of stone, rose prominently above them. The weave of naked wisteria vines clung to the fascia of the building. In the early summer, they would bloom vibrantly purple. Off to the left was the archway leading to what had once been the Great Hall and the rest of the castle.

Inside the museum they started wandering through the various galleries, taking their time to read about the relics locked behind glass, and listening to Jeremy as he elaborated on the facts punched out on the signage. He had such an engaging way of expressing himself and Ruth had no doubt that he would make for a popular lecturer.

Moving on through the many stones and fossils and into the Anglo-Saxon period, they journeyed through history, learning how Somerset had been shaped over time. The gallery ahead of them glowed an ominous shade of red and Ruth's stomach churned. As they walked through she stopped, clutching a hand to her neck as she saw the nooses looped above statues. Her skin began to crawl and tingle, as though nails were scratching and clawing beneath it. She could still feel the presence of Kat, burrowed deep inside her. It was enough to blur the edges of time. She had seen nooses like that before and she had seen the men on the gallows. Images swam through her mind and she heard the jeer of a crowd above the frightened whinny of horses and the splintering of wood. She heard shouts and orders given to try and right the chaos and she could smell sea salt in the air which was odd as they were nowhere near the seaside.

"Ruth?" Tim was shaking her. "Ruth?"

People were turning to look. They gathered in groups, whispering and watching, just as she recalled how people had gathered in groups in another time and place, chattering to one another, glaring at her with hostile eyes through the smeared windows of a carriage.

Everything was merging together in Ruth's head. There was no sense to any of it. She tried to focus on Tim and lifted her arm, but it fell uselessly to her side. Somebody else had control of it and then she felt her head turn as Jeremy began saying her name, trying to pull her out of the gallery.

Ruth's eyes closed and she felt strong arms hoist her upright as she struggled to walk. She longed for the sharp bite of the winter wind and the freshness of the air outside, but everything was changing.

With an almighty effort, she managed to open her eyes, expecting to see the tables in the café just down the corridor from the Rebellion gallery.

Blinking away the haze, she searched for the people who she knew would be in that café: mothers tending to children, elderly couples enjoying a seat at the window, waiting staff bustling about.

She saw none of those things and could no longer hear the worried voices or Jeremy's shouts as he told people to make space to let them through.

In their place, she heard the snort of horses, smelled the tang of leather and sweat and the sound of their hooves clattering against shale as they were driven on, harder and faster.

"Take this! God's teeth, just take it!" Somebody was thrusting something into her hand and she could feel her stomach lurching dreadfully. Her muscles convulsed but nothing came up.

Ruth whimpered but her voice was drowned out by another: "I am quite alright," someone insisted, and Ruth felt her hand batting the object away as the other pressed against the welcome cool of the thin pane of glass.

Slowly, as though being sucked away, Ruth was aware that she had lost all control of her body, but she was no longer in a museum. She was sitting inside a carriage that was racing along on an uneven road filled with potholes. The surface had become slick and slippery from a relentless downpour of rain. When her head turned, it was not Jeremy looking back at her but the concerned face of Mr Giles.

CHAPTER THIRTY ONE

A patchwork of green, brown and gold rushed past the window as the procession continued to gather pace towards Somerset.

Kat glanced across the carriage at Doctor Copping, whose head had dropped to his shoulder as he snored loudly. There would be no waking him. Kat suspected that he had used the remainder of the sleeping draught she had prepared for Lord Jeffreys. Her mind turned to the hemlock that she had eventually thrown away. It had been just as well that she had not given into the madness that had enticed her to even consider such a grand scale poisoning. Nearly every one of these men of authority had required the sleeping draught. It had been the vision of Gideon she had experienced in the stillroom that had interrupted her at the time, and she had realised the madness in her actions. Gideon needed her. He was out there somewhere and he was hurt, scared, alone and betrayed. The familiar sensation of sickness squeezed at her insides again and she swatted Mr Giles away as he tried to help her.

During the journey to Lyme Regis, Kat had travelled with the other women servants. The coachman had complained the carriage had been too heavy, that it would slow them down. A larger lady had been moved in with the male servants and then Kat had been selected. There had been envious stares when she had been plucked from the line and selected to ride nearer the front of the procession in one of the newer, more comfortable carriages with Mr Giles and Doctor Copping, but it did not help with the sickness. The nausea was a consequence of what she now knew about her husband, the depth of his betrayal. It had all been for what? Ambition, money, land, the lies of noblemen who had promised all of those things?

"You look quite pale, Mistress Fox," Mr Giles pointed out. "Are you ailed?"

"I do not always travel well," Kat replied, closing her eyes to try and stop the dizzying sensation but when she did so, all she could see and hear was what she had witnessed in Lyme. Her head was full of horror; the baying crowds in Lyme Regis echoed through her thoughts and she could still smell the sea salt and sweat as she recalled how it had felt to be a part of that crowd, awaiting the public execution of another set of rebels. Kat had been troubled ever since.

Mr Giles had disapproved of her watching. She had seen it on his face. He had thought it unbecoming of a lady to take an interest in the spectacle that was prisoners being hung, drawn and quartered. There had been no way of explaining her reasons though; how could she have admitted that her husband's brother was one of the men sentenced to death? How could she have reasoned that, for Bridget's sake, she had to bear witness to it, to show her solidarity to Robert if he was to be one of the men to meet their end on the beach where the Duke of Monmouth had landed only a few months earlier? So, whilst the horses and carriages were prepared for their journey to Exeter, Kat had ventured towards the gathering crowd…

They were waiting for the selected prisoners to be brought. Kat did not know who she would see or how many, but she caught sight of the executioner, Jack Ketch, who responded to the masses as if he were a man to be celebrated. Like the Lord Chief Justice Jeffreys, his name was renowned and his reputation went before him. Kat thought how very surreal the whole thing was, like actors making their way to a performance as his shorter, lesser known colleague walked behind him. Inadvertently, Kat caught the shorter man's eye. He glared at her, offering something between a leering smile and a grimace. There was thunder on his face. This was a man who had a dark soul. He enjoyed his work.

Attempting to remove herself from his line of sight, Kat sidestepped further into the crowd, but his head swivelled and his murky, grey eyes followed, enjoying her discomfort.

Kat's head began to pound and her vision blurred. Somebody nudged her, told her to watch herself, but Kat barely heard, for around the shorter man's neck she could see a spectral looking noose. Behind him, Kat could envisage Jack Ketch, slipping a sack over his head. One day he too would be caught falling foul of the law and find himself at the mercy of his new colleague. The vision cleared as quickly as it had come and the man turned his head as somebody from the crowd shouted something.

"Pascha Rose, that is." A man had leaned towards her, to inform her all about Jack Ketch's new assistant. "A butcher from London. They say he is mad for blood, that he's been working with a meat cleaver since he was old enough to hold one."

Kat wanted to tell him that Pascha Rose would meet the end of his days before the turn of the year and that it would be Jack Ketch, turning him off. She chose, though, to say nothing and moved on.

The air was salty with brine, and a sea wind had picked up, blowing out towards the vast expanse of water, taking with it the smell of tar and pitch. On the beach, the ropes of the gallows were swinging ominously as though the men had already met their fate and their ghosts had remained.

Kat found that she was standing near to the horses, already tethered to draw the prisoners on a hurdle to their place of execution. They were huge, strong beasts with an impressive show of muscle beneath their bay coats. She caught the wild eyes of one and it snorted, pulling back with fear. Looking around nervously, Kat wondered if anybody had noticed and would accuse her of bewitching the animal. She tried to duck out of the way, out of sight so that no accusation could be made by any of the other bystanders. Then came the shouts, the frenzied whinny and snort of all the horses. The crowds parted as two beasts kicked and bucked. Kat could see the whites of their eyes and the frothy spittle gathering at their mouths. There was the sound of splintering wood as the sledges that were ready for securing to the unfortunate prisoners were kicked to pieces.

People began whispering; something had spooked those horses, they said. It must be a sign that God was displeased. None could agree on whether it was because of the rebels or because of the new King's actions. Nobody said a word about witchcraft or the work of a cunning woman being responsible. Kat overheard somebody whisper that, whatever the reason, it had saved those twelve men from the additional pain and humiliation of being dragged to the place where they would be executed.

There were heckles and hisses as people threw taunts, all in an attempt to show support for the King. Kat knew that these were all actions spurred on by fear.

Shortly, the men were marched past, wrists and ankles bound. Kat recognised none of them. According to several people in the crowd, these were men of far more considerable status than Robert's. Kat could not stay to watch the rest. She had seen the fear on their faces, smelled it on their sweat.

Lord Jeffreys had wanted to stay long enough to see that the men were brought to justice, to be able to report back to the King that his bidding was done in Dorsetshire. Then they would leave for towns in Devonshire and onto Somerset.

Up above, seagulls soared against the scudding clouds, searching for scraps dropped by the crowds, and Kat thought how infinitely better life would be to be able to fly like that, free and untroubled by bloody battlefields and power-hungry men.

"Mistress Fox, we are to make haste!" No sooner than when she had returned to the carriages, Mr Giles was ushering her to where the horses were waiting, impatient to continue their journey.

By the time the procession was pulling away, the first of the condemned was climbing up to the gallows.

Kat recalled how Mr Giles had reached across and pulled the curtain whilst Doctor Copping had whispered a prayer to God before drinking deeply from his flask.

They had made it to Exeter in good time. Only twenty-one souls had been trialled, but hundreds more were awaiting judgement in Somerset.

As they hurtled towards Taunton, Kat tried to blot out the way Mr Giles was nervously twisting his fingers. It did nothing to help her nerves. He had been uptight since the coaching inn they had stopped at, when it had been obvious that the distaste for the legal party of travellers was growing. Every moment they were out on the road they were in danger. News of the sentences the Lord Chief Justice so gleefully dished out had travelled. The landlady had served them with her lips pressed firmly together. There had been no welcoming smiles or friendly conversation, just a cold unpleasantness. Kat had found herself with no appetite. The food had no doubt been spat on or tampered with in some unpleasant way.

When the horses eventually slowed, Kat looked out the window. The magnificent stone of the castle was lit by flaming torches and the uniform silhouettes of the men guarding it were stiff and still. Behind those walls were hundreds of prisoners. By all accounts, more than had been in Dorchester.

Kat leaned towards the window to see that the horses flanking the carriages were drawing back, allowing room for the coaches to make their way down the narrower streets. She pulled the wool curtain. Dusk had already fallen and she was tired, sore and hungry.

There was a shout and they jarred to a halt. Mr Giles stiffened and told her to wait whilst he opened the door and stepped out. An exchange of words was followed by a shout and Kat jumped as something thudded against the door of the carriage. The vehicle rocked ominously as the horses were startled.

Using an elbow to keep herself steady, she pulled back the curtain. A man staggered forwards and then backwards, intoxication threatening to send him off-balance. There was another shout as a watchman moved him along, a drunken nuisance likely to end up in the town gaol, or worse if he was to say anything that hinted his support for the disgraced dead Duke.

Mr Giles returned, wiping spittle from his cheek. "We can walk from here." He instructed the coachman to take Kat's belongings into the new lodgings which, she learned, would also be where both Lord Jeffreys and Mr Giles were to reside. "He wants you close by, Mistress Fox, in the event that he should require your services as a matter of urgency. These journeys are doing his ailments no good."

A sense of dread filled her. She did not like the term, 'require your services'. It conjured images of Lord Jeffreys in his chamber, demanding she look out of his window at the men who had been executed. She wondered what new horrors they would witness in the town so close to where the rebellion had reached its final crescendo. Thoughts of Winchester made her chest feel tight and heavy. Not so long ago life had been much simpler. She would give anything to return to those days, before Gideon had changed and before they had heard anything of the King's handsome young nephew sailing across the seas to lead a small but growing army who had been supposed to put him on the throne.

Even inside the building, they could hear the shouts from the prisoners, some muffled, some loud and coherent. Kat could feel the anxiety and animosity in the atmosphere. Without thinking, she reached for the place where the stone of her necklace was nestled beneath the layers of her clothing. It pressed against her skin as her fingers sought out its shape and she quietly prayed that it would protect her.

The house was deceptively larger than it appeared from the street, with its narrow corridors lit by the flare of candles and sconces. Kat was left standing next to the warmth of a hearth as servants fussed over the important men. Tracing a finger over the surrounding brickwork, she tried to blot out the noise from the prison and hoped that this would not continue through the night. She knew only too well that there would be those guilty of nothing more than being in the wrong place at the wrong time, or who had unwittingly provided a service to the fallen Duke and his men.

The housekeeper was a woman called Beth. She was a willowy woman with sharp features, far younger in appearance than Kat would have expected. "Mistress Fox?" Beth appraised her with a critical eye. "You are the healer?"

"I am the Judge's Apothecary, yes."

Pursing her lips, Beth continued to stare for a moment before nodding. "Of course. You will follow me." Their footsteps echoed down the length of the corridor and Kat struggled to keep up with the woman's brisk pace.

As Kat followed her down a spiralling stone staircase, she felt herself shiver against the drop in temperature. Although the fire was roaring, it had obviously not long been lit. "I am afraid the place hasn't been used in a while. Had we known a healer was to be accompanying Lord Jeffreys, we would have made time to do more with the place." Her tone was frosty and held no note of apology as she bustled around the room, using her rush light on the candle tapers.

Through the smoky haze, Kat could see that her belongings had already been brought down and a half-hearted attempt made to clear the wispy silvery cobwebs that stretched across the hearth and the equipment on the large table.

Beth moved over to a candelabra that had been placed by a work table. "I have been informed that you may require some assistance from the kitchen, with your…" She paused, searching for the right term.

"Are you referring to ingredients and equipment for the dispensary of my medicaments?"

Kat attempted to smile but she knew that it was half-hearted; she was too miserable for it to light up her face. "I shall be sure to ask should I require any assistance. Thank you."

"Well, that is as comfortable as I can make it," Beth said as she finished the job. "Will there be anything else, Mistress Fox?"

Walking around the table, Kat picked up a bottle that was thick with dust. "That will be all. I shall be quite comfortable, I am sure. Besides, it is much quieter down here."

Beth pursed her lips. "The noise can travel. Over five hundred souls in there. It is not so bad down here though." Before leaving the room, she glanced down at her feet to hide the shadow that crossed her face.

Kat waited until she left and then took a seat by the fire. She was too exhausted and hungry to unpack any of her things. All she wanted to do was rest but it occurred to her that Beth had not made mention of supper. After finding her way into the adjoining chamber, Kat smoothed the blankets and sighed. There was little doubt that Doctor Copping would soon bring another lengthy list for the many ailments Lord Jeffreys evidently suffered.

After setting up the table in the stillroom, she made her way up the stairs and to the kitchen where two maids were deep in conversation. Neither noticed Kat as she hovered in the doorway. They had lowered their voices but Kat could hear snatches of conversation. The older lady looked nervous and uncomfortable:

"Mind yerself now, Zella. These walls have eyes 'n' ears now they've brought the others with 'em. You've heard what 'appens to them that show sympathy to the prisoners."

Zella looked barely older than fourteen and she sniffed loudly, wiping the back of her hand beneath her nose. "How is it fair? Eight year old and she's to stand trial. I saw her ma only this morning. Beside herself, she was."

The older lady pressed her lips together until the edges paled. She looked as though she was struggling to keep a hold of her own emotions. "Nought about it is fair." She shook her head sadly. "She knew no better, just doing as she was asked, is all."

"I don't know why Mary Blake had to go and embroider that flag. All flutterin' lashes and silly curtsies she was. Was her own vanity that dragged those blessed girls into it and now this!" Her shoulders began to shake as more tears began to fall.

Shrinking back into the corridor, Kat stifled a gasp. She recognised the name 'Blake'. The school mistress who had died from smallpox in Dorchester prison had gone by that name. As she leaned against the cool stone of the walls, she blinked into the darkness. People had spoken of Mistress Blake when she had been in Dorchester. They had said that she and her young pupils had waved a welcome banner to welcome the handsome Duke into Taunton. Pretty as a picture they had been, all dressed in white and with ribbons in their hair. Could it really be true that one of those girls was now standing trial? 'Eight year old,' the younger maid had said. It turned Kat's stomach, leaving her with no appetite.

It was on her return to the stillroom that she was called to join Mr Giles in the parlour. He had removed the justaucorps he had been wearing during the procession to Taunton and was standing in front of the hearth, one hand in the pocket of his silk waistcoat. It was only when the servant who had shown Kat to the room had closed the door that he turned to acknowledge her with his usual officious tone. "Ah, there you are." The small round spectacles were perched on the bridge of his nose again and she wondered if he had been busy writing to the authorities of Taunton, making more demands of how they needed to prepare for the dispatch of those whose cries could be heard echoing through the castle grounds.

"How can I be of assistance, Mr Giles?" In spite of the shocking news she had overheard, she kept her tone level.

After tucking his spectacles into the pocket of his waistcoat, he pulled the chair back, inviting her to sit. "I should like it if you would join me for supper, Mistress Fox. I assume you have not yet eaten?"

A table had been laid generously with plates of cheese, fruits and bread. The thought of eating anything did not appeal. "Thank you, very kind," she replied as she watched him pour wine into a crystal cut glass and offered it to her.

Running a finger over the deep grooves in the crystal, Kat noted that it was certainly more comfortable in these lodgings than had been the case in Lyme, Exeter or Dorchester.

Joining her, Mr Giles asked if she would say grace. Her mind still turning over the horrifying idea that an eight-year-old child was to face the wrath of Lord Jeffreys and his fellow judges, Kat struggled with the words.

Picking at her food, she watched him hungrily tear at the chunks of bread with his teeth. "You are not hungry?" he asked, noticing the meagre effort she had made.

To defy him, she took a chunk of bread and began to eat it.

He waited until she had finished and then leaned forward. The expression on his face was serious. "There is increasing concern over the safety of members of our legal party. Talk of poison." Allowing the revelation to hang in the air between them, he reached for his wine and took a long sip.

Kat felt her skin prickle with heat. What was he preparing himself to say? Had they found something suspicious that implicated her or had somebody said something about her?

"Lord Jeffreys is particularly concerned and refuses to eat or drink anything that does not pass the lips of another."

Kat stilled the tremor in her legs. "And what does this have to do with me?"

"You know how to make a poison that cannot be detected by smell or taste, do you not?"

Wildly searching for the right response, Kat looked towards the flames of the fire. Had they found the slip of hemlock in Dorchester? After being so distracted by her vision of Gideon, she had discarded it, but she had been haunted and burdened by the weight of her shame. Her concerns were allayed by what he said next:

"There is a trader in Bridgwater who sells assay cups. Lord Jeffreys wants the cup tested before it is purchased. An apothecary is required to make a poison and prove the cup works."

As the relief washed over her, Kat realised what was being asked of her. She would be required to ride out to Bridgwater, but surely that would be a dangerous journey to undertake alone, particularly for a woman? "There must be an apothecary here or in Bridgwater who can do the work?"

Standing up, Mr Giles went to fetch more wine. "I am sure you have not missed the opinions of those around these parts. Taunton is a rebellious town. Same goes for Bridgwater. It is a trusted apothecary who must undertake this work. There are those who may wish to do Lord Jeffreys harm and it is not always easy to flush out the scoundrels."

Kat knew of the cups; fashioned from rhinoceros horn and silver, they would colour if filled with poisoned liquid. An authentic one would be expensive. "You surely do not feel any element of surprise at the resentment directed towards the Lord Chief Justice Jeffreys?" It was an impertinent question but she could not help herself.

Even in candlelight, Kat could see his face had paled considerably. "You should be careful, Mistress Fox," he warned, tipping his chin forward so that it was resting on the steeple of his fingertips. "You have caught the attentions of Lord Jeffreys."

"Oh?" Once again Kat felt her pulse begin to race with worry.

"He appears somewhat…" He looked toward the ceiling, trying to find the most appropriate way to elaborate: "…taken by you." There was an unmistakable sour tone to his words and Kat recalled how tenderly Mr Giles had tended her injuries in Dorchester and the way he had touched her hand on their journey to Taunton. He was quite the opposite to the quick-tempered judge whose fiery, cruel words struck terror in all who crossed his path.

She cleared her throat, her embarrassment obvious. "With all respect, Mr Giles, I think you are mistaken."

"With all respect, Mistress Fox, I believe that it is you who is mistaken." His tone was hard and he looked as fierce as he had when he had found the soldiers attacking her in the cottage. "He has enquired about you: where you are from, why you wear no ring. He does not usually pay this much attention to his servants."

"He holds no desire for a woman like myself. Besides, he has a wife, does he not?" Even as she said it, she felt the deep flush rise from her chest to her cheeks as she recalled their encounter in the corridor, the way his looks lingered longer than they should whenever their paths crossed.

Giving a derisive chuckle, Mr Giles shook his head. "You are far from naïve, Mistress Fox. Do not give me that wide-eyed look. Since when did having a wife stop a man from pursuing other women?"

The thought of it made her insides turn over with disgust. Mr Giles was right, of course, and if the rumours from Dorchester were true, Lord Jeffreys had already proved himself capable of this. There had been talk that a girl had visited the lodgings, requesting a private audience with Lord Jeffreys so that she might make a plea for the life of her brother. Lord Jeffreys had promised her that her brother's sentence would be commuted if she was to lay with him. As the story went, the boy had still met his grim end. Kat did not know for certain if this was hearsay or true. She had not always seen the comings and goings of people, for her own distractions had been too great, but she suspected that there was likely some truth to the story. The thought of it made her shudder and her mind wandered back to Gideon. If she was to find herself in that girl's position, begging for the life of a man dear to her, would she give herself up as a whore in return for his survival? There was no question, she decided, and she grasped the finger where her slim gold wedding band should have been. "And what have you told him about me?"

Mr Giles shrugged. "What can I tell him, other than the knowledge I hold?"

Kat wondered if he was trying to fluster her. It was certainly working. "What knowledge is that, Mr Giles?"

"I know that you do not want to be here, that there is a life waiting for you back in Winchester. And I know that you have not always lived such a modest life."

She shifted in her chair as the heat from the fire prickled her skin. "You have been making enquiries about me? Why should the life of an apothecary interest you so?"

Crossing his leg over his knee, Mr Giles took another sip of wine. "I did not need to make any enquiries to learn that you were seen speaking with one of the women whose husband was sentenced for treason."

It felt as though a cold fist had taken hold of her heart and was clenching it. "Is this what you have told Lord Jeffreys? It is not a crime to offer comfort to a woman who is overcome with grief."

"You are quite correct, offering comfort is not a crime. For that reason, I have not told Lord Jeffreys anything." He eyed her thoughtfully before speaking again. "It is strange that an attractive young woman such as yourself, who is clearly educated, is neither married or betrothed. That has not gone unnoticed."

She imagined the circle of pompous men speaking about her in the same suspicious and scornful way that they spoke of some of the prisoners who were put before them on trial. "That is surely only my business, Mr Giles? Why should it be any concern of theirs, or yours for that matter? I am here to do a duty, not answer questions about whether I am spinster, widow or wife."

Mr Giles lifted his cup to his lips. "I think you will find that every countryman's business, whether that be man, woman or child, is indeed the business of the Lord Chief Justice Jeffreys."

Pushing her dish aside, Kat glowered at him. "Are you insinuating something?"

"Not at all." He took a swig from his cup. "I am merely warning you to tread carefully with him." He lowered his voice. "Lord Jeffreys is a powerful man and he has a temper."

"As we are all painfully aware, but there is no point in you warning me or telling me any of this. I am just the Judge's Apothecary and I have not encouraged any of this…attention." She looked away, terrified that Mr Giles would somehow know of the visions that had come to her about her husband and his likely part in the rebellion.

"You are a good woman, Mistress Fox. I mean no offence by what I say to you. I just remind you of how dangerous and unforgiving he is." His eyes shone with genuine feeling and Kat saw the tenderness in them again. It confused her. Was he looking after her best interests or those of Lord Jeffreys? Could she trust him with anything he was saying?

Her food barely touched, she stood to leave. "You remind me of how dangerous and unforgiving Lord Jeffreys is, but may I remind you of something, Mr Giles?" She gripped the back of her chair. "By whose hand are the orders written for the erection of the gallows, the pitch and the faggots? And who is it who makes the requests for axes and cleavers and instructs the authorities of each town exactly where the prisoners shall meet their end? Think on that, Mr Giles, then let us decide who is indeed dangerous."

******

A pale dawn greeted her in the stabling yard the following morning. She was introduced to a man by the name of Amos, who was to journey with her to Bridgwater. Although much older, he appeared strong and sprightly. In spite of his daunting size, he had a friendly face.

Swinging her legs either side of the beautiful Bay, she took hold of the reins. It felt good to be in the saddle again and she was looking forward to the ride cross-country to Bridgwater. According to Amos, the swiftest route was a rough terrain that a coach would not navigate easily without high risk of upturning. If they were to make haste, even after allowing the horses to graze and rest, they would be back before the first day of the assizes was over.

As they reached the edge of Sedgemoor, the pearlescent sheen of morning illuminated a low swirling mist. The horses slowed and Kat shuddered. It was on this land that the two armies had collided. As she stared across the moors, she tried to focus her senses on Gideon, to look through the mist to an earlier time, when it had been the height of summer and thousands of boots had marched these soils. Breathing deeply and slowly, she searched the sea of faces that her mind's eye had conjured – the Duke's army of ghosts and doomed men…

"Don't say much, do ya?" Amos had closed the gap between them, their horses now side by side. The vision was gone and the mist already lifting.

"I do not have much to say." Kat knew that she was behaving in a needlessly prickly manner toward him.

He laughed vociferously. "Never met a woman who 'as nought to say. Ride well too. Yer a rare find." With a raised arm, he pointed into the distance. "Need to guide 'em along 'ere. I know all the crossings over the rhynes. Can be a nasty business if you ride into one. Run deep, they do."

As the ground flattened, they increased the pace to a canter and then to a steady gallop. Amos looked over his shoulder to see that she had no trouble keeping up and Kat smiled as the cool air on her face and the tang of horse sweat and mud awakened her senses. They pressed on until they neared a crossing. "Not far now," Amos said and his gaze travelled the wilderness of unkempt grass that disguised the dangers of the wetlands. His nostrils flared as he sniffed the air. "Smell on the wind changes, see. That's the way to tell when yer treadin' too near to the wetter ground. It can give way to marsh so fast ye won't know it's comin'." He tugged on the reins to guide his horse further off to the right and Kat followed his lead, relaxing into conversation as they rode.

Amos was from the village of Chedzoy, just a few miles from Bridgwater. He said he had heard the battle, that for days after, the air had smelled of gunpowder and that he had been one of the men recruited to ensure the dead were properly buried. "Over at Westonzoy, it was. Too hasty to get rid of the dead, they were, so the graves were too shallow." He stared off into the distance as his mind indulged in the horror of all he had witnessed. "So many of 'em." He snapped his fingers. "All gone. Workin' the fields not a few weeks before and buried beneath the earth so soon after."

"I am sorry for it, all of this death," Kat said and although she could not see his face, she thought that his eyes would be glistening with tears for the friends and neighbours whom he had no doubt lost. He gave nothing away about his political opinions and where his loyalties lay and Kat did not ask.

As they approached a crossing, Amos became agitated. It had suffered damage too great to risk using. "I know of one farther along." He shifted uncomfortably in the saddle. "But it's not where I wanted to take ye." He reached into his pocket. "Do ye have something with ye to hold to the nose?"

Kat's heart plummeted. It was foolhardy to think that they could have escaped any of the bloody aftermath of the final battle. She shook her head. A nosegay had not been something she had thought to bring.

He spat on the ground. "Just hold on to her tight when I say so and ride with yer eyes shut."

Swallowing hard, Kat felt the worry creeping over her body as her mind turned to what Amos had told her of the days and weeks after the battle. When they eventually found the crossing point needed, Kat could feel a shift in the atmosphere. The air felt thicker and heavier and her head was beginning to pound. Everything looked familiar, yet she had never crossed these moors.

"Just over that small rise in the land over there, that's where ye shut yer eyes," Amos instructed, his tone firm. "Hand me the bridle. I'll keep yer on the right path."

Overhead, the impatient caw of carrion birds could be heard. A murder of crows circled the other side of the mound, the sky suddenly darker as it became dotted with the black plumage of scores of wings. "Close 'em now," Amos shouted over his shoulder and she did as he asked.

The smell that hit her was sudden and repugnant, forcing them both to cough. She leaned into the mane of her horse, still trying to dispel the putrid air from her chest.

In spite of the cool temperature on the moors, Kat felt damp beneath her arms and her body pulsed with heat. The swooping and cawing from the birds was making her feel off balance and she clutched at the ebony mane of her horse, focusing on the coarse hair between her fingers. The steady plod of hooves beat out a monotonous rhythm across the moorland and she thought she could hear the distant cries of men. In her mind's eye she could see the spirits reaching out to her. Buried between her cleavage, she could feel the heat of the necklace. It was beating like a small, black heart, determined to show her what had come to pass on this soil, but she did not want to see, she did not want to think about any of it.

"How far?" she asked between waves of nausea.

"Ye've just got to hold on tight." Amos's voice seemed far away and Kat began to panic that he had let go of the bridle, that her horse would walk her right through whatever ghastly spectacle was lining their route. She tried to take a shallow breath but it caught in her throat. As she coughed and retched, she fell off balance, tumbling from the saddle and hitting the ground. Pain jarred up her arms and on the side of her body and she cried out, her eyes opening. It was impossible to keep the sour, hot bile from rising into her mouth.

Dismounting his horse, Amos tried to calm both animals. His voice was soothing as he gently circled them. This was not a place for them to lose their only source of travel. Kat tried to listen to the gentle tone of his voice but it was disappearing, swallowed by a lifting wind.

Wiping at her mouth with the back of her hand, Kat was aware not only of the crows but of the incessant buzz of flies. Amos's instruction for her to get up sounded far away. Struggling, she rose to her knees. As her vision began to focus on the strange, out of place shapes amidst the trees, a scream wedged in her throat. Images started pouring into her mind, unfiltered and merciless in what they showed her. Unable to take her eyes off the sight in front of her, Kat realised that she was kneeling before the remains of the men who had fought and lost their war against the King. She did not need to be told who these men were as the vision hit her hard…

CHAPTER THIRTY TWO

My eyes are shut but I can still see them – all of them. I see the men who had marched with me, fought with me. Their faces are twisted with horror as they hang from the trees like gruesome trophies that the King's soldiers are hunting down. One by one they have picked them off, some taken prisoner and others maimed and killed where they stand.

Amidst my nightmare memories, I can feel the rise and fall of the horse whose saddle I have been slung over. I open my eyes and try to work out where I am. The last I remember is the searing heat of a fist connecting with my face before it all went black. I see the earth that has been churned up by hundreds of hooves and I know that we must be near to where the battle took place. Pain in my jaw brings a strangled cry from my throat but the steady plod of the horses drowns out the sound.

Turning my head, I see the gleam of a church tower. With a groan, I try to move but my ankles have been bound. They know that I could outrun them, even when they are on horseback. My body aches. When we stop, rough hands jostle with the weight of my body. They do not realise that I am awake and a bucket of water is thrown over me, the cold of it is like icy splinters against my skin. I cry out and I am silenced with a hard shove. They want my name but I do not speak. If I give it to them, she will know how I have betrayed her and I will lose her forever. They think fear has struck me dumb and they laugh, calling me cruel names. Then they march me into the church.

I hear somebody say we are in Westonzoy and I wonder what Hell I am in to be brought back here. A door is unlocked and when it creaks open, images from the battlefield come to me once again as I see the faces of men, once so brave and determined, now huddled in front of me rotting and stinking in their own filth. Many look half dead and I hear a soldier proudly commenting on how many rogue escaped rebels they are still plucking from the countryside. I am one of those.

I am not put in the same room as the others but taken elsewhere. They still need my name and possibly any others I can give. They take great pleasure informing me of how many men were held here in this church straight after the battle, and how they are now either being led to the gibbet after the Dorchester and Exeter trials, or awaiting their fate in Taunton.

Another man is brought in. He is a round man with what I imagine can be a very jolly face. I think he must have great authority in the parish because of the way the others behave around him. He wears a grim expression as he tells me what happens to those who refuse to admit their guilt. The soldiers no longer look pleased and I think it is because they see me for what I am – a man who was on the wrong side. It could have been them, had fate taken a different turn. Solemnly they leave me to consider all that has been said. In the darkness I am left with nothing but the sound of the blood pumping through my body and my dismal thoughts.

I think of the farm boy whom I had struck a rapport with before Monmouth led us to the moors that are not so far from these walls. As my thoughts drift into another space and time, I become aware that my body will not stop shivering, but it is not from cold. I am afraid. It is a strange sort of fear, as though it belongs to another and I am simply observing it. None of this seems real.

I keep thinking that at any moment I will open my eyes and see her beside me, warm in our bed together in Winchester. I will smell the herbs, root and bark on her fingertips as she brings them to my cheek, stroking my face between kisses. The sun will be burning a rosy tinged hue into our chamber, bringing out the lighter tones of her rich brown hair as it falls softly over her milky skin. We will make love and she will promise me a son with a bonny smile and the heart of a lion. She has always been the brave one, my Kateryn. Just like her grandmother with that fierce independent streak. It should have been enough. I should have been content with that. She wanted me for who I was and I see that now.

I choke back a sob. I wonder what she is doing. I try to imagine her happy, helping her grandmother in the apothecary, laughing at some exchange they share but all I can see is the anger in her face, the hurt and accusation. Neither widow nor wife. That is what she will be and all because I am a coward. I do not want her to know. I would rather she thinks that I am dead in a ditch or run off to find my fortune elsewhere than for her to learn of the truth.

The sound of the iron bolts being drawn back give me cause to raise my head. Stark shafts of sunlight flood the room and two men stand there observing me.

The gentleman of authority appears with another soldier who has a face not unlike a snarling dog, with his hard jawline and shiny brown eyes. They interrupt my thoughts of Kateryn and my thoughts of the farm boy as, once again, I am ordered to give my name and from where it is that I hail. The snarling dog-faced one is not afraid to use his fists or boots to get it out of me.

They address me as 'The Runner'. I should be filled with pride for this could be a reflection of my ability to outrun their horses, but the way that they say it gives off another meaning; 'The Runner' paints a picture of a coward, but if cowardice brings survival I would do it all again.

Round and round they go, beating, shouting, threatening me. It is like this for some time and in the moments that they leave me alone in that room to contemplate the consequences of my stubborn silence, I return to my thoughts of what happened to the farm boy who I had struck a bond with, and so many others on that battlefield. Still I cannot recall his name. My memory taunts me with visions of the King's soldiers setting fire to the hardworking hands of men before they hang them, kicking and screaming. I outran all of that but now I find myself back here, dwelling upon the irony that the boy who had marched and fought by my side had been so proud of his fight that he would have told these men his name with such pride. Instead, he died with no name.

It then rushes back to me as I recall his name and how it was that we first met, Christopher Carter and I. It was in Bridgwater, the day that the Duke climbed the spire, looked through his spyglass and made his plan that led us all to our fate and ultimately, our damnation. The boy standing beside me had a quiet, solemn way to him. He was at least a few years younger than me, but he had such wise eyes. The dry heat and dust had brought on a coughing fit and I had offered him a drink. He had been grateful for it and I felt compelled to ask him what reasons had brought him to join the Duke's army. He had replied that he had nothing to lose and everything to gain. His father had worked as a smithy but had lost the forge to drink and gambling. Christopher had told me that his father was a cowardly, dishonest man who had brought him up with fists and insults. Owing to his father's reputation, nobody in his village much cared for the family. Christopher had secured himself a position working for a tenant farmer. It was the only money the family had coming in. A year earlier, Christopher's mother had run off leaving just him and his father. At least, that was what his father told him. He had always destroyed everything in his life and Christopher had his suspicions that his mother had not run off at all, but that his father had a hand in her disappearance. That was why he had joined the Monmouth army, full of hopes and dreams, determined to rise to something better than the stock he had come from, eager to make good his family name. He had wanted all of his village and all of England to know of his part in the rebellion, for Christopher felt so deeply that it was the right thing and that his mother would have been proud.

When we had marched, he had proudly been at the front. Christopher had heard the rumours about me, the exaggerated boasts that Lord Granville had made. They all knew of the lad who could outrun any beast; the lad who was to make stealthy haste into the Royalist camp, slitting the throats of those in highest authority. None of Monmouth's men, other than Lord Granville, Christopher and my brother Robert knew me by my real name.

Robert. When I think of my brother, I wonder what has happened to him but thinking too hard is no good for my soul. It will break me.

I hear the heavy heeled boots approaching once again. My lip is swollen from the last beating. They won't kill me as they want me to hang and for all who love me to know of my crime. As the door swings open, I grimace and make a noise that rattles in my throat so that it is a sound more akin to a chuckle. This angers the soldier. He stomps towards me and hits me in the chest with the butt of his musket, then brings it under my chin. In spite of the pain, I feel a mad moment of joy and they both see it on my face. They think that it is because I still refuse to give them my name, but that is not the reason for the small twitch I feel at the corners of my mouth. It is because thinking of Christopher's memory has made me realise what it is that I must do. He will get his wish, brave Christopher. I will see to it that whilst Gideon Fox disappears into the murky grave of Sedgemoor, Christopher Carter will get his moment to stand tall and show the country that he is proud and that he would do it all again.

Christopher Carter. It is the name I give before I am hauled away and thrown into the room where I must await my fate.

CHAPTER THIRTY THREE

Diffused shafts of sunlight were piercing through cloud as Kat opened her eyes. Her face and hair were wet. She was lying alongside a stretch of water and the horses were dipping their heads to drink. "Thought I'd lost ye." Beads of sweat had gathered on Amos's forehead as he held his cupped hands over her face before splashing her with more water. "Took some skin off but no breaks. Just as well yer're an apothecary. Yer'll know what to do for it."

Still thrown by the shock of what she had seen of Gideon in her vision, Kat was only half listening. Trying to stand upright, she felt her knees wobble and Amos gripped her by the elbow. "Easy now. You took quite a knock, you did. Had to put you over the saddle to get you away from it all."

The awful memory of the men in the trees returned. "There were so many of them," she said and she wrapped her arms about her chest.

Amos glanced back down the track. "Up and down the main route through here and further on too. Made an example of 'em, didn't they?" The emotion in his voice made his bottom lip quiver and he looked away.

Standing at his side, she followed his gaze. Off in the distance she could still see the crows circling and diving.

"I told ye not to open yer eyes," Amos scolded and then his voice softened, "but that wouldn't 'ave made no difference, would it?"

Kat thought there was accusation in his words, no matter how gently spoken. She did not respond and the remainder of their journey to Bridgwater was quiet and uninterrupted. Everything in the town felt muted, even the sharp and pungent smells from the cheese market did nothing to her senses and Kat thought how very dismal everything and everyone appeared.

The little shop beneath the sign of the green bottle was where she was to purchase the assay cup and the owner appeared eager to do business quietly. She was given a backroom to prepare the test for poison. To be seen trading with anyone with connections to the infamous Judge Jeffreys would clearly cause trouble in these parts and Kat was not surprised at this. There was no need to barter as he gave her a good price in return for a swift exchange and it was not long before she and Amos were looking for somewhere to rest the horses and take a meal, in readiness for the return journey. Mr Giles had seen to it that they had enough money to use a coaching inn rather than an alehouse.

The inn was in the shadow of the church, making it appear a dark and solemn place. They were greeted by a woman with a round face and wide brown eyes. Welcoming them in with a smile, she offered them a seat by a window and brought them some good cider when it was established that they were not chancing a meal without the coin to pay.

As they waited for their food, Kat looked out the window at the imposing church spire.

"They say that's the place they planned the ambush on the King's men," Amos told her in a voice that was barely louder than a hushed whisper.

Recalling the visions of Gideon, Kat stared down at her hands. "I know."

Keeping her eyes cast downwards, she could feel the intensity of Amos's gaze. "My ma was like ye, God rest her soul." He lifted his wooden cup and drank. "Could see the future and the past. Never saw 'er own, mind. Or p'raps she just didn't want none of us to suffer for knowin' what would come to pass. Folk like to indulge in knowin' their fortune and the rich will happily pay handsomely for such knowledge, but displease 'em and yer'll pay the price." His eyes were shining with emotion and he smiled kindly at her.

"They turned on her?" Kat asked and her skin crawled as she thought of the stories Darling had hinted at.

"Aye, that they did, Mistress. Hanged by those who made the demands of 'er to look for answers."

"I am sorry to learn of that, Amos. It is a terrible and sad story."

Giving her a sad look, he nodded. "That it is, but past is past." He paused, hesitating before deciding to continue. "I recognised what was happenin' to ye out on the road through to Bridgwater. I knew it the moment ye looked up. Had the same look as she used to and I knew that ye were seeing what happened to those wretched souls."

There was such sympathy and understanding in his voice that Kat felt the burden of her secret weigh even heavier upon her shoulders and she longed to confide in him, to share what she had seen of Gideon. "Do you have loved ones who fought?"

"A house full of daughters. Two married, two still at home. Course, the King's army were quick to take their 'usbands, like it or not. One got injured, a wound to the leg. He'll live but likely limp something dreadful for rest of 'is days. We were lucky s'ppose.

"What about ye? Ye're from finer stock than most, I can see and hear that much. Ye must be courtin'?"

If another man had asked her this question so soon after meeting her, it would have been impertinent, but Amos seemed to convey a kindly and conversational interest. There was no chance of offering him an answer before their food arrived and they were both distracted by the cuts of mutton soaked in a rich smelling onion gravy. They said grace and tucked in.

"Not had meat in weeks." Amos ate with the enthusiasm of a man who had not enjoyed a good meal for a long time and Kat wondered how hard things must be for him if he was accepting work to accompany an apothecary to Bridgwater.

Amos shared some of the hardships his family had endured after the monarchy had been restored, when he had been just a young man. One of his earliest memories had been of his mother going without for a week just to keep his younger siblings fed, that she had lost the baby growing inside her as a result. It was easy to understand why so many countrymen still heralded Cromwell's rule and hated the King so much.

She ate her food, savouring the taste and the opportunity to share the company of somebody who she felt comfortable with. As she watched Amos polish off his dish, a mad part of her wondered if he would perhaps be open to helping her find Gideon. Given the handsome sum she had been promised for her work as a travelling apothecary for the judges, payment for his service would be no issue. Gideon was close and she could feel him. Amos could be trusted, of that she was certain.

There was a commotion as the door to the inn clattered open and several men who were dressed in bold red uniforms entered. An air of excitement drifted in with them as they loudly requested refreshment and food.

Amos stiffened as a silence enveloped the rest of the inn. People were wary of the soldiers. Their presence was not welcome and arrests could still be made through the confessions of prisoners.

"Don't look at 'em," Amos cautioned her. "Best not attract their attention. We're finished with our business 'ere. Can be on our way soon enough."

"Should we wait?"

"No tellin' how long this lot will be." Amos nodded to the landlady who caught their eye and hurried over to the table, keen to quickly oblige any request so that she could concentrate on serving the soldiers and seeing the back of them. She agreed to them leaving discreetly through the back of the inn, where the horses were tethered to the trough. They paid and left the unnerving laughter and shouts behind them.

The earlier chill in the air had lifted and they took the ride back at a slow pace so as to let their meal settle. Amos planned to lead them on another route back to Taunton, avoiding the places that had been defiled with the dead bodies of those who had been killed rather than captured for trial.

Once they were back on the moors, they followed the route up to slightly higher ground, where three ancient oaks appeared to be stooping towards one another in a ring. Amos said they were known as the Three Hags. Folklore and superstition that led to folk keeping their distance meant that a variety of untamed wild flowers and plants grew. It was an apothecary's dream.

As Kat gathered what she thought would be useful in the stillroom, she observed the twisted, gnarled tree limbs and supposed that they did resemble three old women who had become crooked and hunched with age.

Stepping over the huge exposed roots that jutted from the earth, Amos gave her an account of the history behind the trees. "Legend 'as it that their blood was spilled on this very spot. Killed after some young lad followed 'em out 'ere one night and told the rest of the villagers what he had seen. Over a century old is what these hags were rumoured to be. Stole young children from their beds and took their lives so that they might continue living theirs, so the tale goes. Then they would return them, the life drained from their little bodies so that their mothers would find them blue the next morn, with no rhyme nor reason for their sudden death. They say if ye look close enough in the knots, ye can see all the faces of those whose lives they bled dry."

Kat thought it a preposterous tale but in spite of herself, she still shuddered as she looked at how the thicker branches overhead somehow resembled arms and the markings on the trunks appeared riddled with faces. "Some say it's bad luck to come near 'ere. All foolish nonsense, course."

A feeling of unease crept over her and she suddenly wanted to leave. "We should make haste, Amos. If I do not return with the cup in time enough for Lord Jeffreys to be served his evening wine, there will be trouble." She imagined that Amos would be in more trouble than she would be and she did not care to think of it.

Mounting the horses, they began to round back onto the track they had left, descending the crest of the small hill and back onto the relatively flat moors. Alerted by the sound of hooves and voices, the horses' ears twitched back. There was no time to change direction. A small cluster of soldiers had gathered. As they drew closer, Kat recognised one of them from the coaching inn. "What are they doing?"

"Never mind what they're doin'. Best wait it out back under the cover of the trees," Amos changed direction and Kat swiftly followed.

Safely under the cover of the great leafy branches, they dismounted the horses and used the bridles to tether them to the large roots. Then they waited and watched as the group got closer.

The same air of agitated excitement from the inn had followed them out onto the moors and they appeared to be separating into small groups.

"They got somebody with 'em. Must be one of Monmouth's men," Amos said and Kat could make out the figure of a man whose hands were bound.

As two of the soldiers rode towards the foot of the hill, Kat noted how they were stationing themselves in a large loop. Turning her gaze back to the prisoner, she squinted. Even from a distance, it was plain to see that the man was tall and strong. They brought him slightly closer so that his shock of copper red hair glinted in the afternoon sunlight. Gideon.

CHAPTER THIRTY FOUR

Acutely aware of Amos standing by her side, she wondered if he could hear the pounding of her heart as it began to hammer wildly against her chest. Her breathing quickened and she watched in disbelief as a soldier unbound Gideon's hands but began to tether him to a fine-looking ebony warhorse. The horse was twitchy and impatient. Below them, Kat could hear the odd remark made by the soldiers who had stationed themselves at the foot of the hill.

The taller of the two soldiers looked to his companion. "You think he'll grant him his freedom if he wins?"

With a derisive chuckle, the other shook his head. "He'll never do it. That's the fastest and strongest stallion I've ever laid eyes on."

"They're plannin' to race him!" Amos exclaimed. "Are they mad? They'll kill the poor lad! He'll be dragged to his death."

The tethering rope they were using was long enough to allow Gideon a head start, making clear their intention to enjoy some good entertainment. None of them believed he could do it.

Kat tried to swallow but her throat was dry. Every part of her body was desperate to run towards him, to cry out his name and tell them to stop, but to do so would be to endanger both herself and Amos. Gripping Amos by the arm, she held her breath as they aligned Gideon alongside the flaring nostrils of the huge beast. The soldier standing beside him circled his arm twice, demonstrating that the race would form two large loops. Next to him, the stallion was tossing its head and dragging its front hoof, impatient to charge.

Caught up in the macabre excitement, Amos was oblivious to her distress. "It's as good as murder!" His eyes were wide with horror. "No man can outrun a horse, especially not one the likes of that."

Blood was coursing through Kat's veins as she watched the soldier who was seated in the saddle shorten the reins. Another took his musket, aiming it to the sky. As his finger squeezed the trigger, a smart crack filled the air sending flocks of birds from the trees, their wings beating hard and fast.

The stallion wasted no time and thundered across the ground at impressive speed but the rider tried to keep him held back, determined to give Gideon a chance to build up his speed and gain some distance. By the time they were nearing the curve of the wide ring they had created, Gideon's arms were pumping hard and the men watching were jeering. They rounded the corner to loop back around on themselves and Kat could make out the determined look upon Gideon's face, his jaw firmly set and his gaze focused on a spot in the distance. Clenching her fists, she could feel her nails piercing half-moons into her skin as the soldiers below moved back, their shouts escalating as it became clear that both man and beast were on a par. There had been no need for the rider to try and hold his horse back; Gideon was just as strong and fast, even with the injuries and exhaustion he must be suffering. The stallion's hooves churned at the earth as his rider shouted at him to go faster.

Breaking away from Amos, Kat ran to the clearing just beyond the trees. "God speed, Gideon! Run like the wind!" Her voice was lost amidst the chaos. "Faster! Don't stop, Gideon. Don't ever stop running!"

The horse and rider charged on, completing the first circuit and taking the corner that would force them around again. As the soldiers cheered and whistled, flecks of saliva sprayed from the horse, hitting Gideon who was beginning to lag in its wake. He was tiring fast and had dropped to the rear of his opponent, struggling to keep the pace. They drove on hard, back over the ground that they had already covered, heading towards the top of the loop again. His fatigue was obvious.

Clasping her hands together, Kat willed him to take her strength, to channel it into his own body and run. They hit the curve and the horse faltered, his rider pulling him back slightly so that he could remain seated. It bought Gideon just enough time to win back the distance and as they arced around, everything else around them seemed to stand still. It was as though the whole world was silent save for the explosive sound of the race to the finish. The man marking the line that they needed to cross held out his arm.

Running forwards, Kat meant to descend the hill to greet him at the finish, daring to imagine her husband being granted his freedom, but strong hands gripped her wrists as Amos pulled her back. She gave only a short struggle as the pair of them watched the horse level with Gideon. The sun beat down on them both and Kat could see that, in spite of his determination, Gideon was in pain. With a protracted scream of agony he dug deep for his strength. Then, pushing his head forward and crying out with the resolve to claim his victory, he pushed himself beyond the nose of the horse. As they passed the outstretched arm of the soldier standing at the finishing line, Gideon had nudged forward to a clear lead.

Amos let go of Kat's arm and stumbled backwards with surprise. "He did it! The lad actually did it!"

Easing off the pace, the stallion was taken to canter and finally a brisk trot as the rider brought him back around to the others.

From behind her, Kat could hear Amos's laugh of disbelief. She watched in silence, her body tingling as she considered the idea that she was only moments away from reuniting with her husband. Amidst a great deal of noise from the soldiers, Gideon was freed from the tethering rope and his knees buckled.

Kat stumbled, falling against the rough bark of one of the oaks. Against all the odds, Gideon had won. It did not matter to Kat what he had done to find himself in that situation. Not any longer. The important thing was that he would be free to go home. Trembling with emotion, she rested her head against the trunk of the tree.

"Ye're cryin', Mistress." Amos reached out for her hand and she noted that even his was shaking.

"I am happy for him. I am happy for his wife."

Raising his eyebrows, Amos breathed out a long trail of air. "In all my years, I ain't never see anything like it."

"Do you think they'll release him here and just leave him? He will need help. We should wait and see."

"Ye need to get back. No good for neither of us if they think ye're missin'." He began clambering over the tree roots to where they had tethered the horses.

"Please Amos. We cannot just leave him out here on the moors with no way of finding food or shelter."

"We don't know what kind of man he might be," Amos argued but he was already bending to the pleading look Kat was giving him. With a frustrated grunt he conceded. "Have it yer way then. We will wait. I'll go fetch the 'orses."

Kat squeezed her eyes shut, hot tears rolling over her cheeks. She had not dared imagine the day she would see her husband again, but Darling had told her that she would hold great influence over his fate. Did that mean that she would soon be running down the hill to him so that she could ride with him to safety? Would she be able to convince Amos to keep him at his home in Chedzoy until she could safely leave her post without arousing any suspicion?

From the bottom of the hill there was a shout and she crept forward to see that words were being exchanged between the soldiers. Drained from all that had taken place, Gideon was still on his knees, his head bent. The disagreement increased in volume and, although Kat could not make out the words, it was clear that they were arguing over Gideon. One hauled him to his feet and there were more shouts. Then he was shoved forwards. He was no longer bound but he was not yet free.

"Amos, come quickly. They're not letting him go."

Amos appeared with both horses and he peered down the bank of the hill to where the men were moving on. He looked crestfallen but not surprised. "Come on, Mistress. We best be on our way."

"But what about him?"

"Looks like they're keepin' hold of 'im." With a look of disgust, he spat on the ground before helping her mount her horse.

"They had an agreement though. They must surely honour it?"

"No such thing as honour with that lot." For the first time, Amos showed the true colour of where he put his loyalties. "Not a gentleman amongst 'em." He spat again and hoisted himself into the saddle.

"We have to do something. They must honour it. He earned his freedom!" Kat squeezed her legs against the horse's flanks. "I won't let this happen."

Swiftly snatching the reins from her, Amos expertly took hold of her horse. "Are ye mad? Do ye want to get us both killed? They'll do what they will. Ye need to leave it up to yer Judge Jeffreys now. That's where he'll end up, God 'elp his soul."

Choking back the tears, Kat did not say another word. She knew that Amos was right, that it could do no good for Gideon if she was to get caught up in it all.

In silence, they watched the small band of soldiers disappear, taking Gideon with them along with any hope of freedom that he might have had.

CHAPTER THIRTY FIVE

"There's no point avoiding the question, Ruth. Tell me what is going on?" Tim had been interrogating her the whole journey back from the museum. Whilst she had managed to convince him that she didn't need any medical attention, his frustration was growing as he grilled her again over what had happened to make her lose consciousness.

Max and Jeremy had decided to travel together to give Ruth and her brother some space, but she didn't feel ready to share. Her head was still spinning and the emotion that she had felt from Kat still haunting her. She shook her head. "Please, Tim, I know I gave you a fright, but I will be fine once I've had a hot bath and lie down. Can't you just accept it when I assure you that it's nothing to worry about?"

"Nothing to worry about?" Tim was incredulous. "You just had some sort of fit that rendered you unconscious!"

They both fell silent as the car approached the village by one of the narrower and windier roads. Ruth took the moment to breathe deeply. Giving him a sidelong glance, she wondered whether Jeremy had said anything about what had been happening. She assumed not as Tim would have mentioned it.

"If it hadn't been for Jeremy convincing us otherwise, we would have called an ambulance," he said at last and she noticed how his left cheek twitched. It was what always happened if Tim was ever anxious.

Feeling guilty for it, Ruth bit down on her bottom lip. "I'm sorry, Tim. I realise it must have been a shock for you all, but I don't want to talk about it. I'm not ill. There's absolutely nothing wrong with me. You'll at least let me reassure you of that?"

Sighing heavily, Tim checked the mirrors and flipped the indicator before slowing to take a turn in the road. "Don't be sorry, Ruthie. I just want you to be honest with me. I know that if you're not ill, then what happened today has something to do with your psychic side."

The car travelled slowly up the road that Tim's driveway opened onto. "There's not getting anything past you, is there?"

Tim gave her a look. "I'm your brother. Even Max has most likely guessed."

Rubbing her temples with her fingers, Ruth struggled to hold back the unexpected wave of emotion. "The truth is I'm scared. I've never experienced anything like it before and I really don't know how to explain it."

"Well, Jeremy seemed pretty well versed." He struggled to keep the bitterness from his voice. He had never liked being kept in the dark about anything. "That much was obvious given that he insisted we simply take you home." They pulled up on the driveway. "Just how involved is he?"

Before she could respond there was a ping and the screen on the dashboard announced that there was a message from Max. Ignoring it, Tim suggested they go straight inside and he run her a hot bath.

Once they were settled indoors and Ruth had changed into her towelling robe ready for her bath, Tim informed her that Max and Jeremy had decided to stay out a little longer to give them some time to talk.

Ruth gave a sarcastic cheer. "Yay! Lucky us." It was a response that was impossible for her to resist but it brought a smile to Tim's face.

He draped an arm over her shoulders. "That's more like it, I appear to have my sister back."

Stepping into the bathroom, Ruth turned to look over her shoulder. "If you're going to insist on making me talk, can we at least put on the kettle?"

Giving her a comforting smile, Tim nodded. "Don't be too long in there. You know how I hate cold tea."

He was spooning tea leaves into the pot when she reappeared. Whilst they waited for it to steep, he leaned forward across the island. "Now, when are you going to tell me about this person called Kat?"

So, something had been revealed back at the museum. Her stomach plunging, Ruth finally accepted that she had a lot of explaining to do and that her brother was not the sort of person who would allow her to gloss over any of it.

******

By the time Ruth had finished imparting all the details, they had forgotten all about the tea Tim had made. "Bloody hell, Ruth. Why didn't you tell me about any of this sooner?" Having abandoned the idea of making a fresh pot, Tim was pouring a generous measure of gin into two glasses filled with ice.

Ruth had told him everything about how she had met Jeremy, the necklace and of her experiences with Kat. She had been careful to keep any of Jeremy's personal affairs out of it and omitted speaking of Cathy.

Adding a dash of tonic and lemon slices, Tim handed a glass to Ruth and they moved into the lounge. She raised her eyebrows. "Isn't it a bit early for this?"

"You've just told me that you're getting pulled into the seventeenth century by a woman you suspect was practising witchcraft; that you've witnessed the execution of those involved in the Monmouth Rebellion and that you have met the infamous Hanging Judge himself. No, it's certainly not too sodding early for a drink." Dropping onto the sofa he shook his head.

"This is why I was so reluctant to tell you. It sounds so far-fetched."

Tim took a large gulp of his drink. "Not coming from you, it doesn't. You forget that we grew up together and that you used to scare me half to death with this psychic gift of yours. With that in mind, it doesn't sound far-fetched at all."

"Jeremy thinks it is." Immediately she regretted saying it. "Forget I said that. It's completely unfair of me to get so uptight about it, especially given this is the first time he has experienced anything of a supernatural nature." She gave an ironic smirk. "It's the first time I've experienced anything quite like this actually. In fact, I was on the brink of calling myself a fraud and giving it all up before I met him."

"Fate then?"

Ruth thought back to the day that she had opened the door to him, the way the atmosphere in the house had crackled and how it had reignited her psychic energy. "You could say that, I suppose."

"What exactly is going on between you two?" The intensity of Tim's gaze seemed to collude with the silence, needling her into submission to tell all.

Ruth hadn't touched her gin but the desire to do something to alleviate the pressure from Tim's well practised method of sibling interrogation made her bring the glass to her lips. Carefully considering her response, she took a few sips. "There is an attraction, on my part anyway, but that is as far as it goes. I think that most people would find Jeremy attractive. Besides, it doesn't mean anything. It's probably just a rebound reaction."

Hooking the lemon from his drink, Tim brought it to his mouth. It was a dreadful habit of his. He winced as the sour juice hit his palate. "I think you've been due a 'rebound reaction' for quite some time given all that has gone on between you and Grayson over the years." He dropped the lemon slice back into the glass. "I don't buy it, I'm afraid. There's something more here than just noticing his dashing good looks. I might be the younger, sexier sibling, but I wasn't born yesterday."

With a chuckle she threw a cushion in his direction. "Younger maybe. Sexier? You wish."

"Wittier and far more intelligent in that case. Go on. If we're being open and honest then now is the time to spare no detail. You know you can trust me. I've noticed the chemistry between you both." His eyes lit up and he lowered his voice, leaning towards her. "You know, we could always set things up."

Holding up her hands, Ruth was appalled. "Stop right there. Jeremy is off the market and so am I. I'm married."

Tim screwed up his face. "Married to a lousy, cheating bastard of a husband."

"Regardless of my situation with Grayson, he is still my husband and I made a vow." Even as she said it, she realised she couldn't put her heart into the undying loyalty that she was suggesting she had for Grayson.

"Don't give me that bullshit, Ruth. It's a few words and a bit of paper. Grayson broke the 'honour and cherish' part of your vows at least a decade ago, and you know it. He's cold and indifferent towards you and it breaks my heart to see how over the years he has taken away your shine. Don't make excuses, you deserve to be happy."

"Just leave it, Tim," she pleaded, giving him the sternest look she was able to muster. She could not risk him saying anything to Jeremy or attempting to play Cupid and causing any offence. Their friendship had already been tested by their disagreement the evening before.

"Okay. If you say so." Shrugging his shoulders, Tim's agreement to let it go did not sound at all convincing.

"He has only recently lost the woman he loved, so please do not mention anything like this to him." Ruth blurted it out before she could stop herself.

Tim's face fell and he was immediately full of apologies.

"It's a very personal matter," Ruth said, making it clear that she could divulge no more. "But now you know why there is nothing between us and why there can't be anything between us."

He gave her a sombre look, digesting the information she had just imparted. In spite of being rather crass at times, Tim was always full of empathy for others. The moment was interrupted by the sound of the door opening as Max and Jeremy returned.

Nothing more was mentioned and the four of them settled in for the rest of the afternoon. A reservation had been made at the local pub for an evening meal and after several rounds of Ruth reassuring everyone that she was absolutely well enough to go, they began to get ready.

Just as she had stepped into a pair of leather-look leggings and a print knot blouse, there was a knock at the door. Max appeared, bringing with him the scent of cologne and toothpaste. "Mind if I come in for a second?"

Opening the door wider to let him through, Ruth smiled warmly. "As long as you don't mind me applying the finishing touches to my make up. I don't want Tim complaining that I'm making everyone late."

Taking a seat on the end of her bed, Max twiddled one of the buttons on the edge of the duvet cover. "I won't pry about what happened earlier today as I'm sure Tim gave you the third degree, but I know that you and Jeremy shared some cross words last night. I wanted to check in to make sure you're okay?"

Ruth cringed inwardly. She hated the idea that he and Jeremy had shared a conversation about her. Noting the look on her face, Max was quick to the defence. "I've no idea what it was all about as he didn't share the details but I can tell you that he feels terrible about it." He was watching her reaction in the mirror and Ruth avoided his gaze, picking up a lipstick and gliding it smoothly over her lips.

"He's quite smitten by you, you know," he added and she turned around to face him.

"Not you as well. I told Tim, no match-making. Neither Jeremy or I are in that space. We have other things going on. This trip is just companionship." She pulled out the dresser stool and sat down. "I do appreciate you have my best interests at heart, Max, and I know that you don't want to see me hurt by Grayson's actions, but romance is not on the cards. Not now and not with Jeremy. I really appreciate you telling me that he's feeling bad about it though. I am too. The last thing I want to do is argue or upset anyone."

Tim called up the stairs, warning them that they had five minutes. Standing up, Max gestured for her to give him a hug. "Come on. We don't want to keep your impatient brother waiting any longer." He planted a kiss on her forehead. "You look stunning by the way."

"Ever the gentleman," she said with a wink and they went downstairs.

The atmosphere in The Boar was festive and the whole place sparkled beneath fairy lights. There were groups of people chatting and laughing around the bar and others were sitting at tables, lost in conversation. Both Tim and Max were pulled away to mingle, leaving Jeremy and Ruth to sort the drinks. Jeremy suggested they buy a bottle and Ruth agreed. As she put her card on the bar, Jeremy swatted her hand away, insisting it was his treat. A bottle of champagne and four glasses appeared and the barman advised that he would have somebody show them to their table.

Ruth waved over at Tim to show him that they were going to take a seat. He gave a cursory nod in her direction and she realised that it might be some time before he and Max emerged from their social obligations. They were popular in the village and she knew how long they could be kept chatting on occasions such as these. The waitress who showed them to their table poured the champagne and offered to take the two additional glasses over to Tim and Max. "Quite the celebrities, aren't they?" Jeremy commented as she walked away.

Ruth agreed with a chuckle. "Everyone knows my brother and Max. I lose count of the number of dinner parties those two seem to attend. It's just the same when they're staying at Max's flat in London. Mind you, people seem a bit more genuine down here, not so impressed by the business and clients they have."

"Somerset does appear to be yet another gem in the crown of Britain." Jeremy appraised the room with an appreciative nod. The table was tucked into a cosy corner near the open fire. It was Tim's favourite spot and the one he always reserved. Above the pleasant hum of voices Christmas music was playing and, for the first time, Ruth felt her shoulders relax somewhat.

Jeremy had taken the seat opposite her and he leaned across the table. "Before we even think of lifting our glasses, tell me how you are? I've been worried sick about you all afternoon but didn't want to make a fuss."

Waving a dismissive hand, Ruth smiled. "Aside from Tim's relentless line of questioning, I'm fine. Thank you for stepping in and convincing them that there was no need for hospitals or doctors."

"A casualty of the job?" He gave her an empathetic smile and his eyes twinkled, his handsome features catching her off guard.

She looked down at the table. "A good way to describe it. I've explained everything to Tim." They slipped into silence but neither of them touched their drinks. The awkwardness was still hanging in the air between them.

"I told Max," Jeremy said at last, a sheepish expression on his face. "I hope you don't mind but he seemed to be aware of your vocation."

She gave a curt laugh. "Nobody has ever described it as a vocation before. A 'hobby' or 'dabbling in things I shouldn't' are the usual ways in which people refer to what I do."

"From what I have seen so far, I'd say it's a job with a lot of responsibility. You use a very unique skill to offer people emotional healing. Just look at what you've done for me."

She stared at him, realising he meant every word but she was still smarting from the things he had said to her the night before, the doubts that he had admitted to having. "I'm so sorry about last night," he said and his expression was full of earnest. "You have to understand that I've never experienced anything like this before. I was looking for a way of explaining it all away. If I stop and think too hard about what has been happening, I get scared. I should never have suggested that I doubted you though, especially not after all that you knew about Cathy." He chewed on his lip as he waited for her to respond.

"Don't be sorry. I'm struggling to come to terms with it all too. I find myself questioning everything I'm seeing and sometimes I wonder if I'm going mad."

Shame darkened his expression. "All the more reason why I shouldn't have said the things I did last night. I'm so sorry, Ruth. Can you forgive me?"

"Can you believe me?" The sharpness of her tone surprised her and he visibly winced.

"I do believe you, and I hope you know that I'm being sincere when I say that I'm sorry." He reached across the table for her hand and the sensation of his touch sent shockwaves up her arm and through her body. Trying to ignore it, she picked up her champagne flute.

"Then I can forgive you." She raised her glass. "To new friendships."

"And to solving mysteries tangled in time."

They both took a drink and Ruth savoured the way the bubbles flirted with her tongue and palate. "Speaking of mysteries," she said, "how did your trip to the archives pan out?"

Jeremy frowned. "I would say fruitless, at least in terms of Cathy's ancestor. I did manage to look into the bloody assizes a bit more though."

"You found Gideon?" As quickly as she had relaxed, Ruth was tense again. She had not shared any of the details that she had seen when she had connected with Kat again, but now she knew that Gideon must have faced trial. It had not appeared as though the soldiers had any intention of letting him go.

Giving an apologetic shake of the head, Jeremy paused as the waitress brought over a basket of breads and some olives. "No mention of a Gideon Fox at all. There was a Robert Fox of Dorchester and so I-"

"Gideon's brother." Ruth was startled by the sudden vividness of the memory of seeing him stand trial and the broken look upon Bridget's face, of all the hatred that had been directed at Kat. Noting Jeremy's puzzled expression, she realised that there was so much she was yet to elaborate on.

As she recounted what had happened in Dorchester, Jeremy's face paled. "It's still so much to take in," he admitted and pushed his fingers through his hair. "To hear it like this rather than simply reading the facts is mind-blowing." His eyes glazed over as he digested all that she said. "I suspected that there might be a connection between Robert Fox and Gideon."

"You looked him up?"

With a nod, he explained how he had researched what he could of any families by the name of Fox in and around Dorchester. "From what I found, I would suggest that they were likely to have owned a smallholding that had been passed down generations. Towns like Dorchester, and its surrounding areas, were renowned for being staunch supporters of Cromwell. For many it was the reason why they rose against King James II. He was not popular and the gentry involved in the uprising would have given them hope that they could return to the dream that Cromwell had set out to deliver." A pensive expression deepened the lines on his face as he ran his fingers up and down the length of the glass stem. "The echoes of Cromwell reverberated through the latter part of the seventeenth century. A family like Gideon's, who had very likely suffered as a result of the restoration of the monarchy, would have required very little encouragement to step up."

A shadow crossed his face and her heart sank at the sight of it. "I found a record of Gideon but, like Kat, he disappears. There is no record of his death. He is simply lost in time."

"I saw him," she admitted, "when I was hit by the vision at the museum. I was with Kat in Taunton."

Confusion created two furrows just above the bridge of Jeremy's nose. "You saw him at a trial, you mean?"

"No, on the moors." She was about to tell the story of what had happened when Tim and Max arrived at the table.

"You two are a bit slow off the mark, aren't you?" Tim nodded at the two glasses that were still well topped with champagne. He pulled the bottle from the ice bucket and poured some more. Neither he or Max appeared to notice the sombre mood at the table. After the waitress returned to take their order, the conversation casually diverted to much lighter material.

Dinner was pleasant and Ruth liked the way that Jeremy got on so well with her brother and Max. It was a far cry from the relationship they had shared with Grayson and she realised that she was actually enjoying herself. Usually at Christmas she found herself diffusing potential conflicts or being talked over by Grayson who was interested in nothing but showing off about money or complaining about clients. By the time dessert menus were passed around they were all too full and Max suggested they open another bottle of champagne at home.

The walk back to the barn cleared her head and allowed her meal to settle. Max ignited the dual aspect fire in the lounge so that they could all warm up whilst Tim opened the champagne.

"So, you were telling me what you saw when you blacked out earlier." Jeremy took a seat next to Ruth on the sofa. His cheeks were still pink from the brisk walk home. "Should we grab a moment later so that you can finish?"

Curling her legs beneath her bottom, Ruth reached for a cushion and hugged it to her chest. "Tim knows, and Max is no stranger to any of this. I don't mind sharing now, if nobody else minds."

"Sounds ominous," Max had perched himself on the opposite end of the corner sofa.

"Before dinner, Ruth started telling me about the vision she had at the museum," Jeremy explained. "There's this guy by the name of Gideon who, it appears, our lady Kateryn is searching for."

"And by Kateryn, you're referring to the seventeenth-century ghost?" Max was intrigued and all ears.

"She's not a ghost, Max." Tim set down a tray of glasses along with a box of chocolates. "It's more like Ruthie is the ghost."

"Astral projection?" Max raised his eyebrows.

Ruth sank back into the sofa. "Something like that."

Jeremy continued the explanation: "Kateryn's husband went missing some time before Monmouth landed on English soil. She's been connecting with Ruth, asking for her help in finding him, but there's no mention of his name in the archives."

"He had a brother who was trialled for fighting with the Rebel-army though," Ruth added. "Robert Fox was on the list of those executed. Gideon's name doesn't appear anywhere. I think Kat had been seeing things of him. She is incredibly psychic – a gift handed down from her grandmother, so it would seem. Gideon appeared to her on a number of occasions; it was just snatches of him, but enough for her to put two and two together and work out that he must have somehow been involved in the uprising."

Riveted, Tim gasped. "But you said that she was working for Judge Jeffreys, as a travelling apothecary."

"Judge Jeffreys?" Max asked as he picked up a chocolate and popped it into his mouth. "As in *the* Judge Jeffreys who is famed to have stayed in practically every pub or restaurant around these parts?"

"The very same," Tim said. "So go on then, Ruth. Tell us what you saw."

"I witnessed something that suggested Gideon certainly had been a part of the rebellion and he was captured."

"And you're sure you haven't missed something in those archives?" Max directed the question at Jeremy and Tim gave him an impatient nudge, hushing him so that Ruth could continue.

She detailed the journey Kat had made from Taunton to Bridgwater, and the soldiers they had encountered. Then she explained how they had made Gideon race the warhorse, that he had won but his reward of freedom had not appeared to have been honoured.

"I suppose it's feasible that they could have released him once they were off the moors, making it easier for him to find a way home." Jeremy rubbed his chin as he mulled over the possibility.

Max tapped a finger against his chin. "I've heard of this story." He clicked his fingers as he tried to recall it. "You know the one, Tim. It's the local legend of Westonzoyland. It dates back to the Monmouth Rebellion. They say that there was a man who had boasted he could outrun any beast. When he was captured, he was told that if he could outrun a horse, his life would be spared."

Ruth felt suddenly sick. "What happened?"

The look on Max's face said it all. Clasping a hand over her mouth, Ruth went hot and then cold. "He was convicted anyway," she said, hoping that he would correct her.

"As the story goes, his life wasn't spared, although it's not clear exactly how he met his end because his name has been lost in history."

Aghast, Ruth turned to Jeremy. "But you said that Gideon's name doesn't appear on the list of those imprisoned."

"It doesn't."

"Surely he was spared then? The facts may just never have made it into this bit of local history."

Jeremy looked doubtful. "They weren't all brought to trial. Many were hanged or shot on the moors."

The champagne that Tim had poured was suddenly not so appealing. "Do you think that's what they did?"

"It's more than plausible," Jeremy answered and an unpleasant coldness slid over her as she recalled the bodies she had seen through Kat's eyes on the moors.

Tim appeared just as horrified as Ruth felt. "How do we find out?"

"I don't think we can," Jeremy said and his tone was full of apology as he looked between Tim and Ruth. "Many of those who died at Sedgemoor are unnamed. Don't forget that it's very hard to trace people back unless they had wealth. Official records become much sparser when it comes to the commoners."

Ruth couldn't accept it. Something told her that her work was not finished with Kat but what could she do? If the records weren't there in black and white, there was nothing to be learned that Kat did not already know. Tiredness overcoming her, Ruth apologised for cutting the night short but insisted she needed to get to bed.

Picking up his glass, Jeremy joined her in retiring for the night. "Actually guys, I've got a little more research to try and do tonight. If it's okay with you, I'll leave you to enjoy the rest and head up."

"Of course not, but at least let me top you up," Max insisted, grabbing the bottle from the ice bucket. "Don't fancy this one having too much and snoring next to me all night." He gave Tim a playful wink.

When they reached the top of the stairs, Tim and Max had already put some music on, intent on enjoying the rest of their evening. "Thank you for being so supportive." Ruth reached out to touch him so that their fingers brushed together.

He didn't move his hand away. "I've not really done anything."

"You have been there for me."

"I brought all of this to you. I burdened you with it." He turned away, a shadow crossing his face. "I really shouldn't have kept it going. You were in danger today."

"Continuing to communicate with Kat has been my choice." She took a breath. "I want to do it again. If I can do it on my terms, maybe we can control it. Maybe we can bring her here and communicate with her instead. We can try and piece together what happened to her and Gideon."

He sucked in his breath as he struggled with a response. She could see the temptation in his eyes though, and understood that it must be like gold dust to a historian. "Do you think that if we brought Kateryn here, I could communicate with her through you?"

"If we do it in a controlled environment and I contact her, then yes, I do think it's possible."

He thought about it for a moment and excitement faded back to concern. "What about everything that happened today?"

"I simply wasn't ready for it. Doing it on my terms means I will be."

He licked his lips. "How will I know that I'm speaking with her?"

Ruth shrugged and tucked a lock of hair behind her ear. "I suppose we will need to just test the water, see what works. Tim can help if need be. He's used to the stranger things."

"No, I'll be happy to do it." Jeremy's keen reaction to help took her by surprise.

"Let's talk about it again in the morning," she suggested as she stifled a yawn. "I'm sorry. I think today has taken far more out of me than I care to admit."

"As it would appear. If you're going to do this again over the holiday, I suppose you should try and get some rest."

They stood looking at each other for a few seconds until it was verging on awkward. "Thanks again, Jeremy. You've been a rock." Standing on tiptoe, she grazed his cheek with her lips before going to her room and shutting the door.

The bedroom felt like a sanctuary, somewhere she could just cocoon herself and forget about everything. She knew that she would sleep deeply that night and that Kat would stay away.

Jeremy's face burned in her mind. She thought of the way he looked at her with such intensity and then the sadness that would pool in his eyes. Her stomach flipped over as she did so. Both Tim and Zoe were right to suggest there was an attraction there, but she couldn't entertain it. Her eyelids heavy, she pulled back the covers and slipped into bed. Switching off the bedside lamp, she settled into a deep, dreamless sleep.

******

With a groan of exasperation, Jeremy snapped the laptop shut. It was late and he had made little progress. The timeline for Cathy's ancestors remained firmly on 1732, the date of the death of the earliest relative he could trace. All of his searching had been futile. Being so consumed by the research, he hadn't even bothered to touch the drink that Max had poured for him. Picking it up he wandered over to the window that overlooked the garden and fields beyond it. Every time he stopped being busy, his mind would drift and the guilt returned. Still tingling from Ruth's fleeting touch, he felt the back of his hand. She had a good heart and had shown him so much generosity. It was impossible to push down the feelings that were beginning to blossom. Swallowing some champagne, he looked out the window. The scenery was lit up by an almost full moon, the satin black of the sky offsetting the cotton white of the slowly melting snow. Resting his forehead against the glass he felt the familiar stab of grief as his thoughts lingered on Cathy. In recent days that grief had become sharper and more raw, exacerbated by his feelings for Ruth. Cathy had been his world; having feelings for somebody else was as good as infidelity. Sickened by himself, he put the glass down and checked his watch. It was gone one in the morning. Both Tim and Max had retired to bed at least an hour earlier and if he was to be in any fit state to help Ruth go ahead with her plans the following morning, he would need his sleep. Taking one last glance out of the window, he gasped and stumbled backwards.

The silhouette reflected in the window pane was faint but it was there and it was hovering over his laptop. Pivoting, he faced the room. "Cathy?" There had been no mistaking her or the thunderous expression on her face.

Empty. The room was empty. Nobody was there. Rubbing his eyes, Jeremy turned back to the window, convinced he would see her again, but there was only the reflection of the room. It had to be his conscience messing with him. Drawing the curtains, he marched into the bathroom to get ready for bed, reminding himself that Cathy was now resting in peace. She had forgiven him. The guilt could go. So why did he feel worse than ever?

After washing over the sink, he stripped down to his underwear, intending to climb into bed but he stopped as he noticed his black jeans sprawled across the floor. Frowning, he questioned himself. Had they fallen out of the drawers when he had been dressing earlier? Surely, he would have noticed? One of the drawers from the chest was open, another pair of trousers partially spilling from it. It was as though somebody had pulled something out in a hurry. "Cath?" Even saying her name brought back the pain.

Swallowing hard, he looked around, noting the sudden dip in temperature. Scooping up the jeans, he folded them and put them back before getting into bed. The remote control for the spotlights was on the bedside table. Not quite ready for the room to be plunged into darkness, he only dimmed the spots. Above the steady hum of the lights, he could hear the sound of his heartbeat as it increased in rhythm. Eyes wide open and ears keen, he lay rigid in bed as the minutes ticked by. Every groan or creak in the house made him wonder if it could be Cathy or Kat. When he illuminated the screen of his watch to check it again, it was nearing three in the morning.

Giving into a raging thirst, he reluctantly turned back the covers, wishing that he'd had the foresight to fill a glass of water before going to bed. Once he had located the drinking glass by the bathroom sink, he filled it.

On his return, he stopped in his tracks. A small wooden box was on the floor of the room in the place where the jeans had been. He recognised it immediately. The box contained the letter addressed to Cathy and it had been tucked away in the drawer. Too afraid to leave it unattended in an empty house, he had decided to take it with him but had not intended on opening it. Not yet.

He whispered Cathy's name again but he could no longer feel her there in the room. Carefully, he picked up the box and placed it on the dresser. For a while he stared at it, wondering what it was that terrified him so much. It wasn't just the fact that it had been addressed so that it would arrive with Cathy possibly centuries after it had been written, it was the message that it could potentially contain. A part of him kept wondering whether the content could have somehow saved her from an untimely death, whether it could have given the chemo a chance to work a miracle and keep her on earth, with him. He supposed that if she hadn't done what she had that terrible day in Russell, he would never have met Ruth. The nausea hit him again and he knew what was causing it. Covering his face with his hands, he tried to push away the thoughts that were unfolding. There were feelings there that were growing so fast it frightened him. A fierce longing tugged at him as he recalled their exchange goodnight, the way Ruth's mouth had been so dangerously close to his. Closing his eyes, he imagined how it might have been if he had tilted his head towards hers until their lips had touched. Would she have responded or pushed him away?

Unable to stand being shut away in the bedroom with his confusing and destructive thoughts any longer, he picked up the box containing the letter, put on a robe and went downstairs.

He had been sitting at the island counter, the unopened box in front of him, for ten minutes when he heard a soft click from upstairs. Ruth appeared moments later. "Trouble sleeping?" he asked as she approached the kitchen area.

Bringing her hand to her chest, she jumped. "Jeremy, you gave me a fright."

"Sorry I didn't mean to startle you."

She looked relieved to see him. "I was in such a deep sleep but woke up so suddenly that I knew I needed to grab a hot drink to send me off again. I'm grateful for the company actually." Reaching for the teabags she shook the pack at him. "Chamomile. Want one?"

When he shook his head, she carried on making her own. "Makes a change to be startled by the living, rather than the dead." Noting the look on his face, she frowned. "What is it? Have you seen something? Was it Kat?" She hadn't noticed the box.

"No."

"Then what?"

Moving around the side of the island counter, he pointed at the box. "Before Cathy passed, she was sent something."

"Can I open it?"

With a nod, he pushed it across to her. "Don't lift out what's inside, though. I have gloves to handle it."

"An old artefact?" she asked as she lifted the clasp.

"Yes." He began chewing the ends of his nails as he watched her slowly lift the lid. There it was: the letter bearing Cathy's name, dated only weeks before her death.

Ruth gazed at the deep red seal before giving him a quizzical look. "Where did it come from?"

"It was sent to Auckland from a law firm in England. Then I received it over here with some of the storage boxes that came only a few days ago. I don't have the documentation that accompanied it as some of our stuff went into storage and some to Cathy's parents. When I found it, I was too overcome with grief to think straight. Stupid for a historian, right?"

Dismissing the self-deprecating comment, Ruth touched his hand. "Understandable for somebody whose world had fallen apart."

Jeremy swallowed down a lump. Somehow, she always knew the right things to say. He took a deep breath. "I haven't been able to bring myself to open it."

"Fear of damage?"

He shook his head. "I'm worried about the content. It's the weirdest thing I have ever seen: something that has very obviously been written in the past but dated for a future opening date, and for it to be in Cathy's name."

Ruth had abandoned making the tea. "Jeremy, given the necklace found its way into Cathy's family, far-fetched as it may seem, don't you think this letter could also be something to do with Kat?"

"Seems obvious, doesn't it?" Resting his elbows on the island, he put his head in his hands. "I just don't want to open it in case there's something in there that would have…" He couldn't finish without his voice cracking and he felt the warmth of Ruth's hand on his forearm.

"You're worried that whatever is written here would have stopped her from taking her life, that she might still have had a chance."

Pressing his thumb and forefinger to the inner corners of his eyes, he suppressed a sob.

"But Jeremy, the cancer was terminal. She had already been through so much with the chemo and you said yourself that it was simply keeping her hanging on, that the last lot had all but taken her to the brink. What could a letter say that would change all that?"

"I saw her tonight." The response was sudden, choked out. "She was in my room, I'm sure. And then this was suddenly on the floor, pulled from the drawers."

Ruth's forehead lined with concern. "Something woke me earlier. It was like there was a presence in the house. It wasn't Kat, but I felt something."

Dragging his hand down his face, he shook his head. "Shit. It was her. It was most definitely her. I should have opened the damn thing ages ago."

"Well, there's nothing to stop us opening it now, if we're careful."

"I don't know, I-"

"It doesn't have to be tonight, but we can do it tomorrow. Come on, you should really get some rest. So should I."

They turned out the lights and headed upstairs. "Do you think we could try and contact Cathy again?" The question was asked before he had even had time to think through how to frame it.

She was taken aback. "I don't know how that would help?"

Nor did he, but the guilt he had been feeling over his feelings for Ruth had been playing on him. Maybe seeing Cathy again would allow him to explain, to apologise, to ensure she wasn't mad. "You're right," he said at last with an awkward chuckle. "I'm sorry. I shouldn't have asked. Thanks for talking it all through." He leaned forward to kiss her cheek, only for her to turn away.

"Don't."

Confused by her sudden frostiness, he felt defensive. "It's just a friendly peck goodnight."

Her tone was clipped. "Let's just get the letter opened tomorrow and hopefully put your mind at rest." She left him rooted to the spot, unable to find the right retort.

The look on her face had said it all. Despite her kindness and empathy towards him, she felt used and hurt. He couldn't blame her. She had been through hell with her husband and now she was picking up the pieces for somebody else. She thought he was using her to reach out to his dead girlfriend, but regardless of the circumstances that had brought him to Ruth's door, he knew that he would have found another excuse to see her again. The truth was that, no matter how his conscience tried to fight it, he was falling hopelessly in love with Ruth Meadows.

CHAPTER THIRTY SIX

Dashing away her tears, Ruth sat on the bed, the idea of getting back to sleep a distant memory. There was no contest, of all the Christmases she had ever had, this was easily front of line to be the worst. It was her own fault of course. She had been foolish enough to allow herself to believe that the small gestures, comments and looks were because he had thought there was something special about her. It had all been a ruse. He just wanted to use her to try and connect with his dead girlfriend. Was that why he had asked if he could communicate with Kat through her? Was it really because he wanted to know if it was possible to connect with Cathy again, to perhaps see her, touch her and be with her through Ruth? It all seemed so obvious now she came to think of it. What had she been thinking to invite him away for Christmas? With the benefit of hindsight, she cringed at the very notion of how desperate and pathetic she must have appeared.

Going into the en-suite, she splashed her face with cold water. Once she had cooled down, she considered her reaction. It had been out of character for her, a reaction that, if she was honest, had been fuelled by envy. She had wanted to be the one who he had wanted to connect with, to care for and worry about so much. Over the years Grayson had starved her of affection and to see another man showing it for another woman had left her feeling even more raw and unloved. Under the circumstances she supposed that Jeremy's request had been a reasonable one, but the response she had given him had been uncalled for.

Drying her face and smoothing on some moisturiser, she decided that the best way she was going to be able to get any more sleep that night was to go and make amends. It was probably the only way either of them would get any sleep.

Glancing towards the second floor, she noticed a light behind the door. Feeling a little anxious, she climbed the stairs and tapped lightly on the door. It didn't take him long to answer and she noticed that he had poured himself a glass of the bourbon they had purchased on the way to Somerset. He motioned for her to enter.

Ruth perched on the ottoman at the foot of the bed. An air of awkwardness was hanging between them. "I just wanted to say I'm sorry." Her apology was met in unison with Jeremy's and they both gave a short laugh that mingled with both relief and embarrassment. "I shouldn't have been so clipped about something so sensitive to you." Ruth noticed that he was still holding the box. "I'm sorry if I was unreasonable."

Jeremy began to pace, his agitation obvious. At last he put the box down and looked at her. "You coming up here isn't making this any easier."

Affronted, Ruth stood up. "Are you joking? I've just come to share the pipe of peace with you. How can you possibly construe that as me not making things any easier?"

Jeremy gulped at the bourbon, draining the glass. "For a psychic you're not doing a very good job of reading the situation."

With an incredulous laugh, Ruth shook her head. "I don't have to stand here and take this from you. In the morning we can talk sensibly about all of this and-"

Before she could finish, he took her by the forearms and looked into her eyes. "All of this, Ruth: Me being so overcome with guilt, wanting to contact Cathy to check in with her, sharing everything with you, how can you not see why? The guilt I was feeling wasn't just about the damn letter, it was all of this." Flinging his hands out, he expelled a sigh of exasperation. "Every moment I spend with you, I look at you and I wonder how on earth you can't see it?"

"See what?" Genuinely confused and upset, she began to shrug off his touch, but he was suddenly much closer to her, the fullness of his lips so near to her face and catching her off guard. She could smell the sweetness of the bourbon on him as it mingled with the woody scent of his aftershave and, instinctively she tilted her head, their lips almost touching.

The air was static as they stared at one another, neither making the first move. Ruth felt her pulse quicken and she suddenly felt suffocated by the emotions that she had been trying to suppress. When he pressed his lips to hers, the cushiony softness took her by surprise. Melting into the embrace, she returned his kiss and pressed herself against him. As the warmth of his hands moved from her arms to between her shoulder blades and down to the small of her back, the sensation sent a ripple of pleasure up her spine and through her body. They kissed with a shared urgency, stumbling towards the bed as his fingers pulled at the thin straps of her pyjama top and hers found the tie of his robe.

Bringing her lips to the contours of his chest, she savoured the smell and feel of his skin. Effortlessly he flipped her onto her back, gazing at her with a look of such desire that any inhibitions she may have had were cast aside. He stroked the curve of her breast, his fingertips tracing slowly downwards, lingering over her waist, stomach and hips until they reached her thigh.

Surrendering to the tenderness of his touch, she took a sharp breath, feeling the moistness of his tongue begin to explore her body freely. Any sense of guilt or concern she may have had for her marriage melted away as he brought his lips back to hers. Her skin felt feverish against his and Ruth was charged with an unfamiliar fiery passion. Even in the early days with Grayson, she had never felt such a profound sense of desire. The feeling of him inside her made Ruth gasp, the thrill of it causing her to bite down on her lower lip as his mouth traced its way down her neck and decolletage, seeking out her breasts and the hardness of her nipples. As they made love, their kisses became deeper with a passion so unbridled that she paused only to cry out as a pulsing heat soared through her body.

Breathless, they collapsed onto one another and she could feel the tremble in his arms as he held her tightly. It felt so easy and right, so comfortable in his embrace that Ruth fell into a restful sleep.

The gratifying warm tingle from their lovemaking was still with her when she awoke to the sound of the shower. Throwing back the duvet, she got up and found her pyjamas. Running her fingers through her curls, she hoped she didn't look a complete state. There was a mirror on the dresser, just behind the laptop. Moving it so that she could check her reflection, her thumb nudged something next to it and her gaze landed on the sealed letter that Jeremy had shown her the night before. He must have taken it out of its box whilst she had been sleeping. Lightly tracing the edges of the seal with her fingertips, she felt the imprint of lettering elaborately stamped into the resin. The distinctive earthy smell of the parchment accosted her nostrils as she closed her eyes and tried to imagine the hand that had written and sealed the message between the neat folds. No image sprang to mind, only emotion. This was a deep sadness; the dark feeling of betrayal alongside all the anger and hatred that comes with it. As the emotions of the writer captured her, Ruth's elbow hit the laptop causing the battery to whir into life. The moment disturbed, Ruth opened her eyes and frowned. Jeremy must have been working whilst she had still been sleeping. The cursor was flashing next to a name on the screen and Ruth concluded that it must be the ancestor of Cathy's that Jeremy was finding it impossible to trace. Reading it, she frowned. The name was familiar, although she could not quite place it. She looked back at the letter, wondering if perhaps it could be connected to the man that Jeremy was so flummoxed by.

Break the seal!

The unearthly hissed words took her by surprise, tickling the hairs on the nape of her neck and permeating her skull. Dropping the parchment, Ruth spun around knowing full well that the room would be empty. She felt suddenly giddy. The sound of the shower was still in full force from the bathroom and she tried to focus on it but it was impossible.

Turning back to the dresser, where she had dropped the letter, she found that she could picture the hand that had held the goose feather quill as the words meant for Cathy had been scored onto the page. It was pale and the wrist delicate. Once again, Ruth scrutinised the wax seal and the lettering carved so elaborately into its centre. Had this letter been written during the period of time that she had slipped into?

The voice that had insisted she should break the seal and open the letter echoed through her head again. It was accompanied by a crawling sensation beneath her skin. The room around her was shifting and her head was beginning to spin. A vague collection of images began to take shape, gaining clarity and focus. It had happened just like this in the museum, when she had entered the gallery full of artefacts linked to the rebellion. As her eyelids fluttered closed, the name on the screen of the laptop came to the forefront of her mind, fusing with the extravagant flourish of the initial in the wax. There was something about that name. She had heard it somewhere.

Almost immediately, Ruth sensed Kat's presence. A brilliant white light was filling the room, hurting her eyes. The harsh glare began to soften to a haze and she realised that she was looking through a window and out onto a courtyard.

Ancient moon-bleached walls of a castle rose up from the ground. The tang of meat, vinegar and herbs lingered in the air from a meal that must have recently been served and she turned to see the remains of what must have been a lavishly set dining table. There was a grinding noise as a door opened. The first thought that sprang to her mind was that Jeremy would emerge from the bathroom, but she was far from the sumptuously furnished bedroom in the village of Barrington.

The figure standing in the doorway was dressed in a long blue coat and dark breeches. A lace cravat was worn around his neck with a dark blue ribbon tied tightly around the top. This was not Jeremy.

Mr Giles addressed her in his usual officious tone. "Lord Jeffreys wishes for you to see him. He is particularly ailed this night."

Ruth could feel herself responding, only she was not in any control of what she was doing or saying. She was viewing the world through Kat's eyes, trapped inside her body. "What has Doctor Copping suggested I should dispense?"

"There is no instruction from Doctor Copping. It is your presence that Lord Jeffreys has requested." His expression was as grave as those of all the servants that evening. Distressing news had reached the lodgings shortly after

Kat had returned with the assay cup and with it was uproar amongst the townsfolk. The little girl who had been made to stand before the austere looking judges had been sentenced to prison. So frightened she had been that she had collapsed. The news had come as Kat had been contemplating how best to broach the subject of what she had seen unfold on the lowlands of Sedgemoor. The girl was still alive but barely so. Everyone was shocked and sickened by it.

"Very well. Then I must go to him." Kat walked in the wake of his tread as he led her to the parlour room where Lord Jeffreys was sitting alone. Settled in a high winged chair by the blazing fire, the flame emphasised the redness in his cheeks. Clearly in discomfort, he shifted position and grimaced. Kat knew how painful it must be to have a stone that needed to pass but she was glad for his suffering and felt no sympathy. What he had done to the child was nothing short of monstrous.

The smell of alcohol was strong and Kat glanced at the carafe of wine on the sideboard. Next to it was the assay cup that some poor servant had no doubt been instructed to drink from before even a drop was poured for Lord Jeffreys, lest the candlelight was not enough to detect any subtle change in colour.

"Ah, here she is," he said in a way that suggested he had only just noticed her presence. Licking his lips, he regarded her with eyes that appeared almost as black as her obsidian stone but they could not focus. He was drunk.

Unable to look at him for any length of time, she averted her gaze. "Mr Giles said that you are ailed. I can fetch Doctor Copping." She hoped he would agree to her suggestion so that she did not have to spend any longer in his company.

There was a thud as the flat of his hand connected hard with the arm of his chair. He was full of frustrated fury. "Doctor Copping can be of no use for this. It is my head. Every time I shut my eyes they are there." Digging his fingers into his temples he growled with both frustration and pain. "Endlessly there, all of them. There is no respite. I cannot take another night of it." Giving her an imploring look, he pointed towards the shuttered window. "You can surely hear them now? It is so loud that I think my head might split."

Save the hiss and crackle of the fire, the room was quiet. "My Lord, I hear no noise."

"Do not play me for a fool, woman." Springing forth from his chair he threw out his arms. "Listen! Their chatter permeates the stone of the walls; it skitters about the building and it is as though they follow me wherever I walk, whispering into my ears with their accursed voices. They will not stop until they have made a madman of me!"

Dropping her head to her shoulder, Kat listened with a keen ear, wondering if perhaps he could hear the sound of soldiers bringing more prisoners for trial but there was no noise or disturbance. "I can speak to the servants and ask them to keep their noise down?" she suggested meekly, hoping that it would appease him. "I will ask that they go about their business in a more orderly and quiet manner, Lord Jeffreys."

Stamping his foot and clenching his fists, Lord Jeffreys could barely contain his anger. "It is not the servants whose voices crash against my skull and crush my senses. If you cannot hear them, your ears must be full of cloth. It is as though they are here in this very room with us."

Fearful of antagonising him any further, Kat gave a nod. "I shall make up another sleeping draught, my Lord. That should see you through." Keen to be away from him, she made haste to exit the room.

"You think that I am quite mad." His voice was a dangerous sounding purr, stopping her from feeling the cool of the door handle in her hand.

Kat held her breath, her mind racing as she considered how she might calm the temper that she could sense was ready to boil over. "No, my Lord. I do not think any such thing."

The sound of his boots leaving the rush matting and advancing towards her across the stone flooring echoed through the room. Instinctively, Kat's shoulders hunched as she felt him approach. His breath was hot and sour against her ear and neck. "All women think. They think too much. I have watched you. I see the way you silently judge as you crush your herbs and mix your potions."

His fingers cruelly gripped her arm and she stifled a cry. "You obediently dispense your medicaments without speaking a word, but you cannot hide that expression you wear. Some women know how to shame a man, to make him shrivel with one withering look." Gripping even harder, he shook her. "It is not your place to pass judgement." As swiftly as he had taken hold of her, he dropped his grip and fell back a few paces. Then, like a bear retreating to its cave, he slumped back into his chair.

"I will make you the sleeping draught now. You will feel better by morning."

When he looked up at her, he was no longer the formidable judge who presided over the assizes courtroom. He was a man burdened by the weight of his responsibility, haunted by the cries and pleas of those whom he had condemned to death. "It is never wise to judge what one cannot understand." His eyes glazed over as he drained the last of his wine. There would be no need for the sleeping draught if he was to continue this way. Kat returned to the chairs by the fire and offered to refill his glass.

"Stay a while," he said. "The voices are not so loud when you are here."

Obediently, she waited by the side of the chair and watched him drink, waiting for his eyelids to grow heavy. As she did so, she wondered how he could seem so terrifying one moment and so vulnerable the next. "There has been a rebellion," he said at last and he suddenly sounded sobered. "The King must have retribution. People must pay for their sins." This again, she had heard it before. He was always justifying it to her when her opinion counted for nothing. Still, she could not hold back.

"Even children?" She regretted the question immediately.

Lord Jeffreys did not flinch as he turned to face the flames of the fire. "So it would seem."

"The girl is eight years old. She would not have understood what any of it had meant. Her school mistress gave her an embroidered flag to hold. That was the girl's only crime."

"That school mistress did not stand trial." He was growing impatient again.

"And must a child be punished in her place?" She knew that she was treading on dangerous ground but she could not let it rest. There was too much injustice.

The sound of shattering crystal sliced through the air as the wine glass he had been holding hit the wall. "And what would you have me do?" His lips curled into a sneer. "I shall be interested in the wise counsel an apothecary has to give in the matters of law and order."

Her fear quelled by her outrage, Kat gave him a steely stare. "I would ask you reconsider her sentence and show mercy to others who stand before you, particularly after what I witnessed this very day."

Lord Jeffreys stared at her with interest. "Go on."

It was her chance. Even if it got her whipped, tortured or worse, at least she would know that she had tried to save her Gideon. "When I was returning from purchasing the assay cup today, I witnessed some of your soldiers behave dishonourably." She paused, studying his reaction but he simply nodded for her to go on. Taking a breath, she continued. "They had a man with them, a prisoner whom they tied to a stallion."

"And?"

"I heard them promise that if he could outrun the horse that he would go free."

There was a low rumbling sound and she realised that it was laughter. Lord Jeffreys shot her a look of amused incredulity. "Outrun a horse? And he agreed to it? The man could have only been simple or he had lost his mind."

"He beat the horse," Kat said flatly. "I watched it happen. But they did not honour their promise."

The grin fell from Lord Jeffreys's face as he clutched the arms of his chair and leaned forward. "You are certain that they did not let him go?"

"Very certain. They refused to let him go free."

With a slow nod, he rubbed his chin. "Who else knows of this? Have you told anyone else?"

"No, my Lord."

"This news must go no further," he warned and his eyes were hard again. "Who else knows of this?"

Kat felt unsteady on her feet. "No other, my Lord. I have not breathed a word, and nor will I speak of it to anyone."

He stared at her for a while longer before appearing satisfied that she was telling the truth. "Bring the sleeping draught to my chamber along with some of that cordial tincture you make. I shall not require anything more."

Taunton appeared sombre and grey the following day. After a restless night of worrying about the consequences of what she had imparted to Lord Jeffreys, Kat unlatched the door that led into a small courtyard. She needed air and wanted desperately to escape the oppressive atmosphere of the castle grounds, but to do so would be foolish lest she be seen by any locals. If she had thought that the legal conclave was hated in Dorchester, the townsfolk here did nothing to mute their distaste.

As Kat tilted her head to look at the sullen sky, she heard the muffled knell of a bell. Eight slow successive chimes could be heard reverberating across the town as the clouds overhead began to weep. It could only mean that the child had passed. Sure enough, word had seeped through the castle walls when Kat returned inside.

"Didn't last the night, poor child." The hushed voices of two female servants could be heard from behind the door in the kitchen. "Terrified, she was. Her mother said that she was so frightened of the idea of prison that her little heart gave up."

Her eyes welling with tears, Kat could no longer stand to hear any more. Back upstairs, the lodgings were deathly quiet, all but for the hum of people gathering beyond the castle grounds. It was the final day of the Taunton assizes and Kat had made the decision to go to the court. It was the only way to find out if the soldiers had eventually let Gideon go - or not.

Pulling the hood of her cloak over her head, she passed by the prison where hard-faced men were standing guard. Their expressions gave away no sympathy for the women who were pleading for loved ones. Tears flowed and voices were raised as they begged to be allowed inside, some adamant that their brothers, sons and husbands were innocent, that they should not be in there. Their dishevelled appearances did nothing for their cause, finding no weakness in the emotional armour worn by men who had seen and heard far worse.

The Great Hall was overflowing as people flocked to witness the fate of neighbours, friends and family. She regretted her outburst to Lord Jeffreys the night before. If they had let Gideon go, now that he knew of the incident, Lord Jeffreys could issue an order for him to be found and punished. Still, she prayed that she would not hear his name called. Eventually weaving her way to the front, she waited for the assizes to open.

Men were brought in their scores, all of them pleading guilty. It did not surprise her. Reports of what happened to those who claimed their innocence was rife. Shooting a look at the sombre-faced legal counsel, Kat wondered if news of what had become of the young child had softened them at all, but Judge Jeffreys appeared in no humour for leniency. One after another, the men were sentenced. Those who were not sentenced to execution were to be sent to the colonies. In Dorchester, Kat had overheard a conversation between Mr Giles and Lord Jeffreys, discussing the financial gains to be made from selling men into slavery. Her heart pounding, she watched with trepidation as each unfamiliar face appeared at the bar, guilt pressing on her shoulders at the relief she felt that none of them were her husband.

The day drew on and Kat felt a tiny glimmer of hope as Gideon's name remained uncalled. When the heavy clank of chains of the final group of prisoners being brought forward could be heard, Kat felt dizzy. It was hot in the court and the acrid stench of fear was not one her nostrils could become accustomed to. Hardly daring to breathe, she shut her eyes and listened to the names of those called. The clerk's voice echoed around the room and Kat drew a sigh of relief. Gideon was not amongst these men. Desperate to leave the hideously, stifling atmosphere, she turned to fight her way through the crowd. She did not care to bear witness to more families being destroyed by the wicked judges. It was the murmur of excitement from the crowd that made her stop and turn.

The proceedings had paused whilst a slip of parchment was passed on. Judge Jeffreys snatched it, impatience plain upon his face. As he read, his mouth twisted in such a way that it was impossible to decipher whether it was from pain or disgust. Sweat gathered beneath Kat's arms as she gripped the edge of the pew in front of her. The expression worn by Judge Jeffreys was whipping the crowd into a frenzy. As though sensing her gaze upon him, he glanced in her direction. A slow, deliberate smile pulled at the corners of his mouth.

There was a unified gasp from those watching as the clavicle connected hard with the wooden surface that it struck. Kat winced at the sound of it. The peculiar moment she had shared with Judge Jeffreys had gone. His gaze had returned to the court and he was repeating the name of the final prisoner. "Christopher Carter." He said the name slowly, rolling his tongue as though savouring it.

Kat could barely breathe. The name meant nothing to her, but the man at the bar did.

CHAPTER THIRTY SEVEN

There was no mistaking the coppery swathe of hair and lean, strong body. This was Gideon, but why had he been called by a different name?

Kat's legs and arms suddenly felt weak. She wanted to shout out to him, tell him she was there, that she loved him and would stand by him no matter what. A small whimper escaped the depths of her throat and somebody caught her by the elbow as her knees buckled beneath her weight.

"Take a care, my love. You almost fell." The woman next to her was staring at her with concern. "Somebody you know up there, is there?" she whispered and Kat was quick to shake her head. She could not give away Gideon's true identity. It would only make matters worse for him. Her mind worked fast, remembering what Darling had said to her from her deathbed. She had warned her that she must never look upon Gideon as her husband again. At the time she had thought Darling had been hinting at the fact he had betrayed her in some way but now she understood. Had Darling foreseen this moment? Was that why she had been so wild about making Kat promise?

Composing herself, Kat straightened and looked at the exhausted face of her husband before returning to the unforgiving glare of Judge Jeffreys. There was something like amusement in the judge's eyes.

When at last Judge Jeffreys spoke, he turned to address his fellow judges. "It has come to my attention that this one boasts of being able to outrun any beast." He made a strange noise akin to a chuckle before dramatically throwing out his arm and booming: "The man who can outrun any beast."

Gideon did not move and his expression remained unchanged as the room erupted into a series of gasps and whispers. It was quickly followed by the bang of the clavicle jolting the room into silence again. The crime for which he stood accused was read out to him, but he remained impassive, his expression giving nothing away.

"How do you plead?" Judge Jeffreys asked.

Gideon did not speak. The courtroom waited for his response and, as he glanced around the room, his eyes briefly locked with Kat's. Although it was only a fleeting moment, Kat saw the change in him: Pride melted to shame; courage shrivelled to fear. Kat knew that he would not want her to witness any of this. That was why he was using the name of another. His eyes were wide and startled and she could see the strength being sapped from him. He looked away, unable to look in her direction again.

"Guilty." His response was choked and he appeared smaller.

There was a pause as Judge Jeffreys cleared his throat. Kat began to back away, but not before the sentence was passed. No detail was spared as Judge Jeffreys gleefully imparted to the clamouring crowd what fate awaited the man with the ostensible claim that no beast on the land was faster than he.

Gasping for air, Kat left the roar of the crowd behind. She gathered her skirts and began to run, no longer caring what would happen to her if she was to leave the position she had been given. How could she continue to serve the man who had just sentenced her husband to death?

As she clawed her way out of the building, she did not notice the watchful gaze of Mr Giles from the other side of the courtroom. With a calm swoop of his hand, he dipped the crow's feather into his ink pot and began to write.

CHAPTER THIRTY EIGHT

Everything had clouded again and her mind was swimming. Ruth felt as though she had been shocked by an electric current. Pinpricks of pain were running up and down the length of her body.

Somebody was calling her name and she became aware of a face in front of hers. Her vision and senses began to clear. Jeremy was with her and she reminded herself that she had been holding the letter when she had slipped back into Kat's time, but it had been something on the screen of his laptop that had helped trigger it. She swallowed but her throat was too dry and it made her gag. "They killed him!" she blurted out and her tongue felt too thick for her mouth. "Gideon was executed!" A surge of nausea took hold and she scrambled for the bathroom.

When she felt steady enough to wash her face and return to the bedroom, she found Jeremy sitting on the edge of the bed biting his nails. "Sorry I didn't come through to help. I thought you might need the privacy."

Managing a weak smile, Ruth swept her hair back over her shoulders. "Believe me, I'm grateful you didn't come in."

His gaze fell to her hands. "You're shaking."

Ruth knew she must look dreadful but she was beyond caring. Kat's pain was still with her. Strands of hair were sticking to her face and her cheeks were damp from crying. "I should probably go and take a shower." Swallowing hard, she avoided his gaze. She didn't know how to articulate everything she had just witnessed.

"Here, take this." He handed her a glass of water and she gulped it back. "What did you see? Was she here? Kat, I mean."

"No, I just sort of fell into her time again.' Rubbing her head, Ruth shut her eyes and waited for the pieces to continue falling into place. "If I'm perfectly honest, it's all a bit jumbled right now. It seems to take time to come together. That's how it worked before anyway. I'm sorry I can't say more than that."

Nodding with understanding, he took hold of her hand and kissed it. "You go and try to relax under the shower and shout for me if you need anything."

She left him with the questions that were, no doubt, burning his mind.

After Ruth had left the room, Jeremy returned to his laptop. She hadn't appeared aware of the fact that whilst she had been bordering on the edge of consciousness, her fingers had been furiously tapping away on the keyboard.

Too afraid to touch her in case any harm would come of it, he had waited and tried to gently coax her from the reverie that she had appeared lost in.

Picking up the laptop, he took it over to the bed, propped himself against the pillows and began to read.

******

"So that's it, Kat's story has drawn to a close." They were eating brunch with Max and Tim when Ruth imparted everything she had witnessed.

Tim watched her push the half-eaten poached egg around her plate. "I know it wasn't the conclusion you would have liked but I suppose it means your job is complete."

"You sound so nonchalant about it, Tim." Ruth couldn't keep the emotion from tainting her tone. It was easy for them to shrug their shoulders and move on, they hadn't witnessed the heartbreak, the desperately desolate feeling of being torn apart by grief. Kat had needed her and she had failed to deliver.

Giving her shoulder an affectionate squeeze, Tim apologised. "I don't mean to, sis. It's just that this woman was looking for an answer and you helped her find it. So that should surely be it?" He picked up the coffee pot and topped everyone up.

"How did I help her?" The question was flat as Ruth felt the familiar ripple of disgust and distress every time she considered what had happened to Kat's husband.

It was Max's turn to chip in. "You guided her, Ruthie. You stayed by her side to give her the strength she needed to keep her cool when everything around her was falling apart. If she had given away who this Christopher Carter really was then she would just as likely have reaped the consequences."

Sliding her plate to the side, Ruth had lost her appetite. "Maybe you're right." She glanced over at Jeremy. "You're quiet. All okay?" They hadn't had the chance to speak about what had happened between them the night before and as she found her mind plummeting back into the present, Ruth was feeling increasingly awkward. Jeremy had appeared subdued since he had joined them. He shifted his gaze from the table to Ruth and then to Tim and Max.

Shaking his head, he rubbed his palm across the shadow of stubble on his chin. "I don't think it is over." He placed two sheets of paper onto the island counter, pushing them towards Ruth.

Ruth glanced down to read the print. "What's this?"

"I found it on my laptop when you were in the shower." He shot her an inquisitive look. "Were you aware that you'd typed anything?"

The print was all in one block with no paragraphs separating any of it. She frowned as she began to read and her scalp began to tingle uncomfortably. Everything she had witnessed through the eyes of Kat was there in black and white. Bringing her hand to her mouth, she stifled a cry. "That's it. It's exactly how it all happened."

Max had taken one of the sheets of paper and both he and Tim were reading through it, their faces pale and shocked.

Jeremy jabbed at the final section with his index finger. "This name is the same as Cathy's ancestor. Christopher Carter is the man who I can't trace back any further than his death in 1732. After he died, one of his boys went on to have a son who appeared to have significant influence over the Bridgwater Treaty in the latter part of the century."

Max looked up from his reading. "The treaty that lobbied to abolish slavery?"

"That very one." Jeremy turned his attention back to Ruth. "Everything you documented suggests that in order to save his wife's reputation and possibly her life, Gideon Fox masqueraded as a farmhand whom he had met in battle, Christopher Carter. That's the name that he went by in court when he was sentenced to death for treason."

"Are you saying you think that this Christopher Carter is Cathy's ancestor?"

Animated, Jeremy had jumped up from his seat and was pacing the room. "It makes sense and it explains why I can't trace him back any further. According to your account, Christopher's family were extremely poor. It was likely to have been a hand to mouth existence for them and there are no records to be found."

"But it's impossible that your Christopher Carter is the same person. He was sentenced to a traitor's death. I heard it with my own ears and I felt Kat's despair. Judge Jeffreys took such spiteful pleasure in handing that particular sentence out and all because Kat had offended him the evening before by beseeching him to show some mercy to those due to stand trial the following day. She attempted to emotionally manipulate him by playing on the weight of the guilt already on his shoulders. She tried to appeal to his more vulnerable side and he hated her for that. He wanted to punish her, to make a show of the authority he commanded. There is no way that he retracted that sentence."

"Maybe not, but it wasn't unheard of for convicts who were awaiting their execution to be given the opportunity to answer to the name of another called to get in line for transportation. There was a lot of money to be made from the slave ships and there are also accounts of bribes, although the bribes were reserved for those with wealth." Wild with excitement, he raked his fingers through his hair. "I checked the list of rebels again. That's why I took so long coming to join you guys down here. I found his name. I found a record for Christopher Carter from Bridgwater."

"And?" Ruth felt her chest tighten as she waited for him to divulge what he had seen.

"His sentence was commuted to transportation and he sailed to Barbados in November 1685."

Shaking her head, Ruth struggled to comprehend what he was telling her. "What? How?"

"The clue is here." He tapped at the bottom of the page containing the final details of her account. Tim and Max had joined them so that they were all crowding around the pages. "You observed something that Kat did not see and it fits with everything you have told me."

When none of them made any indication that they followed what it was that he was trying to explain, Jeremy gave an exasperated sigh. "Read it."

As she did so, she recalled the way that Mr Giles had been carefully watching Kat's reaction and how, after she had turned to flee the Great Hall of Taunton, he had written something down. "You think that Mr Giles was responsible for the switch in sentence?"

"It's plausible."

"But why? That would have been a huge risk for him to take."

"Was it? There were that many rebels sentenced to death that it was impossible to carry out the sentence for all of them anyway. From what you said, he was in part, accountable for records of the rebel convicts and the orders given to the authorities of each town. He was a clever man, the one who appeared to handle the financial affairs."

"But even if he had guessed the relationship between Kat and the convicted Christopher Carter, what incentive would he have had to change the sentence?"

Jeremy stared at her for a moment, his eyes twinkling. "Love."

Max was enthralled by the story. "He must have been one of the rebels to return to English soil after William of Orange and Mary issued the pardon."

"If it is the same Christopher Carter who Ruth has seen during these…" Jeremy struggled for the right way to phrase it, "…psychic events, then yes, I believe that is what happened and he is connected to the family tree I have been researching. It would certainly explain the influence that his grandson had on the Bridgwater Treaty."

"But didn't you say that, even before he was convicted, he appeared to have had no wealth or connections, either as Christopher or Gideon?"

Jeremy nodded and waited for Max to finish making his point: "How do you think a man who was likely very broken from all those years in slavery, and who appears to have remained on a less than modest income, managed to provide one of his children the sort of education that completely changed the direction of this family tree? Because it was the influence and outcome of Christopher's son's education that must have set the wheels in motion for the grandson to follow suit and gain the right authority and contacts to have the sort of influence he did."

"The boy could have been particularly gifted and sent off to a wealthy household where he was companion to a nobleman who decided to have him educated. Christopher's wealth would have been relatively immaterial if that had been the case. And if he had been particularly close to his son, he may have imparted some of his experiences. In turn, the son may have passed this information down the family line."

Max was quiet for a moment. "I suppose."

"Many more men from Bridgwater were also sold to slavery as a result of the Bloody Assizes and the town remained embittered about this. Enslaved convicts were treated poorly and they would have witnessed the brutal and cruel treatment of their West African counterparts. It's thought that some did share an account of what had happened to them, what they had witnessed in those colonies. Even a diluted version of the truth would have been pretty horrific. If any of that detail had been passed on down the generations, the bitterness would have remained, possibly grown. It would only take one with the strength of mind and the right connections to have made a stand."

"If all this is true, I have to find Kat and tell her what we know." Ruth could not forget the deep hollow crevice that she had felt splitting Kat in two when she had seen her husband sentenced to death. "That's the purpose of all this; the knowledge she has been left with will carry her to a different course in life. Who knows what will happen to her?" Hurrying towards the staircase, she went to fetch the obsidian stone.

"Ruth?" Jeremy's face was sheet white. At the sight of it, she stopped abruptly.

"What if she's meant to think that? What if Kat finding out about the true fate of her husband changes history and of the chain events that would have led to his safe return, to the birth of his sons, to the success that came of the Bridgwater Treaty, to-" He paused to take a ragged breath. "What if it changes Cath's ancestral line?"

The question hung between them and the air was static. The repercussions of getting it wrong were significant and she knew that, but every instinct inside her told her that reaching out to Kat again was the right thing to do. "What if not doing it is what changes everything?" she asked and the house fell silent.

It was Tim who stepped forward. "Ruth is right. I think she has to do it."

Jeremy passed her, taking the steps two at a time. There was no disguising the emotion on his face. To him, this wasn't only a ripple in time that could change history, this was Cath's life – his own history.

The door at the top of the house opened and closed and she imagined him behind it, torn apart and distraught. "Let me go to him," she said to Tim.

There was no response when she knocked and so she gently pushed down on the door handle. He was holding the sealed letter in his hand, staring down at Cathy's name etched into the parchment. Although faded over time, the letters were still visible. Swallowing back her own emotion, Ruth tried her hardest to remain empathetic, to not allow the creeping feeling of jealousy poison her from within. "I understand your reluctance for me to make contact with Kat and tell her the truth of it. I realise what it could mean for you and everything you had with Cathy. And I know that you're not solely focusing on that, but that's the part that is intimately personal to you."

He took a breath to speak but did not lift his head. "The other stuff, everything that has played out through history might still happen, but simply orchestrated by different players – people who were given the chance to live and not had their potential existence snuffed out by a few folk who have found a way to slip back through time and do things the way they think they're supposed to be done." He stopped and it was obvious that the thought of Cathy never being given the opportunity to even exist was playing on his mind.

Ruth wanted to reach out to him, to comfort him but he looked as cold and hard as stone. "I know how much Cathy meant to you, how much she still does. Your memories with her define a huge part of who you are. I do get that. I don't want to risk taking it away, but it's fifty-fifty now and my instincts tell me this is the path we need to take. We need to find Kat again."

He whirled around and emotion was etched into every line of his face. "This isn't just about me and Cath, though, is it?"

Ruth opened her mouth to retort but found herself lost for anything to say. "This is about you and me, Ruth. The repercussions would be far more reaching: I won't just lose one woman whom I have loved, I'll lose another too. Without Cath, we don't meet."

The gravitas of what he was saying struck her hard and she fell against the doorframe. He was right. The sense of loss made her feel hollowed out, devoid of any feeling. When she spoke, her eyes were bright with unspent tears. "It's my calling, Jeremy. I have to do what I think is right."

He sniffed and nodded. "You're right, of course." Holding the letter up, he gave a morose smile. "I need to face the demon that has been holding me back from opening this. I've been so scared that whatever is inside could have prevented Cath from-" Breaking off mid-sentence, he couldn't finish.

Ruth rushed over to his side. "We can open it together. And we should open it. You know that everything could be connected." She reflected on how she had felt when she had traced her fingertips over the ridges of the wax seal. It had been deep sadness that had been there, the end of life and a sense of great loss. The name that had come to her mind was different to Kateryn's. Until that moment, she had wondered if the letter had been written by Kateryn but what she had seen and the marking on the wax seal suggested otherwise. The embossed lettering that had been engraved into the stamper was a 'C'. It would appear that it had not been written by the hand of Kateryn Fox. Still, she felt certain that there had to be a link.

"We should really be wearing some cotton gloves to open this. It's supposed to help prevent any oils from our skin destroying it. I have some but did not bring them with me. This was not something I had expected to be doing. No time to concern ourselves over that now, I suppose." He rested the letter back on the dresser and gestured for her to follow him into the bathroom. "Washing our hands thoroughly is about the best we can do."

They took the letter downstairs to give themselves the necessary space and light. Ruth delicately explained the situation to Max and Tim who promptly made themselves scarce. Emotions were running high for Jeremy and the last thing he needed was an audience.

"It's a tricky job, I'm afraid." She noticed that his hands were shaking as he began to work. "They had a very intricate way of making these things secure. See this?" He gently pulled at a strip of the parchment that had been cleverly spiralled through it. "It shows the seal has never been broken. We'll be the first to lay eyes on what's inside. It's a historian's dream."

She watched as his fingers began to unfold the edges, neatly pressing out each fold. "I can imagine." In ordinary circumstances it would be a wonderfully exciting find for him, but she knew that there was too much of his personal life riding on the content.

Slowly, painstakingly, the letter was revealed. Eventually, he was able to lay it out. Ruth stared at the writing, the beautifully-penned lettering that had faded a little with age. It was difficult to read but Jeremy's lips were moving silently, his eyes bulging, as he digested the content.

"You can read all of that?" Ruth was astounded. Even though she could read the words, it made little sense to her.

At first he did not reply, but then he gave a nod. Ruth's gaze scanned the page until she reached the bottom and her heart skipped a beat. The author of the letter had signed off with their full name and then an alias. There was no mistaking it. This letter had been written by Kateryn Fox.

CHAPTER THIRTY NINE

Sliding back his chair, Jeremy hurtled back upstairs to fetch his laptop. The deep red lettering was scored into his mind. Two names had been signed: Catherine and Kateryn. She had been given a different identity but there was no doubt that this was the same woman who Ruth had been communicating with. Impatiently, he added her name to the search bar and tapped away until he found what he was looking for. At last, Cathy's family tree was connected. The birth, death and marriage records did not give the full picture; he and Ruth would need to fill in the gaps, but knowing what they did now, it was not hard.

Gazing at the fine black lines that branched from Catherine's name, he studied the names, dates of births and recorded deaths of her husband and each of her children until he found the one that he was searching for. Flicking back to Christopher Carter's tree, he found the match and drew a breath. Ruth had been right. It was imperative that she contacted Kat again.

CHAPTER FORTY

The dining table had been cleared and set just as Ruth had instructed. They had called Tim and Max and asked them to return to the barn.

An assortment of pillar candles had been placed around a dish of salt water, the curtains and blinds closed and the main lights dimmed. Ruth placed the obsidian necklace into the dish whilst Max went to turn off the fairy lights. The smell of sulphur filled the room as Tim and Jeremy both struck matches to light the candles.

Once the light in the room had been dimmed to only candle flame, Ruth instructed them all to take a seat. Anxiety had quickened her breathing and she was vaguely aware of the ache in her fingers as they gripped the table edge. She blinked away unshed tears as she thought about the emotion she had shared with Kat when her husband had been sentenced. There had been an unstable edge, something dreadfully dark spreading its wings inside of her as she had run from the Great Hall of Taunton. In that moment, Ruth knew that the darkness would grow and spread, festering; whilst it would be a long time before it broke Kat, when it did, it would change everything. Hoping that she was not too late, she felt Jeremy's fingers lace through hers, giving her the strength she needed to make contact. She could see the worry in his eyes and she knew that his concern was for her safety.

Giving his fingers a gentle reassuring squeeze, she looked him in the eye. "I'll be in control on this occasion, not Kat. You will all be here and you can bring me back any time." The confidence in her voice betrayed her true feelings of trepidation. This was not something she had any experience of doing. She was a healer, not a time traveller or the High Priestess that Kat had thought her to be. Every other time she had travelled back to Kat's time, it had not been of her own volition. What if doing it this way had disastrous consequences? What if Kat was so enraged that she hadn't helped her free Gideon that she attacked her?

"We're here for you," Tim said from across the table and she knew that it was now or never.

Closing her eyes, she recalled how Kat had used fire and water to scry. It wasn't something that Ruth had ever tried but it was worth a go. She knew that she needed to focus her mind, to claw her way through her own memories until she found the vague collection of images that had once been a part of Kateryn Fox's mind. It had happened that way in the museum, when she had entered the gallery full of artefacts linked to the rebellion and when she had read the name of Gideon's alias. As her eyelids fluttered closed, she returned her mind to the items she had seen in the museum's glass casements. She could picture all of them just as they had once been, hundreds of years earlier.

In her mind's eye she could see the swords that had been found on the battlefield, the blades glinting in the sunlight. Lying next to them were others, the silver dirtied to a red-brown where blood had been drawn and wounds inflicted. The images stimulated her senses and she found that she could smell the stench of death muddled with wet soil. That was where those swords had been found, discarded on the vast planes of Sedgemoor, the bodies of the men who had used them lifeless and bloody as the marshland attempted to swallow them before the carters came. She thought of Kat's time in the apothecary shop with her grandmother, of the vastness of the sweet, sour and foul odours from the countless jars and bottles, and a memory slowly began to take shape, like the petals of a flower steadily unfurling.

Shocked at how quickly the energy in the room had started to change, she opened her eyes. Tim was watching her from across the table, Max sitting next to him and, next to Ruth, was Jeremy. His gaze was fixed upon the necklace in the bowl of saltwater. The blackness of the stone appeared to flow into a dark shade of purple. Ruth pulled it from the bowl of salt water and they all watched as the surface gradually melted into an array of colour: purple to magenta, to orange, to yellow, to green…

Nobody said anything as she felt the energy in the room begin to engulf her. Silently she returned to the deep chasm of her mind where the memory she had found was becoming stronger - Kat's memory.

The candle flames grew taller and brighter, swaying hypnotically in unison, lulling her into a state of deep relaxation. Burning wax mingled with the smell of Christmas and she reached out to take a drink from the glass in front of her, suddenly aware of the giddying sensation…..

******

This was intoxication. It was the welcome, hollow numbness that she had grown so accustomed to during the evenings she sensed the nightmares returning. Over ten years had passed since she had lost Gideon but the terrible memories and feelings had never gone away. After the assizes courts, had come the blood. Without mercy it had spilled across the towns, roads and villages as more men had been disposed of at the King's pleasure. So foul was the smell that those who needed to travel through the West Country had avoided the roads if they could.

Eventually the news had come in waves: More unrest across the country and the King finally deposed of his throne by his own daughter, Mary and her husband, William. The wicked judge, whose voice and temper still haunted her dreams, had faced a cruel twist of irony shortly after that; he was no longer the hunter but the hunted. That had been five years earlier. Kat would never forget the day she had learned of the capture of Lord Jeffreys. She had been visiting friends and word had come whilst they had been dining. With her appetite lost, she had retired early. All night her head had spun. After William of Orange had overthrown King James, Lord Jeffreys had attempted to escape English shores to join his employer in exile. The man who had recognised him, who had thwarted his attempt to conceal his identity and sail away, had evidently stood before him four years earlier during the infamous assizes. She should have been pleased for the news, have delighted in the glorious retribution it appeared to be but instead the news had ailed her. She had reminded herself that no matter what happened to King James or Lord Jeffreys, nothing would return her husband to her arms.

William and Mary had taken the throne shortly after that and Lord Jeffreys had never faced the executioner. It had been his kidney that drained him of life and he had passed away in the tower.

Even when the official pardons had come for those involved in the Monmouth uprising, Kat had not rejoiced. All of it had left her wondering what point there had been to any of it. Being widow to a martyr felt quite different to being widow to a rebel. The anger she felt was always so quickly quashed by the misery.

She had another husband now, of course. It would not do for him to see her so morose. Turning to check that the doors to the dining room had been properly shut, she reached for the newssheet he had been holding before he had retired from dinner.

Taking one of the candlesticks from above the fire, she held it up to read. The words blurred as her vision was obscured by the gathering tears but she already knew what they said, she had just wanted to see them for herself. Nobody had believed that any of those transported to the colonies would return but here it was in front of her - news of more of them who had returned to England. It was all more words, carefully crafted to remind the country how good and noble King William was for securing the return of those men. They had a second chance. What use was a pardon for those who had lost their lives? What good was it for men like Gideon? As she dropped the newssheet to the table, Kat's hand knocked her glass. The sound of splintering crystal brought one of the servants running into the room. Kat did not move as the mess was cleared and the wine mopped. She could not take her eyes off the deep red liquid rapidly spreading across the page. It had been over a decade since Gideon's blood had been spilled for his part in the uprising; a decade of burying her grief and hiding it away, especially from Pelham, the man she had eventually married.

"Leave us." The gentle but authoritative voice of her husband brought all the fussing to an abrupt end. When they were alone, he placed a hand upon her shoulder, asked her if all was well and suggested she retire to bed. Kat could not turn her head to look at him. There was too much rage inside her, rage that she had kept swallowed down for years. She did not want him to see it burning in her eyes, the unspoken accusation that was always between them. She felt the warmth of his lips on top of her head and closed her eyes. If she was to look, she would be reminded of the dark times she had endured all those years ago when they had first become acquainted, back when he had addressed her as Mistress Fox and she had known him as Mr Giles.

******

"Thank goodness for that." Tim's voice ripped through the silence as Ruth's eyes snapped open. "Did you speak with her? Is it done?"

Ruth did not reply. She was in another place and time.

"I don't think she's actually back in the room." Max chipped in.

"I've seen her do this before," Jeremy said and the sound of his voice seemed to stir her slightly. "Ruth, did you see her?"

She remained rigid and staring ahead as though looking at something else entirely, but her head nodded back and forth in response to his question.

"Ask her what happened." Tim's impatience was creating an atmosphere and Max nudged him to calm down.

Jeremy leaned closer to her. "Did you speak with Kateryn? Is she with you now?" As she turned to look at him, the blood in his veins ran to ice. The brilliant azure shade of her irises had darkened. In the fractured light she looked different, not at all like herself.

Her brow creased into a frown. "Who are you?" she asked and the candles went out.

******

"Who are you?" Kat demanded into the darkness of her chamber. In spite of the chill in the air, her skin was clammy. The pale light of dawn was seeping through the rich material of the curtains that had recently been hung. Soft snores were coming from the truckle on the floor. It seemed that her spectral visitor had not managed to disturb the maid. That was a blessing. She did not want word to work its way back to Pelham, informing him that she was having the nightmares again. All those years ago, after she had fled Taunton, she had returned to the apothecary shop in Winchester and had been plagued by them. Every night she would wake screaming as thoughts of Gideon's suffering had scarred her mind. It was only when Pelham Giles had arrived on her doorstep that the nightmares had started to ease.

After the assizes, he had left his important and wealthy position to find her. Kat had been a mess. He had been staying at a coach house and had visited the apothecary every day. At first, she had shut the door on him. He had persisted though, had shown her great empathy. Then one day she let him in.

Kat had not realised that on the day when Judge Jeffreys had finally destroyed everything she had held dear, Pelham Giles had been watching her from the other side of the Great Hall of Taunton Castle. He told her that he had seen the glimmer of recognition that had so briefly glanced upon her face and he had guessed that the last defendant, Christopher Carter, meant something to her. Relieved to share the burden of her grief with another, she had confessed and told him everything. At the time of her confession, it had seemed that she had nothing more in life to lose.

Pelham had stared at the ground and she had been unable to tell whether it was from awkwardness or shame. Perhaps it had been both. In the plain way that he expressed himself, he had said that he was sorry for her loss and that she did not deserve such tragedy.

After that they had spent each afternoon walking the banks of the River Itchen, giving one another companionship. They had not spoken of Gideon again. It was enough that Pelham Giles would carry her secret so that she could keep her story that Gideon had been lost when travelling on business. On one of those walks, as the vibrant shades of autumn were fading to the waxen hues of winter, he had admitted that he had grown to love her during the time they had spent together in servitude to Lord Jeffreys. Love had been the reason that he had left his position - to seek her out in the hope that they might start a new life together.

When Pelham Giles had offered her the chance to be a wife once again, it had been with a heavy heart that Kat had reminded him that, although it was only the two of them and God who knew of what had become of Gideon, in the eyes of the law she was an abandoned wife, so it would be many more years before she could marry again.

As cool and efficient as she had always known him to be, Pelham Giles had simply nodded his head before informing her that such matters could be fixed and that it would also be wise to change her name for fear of Lord Jeffreys exacting his revenge for the great insult that her departure had evidently caused.

Using a quorum of his wealthy and influential acquaintances, Pelham had executed the plan with ease. He was a well-connected and respected man and he knew the affairs of many important men in the country, financially, legally and otherwise. There was no shortage of willing assistance for a man like Pelham. It had not been hard for a suitable body to be found and for the fate of Gideon Fox to be recorded as death by misadventure - another poor, anonymous soul whose untimely demise had helped disguise the truth of Gideon's betrayal.

Kat's name had been changed to Catherine St Clair and the apothecary shop had been sold. Weeks later she had become Catherine St Clair Giles and they had moved into a beautiful country manor. There was nothing of her old life left, aside from a few of the chattels she had kept from her grandmother's apothecary and of course, the necklace. With her new name and new life, she was the kept woman Darling had beseeched her to never become.

Shaking her head free of the memories, she returned her focus to the strange, transient man by her bedside, who was swiftly fading into the creamy light of a new day. When he had vanished, she wondered if he had even been there at all. With a heavy sigh, she fell back against the bolster and waited for her maid to stir from her slumber.

At breakfast, Kat stared miserably at the knife on the table, unable to eat, unable to smile or even muster a response to anything said to her. It wasn't that she failed to recognise the fortuitous turn her life had taken, providing her with three beautiful children, comforts and luxuries and food on the table; it was that nobody could see the darkness inside her, its malignant bloom growing each day. Deeply troubling thoughts peppered her imagination. They were thoughts that had bothered her since news had come of the royal pardon that was so useless for so many. Every day she thought of the men who had returned by sea to their loved ones and their old lives and she felt cheated. She had no pleasure in anything any longer. Even her children could not hold her attentions long enough to prevent her mind wandering to the various ways that she could stop the pain and misery. She no longer felt any connection to the spirit of her grandmother, or took any comfort from prayer. What use was her mortal body on earth any longer? Pelham had his work and the children had Kitty, the governess. Kitty loved those children with the ferocity of a mother's love and they loved her back.

Kat's gaze returned to the knife. What harm could it do, she asked herself, if she was no longer there? Her misery only served to sap the life from the house and make even the brightest days appear grey.

"What is it, my love?" Pelham had dropped his bread and was giving her a look of concern. "Are you ailed? Should I call for Doctor Brownlow?"

Managing a weak smile, Kat shook her head. "I am just fatigued. I did not sleep well."

Pelham appraised her silently from across the table. "You have remembered that I am travelling to London this morning? Should I cancel the plan? You really do not look well."

"Please go, husband. It is nothing a little fresh air and a gentle walk will not resolve. I shall be quite alright."

"Very well." He returned his attention to his reading material, leaving her to return to wallowing in the dismal fancies of her own departure. Perhaps she would be brave enough to do it whilst he was away? It would be far easier without him keeping an eye on her or finding a way of stopping her. Kitty would be busy with the children and they would all be far too involved in their studies or games to notice that their mother was missing. Kat could no longer take the anguish of living another day with the knowledge that, whilst other men were still being returned to their families and loved ones, her real husband was dead.

"Mother! Mother!" The wailing voice of Charlotte, her eldest child, tore through the house as the doors to the dining room were flung open.

Before Kat could speak, Charlotte was running towards her and flinging her arms about her shoulders and crying so desperately that Kat looked towards Pelham for help.

"Charlotte," Pelham began, a note of impatience in his voice as he snatched his reading spectacles from the bridge of his nose and stood up, "whatever is this fuss?"

"There was a lady, but she wasn't really there," Charlotte sobbed making no sense. "I saw her though, mother. I really did."

"Lottie thinks she has seen a ghost," her brother chipped in, his tone taunting.

Her face flushed from tears and frustration, Charlotte turned on him. "I did see a lady. I did!"

"We all know that she's making it up. Ghosts are-" He jumped at the sound of Pelham smacking the surface of the table.

"Quiet!" He shot Kitty a look of irritation for her failure in keeping the children under control. "There shall be no speaking of any of it! All this speak of ghosts. It is nonsense and it is not Godly!" Outraged by the disturbance, he ordered Kitty to take the other children away whilst Kat was to deal with Charlotte's outburst.

Leading her daughter through to the parlour, she waited until she was certain that they were alone before encouraging her to talk.

The room was bathed in sunshine and smelled of fresh flowers, making it appear instantly more comforting. Charlotte blinked away the tears and looked at Kat in earnest. "I did see a ghost, mother. You have to believe me!

I am not making it up." She looked very small sitting in the large fireside chair that was usually reserved for Pelham.

"I know," Kat replied gently. She thought of the faded silhouette of the man she had seen earlier that morning. "Have you seen her before?" she asked softly, careful not to upset her any further.

"No, mother." Her eyes were wide and unblinking.

"And where did you see this ghost?"

The little girl gave a sheepish look before her face crumpled. "When we were playing hide and seek. I ran to the hidden room."

Kat felt her breath catch in her chest. The children were forbidden from going into that room. It was where she had stowed away everything from her past and all items that were connected to her 'gift'. "The hidden room, you say?"

"I didn't mean to!" Charlotte protested and her bottom lip began to quiver. "But I could not think of any more places to hide and William was counting too fast."

"And the ghost was in there?"

Charlotte looked frightened. "Not at first, but something dropped on the floor. When I went to pick it up, she was suddenly there in front of me." Her voice was timid and she looked even smaller as she sank back in the chair.

Barely daring to breathe, Kat watched her daughter carefully. "What did she look like?"

Charlotte was sobbing uncontrollably again. "I cannot remember, mama. But she was looking for somebody and then I could hear a man calling out to her and she wasn't there any longer."

Standing up and pacing about the room, Kat felt panic surging through her body. "What have I told you about the hidden room, Charlotte? It is a place that you must never venture."

Charlotte's eyes were wide with terror. "You won't tell father?"

"No, of course I won't," Kat reassured her. Telling Pelham about their daughter's find would be a dreadful mistake. She recalled how she had come to hide the necklace in the first place, shortly after the birth of Charlotte. It had been after another vision that she had confided in Pelham about the necklace and of her second sight, how it was both a gift and curse. At first, he had appeared confused, then he had become scared. He had looked upon her as though she was a stranger to him, but he had become cold and withdrawn before telling her that it was an unholy thing, that she must rid herself of and stop working with the herbs. "In turbulent times they look for women like you," he had said, a quiver to his voice.

"People are not so foolish these days," Kat had protested. "Why should I give up my skills in healing and medicine for the fear of some uneducated fool's superstition?"

At that he had turned on her and it had been the first time she had ever seen him so angry with her. They had argued dreadfully and then he had reminded her that, owing to the way she had left her service with Lord Jeffreys, in spite of all the precautions they had taken to conceal her identity, they might never be safe. "He was obsessed by you," he had said. "He referred to you as 'little witch'. Whatever it was that you said to him the night before the last of the Taunton assizes, it broke him. And leaving your position the way that you did made things all the worse. He was formidable after that."

"He was formidable long before that!" she had countered.

Pelham had looked haunted as he had recalled how it had been. "You did not see him, my love. After you had gone there was a wildness in his eyes. He wanted revenge. He went to Bristol in such a bad temper and when the assizes opened in Wells, he was different. I remember how his eyes had flared when he mentioned your name and I thought that I could be staring into the very pits of Hell." At that point, he had taken her hands in his. "Need I remind you of how powerful he is now that he is Lord Chancellor? I live in fear that his obsession has remained and that one day he might send someone to find you. If we are found together, he will make us both pay. If anyone was to get a mere sniff at what you have just confided in me," he looked at her from beneath hooded eyes, "or anything else for that matter, it would be enough to see you…" He pressed his finger and thumb to the inner corners of his eyes. His request was a simple one – he did not wish for her to ever use the necklace to incite her gift again.

For the sake of their happiness and for the sake of their firstborn, Kat had done as he had asked. She had sold the apothecary too. Disposing of the necklace was an impossible request though, it was too valuable and far too sentimental. Along with some of the other items that she had found herself unable to rid herself of, she had hidden it in the wall of a tiny room that was coveted away behind a bookshelf in the solar. The children all knew that they were forbidden from entering that room. Kitty knew that too. What had she been doing to allow the children anywhere near it unattended? A fresh wave of fear washed over her as Kat gripped her daughter's shoulders. "Charlotte, you must answer my next question honestly now, for God will know the truth," she warned and the little girl stared at her through red, puffy eyes. "Did Kitty or any of the others see this necklace?"

"No, mama! No! I dropped it and ran." The expression on her face was sincere and Kat felt herself calm a little.

"You must not breathe a word to another living soul, Charlotte. And you must give me your word that you will never set foot in that room again. Can you promise me that?"

When Charlotte nodded, Kat pulled her into a comforting embrace. If Kitty had seen the necklace, she might have said something to Pelham. Dabbing at her daughter's cheeks with her fingers, she whispered: "Now let us go and find Kitty and we shall not say another word about this, my love. We can put it all down to being a bad dream and shadows, for your father is quite correct when he says that ghosts are not real."

Trying to look convinced, Charlotte slipped off the edge of the chair and began to trail along behind her out of the room. "But mama, what will I do if she comes back?"

"She was not real, Charlotte. If you ignore her, she will go away." Even as she said the words, she felt a crushing wave of guilt. This was no childish daydream; the necklace was reaching out for her. After all these years, the High Priestess had returned, or perhaps she had always been there, shut behind the secret door.

******

Pelham left fretting over Kat's obvious downturn in health. It had not gone unnoticed how morose she had been of late.

"We shall be quite alright, husband," Kat reassured him and kissed his cheek. "All is well, I shall see you soon enough." He smelled of lemon balm and rosemary and Kat inhaled the scent, savouring it whilst her lips lingered against his skin. Silently, she chastised herself for becoming so despondent with life when she had a husband like him. Pelham had always been gentle, shown her respect and love, given her three beautiful children, so why could she not shake the dreadful sadness that had grown with intensity since she had read the newssheet about Monmouth's men only days earlier? Pushing the sombre feelings aside, she smiled at her husband as he bid them all a farewell.

They watched the stagecoach leave the grounds of the house before Kitty began ushering the children back inside to start their lessons.

Once she was alone, she climbed the stairs to the first floor. In the solar, she glanced over at the bookshelf that hid the little room where Charlotte had found the necklace. Inside, dust had gathered on the various boxes and bottles that had been stored in there. Kat picked up a silver scent bottle that had belonged to her grandmother and blew away a layer of dust before removing the stopper. The scent of lavender oil was still there, bringing with it memories of her time in the apothecary with Darling. A snuffbox had been placed next to it. This one had been a wedding gift that Kat had saved for. She had arranged for it to be engraved with a G and K. Gideon had left it behind when he had left to chase his dreams and perhaps just as well; the soldiers would have removed it from him upon his capture and guessed that he had lied about who he really was.

Kat felt the unbearable weight in her chest once again. After so long, how was it still so raw? It was as though his spirit was near. She could feel him again. Her gaze fell to the floor where Charlotte had discarded the necklace. She swallowed but her mouth was dry, causing her to cough. Although inanimate, the obsidian stone appeared to stare with its black unblinking eye. This was an evil thing. All that it had done was to bring forth a spirit who had done nothing to help save Gideon, had scared her daughter and now she felt certain that it was invoking her husband's lost soul. It needed to be removed from the house and taken far away from her children.

As she snatched it from the floor, Kat felt her palm heat up. In her mind's eye, she could see Gideon. His face was brown with starbursts of lines around his eyes. He looked older than she remembered, wiser and no longer the carefree young man whom she had married. His copper hair, still the colour of rich autumnal leaves, was blowing behind him.

Dropping the necklace into her pocket, Kat cried out. This was how Gideon might have looked had things been different. Memories from over a decade earlier began swimming through her head, dizzying her.

Sleep would not come to her that night. Daybreak would soon be melting away the inky darkness and the first of the songbirds would be calling to their mates. When Kat tiptoed downstairs, it was still early enough for the servants to be in their beds. Around her neck, she could feel the weight of the obsidian pendant. In spite of her reserves for the necklace, she had been unable to part with it. The image of Gideon had been impossible but so beautiful that it had given Kat some moments of false respite from the years of guilt and heartbreak. Even if it was one more time, she needed to try and look again, but it would have to be somewhere private where she would not be seen.

At the far end of the garden, just beyond the muted blush of roses and hollyhocks, was a stream that eventually joined the river Itchen. The sounds of the nocturnal beasts would soon give way to the early risers and Kat knew that she would have to hurry. Kneeling on the grassy bank that sloped down to the stream, she listened to the calming trickle of water. This was a noise that never failed to soothe her mind. Beneath the moonlight, the water shimmered and rippled. Tiny bubbles popped on the surface now and again as the odd fish swam upstream.

Unhooking the necklace, she held it above the water's surface. It had been a long time since she had done anything like this. Closing her eyes, she tried to picture Gideon's face just as she had seen it before their troubles had begun.

It was still there, bold and beautiful in the deep pockets of her memories. As her eyelids fluttered open, she stared at the shiny black surface of the stone, willing it to make something happen. Nothing did. Realising that everything around her had grown silent. Kat knew that this was that moment in time when creatures of the night would scuttle away as those whose busy chatter would emerge with dawn. The silence left her disconcerted and disorientated. It had been so long that Kat did not even know whether she even had the ability to communicate with the other realm any longer. She did not speak, the words would not come, and so she waited.

******

When Ruth turned her head, she was glaring at Jeremy. This was not Ruth. "Kateryn?" he asked. Neither Max nor Tim said anything but he was aware of their mounting tension.

Her eyes narrowed, cold and accusing. "I no longer go by that name. What are you?"

Jeremy glanced at the others, searching for guidance on what to do next. Tim nodded, encouraging him to give her an answer. "I am a friend of Ruth's."

"The High Priestess has sent you?" She recoiled and he noticed that her fingers were moving over the stone pendant. "What wicked magic is this?"

"We are here to help you, Kateryn."

Her breath was frosty against his cheek as she moved closer to him. "I have told you that I no longer answer to that name. My name is Catherine and I will banish you, spirit. Plucking a strand of hair from her head she began to bind it around the stone. "I banish you demon spirit. I will banish both you and your High Priestess from this world. I send you back to the evil place from whence you came."

Panic stricken, Jeremy thought fast. "We can help you find your husband."

There was a thud as she dropped the necklace. "My husband is not lost," she said, her voice laced with misgiving. "Pelham is safe and well. This is all trickery."

Choosing his words carefully, he took a deep breath. "I am speaking about Gideon." He reached for her hand. It felt ice cold.

"Gideon?" The flinty gaze warmed. "It is not possible. Gideon is-" Unable to bring herself to even say what she had thought had happened to him, her eyes pooled.

"Gideon is alive. I know what happened in Taunton, how he went by a different name to protect you from the shame of his part in the rebellion and I know that he was sentenced for high treason. I know what you heard, what the judge stated would happen to him but you must know that the sentence was commuted to a lesser one."

Shaking her head with confusion, she dashed at the tears that had begun to fall. "Why are you saying all of this? Why do you taunt me with these evil lies?" She tried to free her hand from his grip, but he held on.

"I know what happened to Gideon after he was trialled as Christopher Carter. He did not face the executioner because on the very day that the sentence was given, the man responsible for preparing the documentation changed it."

Her jaw dropped as she struggled to digest the information he was giving. "On the 25th November 1685, Gideon was transported to Barbados under the name of Christopher Carter. Kat, it was Mr Giles who saved your husband's life."

CHAPTER FORTY ONE

Morning had long since broken to the high trill of lark song when her eyelids fluttered open. She must have fainted after falling into a reverie and now she was stirring. Blinking away the spots of sunlight that were blurring her vision, she frowned with confusion before remembering why she was lying on the grass. Panicking that she may have been seen, she sat up. Save for the birds, insects and gentle plip-plop of minnows, there were no other signs of life by or near to the river. The necklace was nestled between a patch of buttercups, the surface of the stone catching the sunlight. Hooking it around her neck, Kat returned to the house.

In her chamber she shook out her skirts and called for the maid to come and light the fire so that she might warm herself again. The feeling of cold had bitten through her flesh. It was, she decided, a good idea to arrange for the tub to be brought through and filled. The protests from her children carried through the house as Kitty informed them that they would be beginning their day with a wash just after their mother had dried and dressed. Kat was barely aware of the commotion as she stared in the mirror at her reflection, recalling what the spirit man had told her. If Pelham really had arranged for Gideon's transportation to the colonies, why had he not told her any of this and allowed her silent suffering to continue? A pulsing rage was slowly growing inside her. The walls of the house felt like they were closing in and with them was Pelham's deception.

Kissing each of the children, she advised Kitty that she would be taking her horse out into the meadows. Without stopping to even break her fast, she left. Riding fast and hard out amongst the wildflowers was the only way she knew how to exorcise the dreadful feeling that had been building since learning that Gideon was possibly alive.

The horse was ready for her shortly after her instruction was sent to the stabling yard. This was Sundance, her favourite gelding. His pearly coat shimmered beneath the late spring sunshine. Kat trotted him through the paddocks and out onto the neighbouring meadows before kicking him on faster, tightening the reins as they gathered speed. The beat of his hooves sent birds flying from the lower perches of the trees that lined the chalk stream running alongside. Tears clouded her vision but she did not care; Sundance knew the routes they rode well and he would take the lead. They galloped for some time before Kat eventually pulled on the reins to gently slow him to a brisk trot. They were on the edge of the water meadows that opened out onto Winchester. The grey flint and stone palace could be seen from here. Guiding Sundance to the mill at the end of the river and towards a trough outside a coaching house, she waited whilst he quenched his thirst. It was not often Kat ventured into Winchester. The steady churn of water from the mill's wheel and the familiar smells and sounds brought back too many memories.

When Sundance appeared satisfied that his thirst was quenched, they headed back the way they had come, oblivious of the curious watchful gaze upon them.

As she rode, she reflected upon the words of advice that the strange spirit man had imparted after he had told her of Gideon's true fate. He had told her of a letter sent through time, to whom it had been sent and the year it had been opened. This man was a time traveller and he was collaborating with the woman called Ruth. He explained that Ruth was a sensitive, just like Kat, and then he told her what must be done to ensure that history would remain unchanged. It had all been so much for her mind to accept. Kat had assumed that she had summoned a High Priestess who had lived amongst the Druids on St Catherine's Hill centuries earlier, not a woman whose birth date was still centuries into the future. The idea of it was shocking, but she knew what needed to be done – one day. Now however, she just needed to breathe, to be grateful for the fact that, although her path would be unlikely to cross with his again, Gideon had been saved. He was alive and he would live a long life, have several children and then grandchildren, one of whom would become a successful lawyer who would play a part in an important event that would make significant changes. The man did not share anything more, for fear of saying too much, but Kat had been given an insight into the future that filled her with such pride and love for the husband whom she had lost. She rode on, reflecting on all of it, feeling the bittersweet emotions of love and pride mingled with relief, loss and longing.

The dry mud track leading to the Almshouses was empty. As the track opened onto a meadow, Kat took the horse back into a canter, pushing him on to a gallop. Warm air scented with the early tones of summer pervaded her nostrils and she let her mind drift back to the days when Gideon had run alongside her, never tiring. She could almost feel his presence, hear the pound of his feet in perfect sync with her horse's hooves. Pressing on faster, she imagined his face, pink from the heat, strands of his copper hair sticking to his forehead. If she imagined hard enough it was as though he was with her, bringing her the comfort she desperately needed.

A whinny from Sundance and the moment was interrupted. Kat opened her eyes. The steady pounding of his hooves was hypnotic, striking a perfect harmony with the echo of her thoughts, and she could still hear the sound of Gideon's feet, running alongside her. Smiling through fresh tears, she realised that her daydream was still with her. She was not ready to let go of it just yet.

As she turned her head to marvel at the majestic rise of St Catherine's Hill to her left, she saw it; the bright glint of copper against glorious sunlight. Crying out with fright, she shifted in the saddle. At the sudden motion of his rider, Sundance shied, almost unseating her. Had the obsidian brought her the past or had it conjured a demon spirit intent on torturing her fragile mind? Feeling the weight of the pendant nestled between her breasts, she shouted out as she squeezed the horse's flanks, willing him to pick up the pace. "Be gone, Demon!"

Sundance resisted the bridle with a petulant shake of his head but Kat would not allow his speed to plateau. Flecks of saliva were gathering at the corners of his mouth. He was already tiring from their earlier ride into Winchester and she had not given him enough respite. "Be gone with you," she screamed but the image of Gideon did not fade into the landscape as she had hoped. There was such determination upon his face that she was certain he would chase her to the pits of Hell. Fear began to take her sanity and, without thought for her safety, she jumped. The ground was soft enough to cushion her fall but the pain in her right shoulder burned as she hit the rich pasture and rolled over and again. The steady rhythm of Sundance's hooves slowed as he realised that he was alone and she saw him circle, but not before the flash of copper was upon her again and Gideon's face was above her, full of concern. She recoiled as he reached to help her up.

"Leave me!" she cried out, snatching her arm away from him and wincing from the pain. "You are not real."

His reply was choked. "God's teeth, it really is you." As his face crumpled, he fell to his knees so that he was beside her. "I didn't think I would ever…" Warmth radiated from his body as he got closer to her and she felt her own respond to it as she tried to catch her breath. Looking at the leathery brown skin on the backs of his hands, the creases around his eyes and the pale ridge of an old scar that reached up from his neck to the edge of his chin, she whispered his name. "Gideon?"

As he gently took her in his arms, he did not need to reply. This was no vision or other worldly thing. It was Gideon.

"Gideon, I thought you were-" Before she could finish, he pressed a finger to her lips.

"I am passing through Winchester and have come to these parts every day, but I did not dare imagine that I would find you here, in the place we used to come." He stared at her with a look of disbelief that matched her own amazement.

The surge of emotion too great, Kat fell against his chest and felt the comfort of his arms wrapping around her. They were stronger than they had once been. For a long while they cried together, their sobs becoming one until Kat tilted her head so that her gaze met his. Bringing his lips to her cheeks, he kissed the tears, moving down her face until his mouth pressed against hers and they were kissing, the urgency of their passion intensifying as they fell amongst the campion and musk mallow. They cared for nobody as they impatiently fumbled with their clothing in between kisses and when he brought his lips to her naked breast she cried out, begging him to take her. They made love as the sunlight baked their exposed skin and Kat's eyelids fluttered as his fingers slipped from hers. "Don't let this end," she murmured.

Exhausted and emotional they lay in each other's arms. "I wish we could stay here," he whispered into her ear. "A moment in time, bottled forever. Never to be doubted and never to be forgotten." It was the phrase they had always used when they had been courting in secret.

Kat's mood darkened as she sat up and brought her knees to her chest. The warm tingle of him was still upon her, but this sensation was transient, something that could never be bottled or locked in time. They were no longer Kateryn and Gideon; now they were two different people going by different names and leading separate lives, joined only in the shadow of what had once been. He had told her of his wife, a young woman who had nursed him back to health after he had returned to English shores with a fever that had almost killed him. They had married weeks later. The news wounded her deeply and he could see it. Kissing her on the cheek and the lips, he told her that he would give it all up in an instant if they could be together again. The thought was a delicious one. They could be illicit lovers, meeting in secret and indulging in their love for one another until they found a way of being together again. She thought about it for a while, permitting herself to imagine how it could be and then she shook her head. This was the daydream of a foolish young girl, not the thoughts of a mature woman with a family to consider.

Kat brought her finger to his naked shoulder, touching the pale ridged skin of a rough furrow of flesh that snaked down his back. It joined a network of scars inflicted by the whips and other methods used to control the slaves on the plantations. In that moment, she wondered what horrors he had experienced for all those years. Suddenly irritated, he threw on his shirt.

"Once again we are a forbidden love. We were not meant to be." His voice was deadpan and the words stung.

"You married another," she commented, her tone tinged with jealousy that was impossible to disguise.

Turning to look at her, his eyes were ablaze. "As did you."

Dropping her head to her knees, she felt the weight of their sin. What had happened between them could never be undone. "I thought you were dead," she muttered but he was already standing up, marching towards the water's edge for refreshment. He meant to say goodbye to her. There would be no way they could see one another again. She knew that but it did not hurt any the less. "Do not let it end like this, Gideon. Not this way."

He splashed the cool water on his face and sighed. "It will never end, Kat. For the rest of our lives, no matter how far apart we might be, how different our lives have become, our hearts will always beat as one." Taking hold of her hand, he brought it to her chest. "You will always be here."

"You will walk me home? We can stop at the woodland that fringes the house."

"And if we are seen?"

"You are simply a kind hearted gentleman accompanying me on my journey to see to it that no rogues bring me any trouble."

Helping her mount Sundance, he walked alongside her sometimes in companionable silence and sometimes talking. They reached the woodland of hazel trees all too soon. "I am glad that he takes care of you." He smoothed Sundance's pearly coat as he referred to her marriage to Pelham. "It is what I wanted for you – a better life, one that you deserved. I thought of nothing but you on that ship, through the storms and the sickness. The knowledge that you would be safe and not tarnished by the trouble that my real name could have brought to you gave me peace of mind. It is what I clung on to, to survive."

"Pelham treats me very well. I can assure you of that." Her response was tight lipped. She was still so angry at the deception.

Gideon's arm fell to his side and he nodded, his expression thoughtful. "So that is the name given to him by God." Giving her a morose smile, he patted the rear of the horse. "Farewell, my love. God bless you."

Riding past the pink of the foxgloves and into the grove of hazels, Kat did not look back for fear that she would shatter into a thousand pieces. Her vision blurred from tears, she wondered whether it was possible to die from a broken heart.

CHAPTER FORTY TWO

The air in Pelham's office was stale. Clearing her throat, Kat opened a window and waited. It would not be long before he returned from his trip and she wanted to ensure that they were alone.

Several days had passed since her encounter with Gideon, but the time had done nothing to settle her anger and frustration. When she heard the distant sound of hooves and the clatter of wheels, she straightened so that she was sitting rigidly in his chair.

There was much fuss when Pelham returned. It was always the way. He was a kind employer but he had a firm manner, one that promised repercussions should there be reason. Whilst his past was as much a secret from the servants as her own, Kat knew that there were whispers amongst them that he had once served the Hanging Judge.

The sound of his boots treading the staircase was accompanied by the gleeful shouts from the children. He would be wondering why his wife was not there to greet him. Fearful that the shame of her own betrayal would show, she lowered her head as she waited. At last, voices could be heard ushering him towards the study.

He did nothing to hide his annoyance when the door was opened. "You know my study is private. What is the meaning of this?"

Laying the flats of her hands on the table, she spread her fingers and firmly held his gaze. "What troubles you, husband? What secrets might you covet away in here that you do not want me privy to?"

His eyes shifted from the desk to the rest of the room. Nothing had been disturbed but that did not help his obvious discomfort. "This is the welcome I receive, after a week of being away?" He was angry and striding across the room towards her.

"It is more welcome than you deserve."

That stopped him. Confusion deepened the lines on his face. "Are these the ramblings of a fever? You look pale." Placing his hand on her forehead, he looked for signs of malady.

Kat stood up sharply and moved away from him putting the bulk of the desk between them. "I am perfectly well, thank you."

His cheeks had started to flame. "Then there can be no excuse for this, this..." Arcing his arm through the air between them, he struggled to articulate himself in the face of her audacity. Kat was not surprised. She had always been relatively subservient to his requests, but Gideon had awakened her old spirit.

Pelham continued his rant: "When a man returns from a week of business, it is more than reasonable to expect his wife to greet him in the appropriate manner."

Kat's nails bore down into the soft wood of his desk. "I am not though, am I? I am not your wife."

With an exasperated chuckle, Pelham shook his head. "I will have one of the servants fetch Doctor Brownlow. You are clearly quite unwell."

"Do not avoid answering me, Pelham. Even the men who helped you make our marriage legitimate in the eyes of the law cannot make it so in the eyes of God. It is bigamy and you have always known this. There are ways I can find out the truth, and I will." The determined glint in her eye told him that she meant every word. He knew her capability and that was the true reason he had demanded that she leave it all behind, give up the apothecary and everything her grandmother had left to her. He had not wanted for Kat to find a way of uncovering the truth.

Edging around the table, she closed in on him as a predator might stalk its prey. "What really happened to the man who was trialled as Christopher Carter? What happened to my husband?"

She thought that he would deny it, tell her she was mad and call for help to restrain her, but he did not. His shoulders fell forward and his gaze hit the desk. "When I saw you across the courtroom that day, I knew that he meant something to you." Drawing a breath, he continued. "I saw the way you looked at him and I saw your heart break."

"You have already told me that part, Pelham. Before we were betrothed you told me that you had guessed. Tell me the rest."

Moving some paperwork, he sat down and his voice shook. "I altered things, made sure that he would be transported." His complexion pallid, he looked suddenly afraid. "I loved you. I did it all for you."

Kat felt her top lip peel upwards in a snarl. "You let me go on believing that my husband was dead, that he had been butchered to death with the henchman's axe and left to rot." Years of buried emotion were rising to the surface, threatening to boil over in a tearful fit of rage. "How could you, Pelham? It is unforgiveable."

Nervously rubbing his chin, he looked at her firm in the eye. "And if I had told you that he had been transported, what then? Would you have still agreed to marry me?"

There was no answer she could give. Her silence said it all.

Crestfallen, he sighed heavily as he prepared to elaborate with more of the truth. "I spoke to him later that day. I told him that he would need to calmly answer to his name when it was called and get in line with those being transported. I did not want it to take him by surprise and cause any disruption. He was a shrewd man though and he guessed that there was a reason for the switch. At first, he had thought you had somehow paid for his life, that you had-"

"Don't." Nausea squeezed her insides. How many women had done that? She thought of the poor girl who had suffered the degradation of spending the night with Lord Jeffreys only to find out the following morning that her brother had still been executed.

"I told him how it was that we had come to know one another and I said what a fine woman I thought you were. He begged me never to tell you what had really happened to him, that it was better for you to believe that he was dead or that you would not live your life. He wanted for you to remarry, have children and move on. He made me promise, Kat. And I honoured it."

Silence filled the room and Kat moved over to the window, looking out onto the gardens that backed onto the woodland. Images of Gideon's face as they had made love in the water meadows flashed before her and she bit down on her lip as she also recalled his expression when she had shared with him the name of her husband. "Did he know that you intended to marry me?" she asked at last.

"It was his last request." He stood up, holding her reproachful gaze. "He had no need to request it of me, though. I would have asked you anyway. I meant every word when I told you that when we left Dorchester I had already fallen deeply in love with you." He regarded her with shiny eyes and frowned for a moment as though something occurred to him that he wanted to ask her about before thinking better of it. "It has only ever been you, my love." His expression appeared tortured as he turned to leave the room.

It was the last they spoke of Gideon, or of his alias, Christopher Carter. Weeks passed and then months. When Kat's belly rounded and her breasts enlarged, they rejoiced the imminent arrival of a new child. In spite of it all, Kat realised that both men in her life had deceived her out of love.

Summer became winter and then the hard frosts gave way to the softer shades of spring. Kat had been in confinement for four weeks when the house was filled with the heightened wails of a newborn baby. Her body aching and her energy spent, she held him in her arms marvelling at the tiny but perfectly formed features of his face. When it came to her children, she had always stood firmly by her belief that mothers should never have favourites, but this little boy had stolen her heart.

"He is a fine young boy," Pelham remarked as the swaddled child was handed to him, sated and sleepy from his feed. "His name will be Nathaniel Austin." As he handed the child back, he did not smile or commend Kat for delivering him another healthy son. There was no hint of the elated joy he had shown at the birth of their previous three. Oblivious to his change of mood, the women by the bedside all commented on how handsome the child was with his stormy-coloured eyes and shock of red hair. Tight-lipped, Pelham simply nodded and returned to his study.

No sooner than she was alone, Kat took her son into her arms and looked out the window. The first of the bluebells were already beginning to appear at the edge of the woodland beyond the lawns. In a matter of months, the meadows would be filled with campion and musk mallow, just as they had been the day that she and Gideon had found each other again.

Bending her head to kiss the shock of fiery hair on her son's head she whispered to him: "One day my son, I will tell you all about where you came from and the sad, brave story that brought you into my arms."

Outside, the clouds parted for the sun so that the child was bathed in a golden light. "I know that you will grow up to be a man of great things. You are Nathaniel Austin: boy of a gentleman and son of a warrior."

CHAPTER FORTY THREE

It took her several moments to realise that the faces staring back at her were those of other people from an entirely different time. Her arms felt heavy and her breasts ached as she recalled the feeling of the baby nestled in her arms. "She's gone." She choked back a sob. "Kat is gone."

Jeremy put his hand on her shoulder and she blinked away the tears. "I held him." She smiled wistfully as the memory remained with her physically and emotionally. "I was holding Cath's ancestor in my arms, Nathaniel Austin."

Jeremy's face was animated. "You saw him?"

Taking a sip of water from the glass that Tim had handed her, Ruth nodded as she relayed everything she had experienced through Kat. Picking up the necklace, she marvelled at the journey it had made through lifetimes, connecting souls from different eras who would influence one another's fate. "That's why Cath was still with us. In death she knew. She needed you to read that letter." All eyes were upon her as everyone waited for her to elaborate further.

"When I connected with Kat, I felt the huge burden that she was carrying. She was ready to end it all." The weight of Kat's suffering was still encumbering her and she glanced up at Jeremy. "The burden of the death she thought Gideon had suffered had been too great for her to carry any longer. If her daughter hadn't found the necklace and you hadn't reached out to her through me, I dread to think what she would have done whilst Pelham was away."

Ruth glanced out the bi-folds to see the sun was already beginning its descent. Their own time had clearly ticked on whilst she had been with Kat. The lights flickered before the barn was filled with a warm yellow glow.

Max was visibly shaken. "Sorry to spoil the mood but this whole thing has rocked me. Not sure I'm going to be able to sleep without the lamp on tonight." He pulled a bottle of red from the wine rack and began to open it. "It wasn't you who we were seeing, Ruth. You looked and sounded so different." Sharing the wine amongst four glasses, he pushed them across the island counter. "And when Jeremy started speaking to you, it was like this curtain of haze fell over you both. I've never seen anything like it."

Tim picked up a glass and took a swig before opening the doors leading to the decking. "I have to say, sis, I'm with Max on this. I grew up with you but I have never seen you do anything quite so spectacularly supernatural. How?"

They moved outside and Ruth inhaled deeply. "I don't know how I did it really. The necklace? Kat? Maybe it was a combination of the two. The irony is that I was ready to chuck all of this in before Jeremy turned up on my doorstep."

Jeremy was aghast. "You wouldn't! Why?"

"Because I thought I was losing my touch and Grayson was never happy with me doing all that 'hocus pocus' as he put it."

Jeremy joined her, slipping an arm around her waist. "But you're so gifted. You radiate such warmth and empathy. It's not just the psychic side of you that's special, Ruth. I genuinely believe that you are a healer."

The compliment made her blush and she noticed the knowing smile that Tim shot in Max's direction. "Come on." He linked his arm through Max's. "Let's leave these two to get the fresh air they need and we'll finish the last of the gift wrapping upstairs."

Taking two faux fur blankets from the small storage box beneath the pergola, Ruth handed one to Jeremy and sat down on the bench. Just beyond the security lights that flagged the perimeter of the garden, Ruth could see the spindly silhouettes of the trees. She wondered how many of them had been there standing guard of the countryside during Kat's time. Turning to Jeremy, she hooked a knee under her. "After you told her what had happened to Gideon, she was furious and took her horse out. That was when she found him again. If she hadn't found him, Nathaniel would never have existed and-"

"Cath's ancestral line would never have existed." As he looked out across the wintry landscape, he appeared lost in profound thought. "So, we changed history."

Ruth shook her head. "We didn't change history. We were simply a part of it."

They sat in companionable silence, contemplating the enormity of it all before either of them said anything more.

Staring out at the space in front of him, Jeremy frowned. "But she didn't write all of that in the letter. Something could have so easily gone wrong, the wrong things said, the incorrect decisions made."

Smiling, Ruth was able to recall everything that Kat had learned from her grandmother, Darling. It was knowledge that was new to her too, golden nuggets of advice that she would take away and use in her own career. "Kat had learned from a very wise woman – one who had lived through the Civil War, who had predicted many events and warned many people of dangers over time. She had lived by the rules of balancing how much was imparted: say too much and one can create the sort of panic that brings discord to the natural flow of events. Only tell somebody what is required. We are spiritual guides, not fortune tellers. Just look at the anguish you faced with making the right decisions to keep Cath and me in your life. You were so terrified of losing us both that you procrastinated and even that could have cost you everything you have held dear."

Jeremy exhaled a fine mist of silvery breath. "It bends my mind."

"Mine too." She chuckled. "I think I've learned not to overthink it. We are all part of a greater force and sometimes we just have to stop and listen, or look." She touched his knee affectionately. "That's what you did with the necklace. It's the reason why we are sitting here now reflecting on this particular piece of history that has shaped life as we know it today."

"There's so much that is likely to be lost in history, though. I'd be interested to take a look at the parish record that recorded Nathaniel's baptism. Somehow, during the course of his lifetime he was introduced to his biological father and they bonded. The birth record must have been altered at some stage. Max wasn't wrong when he pointed out how strange it is that, of all the children belonging to Christopher Carter, it was Nathaniel who was so much more elevated." He sighed and leaned back against the seat, crossing his leg over his knee. "There are so many things we can only assume to piece the whole story together, but I think Cathy would be pleased with the outcome."

"Can you feel her any longer?"

Placing the palm of his hand against his chest, he shook his head. "Only in here. I think she's gone too." He blinked away the emotion. "I feel peaceful."

Ruth slept in her own room that night. It felt somehow more respectful to the memory of Cathy. Jeremy did not object.

******

Christmas morning was bright and sunny and the snow was beginning to melt in far more visible patches. They avoided talking about anything that had happened over the previous two days, instead focusing on the joy of being together in the present. After a late brunch, Jeremy suggested that he and Ruth take a walk.

The weather was milder than it had been and they agreed to burn off brunch with a trip to the memorial site that marked the Battle of Sedgemoor. It was an opportunity to finalise everything and pay their respects.

They stood at the gated entrance to where a remembrance stone had been placed amongst four other pillared structures. The site glimmered beneath the bright sunlight and Ruth leaned on the gate as Jeremy quietly read the signs.

There was no need for her to read any of it. She could recall everything. The obsidian had not only shown her Kat's experiences but Gideon's too.

She lifted her gaze to the fields beyond and then turned her head to see a clump of trees in the distance farther to the right. That was where they had raced Gideon. She looked around for the small hill with the trees known as the three hags that Kat and Amos had watched from. It had long gone – ruined by machinery, farming, superstition or even war, she had no idea. Gripping the gate post until her knuckles were white, she hadn't noticed Jeremy approach her.

"You okay, Ruth?"

She unlatched the gate. "I'm okay."

The air around her felt suddenly still as Ruth crossed the threshold, walked slowly over to the memorial stone and removed her gloves. It was ice-cold to the touch.

To the glory of God
And in memory of all those who doing the right as they gave it
Fell in the Battle of Sedgemoor, 6th July 1685
And lie buried in this field
Or who for their share in the fight
Suffered death, punishment or transportation. Pro Patria.

Moved by sorrow, she recalled all that she had witnessed through Kat's eyes. "I am sorry for it," she whispered. "I am sorry for it all." As she spoke, she felt the warmth of a hand in hers and the stone in front of her appeared brighter. Comforted, she smiled, pleased to have Jeremy by her side. It was a warm and reassuring grip, filling her with a sense of peacefulness. Ruth turned to face him but the space behind her was empty. Looking over her other shoulder she saw Jeremy still at the gate, lost in the words that he was reading.

Her hand still tingling from being held, she lifted it to her face and bent her fingers. "Gideon?"

Only the shriek of a sparrowhawk could be heard from a nearby tree.

Stuffing her hands in her pockets, Ruth waited whilst Jeremy finished looking around.

"We should really get going, I suppose," she said. "Tim will be on the warpath if we make him wait any longer for the main event." They had promised they would be back in time for the canapes that were to be served at four, along with the giving of presents before they started on the main meal." It was already nearing three in the afternoon and the drive was a half hour.

At Jeremy's insistence they finished with a short walk through the village when they returned. Pathways of slushy snow and mud crunched and squelched beneath their boots and Ruth found herself lost in easy conversation. They stopped at a wooden gate, turning to take in the pretty views behind them, then he reached into the breast pocket of his coat. "I have something for you." He gave her a bashful look. "It feels too embarrassing giving it to you in front of anyone else."

"You shouldn't have." She gasped as he placed a neatly wrapped package in the palm of her hand.

"I wanted to, as a way of saying thank you." Scratching the back of his head awkwardly he watched as she pulled at the gold ribbon. "I knew what I wanted to get you and Max took me to a place he knew of the other day."

Peeling back the paper, Ruth found herself holding a port red box. She carefully lifted the lid so that the contents glimmered in the light. A polished orange stone set in sterling silver casing was on the end of a beautiful chain. "Jeremy, it's absolutely stunning," she said breathlessly as he helped her fasten the chain.

"I felt so awful for bringing you the trouble I did with Cath's pendant that I wanted to get you another. This one is for protection. It's supposed to help ground psychics when they make contact with the spirit world."

The gesture was so incredibly touching and thoughtful that Ruth found herself lost for words.

"And," he added, "I thought you might wear it next time I take you out for dinner. If you'll say yes to the invitation?"

"That depends on whether you're going to just get up and walk out on me again," she teased.

He gave her an apologetic smile and reached to tuck a strand of hair behind her ear. "I don't intend on going anywhere without you again." The sincerity in his eyes drew her towards him and they kissed, their mouths lingering and their fingers intertwining. "Now that we're done with making history, I'm hoping we can start focusing on our future."

"I'd like that very much," she said before falling into his arms once again.

EPILOGUE

Pushing back the thick curtain, he pressed his hand to the window pane. Pelham knew that the boy was out there somewhere and he could guess where. The water meadows had been the place where she had loved to ride and walk. Often Pelham had found her sitting in quiet contemplation staring up at the great shoulder of hill in front of her. Ever since Nathaniel had been a babe in arms she had taken him there, shown him her special place and shared the magic of it with him. It had taken a lot of strength over the years for him to brush aside the jealousy. Nathaniel had changed her. He had changed everything, but Pelham had made a promise and he would never turn his back on either of them.

Making his way to the stabling yard, he had one of the horses readied for mounting. It would be the swiftest way to reach the boy and bring him back. The stagecoach was already waiting at the front of the house and the journey would be a long one. It was a journey that he had made with Nathaniel's mother many years before when things had been so very different.

The soft lull of a cuckoo came from the trees, its call making the day appear deceptively pleasant. No day could be pleasant any longer, not without her. They had lost her to the sickness almost a month earlier. For weeks they had watched her weaken as the fevers came, each one worse than the last. There was nothing any doctor could do to help. Even she had been unable to instruct on the right plants that were needed. Her thoughts had been scrambled and her words confused, but he had not needed her to tell him what he must do for their boy.

On horseback, he followed the gentle wend of the Itchen until he could see the almshouses nestled amongst fields of roaming cattle. Training his gaze along the riverbank, his eyes rested on the boy almost immediately. There was no mistaking him. Pelham felt the familiar lurch in his gut as he noted the striking resemblance: the same rich red hair, startling stormy green eyes and lean, muscular physique. He sighed heavily, the weight in his heart growing.

Nathaniel was sitting in the favoured spot of his mother's, staring up at the hill rising magnificently over the line of trees on the opposite riverbank. He wondered if he would ever be able to coax the boy away.

The boy had his mother's heart, and Pelham feared that he also shared her sensitivities. This he had always found discomfiting. It was as though he had the ability to read one's thoughts and there were far too many secrets, too many untruths. The boy was pensive but as sharp as a blade. It was a trait that would serve him well when he finished his studies in law. Men all over the country would look to him to manage their affairs, to straighten out their complex webs of lies and deceit that great fortunes had been built upon. But Pelham knew that his boy would turn the other way. His mother had brought him up differently; exposing the wicked deeds of a nobleman's rivals or hiding those of another were not the sorts of things that drove the fiery ambition in his son. Nathaniel was fierce for honour and justice, but his fight would be for the everyman, the ones who would never be able to afford the services of the accomplished man he would become.

Dismounting his horse, Pelham cleared his throat awkwardly. "It is time."

At the sound of his voice, the boy turned. His face was still damp from crying. Without saying a word, he got to his feet and nodded.

Everything had been loaded into the carriage by the time they had returned to the grounds. All that was left was for Nathaniel to climb in too. Pelham felt a rush of nostalgia as he recalled the first time the boy had left the country house in a carriage on his own. That had been when he had started his studies. It had been an emotional day, but back then Pelham had always known that he would return. This time things were different.

He handed him the slip of parchment that gave him all the details he would need. "God speed, son."

"Will I see you again?" Nathaniel asked and Pelham noticed that his fist was clenched around something.

"That will be your choice," he replied.

He stood back to watch the boy mount the step into the carriage. When the door was closed and the wheels began to move, Nathaniel lifted his hand to wave. Noting the glint of the dark stone on the end of the tarnished chain now resting on the boy's knee, Pelham knew that it would indeed be the last time he would see him again. They would write but there would be no reunion. Nathaniel was his boy, but he was somebody else's son.

The birth record had been amended. It had been Pelham's last promise to her. Her heart may have beat alongside his for all those years but it had always belonged to someone else and so had their son, Nathaniel.

As the black carriage disappeared from the courtyard, he felt a warmth by his side and he knew that she was standing with him for the last time. The sun was growing stronger and he could smell the cooking from the kitchen in preparation for his other children and their young families returning home later that day.

As swiftly as it had appeared, the warmth drifted away and overhead came the screech of a harrier. Its great wingspan cast a shadow over him before he watched it fly towards the bold silhouette of St Catherine's Hill.

Thank you for reading 'The Judge's Apothecary'. I hope you enjoyed reading it as much as I did writing it. If you can, please do leave a review on Amazon and Goodreads.

You can also get in touch with me by using the contact form on my website: emmanicolelewis.co.uk.

More books and novels by Emma-Nicole Lewis

Also in paperback:

'A Shadow Beyond' features the moving and tragic story of Eyam, the plague village.

Lost in the folds of time, behind one village's brave sacrifice, is the tragic and chilling secret of Thornycroft Hall....

Locked away in the top quarters of Thornycroft, a large house on the edge of the historic village of Eyam, is a centuries old secret.

Escaping the chaos of a complicated break up, Kate Saunders travels to the Peak District to stay with her Great Aunt Edie who has suffered a fall. Thornycroft is the perfect bolthole for Kate, peaceful and providing plenty of distance from her obsessive ex.

But when Kate stumbles across a diary and an ancient bogwood jewellery box in the top of the house, the tranquillity she had expected is shattered. She is shocked to discover that Edie has been tampering with the supernatural and as Kate reads the contents of the diary, the shadows of Thornycroft's past begin to stir.

Kate becomes fascinated by the history of the house and the legacy of the villagers who made a brave yet devastating decision during the outbreak of plague. The more she discovers, the more she realises that, hidden behind Eyam's tragic story, is a dreadful family secret.

Stalked by her ex and restless spirits who harbour a dark secret, Kate realises she's in danger - not only from the living, but from the dead.

As the haunting intensifies and layers of time peel away, Kate starts to uncover a chilling truth that has remained buried for centuries…

Available on Kindle:

'The Wishing House' is set in 1642, at the turn of Civil War. Constance Yorke experiences terrifying visions she does not understand. The visions soon lead to accusations that dramatically change her life – and the village she lives in.

Just one wish....

Behind an old dilapidated cottage in a peaceful Shropshire village, is an ancient wishing well. Surrounded by superstition and folklore dating back to the civil war, the well and the house have been left untouched by the locals. When a stranger to the village buys the house, the well is disturbed....

Present Day - Unexpected circumstances lead Milly Lyle to move to The Wishing House, a quintessential country cottage recently restored and renovated by her lover. With its chocolate box looks, quaint location and the pretty well outside, it seems the perfect place for a fresh start. Then she hears of the legend of the Wishing Well Witch and the noises, dreams and strange events begin.

1642 – the turn of the civil war. Constance Yorke, the troubled wife of the parish Clergyman, finds herself turning to the wishing well behind her house for answers to her prayers. Plagued with visions portending a country torn in two by a bloody war waged by the King, it seems that Constance may have dabbled with things that she shouldn't. Growing more isolated from her distant husband and the other villagers, she is left with nothing but her wishing well and the curious white dog that keeps appearing. When Prince Rupert and his Cavaliers ride through Sleepers Brook after a skirmish at Powick Bridge, it seems that Constance Yorke's visions are coming true and that perhaps, she really is falling foul of witchcraft.

As times collide, one woman's quest for retribution becomes another's peril in a chilling story of love, jealousy, betrayal and revenge.

'The Hidden Door' is a beautifully bittersweet novella about a door in a garden wall that opens into a mysterious wood.

In the private grounds of a Hampshire estate is a cottage called Keeper's Lodge. With its rambling, wild garden and quaint little summerhouse, the cottage is the perfect retreat for writer, Natasha.

When she is exploring, Natasha finds a poem that leads her to find an ornate looking key, tucked away inside a little dovecote. The key fits into the lock of a door, hidden in the wall, behind the overgrown garden. Natasha has been warned not to breach the boundaries between Keeper's Lodge and the Crabwood Estate, but curiosity gets the better of her and she opens the door to find out what is behind it.

Amidst the haven of a woodland glade, she meets Will, son of Mr Randall, the owner of Crabwood Estate.

Will and Mr Randall have a secret though and as Will and Natasha grow close, she learns that all may not be what it seems.

'Three' is a supernatural thriller with twists and turns, told from three points of view and unravelling the mystery behind a murder that happened at Hillcrest House thirty years earlier.

A criminally insane convict. A haunted house. A shockingly twisted truth.

Hillcrest House is where Annabelle Montague was killed, on New Year's Eve, thirty years ago. Convicted of murder, her husband, Sir Edward Montague, has spent the last thirty years of his life in a high security unit for the criminally insane. Now, as part of an experimental treatment pathway, he has returned to Hillcrest House. Much like his rapidly deteriorating mind, the house is a derelict and wasted version of its former grand self. Inside the dimly lit corridors, lurking amidst the shadows and the dusty, empty rooms is the truth – and Annabelle.

Under the supervision of two clinical professionals, one desperate for money, the other for recognition, the experiment begins. As it does, the unsettling rumours surrounding Sir Edward and Hillcrest House begin to surface.

Is Sir Edward more dangerous and disturbed than anyone had realised, or is there something more sinister creeping about in the darkness at Hillcrest House?

A story told from three points of view and over the course of two days, a twisted truth begins to unravel. Everyone has something to hide. Especially Annabelle.

Printed in Great Britain
by Amazon

15935235R00193